Eye of the Beholder

"Kathy Herman delivers a taut suspense story with national implications and a vibrant call for godly action. Well done!"

KATHRYN MACKEL
AUTHOR OF *THE DEPARTED*

"Kathy Herman's best suspense novel yet—*Eye of the Beholder*—will grip you from beginning to end. The characters and mystery are as current as today's front page and as timeless as Scripture. Truly a fulfilling, challenging read. Buy it!"

LYN COTE
AUTHOR OF *THE WOMEN OF IVY MANOR* SERIES

"*Eye of the Beholder* enticed me from the first page with familiar and beloved people. Then it took a twist that both delighted and convicted me. Kathy Herman gets inside her characters' hearts, using both compassion and wisdom to show us what hides within our own souls. This visit to Seaport will change your life."

JANELLE CLARE SCHNEIDER
AUTHOR

"Little white lies. Preconceived notions. Racial, social, and educational prejudices. These are the elements of Kathy Herman's *Eye of the Beholder*. As if pulled from today's headlines, this novel touches on the fear that overtakes a town when rumors of terrorists are afoot. Filled with unexpected twists, *Eye of the Beholder* held me captive until the very end."

TRACI DEPREE
AUTHOR OF THE HIGHLY ACCLAIMED
APRONS ON A CLOTHESLINE

A Shred of Evidence

"When I get myself out of bed *an hour early* in order to keep reading a book, I know I'm hooked! But I also squirmed as Kathy Herman's suspense novel probed that uncomfortable gray zone between what's concern and what's gossip. The book begs for discussion and couldn't be more timely for both church and society."

NETA JACKSON
BESTSELLING AUTHOR OF
THE YADA YADA PRAYER GROUP NOVELS

"*A Shred of Evidence* will definitely keep readers turning the pages."

CHRISTIAN BOOK PREVIEWS.COM

"Kathy Herman gives her readers true-to-life characters, a plot that could be fresh from today's headlines, and plenty of food for thought."

DEANNA JULIE DODSON
AUTHOR OF *IN HONOR BOUND, BY LOVE REDEEMED,*
AND *TO GRACE SURRENDERED*

"Deception, lies, and slander ensnare the town of Seaport, but there comes as well the power of words to heal and move mountains."

DORIS ELAINE FELL
AUTHOR OF *BETRAYAL IN PARIS* AND *THE TRUMPET AT TWISP*

"A missing child, fearful heartache, and unfounded rumors make *A Shred of Evidence* a powerful suspense you won't want to miss."

GAIL GAYMER MARTIN
AUTHOR OF *MICHIGAN*

EYE OF THE BEHOLDER

A NOVEL

KATHY HERMAN

Multnomah® Publishers *Sisters, Oregon*

EYE OF THE BEHOLDER
published by Multnomah Publishers, Inc.

© 2005 by Kathy Herman
International Standard Book Number: 1-59052-349-0

Cover images by Stephen Gardner, PixelWorks Studios, Inc.
(www.shootpw.com)

Unless otherwise indicated, Scripture quotations are from
The Holy Bible, New International Version (NIV) ©1973, 1984
by International Bible Society,
used by permission of Zondervan Publishing House.

Multnomah is a trademark of Multnomah Publishers, Inc.,
and is registered in the U.S. Patent and Trademark Office.
The colophon is a trademark of Multnomah Publishers, Inc.

Printed in the United States of America

For information:
MULTNOMAH PUBLISHERS, INC. • 601 N. LARCH ST. • SISTERS, OR 97759

Library of Congress Cataloging-in-Publication Data
Herman, Kathy.
Eye of the beholder : a Seaport suspense novel / Kathy Herman.
    p. cm.
ISBN 1-59052-349-0
I. Title.
PS3608.E762E97 2005
813'.6—dc22

                                2005008709

06 07 08 09 10—10 9 8 7 6 5 4 3 2 1

To Him who is both the Giver and the Gift

ACKNOWLEDGMENTS

I would like to express my gratitude to Farideh Arianpour, my Iranian-American friend, whose gentle resolve to treat all people with respect and dignity inspired me to weave an unanticipated thread through this story.

I extend a special thank you to Paul David Houston, assistant district attorney, Nacogdoches County, Texas, for his valuable input regarding law enforcement and legal procedures; and for taking time to read pertinent chapters and make suggestions that have added to the realism of the scenes. Paul, thanks for being accessible and also for searching out answers to my questions about drug trafficking. I'm grateful for your willingness to help.

Also, a special word of thanks to my friend, Will Ray, professional investigator, State of Oregon, for taking time to advise me on scenes pertinent to DNA evidence and private investigations. Will, you're always so generous with your time and knowledge. You're starting to feel like family!

I also wish to thank Kim Prothro for her perfectly timed e-mail giving me a link to an interview on the Moody Broadcasting Network regarding North American Muslims.

A warm thank you to my zealous prayer warrior and sister, Pat Phillips, for her unceasing prayers, especially when it seemed as if the story had come up against a brick wall; and also to a host of friends and readers whose prayers strengthened me as I sought to bring the story together: Susie Killough, Judi Wieghat, Carolyn Walker, Mark and Donna Skorheim, Pearl Anderson, LaVerne McCuistion, Deidre Pool and her entire fourth-grade class, my ever-faithful friends at LifeWay Christian Store, and others too numerous to mention. You know who you are and so does the Lord. Thank you!

To my readers who encourage me with e-mails and cards and personal testimonies, thanks for sharing how God has used my words to touch you. He uses you to bless me more often than you know!

To my novelist friends in ChiLibris, thanks for encouraging and challenging me in my work—and for your many prayers on my behalf.

To my editor, Rod Morris, there's no doubt in my mind that I would be less of a writer if you were less of an editor. Thanks for using your gift to help develop mine.

To the staff at Multnomah Publishers, thank you for sharing my heart and for working so diligently to get my books on the shelves.

And to my husband, Paul, who overlooks in me the obvious signs of aging, the challenging physical limitations, and even the character flaws—and makes me feel cherished. What a gift you are, and a powerful demonstration that beauty is indeed in the eye of the beholder.

And to my heavenly Father, who, because of Jesus, looks upon me as if I had never sinned—use the words of this story to cause Your people to see others with Your eyes of love and mercy.

PROLOGUE

Live in harmony with one another.
Do not be proud, but be willing to associate with
people of low position. Do not be conceited.

ROMANS 12:16.

The tires squealed on Owen Jones's black Jaguar convertible as he turned on Half Moon Drive and again on Barefoot Trace. Some father–son talk *that* had been! Why had his parents waited until he moved all the way to Florida to be closer to them to start having problems?

The pastrami sandwich he hardly remembered eating now felt like a hot coal in his stomach. He reached in the glove box and took a couple of Tums out of the bottle and popped them into his mouth.

Owen slowed the car and passed by a row of flowering crape myrtle trees, then turned into the driveway of a plantation-style house with white columns framing the front porch.

Except for his growing concern over his parents' marital problems, his life was perfect. It seemed as though he had been handed the dream he would have wished for had he dared to hope for something this good.

After several years of working for a CPA firm in Raleigh, one of his father's law partners had submitted his name to the president of Global Communications to be considered for the chief financial officer position.

The president had contacted him and made the overture, citing Owen's creative vision and financial acumen as the primary reason for their interest. Three weeks later, the job was his. And making it even more attractive was the fact that Global's home office was based in Port Smyth, easy driving distance from Seaport, where his parents lived. Had he handpicked a job and a location, it couldn't have been more ideal. Or so he thought.

He pulled the car into the detached garage and looked in the rearview mirror in time to see Hailey's white Lexus coming up the drive. He got out and waited for her, his briefcase in one hand, a waiting hug in the other.

"Hi, sweetheart." Owen slid his arm around her shoulder and pressed his lips to hers. "So how'd the interview go?"

Hailey Jones shrugged. "Who knows? They never tell you anything."

"Think positive. There's bound to be a position for a good HR person somewhere in this town."

Hailey arched her eyebrows, her round blue eyes filled with skepticism. "I'm interviewed out. There are qualified people in line for every position. I may never find what I want."

Owen pulled her closer. "You don't *have* to work."

"What would I do all day in this big house by myself?"

"I don't know, enjoy it?" The reproving look in her eyes made it clear that he'd better not push it. "Don't worry. Someone will snatch you up when they realize what an asset you are."

"Thanks for the vote of confidence. Too bad you're not doing the hiring. I could use someone who's applicant friendly. I feel like a number."

"Maybe Brent McAllister would put in a good word for you. I still can't believe his phone call to Global got my foot in the front door."

"Me either. It was a real gift."

Owen unlocked the front door and held it open, then followed her inside. "I'm certainly grateful for getting a break, but it's not as though I'm unqualified for the job."

Hailey turned around, blond tresses draping her shoulders, her expression contrite. "I didn't mean it that way. You're going to be a fantastic CFO. I'm just feeling insignificant at the moment."

Owen took her into his arms and held her close. "Then I'll just have to make you so happy you'll have no regrets. I didn't think we'd ever be able to afford a house like this. What a great place to raise a family."

Hailey wiggled out of his embrace. "Don't even go there. Right now, I just want to get settled and find where *I* fit. I have no desire to be dependent, house or no house. Why are you staring at me?"

"You're so much like my mother," Owen said, fighting the urge to smile. "I guess we Jones men are irresistibly drawn to women who have a mind of their own."

"As well you should be. And I consider being compared to Ellen the ultimate compliment."

He laughed. "Mother can get a bit overzealous."

"I admire her zeal. She's articulate and opinionated, yet she's open to new ideas."

Owen nodded. "I wish you had known her when she was a newspaper editor. She's not as revved up now that she's writing novels."

"Maybe she's sounding off through her characters."

"Speaking of *characters,* my mother's collection of friends is about to drive my dad nuts. That's all he talked about at lunch today—*again*. Gave me indigestion."

"I don't get it. Guy's out of town as much as he's in. Why should he care who Ellen's friends are?"

"Boggles his mind that she's drawn to the 'strays,' as he calls them. He's embarrassed to be associated with them. Thinks it's bad for his professional image."

"They seemed nice to me. Don't some of them go to your folks' church?"

"Yes, but he'd just as soon keep a comfortable distance."

"Well, he'd better get over it. When have you known your mother to be uppity?"

Owen put his finger to his chin and looked up, his eyes moving one direction and then the other. "Let's see...there was that time back in 1985..." He smiled. "Actually, Mom's always had a range of friends from different backgrounds, and Dad's never objected before." He lifted his eyebrow. "But expecting him to share Sunday dinner with a pair of kidnappers, the kidnapped, and the falsely accused is a bit over the top. And then there's that nosey neighbor lady and the Muslim woman she met out jogging."

"But they all seemed very nice."

"That's not the point."

"Then tell me the point."

Owen put his hands on her shoulders and looked into her eyes. "For the first time in his life, *Guy Langford Jones* is on his way to the top. And if Mom doesn't care that her choice of friends is tainting his image, it's liable to split them up."

"Come on, Owen. Your folks' marriage is rock solid. They're mature enough to work through this."

"Yeah, that's what I thought."

I

Guy Jones slammed down the receiver when the answering machine clicked on, lamenting that he couldn't even connect with a real person at his own home! Ellen was probably out gallivanting somewhere, no doubt being used by of one of her needy friends. A knock on the door stole his attention.

"Will you look at this?" Kinsey Abbot squeezed through the doorway, her arms around a huge basket covered in green cellophane. "Brinkmont Labs sent this gift basket for you. You want it on your credenza?"

"Sure. Here, let me help you with that."

"We're all so proud that you pulled off a win on the Brinkmont case," she said. "The entire office is buzzing."

"Thanks. But I couldn't have done it without you."

"True." Her smile told him she was only half kidding. "Is Ellen going to drive up to celebrate with us?"

"I'm still trying to reach her."

"I've been meaning to ask—has she heard back from any of the publishers she submitted her novel to?"

"She's had several rejections. But she's still got several manuscripts out there."

"Must be discouraging."

"Ellen doesn't have *time* to be discouraged."

Kinsey lifted her eyebrows. "Has she started the second novel?"

"Says she's going to. But at the moment, she's consumed with writing a Bible study for Billy and Lisa Lewis. I think she's broken Mother Teresa's record for the most time spent with the underprivileged."

Kinsey smiled. "Ellen's a sweetheart. Most of us wouldn't make the effort to relate to the mentally challenged."

"I just don't understand what they have in common."

Guy heard a knock at the door and looked up into the face of Brent McAllister.

"Am I invited to the party?" Brent said.

"Sure. My sidekick here just brought me this giant gift basket Brinkmont sent over. Looks like there's enough coffee and chocolate in there to keep this place buzzing for a long time. Also caviar and crackers and a bottle of champagne. Help yourself."

Brent extended his hand to Guy. "Congratulations on a job well done. Donna and I are driving down to Seaport for the weekend. What do you say we spend some of that money you earned for the firm and take you and Ellen out on your own turf?"

"Better yet, why don't you come to our house for dinner? It'll be quieter and more conducive to conversation."

"You sure?"

"Absolutely. We'd love to have you. How about Saturday night at six? No ties allowed."

"Sounds great."

Guy made a note on his desk calendar. "Ellen makes a wonderful pork tenderloin. How's that sound?"

"You kidding? I'm so used to eating out, a home-cooked meal sounds terrific."

"Good. I'm looking forward to it. I also want you to see the house."

Brent chortled. "I guess it's about time. How long have you been with the firm—seventeen, eighteen months?"

"Sounds about right."

"Time flies. Seems like only yesterday we added your name on the door."

Kinsey walked over and stood in the doorway. "If you gentlemen will excuse me, I need to get back to work."

"Don't you want some of this chocolate?" Guy said.

"No, I could gain weight just looking at it. But thanks anyway."

Guy's eyes followed Kinsey's trim figure as she left his office and took a seat at her desk.

"You're staring," Brent said.

"She's a cute gal. Smart as a whip."

"I wondered if you were ever going to notice her *attributes.*"

Guy caught Brent's gaze and held it. "My interest in Kinsey is strictly professional. You're the one who's on the prowl."

"Not at the moment. Donna's working out nicely."

"This month."

"I've never been good at long-term relationships," Brent said. "So what?"

"Suit yourself. Just don't project your lust onto me."

Brent smiled and shook his head. "Same old Guy. You haven't changed since law school. Other than you've been born again or whatever you call it."

"I was faithful to Ellen even before I became a Christian."

"Yes, you were. I've always admired that about you. I, on the other hand, refuse to be limited to one woman." Brent slapped Guy on the back. "Don't you ever wonder what you're missing?"

"Don't you ever regret that your affair with Renee Bateman broke up two marriages and forced Renee to leave the firm? You could have just as easily pursued a single woman who wasn't a partner."

Brent shrugged. "Renee's got her hooks in some wealthy neurosurgeon. My Ex got a big enough settlement to do whatever she wants. You got to take Renee's place. And I get to play the field. Everybody's happy."

Guy stared at Brent, more out of pity than disgust, and decided not to say anything else.

"You mind if I chill that bottle of champagne?" Brent said. "I know you're not going to drink any of it. But we're going to toast you anyway before we take you out to Savvy's tonight."

Guy smiled and basked for a moment in his achievement. "I love it when cases turn out the way we want."

"That's an understatement. This win practically guarantees that Brinkmont will remain a client. You deserve the kudos."

Ellen Jones pushed open the kitchen door with her shoulder, a plastic bag of groceries in each hand. She glanced at the clock: 4:57. At least she had made it back before Guy got home from Tallahassee. Where had the day gone? She had planned to get the bills paid and do some writing on her novel, neither of which had gotten done.

She set the groceries on the breakfast bar and began putting the perishables in the refrigerator when she noticed the light blinking on her answering machine. She reached over and pushed the button.

You have four messages...

"Ellen, it's me. It's 10:00 A.M. I won! Call my cell." Beep.

"Honey, it's noon. I keep hoping to hear from you. Please call my office." Beep.

"It's me again. It's 2:15. I need to talk to you. Call me as soon as you get this." Beep.

"Ellen, it's Guy. It's 4:45. You didn't answer your cell phone either. Everyone's taking me to Savvy's for a victory celebration. I wanted you to drive up so you could join us, but it's too late now. Anyhow, don't wait up. I'll see you when I see you." Beep.

End of messages.

Ellen sat on a stool at the breakfast bar and rummaged through her purse. She turned on her cell phone and saw that Guy had left her a message. She listened to the message and winced at the irritation in his voice, then scrolled till she found his number and hit the talk button.

"McAllister, Norton, Riley, and Jones. How may I direct your call?"

"This is Ellen Jones. May I speak to Guy please?"

"One moment."

Ellen tapped her fingers on the breakfast bar, hoping to get through to Guy and not end up with his secretary as a go-between.

"Ellen, it's Kinsey. Guy's meeting with a client. Can I have him call you back?"

Ellen exhaled more loudly than she had intended. "Yes, I need to talk to him as soon as possible." The doorbell rang. "Please be sure he gets my message."

"I will."

Ellen hung up and hurried to the front door and looked through the peephole. Her neighbor Blanche Davis was standing on the porch.

Ellen unlocked the door and held it open. "Hi."

"I saw you drive up and had to come over," Blanche said. "I've hardly seen you this week."

"It's been wild. I'm putting away groceries. Why don't you come out to the kitchen?"

"Thank you, dear."

Ellen let Blanche inside and then followed her out to the kitchen. "Would you like something cold to drink?"

"No, thanks. It's nice just being here. I've been a little lonesome."

"You got your hair done," Ellen said, aware that Blanche's curls were tighter and bluer than usual.

"I had my girl color it and give me a perm. I always feel so much better when it behaves and I don't have to fuss with it. When you get to be my age, you go for what's easy."

Ellen smiled and slipped a carton of eggs in the refrigerator. "At my age, too. Though my curls are natural and do whatever *they* want. Especially in this humidity."

"Is the Bible study you wrote working out?"

"Yes, very well. Billy and Lisa are surprisingly astute spiritually. But they express themselves slowly and I'm sure they'd be frustrated in a group setting." The phone rang and Ellen reached for the receiver. "Excuse me, Blanche. Hello...?"

"Ellen, it's Julie Hamilton. The dairy is serving up banana splits at half price. You and Guy want to go?"

"Well, that's too good to pass up. Count me in, but Guy won't be home from Tallahassee till late." Ellen turned and looked over her shoulder. "I'll bet Blanche would like to go."

"Great, ask her. Why don't we pick you up at seven?"

"Wonderful. See you then." Ellen hung up the phone and turned to Blanche. "Do you like banana splits?"

"Oh, my, yes."

"The Hamiltons invited us to go out for half-price banana splits, unless you've got other plans."

"No, I'd love to go."

"Have you had dinner?"

Blanche shook her head. "I don't give much thought to it when it's just me."

"Why don't we go out for dinner? My treat. The Hamiltons aren't picking us up till seven."

"It's awfully nice of you, but I don't want to overdo my welcome."

Ellen tried not to smile. *Since when?*

Guy walked his new clients to the door and engaged in a few moments of small talk before sending them on their way. He turned to go back to his office when Kinsey stopped him.

"Ellen called forty-five minutes ago. She sounded disappointed she missed you."

As well she should be! "Thanks, I'll call her back."

"Everyone's ready to go when you are. We've reserved the

back room at Savvy's." Kinsey arched her eyebrows. "Brent's got the chef cooking up some culinary masterpiece."

"Great. I'll just be a minute." Guy walked into his office and picked up the phone and dialed. He hung up when the answering machine went on, and then dialed Ellen's cell number.

"Hello."

"Ellen! Where have you been all day?"

"Exactly where I told you I'd be: at my Wednesday Bible study till noon; then out to lunch with the ladies in my group. After that I worked with Billy and Lisa. Then went to the bank, the cleaners, the pharmacy, the tailor to pick up your suit, and the grocery store. I didn't get your messages till almost five. I'm just sick that it's too late to drive up there."

"I left a message on your cell phone, too."

"You hardly ever call me on the cell so I didn't think to check it for messages."

"That's the problem lately—you don't *think*. At least not about me!"

A few moments of steely silence told him he'd made his point.

"Hold on," Ellen said. "I'm going outside."

It sounded as though she had put her hand over the receiver. A minute later she started talking again.

"There's no need to get huffy with me," Ellen said. "It's not as though I missed your calls on purpose. I had a busy day."

"What was all that noise I heard before? Where are you?"

"I'm having dinner at Gordy's with Blanche."

"Great. I just won the biggest case of my life and have been invited to Savvy's for a victory celebration, and my wife's down at the local crab shack breaking bread with the neighborhood gossip."

"Cutting Blanche down is beneath you. And you know I would've gladly driven to Tallahassee on such short notice had I gotten the messages in time. But I don't like being taken for granted. I have a right to expect adequate notice when you want me to change what I have planned."

"How much notice do you need, Ellen—a week? Two? You were more flexible when you were editor of the *Daily News*! I suppose next you'll be wanting to hire a secretary to manage your busy schedule!"

"Are you finished?"

"No, I'm just getting started! But I need to go; everyone's waiting. I can't tell you how let down and embarrassed I am that you're not here. Do you know what kind of message that sends?"

"Will you calm down and let me get a word in?" Ellen exhaled into the receiver. "I couldn't be happier that you won the Brinkmont case or sorrier that I didn't think to check my phone for messages. I'm as disappointed as you are that I can't be there."

"Yeah, I can tell. You're so broken up over it you're already having dinner with one of your quirky friends."

"Guy, what do you expect me to do, deny myself food as a punishment for—"

"Since when does it matter what I expect? You're going to do whatever you want anyhow!" Guy slammed down the phone.

He stood leaning with his palms flat on his desk, his heart racing. At least she got *that* message. He heard a gentle knock and was aware of Brent standing in the doorway.

"Everyone's ready. Is Ellen going to meet us over there?"

"No, I talked her out of it. She's been tied up all day, trying to negotiate a book deal. I convinced her to stay close to the phone."

"That's exciting. Which publisher is she talking to?"

Guy manufactured a smile and hoped it didn't look phony. "You know, I got so excited I forgot to ask her."

2

Ellen Jones stood in line at the cash register at Gordy's Crab Shack, waiting to pay her bill and determined not to let Guy's hanging up on her spoil her evening. Someone tapped her on the shoulder.

"Good to see you," Gordy Jameson said. "Where's your other half?"

Ellen handed her bill and credit card to the cashier. "He's coming home later tonight. He won a big case and went out with his partners to celebrate."

"Tell him congratulations. Next time he comes in, the clam chowder's on me."

"You can't keep giving us part of our meal free every time we come in."

Gordy smiled. "Been doin' it a long time. Who's your friend?"

"Excuse my manners," Ellen said. "This is my neighbor, Blanche Davis. Blanche, this is Gordy Jameson, the owner."

"Pleased to make your acquaintance." He winked at Ellen and handed Blanche a coupon. "Come back for a piece of Key lime pie—on the house."

"Why, thank you," Blanche said. "I certainly will."

Ellen signed the credit card slip and handed the white copy to the cashier. "Is Pam here tonight?"

Gordy shook his head. "She's hemmin' her wedding dress."

"My goodness, your big day will be here before you know it."

"Yeah, let's hope the weather cools down by then. We're doin' the whole shebang outside. We'll say our vows down at the lighthouse, and then have a big shindig on the beach afterwards." Gordy's smile stole his face. "The church is way too small and neither of us wanted a reception in the civic center. We decided to do it outdoors and invite as many as we want."

"Guy and I got the invitation and are really looking forward to it."

"Good. Since I can't talk Pam into elopin', I might as well enjoy the party. You ladies have a nice evenin'."

Ellen held open the door and followed Blanche outside, then walked down the pier toward the parking lot, trying to think of a fitting way to punish Guy for hanging up on her.

"You've been awfully quiet tonight," Blanche said. "Are you annoyed with me? I do tend to go on and on."

"No, my busy day finally caught up with me and I'm a little tired. I'll get a second wind here in a minute."

"Hi, Mom!"

Ellen looked up and saw her son and daughter-in-law walking toward her. "I wish I'd known you two were coming here for dinner, you could've joined us. You remember Blanche?"

Owen Jones held out his hand. "Yes, nice to see you again."

"Hello, Blanche," Hailey Jones said. "We met at Ellen and Guy's."

Owen looked over Ellen's shoulder, his eyebrows scrunched together. "Where's Dad?"

"Still in Tallahassee. He'll be home late."

"Isn't it great he won the Brinkmont case? He sounded so happy."

"When did you talk to him?" Ellen said.

"Right after the verdict came in. He called me at work. I understand Brent McAllister and his girlfriend are coming to your house for a victory dinner Saturday night. Why do you look surprised? Did I hear Dad wrong?"

Ellen managed a weak smile. "We haven't hammered out the details yet."

"Since you've already eaten," Hailey said, "do you want to come back inside and have coffee so we can visit?"

"Oh, honey, I'd love to," Ellen said apologetically. "But the Hamiltons invited us to the Old Seaport Dairy for banana splits."

"They're half price." Blanche nodded her head matter-of-factly.

Owen smirked, his hands buried deep in his pockets. "Mom certainly doesn't have to worry about the *cost*."

Ellen held her son's gaze until she was sure he read her irritation. "For your information, I *love* a bargain, especially if it involves something sweet."

"Oh, uh, right. Well, you ladies have fun. Nice to see you again, Blanche." Owen took Hailey by the arm and hurried her down the pier toward Gordy's.

Ellen walked to the car, thinking the men in her family needed to come down off their high horse.

Guy Jones raised his water goblet and listened for the tinkling sound as Kinsey Abbot's champagne glass touched it. "Cheers."

"Cheers." Kinsey took a sip of champagne, her eyes seeming to study his. "It's your big victory celebration and you're drinking water?"

Guy smiled in spite of his mood. "Ah, but it's Perrier."

She took another sip of champagne. "I admire a man who stands by his guns even when he's the odd man out."

"Odd man out?" Guy chuckled. "I thought we were here to hail my strengths."

"We are. It takes a strong man to stand by his convictions."

"Plus it frees me up to be a designated driver."

Kinsey smiled and poked him with her elbow. "I'm serious. You're a wonderful asset to the firm. Things started to slide after Renee left. I'm not sure Brent could have held it together without you."

"You're kind, Kinsey, but I have three very capable partners. I've just begun to make a contribution."

"And on top of everything else, you're actually humble." Kinsey tilted her glass and drank the last drop of champagne, then turned to him. "If I'd married someone like you, I wouldn't be divorced. I sure hope Ellen appreciates what a gem she has."

"I'm sure she does." *Not that she acts like it lately.*

The sound of metal tapping glass caught his attention, and he noticed Brent McAllister standing at the head of the table.

"Before dinner is served, I just want to say how pleased I am that my law-school-chum-turned-partner is working out so well. I've long admired Guy's command of law and the authority he exudes in the courtroom. He's a gentleman and a professional— and a valuable part of this finely-tuned machine of McAllister, Norton, Riley, and Jones.

"Of course, outside the office, he and I travel to the beat of different drummers. But who knows? If there really is a God, maybe He sent Guy to straighten me out. If that's the case, the poor chap's really got his work cut out for him." Everyone laughed, and Brent winked at Donna. "Seriously, Guy. Thanks for a job well done. And for all you've brought to this firm. We're proud to call you partner." Brent raised his glass. "Hear! Hear!"

Guy raised his water glass and then took a sip, painfully aware of Ellen's absence—and of Kinsey Abbott sitting much too close.

Ceiling fans whirred like helicopter blades above the white tile floor and red brick walls of the Old Seaport Dairy. Customers packed the booths and tables, and the noise level made it impossible to be heard when speaking in a normal tone of voice.

Ellen Jones sat next to Blanche Davis, eating the last of her banana split and enamored with two-year-old Sarah Beth Hamilton seated with her parents on the other side of the booth.

"Is that good, sweetie pie?" Ellen said.

Sarah Beth gave an unequivocal nod, then opened her mouth and shoved in a spoonful of drippy ice cream.

"She seems so happy and well-adjusted," Ellen said to Julie and Ross Hamilton. "I'm proud of you for dropping the charges against Billy and Lisa and allowing them time with her."

"Sarah Beth's crazy about them," Ross said. "There's no way they understood that hiding her from us was kidnapping."

Ellen was aware of the stares and whispers going on around them and wondered how long it would be before people forgot the false sex abuse allegations that had been hurled at Ross, the eight-day search for Sarah Beth, and the shocking discovery that she had been hidden by a mentally challenged couple.

"Billy and Lisa were so cute when they came for lunch Sunday," Julie said. "They handled Sarah Beth like a treasured baby doll. It was really sweet."

Sarah Beth took her tiny thumb and forefinger and pulled out a piece of banana from the soupy ice cream and offered it to Ellen. "Here you go, sweetie pie."

Everyone laughed.

"Why, thank you," Ellen said. "But I already ate my banana split. Why don't *you* eat the banana?"

Sarah Beth's blue eyes were wide and animated, her cheeks dimpled. "I *wuv* fruit." She popped the banana into her mouth and looked as though she were waiting for applause.

"Well, isn't she the little entertainer?" Blanche said. "And such pretty red hair."

Sarah Beth took her sticky hand and grabbed a fistful of curls. "I gots hair like my mama."

"Yes, you do," Blanche said.

Ross looked at his watch. "I can't believe it's already eight-thirty. I guess we should get you ladies home and little princess here down for the night so she won't rival Oscar the Grouch tomorrow."

Julie dipped a napkin in water and washed Sarah Beth's face and hands. "This was fun. Let's do it again when Guy can join us."

Don't hold your breath. Ellen got up from the table and walked toward the exit, once again reminded of her anger at Guy. She didn't relish the thought of getting into a late-night argument and wished he would stay over in Tallahassee and drive home tomorrow after they'd both had time to sleep on it.

Guy Jones finished the last bite of triple chocolate mousse and passed again on the dessert wine. As far as he could tell, Kinsey'd had enough for both of them—and then some. She had gotten flirtier after each drink, and he was sure the others around the table were starting to notice. Then again, they seemed as glassy-eyed as she was.

Guy felt a pang of loneliness as he looked around the table. The other wives seemed to be having a good time.

He took a sip of Perrier, then sat back in his chair, his arms folded, and studied his partners. These were the men whose names were set apart by comas, but whose goals were one with his: Brent McAllister, Kyle Norton, Franklin Riley. Professionally, he considered each a storehouse of knowledge and legal experience to be regarded with utmost respect.

So they got a little carried away with imbibing tonight. What right did he have to expect them to live by his standard when they didn't even know his God?

But what was Ellen's excuse for bad behavior? Her actions certainly didn't measure up to the biblical command that wives should respect their husbands. Guy felt as though he had been dropped to the bottom of her priority list. For weeks she had seemed distracted by one oddball friend or another. Why wasn't she content just to write novels and be his wife? Was it asking too much for her to greet him with open arms and give him her attention from Wednesday night until Monday morning? She had the biggest part of three days to do whatever she wanted.

Guy wanted to get on the highway and head for home, get this off his chest. But at the moment, it seemed important to be a good receiver. Brent had gone to a lot of trouble to get everyone together to celebrate the Brinkmont victory. And Guy felt increasingly responsible to make sure the others didn't drive drunk.

Kinsey leaned back in her chair, her right arm resting against his left.

Guy sat forward, his elbows on the table, his fingers linked together.

A second later, Kinsey assumed the same posture, her bare shoulder resting against his arm. "Am I so repulsive?"

"You're drunk, Kinsey."

"Is *that* why I feel so good?" She giggled, an unruly curl dropping down over one eye. She brushed the hair off her face and began giggling again.

"I think you've had enough," Guy said. "Why don't I order us some coffee?"

"Party pooper."

Guy held up his hand and the waiter came to the table. "Two coffees, please."

"Would the lady like a little more dessert wine?" the waiter asked.

Guy shook his head. "The lady would definitely *not*. Thank you."

"I like a man who takes charge," Kinsey said. "Charge!" She belted out a deep, resonant laugh and then got tickled with herself.

"What's so funny down there?" Brent lifted his eyebrows, an amused look on his face. "Or is it too *personal* to share?"

Guy shot him a don't-you-even-joke-about-it look. "Kinsey's just feeling the merriment, that's all. Nothing a little coffee can't fix."

"Coffee?" Brent reached over and picked up a short, slender bottle. "We haven't finished the Muscat. There's plenty of time for coffee later. The night's young, Counselor. Eat. Drink. Be merry. You only go around once. Live a little on the edge. Waiter, more Perrier for my friend!"

Everyone roared.

Guy smiled and shook his head, then settled back for a long evening. He would just have to stay over another night. How could he insult his colleagues by cutting short a celebration in his honor?

3

Ellen Jones lay on her side on the couch, her knees bent, and a throw pillow held tightly to her chest. She was aware of the September humidity, cold air pouring out of the ceiling vent, and the cuckoo clock in the kitchen striking eleven. How she dreaded another confrontation with Guy! How could he possibly think she wasn't excited that he had won the Brinkmont case? That's all he'd talked about for months.

Ellen tucked her chin to her chest to stretch the muscles in her neck. There was no justification for Guy hanging up on her. She had apologized all over herself for failing to check her phone messages. It was his turn to apologize.

Plus, he'd had a lot of nerve inviting Brent and his latest conquest to dinner Saturday night without asking Ellen first. She had never told Guy how glad she was that the firm's offices were located in Tallahassee, and that she wasn't pressured to put on dinner parties for the partners or flit from one cocktail party to another, schmoozing with corporate clients. Guy held his own in those situations. Ellen could endure it, but could think of no greater torment than having to mingle, Shirley Temple in hand, and make meaningless small talk. At least in her own dining room, she would be able to control what was poured into the goblets.

Ellen breathed in and forced it out. It shouldn't take Guy more than two hours to drive home since he wouldn't have to fight the rushing river of daytime traffic. Surely the victory dinner would have been over by ten.

Ellen knew she had to address the deeper reason for the tension between them. Why couldn't Guy understand that she found befriending people of varying ages and backgrounds satisfying? It's not as though she had abandoned her writing or her husband. But wasn't her response to people's needs more important to God than whether or not she got published? Or whether Guy's inflated ego could handle it?

She could still feel the sting of the unpleasant exchange they'd had Monday morning before he left for Tallahassee...

"I'm leaving now," Guy had said, giving her a seemingly half-hearted hug. "You've got three whole days to tend your menagerie of friends. But I expect peace and quiet when I get home. And I don't want people coming and going all weekend."

"Don't refer to them as if they're pets I feed and water. They're loving people I'm happy to know."

"They're an embarrassment, Ellen. Do whatever you want when I'm gone. Just remember they're your friends, not mine."

"Why the big objection? You didn't seem to mind sharing the media limelight when I stood by the Hamiltons until Ross was finally vindicated."

"Standing by someone is one thing. But why you're encouraging an ongoing relationship with a stay-at-home mom and a body shop worker is beyond me."

Ellen bit her lip and counted to ten. "Julie and Ross are wonderful kids. I enjoy their company. Sarah Beth is a delight, and I consider myself her adopted grandmother."

"You could just as easily attach yourself to a child whose parents are more socially suited. Did you ever stop to think how your choices reflect on me? I have an image to uphold."

"I'm sure the entire world is watching."

"You can cut the sarcasm, Ellen. The Hamiltons are just *part* of the problem. You're also consumed with trying to be a self-appointed Bible teacher for Billy and Lisa Lewis, who probably don't understand half of what you're trying to convey."

"Hold it right there," Ellen said. "They may be mentally challenged, but they are amazingly sharp spiritually."

Guy rolled his eyes. "Yes, I'm sure they're right up there with the apostle Paul."

"Before you pass judgment, Counselor, maybe you should sit in on one of our Bible study sessions. Some of their insights would surprise you."

"You're not trained to deal with the mentally challenged."

Ellen threw up her hands. "How else are they going to get spiritually nourished? They don't express themselves well enough to be part of a group study, but they understand far more than people realize. Should I just abandon them because they're slow?"

"Ellen, you're not a special ed teacher or a Bible scholar—you're supposed to be a novelist. Why can't you just focus on what's important?"

"That's exactly what I'm doing."

"What you're *doing* is compounding the problem by adding more characters to your collection."

"What's that supposed to mean?"

Guy scrunched his eyebrows. "Do you really need to associate with the neighborhood gossip to feel fulfilled?"

"Blanche Davis is just lonely. She's done a one-eighty since I took an interest in her."

"And that Muslim woman you met out jogging, what's-her-name...?"

Ellen shook her head and held Guy's gaze for a few seconds. "Mina Tehrani is precious. What's your problem with *her*? She's an RN and her husband's a respected oncologist."

"She's Iranian, Ellen. Have you no sense of political hot buttons?"

"She's an American citizen. Have you no sense of what it took for her to achieve that? She came to this country as an adult, had to learn the language, then studied to be a citizen while she went to nursing school. Neither you nor I had to work that hard to achieve our goals."

Guy picked up his briefcase and went and stood in the doorway. "You're never going to succeed as a novelist unless you change your focus. I can't tell you what to do, Ellen. But I suggest you reevaluate the people you surround yourself with. It seems to me you've lost your perspective. I didn't marry a social worker and have no interest in involving myself in the lives of all these people you drag home. At least have the courtesy to get it out of your system before Wednesday night..."

Ellen blinked away the irritating memory. She thought she heard the garage door open, and then realized it was just the refrigerator making noises.

She let out a desolate sigh. *Lord, help me understand what Guy wants from me, and what You want me to do about it.*

Guy Jones put Brent McAllister and his girlfriend in a cab and paid the driver. The others had already left—everyone except Kinsey Abbott, who couldn't articulate directions to the stop sign, much less her condo.

"Take me to your leader!" She looked at Guy and started giggling.

"Come on, Kinsey. Just tell the cab driver where you live."

"I live in an itty bitty gray house. With an itty bitty gray cat." She laughed so hard she stumbled and one of her high heels came off. "I want *you* to take me home."

Guy slipped her heel back on, then looked at the cab driver and shrugged. "I'm afraid she might not make it to the door, even if you got her there. Thanks anyway."

Guy gave his valet parking ticket to the attendant and waited in the sticky night air for his car to be brought around.

When he saw his Mercedes coming up the circle drive, he walked Kinsey over to the curb. He opened the front passenger door and buckled her in the seat, then took her wallet out of her purse and read the address on her driver's license.

"Any idea where Allendale Court is?" Guy asked the attendant.

"No, sir. Sorry."

Guy gave the attendant two dollars, then walked around the car and got in on the driver's side. He put Kinsey's wallet back in her purse, then sat for a moment, trying to decide what to do with her.

She sat smiling at him, curls softly framing her face, her black dress hugging her in all the right places. She was beautiful. Drunk, but beautiful. He dismissed the inappropriate thought that crossed his mind and started the car.

4

Ellen Jones woke with a start, the clanging of the cuckoo clock sounding long and exaggerated. She sat up on the side of the couch and rubbed her eyes, then got up and stretched her lower back.

She walked to the bedroom, and saw the bed had not been slept in. She squinted until she could read the clock: 5:04. Had she known Guy was staying in Tallahassee last night, she would have slept in the bed and saved herself a miserable backache.

She crawled under the covers and pulled them up around her neck. Maybe when Guy finally got home, they would both be rested and able to deal with yesterday's misunderstanding in a way that was fair to both.

Ellen closed her eyes, her mind racing, and quickly realized she would probably not be able to go back to sleep.

Guy Jones stepped out of the shower and dried off, then put on his terrycloth robe and opened the door. He stood at the sink and took a sip of coffee, his thoughts focused on how he would respond to Ellen when he got home. She would no doubt be furious with him for hanging up on her. Tough. He hoped she'd had a miserable night. He certainly wasn't planning to apologize. He couldn't remember a time when he felt less important to her—or when he'd had to lie to keep from being embarrassed by her indifference.

He wasn't sure yet how to cover his lying to Brent about Ellen's nonexistent book deal. Or how to break it to Ellen that he'd invited Brent and Donna for dinner Saturday night. But as long as Ellen felt guilty about missing the victory dinner, he knew he could manipulate her emotions to work in his favor.

Guy filled his palm with shaving cream and lathered his face, then picked up his razor and cut a swath from his sideburn to his chin. In the foggy mirror, he could see Kinsey standing in the doorway, swallowed up in his pinstriped shirt, mascara smeared under her eyes.

"I would've bet you were an electric razor man." Kinsey looked down and held the shirttail between her thumbs and forefingers. "Thanks for letting me borrow your shirt. I'll have it laundered and starched for you."

"That's not necessary. Just leave it in the closet. I'll take it home next week."

"I hope last night won't change our working relationship."

"Only if *you* let it," he said. "As far as I'm concerned, it's business as usual. No one else needs to know."

"Thanks. Not every boss would be so discreet. Are you driving back to Seaport now?"

Guy leaned his head back, razor in hand, and cut three swaths under his chin. "Yeah, I'll be out of here in a few minutes, then the bathroom's all yours. When you're ready to leave, just pull the front door shut. It'll lock by itself."

Ellen Jones finished her fourth cup of coffee and went into the living room to cool off under the ceiling fan. She picked up the remote and turned on the TV, fighting the temptation to call Guy's apartment and see whether he was still there. How hard could it be for him just to call and tell her he was on the way so she wouldn't worry?

Ellen thought about the dinner party she was purportedly throwing for Brent McAllister and his girlfriend on Saturday night. As much as she dreaded the thought of struggling to make small talk with whomever Brent had attached himself to at the moment, she knew it was the perfect opportunity to redeem herself with Guy. Suddenly she was aware of the news commentator's voice. She glanced up at the TV.

"CNN is still trying to confirm a report that early this morning the Coast Guard boarded and seized a fishing vessel filled with bomb-making materials between Seaport and Port Smyth, Florida. Sources told CNN that five men of Middle Eastern decent were arrested. Officials have neither confirmed nor denied the report. However, in light of the recent chatter picked up by U.S. Intelligence, and the country being placed on high alert for terrorist attacks, the mayors of Port Smyth and Seaport are demanding answers—"

Ellen heard the kitchen door open and turned off the TV. She sat quietly, her heart pounding, aware of Guy's footsteps approaching the living room.

He came and stood in the doorway, his briefcase in his hand, his face expressionless. "I'm home."

"You could've called so I wouldn't worry."

"I didn't feel like leaving another *message*."

Ellen started to defend herself and then decided not to. "I'm really sorry I missed the dinner. I made the assumption it went late and you decided to stay at the apartment. But it would have been nice to know that."

"I was too tired to drive home last night. But I wasn't ready to talk to you anyway."

"Are you now?"

"If you're ready to listen."

Ellen nodded, then folded her arms and waited for his apology.

"For the past few months or so, things have begun to change with us. You're consumed with everyone else and seem distracted any time I try to talk to you about what's going on with me. I resent being made to feel like an afterthought. And now I can't even reach you by phone. It's got to change."

Ellen bit her lip. "It's interesting how our perspectives differ. It seems to me that the Brinkmont case and our discussions about it have dominated our conversations for weeks. I honestly don't see that I've been inattentive. But if it happens again, call me on it right then so I'll understand what you're talking about. I've already apologized for not checking my cell phone for messages. I don't know what else to say."

"Good, because I'm really not in the mood to argue. The dinner last night was very nice, no thanks to you. I was so embarrassed you weren't coming that I told Brent you were home negotiating a book deal."

"*What?*"

"He mentioned it to the others in the course of the evening, but I'll just tell them it fell through."

"Why didn't you just tell them the truth? It's hard to believe you found it that embarrassing."

"I did. And don't ask me to apologize for how I chose to handle it."

"You could apologize for hanging up on me."

"Why? I thought it was the appropriate response."

Ellen held his gaze. "Because I dared to have dinner with Blanche instead of beating myself up over the missed phone messages?"

"I don't think you realize how disappointed I was."

"And I don't think you realize how disappointed *I* was. Don't you think I'm proud that you won the case? It killed me not to be there last night. But wallowing in my mistake wouldn't have accomplished anything."

"Oh, I don't know, it might have convinced me of your sincerity."

Ellen breathed in and let it out slowly. "Guy, I'm not going to grovel. I'm truly sorry I missed the messages and missed the chance to revel in the kudos with you. But I didn't do it intentionally. Can't you just forgive me and put this behind us?"

"When I'm ready. I'm too mad right now."

Ellen threw up her hands. "Okay, Counselor. The ball's in your court."

"One more thing," Guy said. "I invited Brent and Donna to dinner Saturday night."

"Yes, *Owen* told me. Seems I'm not the only one who isn't communicating."

"I would have cleared it with you first, but you weren't returning my messages. When Brent told me he and Donna were going to be down here this weekend, I extended the invitation right then. I was afraid if I waited until you and I had a chance to connect, it might seem like an afterthought."

Try showing me the same consideration, she thought.

"Also, after the party broke up last night, I put Brent and Donna in a cab and sent them home. But Kinsey was too—"

The phone rang. Guy turned around and walked into the kitchen and picked it up. "Hello...? Hold on...Ellen, it's for you."

Ellen got up and went in the kitchen. Guy dropped the receiver in her hand and rolled his eyes.

"Hello?"

"Ellen, it's Mina Tehrani. The FBI came to Cancer Center and took Ali! I'm scared! I don't know what to do!"

"Why did they take him?"

"Because of boat with bombs Coast Guard found. Ali knows nothing of such things."

"Where is Ali?"

"I don't know! Please, they won't hurt him, will they? He has nothing to hide! He is American citizen! He is fine doctor!"

"Mina, calm down. Where are you?"

"At home."

"Stay right there. I'm coming over."

Ellen hung up, her eyes colliding with Guy's.

"I wasn't finished talking," he said. "Which of your mixed up friends am I competing with now?"

"Mina's husband has been taken in for questioning by the FBI. She's confused and terrified. I can't just leave her home by herself."

"What does the FBI want with her husband?"

"Something to do with a boat the Coast Guard seized this morning. Apparently they found bomb-making supplies onboard. I heard something about it on CNN just before you got home. I'm sure it's a big mix-up."

"There's no way you can know that! I told you associating with Muslims would come back to haunt you. At least it's reassuring to know the FBI's on top of their game."

"Not to a Muslim-American whose husband has just been hauled away."

Ellen read the name Tehrani on the mailbox. She went through the wrought iron gate and up the steps of the elegant three-story home and rang the doorbell.

A second later, Mina opened the door and ushered her in, then fell into Ellen's arms and began to sob.

"What will happen to Ali? He's good man. He loves freedom in this country. My daughter Sanaz wants to come home from university and stay with me. I tell her no. She must not allow this to take her mind off education. I tell her everything will be all right. But I don't know that."

"Listen to me," Ellen said. "The FBI won't detain Ali for long; he's done nothing wrong. I'm sorry you have to endure this. Maybe someday we'll figure out a better way to sift out terrorists."

"Ali became citizen ten years now. He works long hours and pours heart and soul into being fine doctor. He would have nothing to do with terrorists or anyone who would harm United States of America."

Ellen kept her arms around Mina and rocked gently from side to side. "I know that."

"If FBI thinks Ali is friend of al-Qaeda, they not let him go!"

"Shhh, don't think that way. Ali has an impeccable reputation. As soon as the authorities realize he has no connection to any terrorist group, they'll let him come home."

"But who will respect him after this? Reputation will go straight down toilet!"

Guy finished watching the "News at Noon," then turned off the TV and sat quietly for a moment. This morning's confrontation between the Coast Guard and a suspected terrorist vessel off the coast of Seaport was all over the news. It seemed as though every conceivable branch of law enforcement had been called in. All he needed was for Ellen to be seen with Mina Tehrani right now. Why couldn't she get involved with *normal* people who weren't controversial and high profile?

Guy heard the front door open. He picked up the newspaper and pretended to be reading, aware that Ellen had stopped in the doorway.

"I got back as quickly as I could," she said. "Mina is just devastated. Some women from the mosque finally came over to stay with her."

"There must be a reason the FBI singled out her husband, Ellen. It's not as though they draw names out of a hat."

Ellen sat in the chair facing him. "Mina said Ali has a nephew who recently graduated from FSU. He's been quite vocal with his disapproval of America's involvement in the Middle East. Last month the Tehranis had a get-together of family members who live in the U.S., and this nephew was at their home throwing around his anti-American sentiments. Finally, Ali grabbed him by the arm, and the two left the house. Ali came back without the nephew and told the others that he was no longer welcome in their home. That's the last she saw of him."

Guy shook his head and exhaled loudly. "The FBI had

probably been watching the house! Why can't you just stay away from these people before you get pulled into it?"

"*These people* are innocent of any wrongdoing and aren't pulling me into anything. Why should I cower in fear of the FBI? The Tehranis cherish freedom more than both of us put together. One of these days you're going to realize what beautiful people they are."

Guy turned the page of the newspaper. "Well, like they say: Beauty's in the eye of the beholder. All I see is trouble brewing."

5

Just after one o'clock on Thursday afternoon, Gordy Jameson looked around the dining area of Gordy's Crab Shack and decided the noon traffic had thinned out enough for him to take a lunch break. He stuck his head in the kitchen and hollered at his fiancée.

"Pam, I'll be out back with the guys, okay?"

"All right, love," Pam Townsend said. "I'll keep an eye on things."

Gordy went out on the back deck and sat at the table with his lunch buddies, Eddie Drummond, Captain Jack, and Adam Spalding.

"You guys get enough to eat?" he said.

Each man nodded.

"Did you hear about the boat the Coast Guard seized between here and Port Smyth?" Eddie said.

Gordy shook his head. "What's the deal?"

"They found five terrorists on board," Captain said.

"Terrorists? Are they sure?"

Eddie lifted his eyebrows. "Gee, I don't know…five Arabs…materials on board to make suicide bombs. Maybe they got lost on the way to the fishing tournament."

"Come on, you're pullin' my leg," Gordy said.

Adam's eyebrows scrunched. "It happened just a mile off the beach where I hang out. Would I joke about a thing like that?"

"Where'd you hear this?" Gordy said.

"On the news, on the way over here." Eddie chugged the last

of his iced tea, then stood and put a dollar under the saltshaker. "I've gotta get back to work. Want me to call if I hear anything else?"

"Yeah, keep me posted." Gordy's eyes followed Eddie to the back door.

"You look rattled," Captain said.

"I was just thinkin' of Pam and our wedding plans. Sure hope nothin' awful happens to make us postpone it. I'm ready to take that woman home with me."

Adam smiled. "So go for it. You can't let the threat of terrorism put your life on hold."

"Yeah, I know, but if somethin' like 9/11 happens again, who's gonna feel like celebratin' a wedding?"

"By the way..." Captain leaned forward on his elbows. "Did you and Pam ever find a place big enough for the reception?"

Gordy arched his eyebrows. "Yeah, the beach. We've rented a couple of those huge gazebo-lookin' tent thingies. Pam wanted to have one of 'em set up for a seafood buffet and the other for servin' cake and punch."

"Ah, did I detect a hint of traditional?" Adam said.

Gordy laughed. "In the rings and the preacher maybe. Everything else is gonna be anything but."

"What if it rains?"

Gordy smiled and punched Adam on the arm. "It wouldn't dare. But on the slight chance that Mother Nature decides to double cross us, bring your umbrella. I might do a little Gene Kelly number right there on the sand."

"I never thought I'd see you this happy again after Jenny died," Captain said. "Seems like Pam'll make a good partner in the business, too."

"Yeah, she's lovin' it. That's the icin' on the cake." Gordy looked up, surprised to see Pam come out the back door and approach the table. "Speakin' of cake, I bet I know what this is about."

Pam sat in Gordy's lap, her arms around his neck, her deep tan set off by her yellow sundress. "Okay, love. The cake will be chocolate inside and out, though I'm sure the bakery chef was cringing."

Gordy kissed her on the cheek. "Works for me, darlin'."

"Why is the bakery chef cringing?" Adam said. "Chocolate sounds great. You're talking about the groom's cake, right?"

Gordy winked at Pam and then turned to Adam, a broad grin stretching his cheeks. "Who said anything about a groom's cake? Our wedding cake's gonna be chocolate—and in the shape of a crab. Seems rather fittin', I'd say."

Guy Jones went in his study and shut the door, then picked up the phone and dialed the office.

"McAllister, Norton, Riley, and Jones. How may I direct your call?"

"It's Guy. Let me talk to Kinsey."

He sat back in his chair and put his feet on his desk.

"This is Kinsey Abbott."

"How's your head feeling?"

"Huge. I haven't partied that hard on a weeknight in a while. Thanks for taking care of me."

"You're welcome. Lucky for you I'm a gentleman."

Kinsey dropped her voice an octave. "Oh, I don't know. It might've been fun to have *something* to repent of...oh, come on, laugh. I'm just kidding."

"I don't joke about things like that." Guy turned over a pencil and bounced the eraser on his desk. "You didn't say anything to the others about staying at my apartment, did you?"

"Of course not."

"Did everyone make it in?"

"Uh-huh. *I* can tell they're dragging, but it's business as usual."

"Were you able to get your car?"

"Sure, after I paid a whopping parking fee."

"Better than a whopping fine—or a serious accident. You were in no condition to take the wheel."

"I know. You're a prince. And that Ellen's one lucky lady. By the way, did she close the book deal with the publisher?"

"Actually, no. It fell through."

"I'm sorry."

"I think she's holding out for something better. Oh, I almost forgot...I guess you heard about the boat the Coast Guard seized this morning between Seaport and Port Smyth?"

"No, what boat?"

"The one masquerading as a fishing boat and carrying materials for making suicide bombs. The latest report is that a surface-to-air missile was also discovered on board. The Coast Guard took five Arab men into custody. It's all over the news. You might want to turn on the radio."

"Where have *I* been? No one in the office mentioned it so I doubt if they've heard anything either. I'll go turn on the radio. Thanks for the heads up."

"Sure. You need me for anything?"

"Not yet. I'll call if I do."

"Okay, I've got to get back to work."

"Thanks again for keeping me out of trouble last night."

Guy smiled. "See you Monday."

He hung up the phone and heard a gentle knock at the door. "Come in."

The door opened and Ellen stood in the doorway. "Sorry to bother you. Do you want spicy shrimp pasta or grilled chicken for dinner?"

Feeling guilty, are you? "Pasta sounds good. Heavy on the spicy. Did Mina's husband come home?"

Ellen shook her head. "Not yet. I can't imagine the FBI will hold him much longer. None of the men they arrested were Iranian."

"Need I remind you that al-Qaeda is an equal opportunity recruiter throughout the Arab world?"

"Mina said the Iranian people are Persian, not Arab. And their two cultures are as different as the United States and Mexico."

"In case you hadn't noticed, Muslims stick together."

Ellen glared at him. "Not every Muslim supports the violence."

"No, just the throngs taking to the streets and burning the U.S. flag and effigies of our president."

"That's a small percentage. And you don't see American Muslims taking to the streets."

"Only because they're outnumbered. Any way you slice it, your befriending the Tehranis will be perceived as anti-American."

Ellen folded her arms tightly, her mouth a rigid line. "I resent the implication that my friendship with them somehow makes me disloyal. You don't know anything about them."

"Why would I want to?"

Ellen exhaled loudly. "That kind of narrow thinking is part of the problem."

"Oh, so now it's *my* fault?"

"Guy, don't let this complex issue come between us. I loathe the violence as much as you do. But it's ludicrous to turn my back on the Tehranis just because they're Iranian."

"You keep dancing around the fact that they're also Muslim. Have you taken a good look at the news lately? These people are crazed and out of touch with the real world. You can't trust any of them!"

"That's an unfounded generalization, Counselor, and you know it!"

"Then they'd better clean out the mosques because that's sure how it looks!" Guy looked down at the stack of papers on his desk. "I need to get back to work."

"I'm curious what impression you think Muslims have of Christians?"

"I really don't care."

"Not even that they perceive the U.S. to be a Christian nation—and therefore our moral decline a by-product of Christianity?"

"Why do you always have to analyze things to death? We're supposed to hate evil. Can't you just leave it at that?"

"We're also supposed to love our neighbors as ourselves. What if I'm the only Christian Mina and Ali ever know? How will they know what true Christianity is all about if I don't model it?"

"Oh, please. Muslims are just waiting for the chance to shove their entire twisted belief system down *our* throats. If they can't convert us, they'll destroy us. Why do you think the FBI doesn't care if Mina and her husband are Iranian or Saudi or Pakistani or Iraqi—only that they're Muslim?"

"Fine! Then let the FBI determine if the Tehranis are a threat to our national security! *My* job is to treat them the way *I* would want to be treated!"

Guy put on his reading glasses and picked up the paper on top of the stack on his desk. "If you're finished with your tirade, I need to get back to work."

"Just one more thing, *Counselor.* You were relentless when I incorrectly judged Ross Hamilton guilty of sexual child abuse. You told me to weigh the facts, that feelings couldn't be trusted. May I suggest you follow your own advice?"

Gordy tiptoed into the kitchen at the crab shack and came up behind Pam and put his arms around her, his cheek next to hers. "How come I always find you out here?"

She rested her back against his chest. "I love being in the kitchen. It's therapeutic."

"Therapeutic, eh? Well, far be it from me to deprive my

future bride of needed therapy. What smells so good?"

"I just took my fruit pies out of the oven."

"So that's what you've been up to?"

She nodded. "Three different kinds. Plus triple chocolate mousse cake and my special pineapple bread pudding. I thought we might try adding more variety to our dessert menu."

"What's wrong with Key lime pie?"

"Nothing. It's delicious. But our regular customers might order dessert more often if they had additional options."

"Hmm...you're right. Smart thinkin'."

Pam turned around, her arms around his neck. "Gordy, be honest with me. If you'd rather I stay out of the kitchen and spend my time out front with customers, I will."

"Nah. I just like showin' you off. I want you to find where you fit since you're gonna be the other half of this ownership soon."

"I enjoy greeting customers for a while. I really do. But I love rolling up my sleeves. There's just something about having flour up to my elbows...I'm in my element."

"Okay, darlin'. Fine with me. I'm just happy to have you here. Those pies any good?"

Pam smiled, her blue eyes twinkling. "Made from my grandmother's state fair blue ribbon recipes. Cherry, mixed berry, and peach."

"I'd better have a taste of all three with a big scoop of vanilla ice cream. Maybe a little of that chocolate cake and some of that bread puddin', too."

Pam gently patted his middle. "You can't make a habit of this if you want to fit into that Hawaiian shirt we bought for the wedding."

"Yeah, I know. But I should sample whatever we're promotin', right?" Gordy picked up her hand and pressed his lips to it. "Just give me a smidgen of everything."

He watched as she took a small plate and began to fill it with samplings of the desserts she had made.

"By the way," he said, "I listened to the radio a few minutes ago. The men the Coast Guard captured had definite links to al-Qaeda. Looks like they were usin' that big fishin' boat to store stuff to make bombs. But the surface-to-air missile really has authorities rattled. I guess that thing can knock out a commercial jet pretty easily."

"Gives me cold chills. I remember watching a program not too long ago about that kind of weapon being available on the black market. I doubt this is the *only* one."

"Yeah, makes you wonder what else is out there and who's plannin' to use it."

"Did you ever get a hold of Will?"

"I left a couple messages on his voice mail, but he hasn't called back. I'm sure every available cop's been pulled into this thing."

Pam put a scoop of ice cream on the pie slivers and handed the plate and a fork to Gordy. "We've all been waiting for the other shoe to drop since 9/11. I hope and pray this isn't it."

6

On Thursday night, Gordy Jameson was just turning off the eleven o'clock news when the doorbell rang. He put down the remote and went to the door. Through the screen he saw Will Seevers standing on the stoop.

"I knew you'd be up," Will said. "Mind if I come in and unwind before I go home?"

Gordy pushed open the door. "Course not. I've been waitin' for you to return my calls. You just gettin' off work?"

"Yeah. Do you believe this mess with the boat?"

"Still tryin' to absorb it all. Let's go out to the kitchen. You want a Coke?"

"Sounds good."

Gordy grabbed two cans of Coke out of the refrigerator, then sat at the table and handed one to Will. "I've got a few questions."

"Fire away. But I probably don't know any more than you're already hearing on the news—not that the feds would tell a lowly police chief much else anyway."

Gordy fiddled with the saltshaker. "How'd the Coast Guard know to seize the boat? From what I saw, it looks like a run o' the mill fishin' boat."

"No one's saying, Gordy. But someone must've tipped them off. The feds are being really closed-mouthed. Gripes me to be out of the loop with this thing so close to my turf."

"Is it true these guys are linked to al-Qaeda?"

"Yeah, at least one of them's wanted in connection with 9/11."

Gordy glanced up at the picture of Pam and him that he'd

stuck under a magnet on the refrigerator. "Then I suppose the town's gonna be crawlin' with feds tryin' to figure out where these guys were operatin' from?"

"Count on it. They're concentrating on the neighborhood around the mosque."

"I've got customers who live in that neighborhood. They seem real nice."

"Yeah, well, this is the wrong time to be too trusting."

"Or too paranoid. The Muslims I know don't go along with the violence."

"Really? Try getting them to denounce it. Wanna bet they won't?"

There was a long pause.

"Sorry, Gordy. I didn't mean to take my frustration out on you. But after what happened today, I've got an eleven-year-old holed up at home because she's afraid some suicide bomber might be outside. Makes me want to gather up all the Arabs and ship them back where they came from."

"We start doin' that and it won't be the same America anymore."

Will took a gulp of Coke. "Let's talk about something more pleasant. How're the wedding plans coming?"

"Great. Pam's doin' most of the plannin'. All I'm responsible for is the rings, the preacher, and the best man. Which reminds me, your shirt came in. I'll give it to you before you leave."

Will chuckled. "I can't believe you're really going to have us wear Hawaiian shirts."

"Why? We'd suffocate in suits. Would look pretty dumb with Birkenstocks, too."

"Hey, you get no complaints from me. Do you realize the wedding's two weeks from Saturday? You getting cold feet?"

"Nah, warm as toast. I'm so ready to be married again. After Jenny died, I didn't think I could love anyone else. Then to find Pam...well, I can't thank you and Margaret enough for fixin' us up."

"We've gotten a kick out of it, too. Really, Gordy, it's great to see you so happy."

"I just hope all this terrorist stuff doesn't throw a big monkey wrench into the turnout."

"Why would it?"

"I dunno. People might feel a little vulnerable congregatin' on the beach after what was found on that boat. Plus, if the feds are gonna be here knockin' on doors, the media's not gonna be far behind. You remember what it was like when the Hamilton girl was missin'? This place was overrun with media. It was a big pain in the neck."

"Well, on the upside, at least you'll have more customers. The media always sniffs out the good places to eat."

Gordy spun the lazy Susan and watched the condiments go round and round. "Will, you think there's gonna be a problem with Dr. Tehrani bein' at the wedding?"

"That Iraqi oncologist who was so nice to Jenny?"

"He's Iranian."

"I don't know, Gordy. I sure don't want to shake hands with any of those people right now. Maybe others feel the same way."

"But Doc Tehrani's a great guy. I can't tell you how compassionate he was with Jenny. I'll never be able to thank him enough."

"I hear what you're saying, but you can't trust any Muslims nowadays."

"Sure I can." Gordy dumped a few toothpicks on the table and pushed them around with his index finger. "Doc's an American citizen—a darned good one."

"Then he shouldn't have any problem understanding my right to avoid shaking his hand."

"I've never heard you talk like this before."

"We're at war, Gordy. And like it or not, the enemy's Muslim."

"Come on, the enemy's the nutcases who push all that jihad stuff. You can't lump all Muslims in with them."

"I can when I can't tell who's who."

Ellen Jones lay staring at the ceiling fan going round and round in the dark. For the first time in thirty-three years of marriage, she wondered if Guy had stopped loving her—or if she had stopped loving him. They'd hardly exchanged a civil word in days, and for weeks it had seemed as though he was looking for new reasons to be angry with her.

Ellen felt determination tighten her chest. It would be wrong for her to yield to his petty dislike of her friends and sever ties with them—especially Mina. And especially now.

Lord, surely You didn't bring these friends into my life for me to abandon them because Guy is more interested in his professional image than his Christian witness?

Ellen didn't want to disrespect her husband. But her yielding to Guy's objections would force her to disregard the biblical command to love her neighbor as herself.

Lord, I'm so frustrated. Please help me to do the right thing.

Guy lay on his side facing Ellen, the only sound the beating of his heart. He opened his eyes and saw hers were open, then quickly clamped his shut. He hoped she was feeling guilty, though he doubted his strong objection to her choice of friends would change anything. Ellen's stubbornness could outlast a pit bull's.

He felt justified withholding from her the details of the victory dinner—and what had happened afterwards. So what if he'd let Kinsey use his couch to sleep off the effects of her celebrating? Nothing had happened. And it wasn't as though he were enmeshed in her life the way Ellen was with her friends.

Guy tried to will away the empty feeling. He couldn't remember a time when he had kept a secret to spite Ellen. Since that night thirty some years ago when they'd met at the university coffee shop, their hearts had been inexplicably intertwined...

Guy had sat in the corner booth, drinking black coffee and snacking on doughnut holes. He had one eye on the calculus assignment laid out in front of him, and the other on a curly-haired brunette sitting at a nearby table, her face hidden behind a journalism textbook. For some reason, the young coed was a total distraction. The way she twirled her pencil over and over like a baton. Her occasional chuckling at whatever she was reading. And those pretty, long legs crossed at the ankles and neatly folded under her chair.

She unexpectedly lowered the textbook and locked gazes with him, revealing the clearest blue eyes he'd ever seen. "Is there a reason you keep staring at me?"

"Oh, uh, hi. I couldn't help but notice you're studying, too, and was wondering if you'd care for a doughnut hole?" He cringed at how stupid that sounded. "I'll never eat all these." He slid out of the booth and placed the half-full pastry box on her table. "There you go: brain food. Guaranteed to enhance your learning experience."

The corners of her mouth turned up slightly. With her thumb and index finger, the young lady reached in the box, picked up a chocolate glazed doughnut hole, and popped it into her mouth "Mmm...you've hit on my weakness."

"Then why don't I get you a coffee to go with it? By the way, I'm Guy Jones."

Her eyes seemed to search his. "Ellen Madison. All right. Cream, please."

Guy went to the counter and ordered a coffee with cream and a warm-up for himself, then brought them back to the table. He pulled out a chair and sat across from the woman who'd stolen his concentration and blown his chances of completing his calculus assignment before the sun came up.

Ellen proved to be a good conversationalist—intelligent, thought provoking, succinct. She expressed strong opinions about a variety of issues, yet he sensed her heart was as delicate as a flower petal. She was passionate about her studies, especially journalism—and quick to tell him she didn't drink, do drugs, go to wild parties, or feel obligated to kiss a guy just because he asked her out. He fell in love with her before she polished off the box of doughnut holes...

Guy wanted to reach over and pull Ellen into his arms as if that would somehow fill the aching void. Instead, he turned over and faced the wall, wondering if they would ever again understand each other.

7

On Friday morning, Gordy Jameson stood at the back door of the crab shack, watching Billy Lewis wash down the umbrella tables on the deck with Clorox water. He smiled and walked outside, nearly bowled over by how thick and hot the air felt.

"Hey, Billy, you about ready to call it a mornin'? It's miserable out here."

Billy's head bobbed, perspiration shimmering on his face and dripping down his temples. "I have no more tables to clean, Mr. G. I will go now."

"Why don't you sit a spell, have a cold drink before you head out?"

"Okay. I *like* Sprite."

Gordy smiled. "I knew that. Sit there under that umbrella and I'll be right back."

Gordy went inside, got a couple cans of Sprite out of the refrigerator, then went back outside and sat in the chair next to Billy. "Here you go."

"Thanks, Mr. G."

"So what're you and Lisa up to these days?"

"We are hav-ing a Bible study with El-len."

"That's right. I almost forgot. How's it goin'?"

"Good. I like El-len. She does not care if we are slow."

"So you learnin' anything?"

"Oh, yes. We are learn-ing how to love our neigh-bor."

Gordy was thinking Billy and Lisa already had that one

nailed down. "Which reminds me, I heard the Hamiltons had you over for lunch."

Billy's smile revealed a row of crooked teeth. "We ate cheese bur-gers and sang songs with Sar-ah Beth."

"Aw, that's great, Billy. I know you were real fond of that little girl. The Hamiltons are nice people. I'm glad they decided not to prosecute."

Billy stared at him blankly. "I do not know that word."

"I'm glad they believe you weren't tryin' to hurt Sarah Beth."

Billy nodded. "I am glad, too."

The back door opened and Pam Townsend stepped outside. "Hey, fellas. We need to get those tables set for lunch."

Gordy tipped the can and downed the last of his Sprite. "That's our cue to scat. See you in the mornin', Billy."

"I will do an ex-cel-lent job."

Gordy stood, a hand on Billy's shoulder. "You always do."

Billy left, and Gordy slid his arm around Pam's waist and pressed his lips to her cheek. "Did you paper clip the dessert specials to the menus?"

"Yes. I'm going to feel really foolish if, after all this, everyone orders Key lime pie."

Gordy smiled. "Good news travels fast. I have a feelin' you're gonna be busier than you wanna be. Let me get outta your way so you can have the girls set the deck for lunch."

"As humid as it is, I doubt many customers will want to sit out here. I sure hope the weather cools off before the wedding."

"Don't worry, darlin', there's always a nice breeze on the beach. Come on, let's get inside where it's comfortable."

Gordy opened the back door and followed Pam inside just as Guy Jones walked in the front door with his son.

"Well, look who's here," Gordy said, extending his hand. "Ellen was in the other night and said you won a big case and were out with your partners celebrating."

Guy gripped Gordy's hand. "Yeah, biggest case I've ever won. You've met my son, Owen."

Gordy nodded. "Nice to see you again. You guys are the first customers of the day. Pick your spot."

"I'd like to sit at that back table," Guy said, nodding toward the window.

"Great. Come right this way."

Gordy seated them and handed each a menu. "The clam chowder's on me—to celebrate your big win."

"Thanks," Guy said. "That's generous of you, as *always*."

Gordy winked. "My pleasure. Somebody will be right with you to take your order."

Guy picked up the menu and began to scan the selections, realizing he wasn't hungry.

"You look tired," Owen said.

"I haven't slept well the past couple nights."

"I guess you and Mom are as concerned about this terrorist thing as Hailey and I."

"I am." Guy looked over the top of the menu and lowered his voice. "Your mother, on the other hand, is rallying around that Muslim friend of hers. Never mind that the woman's husband was questioned by the FBI."

"You're kidding?" Owen's eyes were round and questioning.

"I wish I were. After the Coast Guard seized that boat, the FBI picked up Dr. Tehrani at his office. Your mother's convinced herself he's not involved. She's gone over to their house a couple of times to *comfort* the guy's wife."

"She shouldn't get in the middle of this."

Guy lifted his eyebrows. "She doesn't listen to me. I told her from the beginning making friends with that woman would come back to haunt her."

Owen picked up his spoon and tapped it lightly on the table. "Dad, I'm worried about you two."

"So am I. All of a sudden, your mother's friends are more important to her than I am. It's driving a wedge between us." Guy let out a sigh of exasperation. "Sorry. I shouldn't be dumping this on you."

"That's all right. I'm not blind."

"Did you know she missed my victory dinner?"

"Yeah, she didn't get your message in time."

"Because she didn't bother to check. You can't imagine how embarrassed and empty I felt not having her there. I told everyone she was home negotiating a book deal."

"You lied?"

Guy nodded. "When I go back on Monday, I'll tell them it fell through. It sounded better than admitting my wife was inaccessible and didn't return any of my messages."

"In all fairness to Mom, she's out of the habit of checking her cell phone for messages now that she's not working for the newspaper. Don't you usually call her at home in the evenings?"

"You're missing the point."

"Don't get upset, I'm not taking her side. I'm just trying to understand what's going on. Maybe she's wrapped up in her friends because she's lonely."

"She wouldn't be lonely if she'd focus on writing another novel."

"You can't know that. Mom likes to be where the action is. Maybe she's not cut out for that much alone time."

"Your mother's an intelligent, creative, articulate wordsmith. She needs to be writing. If she needs people contact, she should join a writer's group."

The waitress walked up to the table and set a glass of ice water in front of each of them. "You ready to place your order?"

"Yes, I'll have the special," Guy said. "Blue cheese on the salad. Just water to drink."

Owen closed his menu. "I'll have the same. Ranch dressing on the side."

"All righty. I'll have this out to you in just a few minutes."

Guy took a sip of water and didn't say anything else until the waitress was out of earshot. "Owen, I guess what I'm trying to say is, I feel as if your mother and I are living two separate lives. We don't share the same goals, the same friends, the same likes and dislikes, the same *anything*. Sometimes I don't even feel as though I know her anymore."

"Don't you think your working in Tallahassee half the week has something to do with that?"

"No. We were fine for over a year—until she got involved in the search for Sarah Beth Hamilton. And after Billy and Lisa surrendered the girl to the authorities, your mother became obsessed with the whole lot of them—and the other weird friends she spends too much time with. She doesn't seem to care anymore if she gets published."

Owen's index finger moved slowly around the rim of his water glass. "Are you and Mom even talking about all this?"

"I try. Seems to bounce right off her. You know how stubborn she is. But my biggest concern is her relationship with this Mina Tehrani. The Hamiltons, the Lewises, and that gossip Blanche what's-her-name are just annoyances. But the Tehrani woman could be bad news."

Ellen Jones opened the wrought iron gate and went up the stone walkway toward the Tehrani's house, cooled by the shade of the live oaks in the front yard. She went up on the porch and rang the doorbell, noticing for the first time the initial "T" in the rectangular stained-glass window above the front door.

Half a minute later, Mina Tehrani opened the door and threw her arms around Ellen and clung tightly for several seconds. "Come in, my friend."

Ellen handed her a still-warm loaf of homemade oatmeal bread. "I thought this might taste good. I know you're not eating."

"You know too much," Mina said. "Yes, I had not thought of food. But aroma makes me hungry. I'll have a slice if you will."

"All right." Ellen followed Mina out to the kitchen. "How long was the FBI here?"

"Long enough to ask same questions over and over. I tell them same answers, but they ask anyway."

"Mina, I'm sure you know this, but be sure your husband has a good attorney."

"Ali told FBI he does not want attorney. He has nothing to hide."

"I don't think that's wise."

"My husband would never allow attorney to tell him, 'say this,' or 'don't say that.' He will speak truth. FBI will see that. Would you like coffee with bread slice?"

"Sure, but why don't you let me help you?"

Mina motioned for Ellen to sit. "Please, it is good for me to be busy. I've been moping around like rag doll."

"You realize the FBI has to either charge Ali with something or let him go?"

Mina's eyes drooped with exhaustion. "Ali is free to go. He is helping FBI find Bobak."

"Ali's nephew?"

"Yes. Bobak is loudmouth, but not terrorist. FBI will see that, too."

Mina cut a thick slice of bread and halved it. She put it on a blue china plate and set it in front of Ellen, then put a small bowl of preserves and a butter dish on the table.

"Is it possible Bobak isn't harmless? I mean, it's pretty brazen for an Iranian student to protest against U.S. Middle Eastern policies right now. He has to know that he'll draw the attention of Homeland Security and the FBI."

"Bobak is young fool. He has acquired no wisdom and

mouth is much too big for brain. But he is all talk." Mina set her plate on the table and poured coffee into Ellen's cup and then her own. "The men Coast Guard arrested intended to harm people of United States with suicide bombs and surface-to-air missile—horrible weapons. Bobak uses only mouth as weapon. FBI will see that."

Ellen studied her friend's face as she sat across from her at the table. Did Mina believe what she was saying about Ali's nephew, or was it wishful thinking?

"Did your friends from the mosque stay with you last night?"

Mina shook her head. "I sent them home. I could not listen to any more negative talk. That accomplishes nothing."

"They're angry the FBI questioned you and Ali?"

Mina's eyebrows gathered and she took a sip of coffee. "Also scared who might be next."

"What about you?"

Mina dabbed her eyes. "I must trust FBI to resolve matter. Ali has nothing to do with terrorists. He is not violent person and believes..." Mina paused, her chin quivering. "I should not speak of this."

"You can trust me," Ellen said.

Mina looked at her searchingly, a tear trickling down her cheek. "Ali believes terrorists twist meaning of jihad to justify evil pursuits. He speaks only to me about this and is afraid we will not be welcome at mosque if he criticizes publicly. This is no problem for me. My heart grew cold toward Islam long ago. But Ali could not bear such a separation." Mina folded her arms on the table and looked out the window. "Jews, Christians, Muslims—all claim to be children of Abraham. So why do we go on hating each other?"

Guy sat working in his study, aware of the garage door opening and closing, the rumbling in his stomach, and the delicious aroma of Ellen's pot roast. He was ready for a home-cooked meal but didn't look forward to sitting across the table from his disgruntled wife.

The phone rang and he picked it up. "Hello."

"Guy, it's Brent. Listen, Donna and I are going to have to bow out of dinner tomorrow night. Her sister is coming in from Fort Lauderdale to escape a nasty weekend. That tropical storm is expected to hit along the east coast sometime tomorrow and dump ten inches of rain."

"Yeah, that's what I heard."

"I hope our canceling won't be a problem."

"No, not at all. We'll do it another time. You and Donna have a nice weekend with her sister. I'll see you Monday."

"All right. Thanks for understanding."

Guy hung up the phone and went out to the kitchen where Ellen was unloading a sack of groceries. He noticed a package of pork tenderloin on the countertop.

"Who was on the phone?" Ellen said.

"Brent. He and Donna can't make it tomorrow night."

Ellen stopped unloading the sack and let out an exaggerated sigh. "I just bought everything I need to make dinner."

"Sorry. Donna's sister lives in Fort Lauderdale and is coming to Tallahassee to escape the tropical storm. Can't you freeze the meat?"

"I could. I like it fresh."

"Sorry. At least you don't have to spend the day tomorrow preparing for dinner guests."

Ellen opened the refrigerator and put the meat in the bottom pull out drawer. "It's not the preparation I mind, it's Brent flaunting his conquests."

"Yes, he has a weakness for women, but he's also a great attorney with an enviable professional reputation. Don't forget he helped Owen get the CFO position at Global. Plus, Brent's a stimulating conversationalist. The guy's really smart."

"He may be intelligent, but his actions tell me he isn't *smart*." Ellen walked over to the pantry and took out a jar of horseradish.

"That's unfair, Ellen. The people you spend time with can't hold a candle to Brent in education, success, or anything else."

"How about morals?"

"Brent's okay. He just needs the Lord."

"Amen to that." Ellen picked up two potholders and opened the oven door. "It's not my place to judge Brent. It just irritates me that you act as though he's a class act just because he's a Harvard grad and has a successful law firm. It takes more than financial success to make a person classy. Brent's an alley cat. And frankly, I'm tired of you always coming to his defense."

"Then maybe you can understand how *I* feel, listening to you defend those Muslim friends of yours!"

Ellen pricked the pot roast with a fork, then carried the roasting pan from the oven to the stovetop and set it down. "That's an unjust comparison, Counselor. The Tehranis have done nothing wrong."

"That's what you keep saying, but I think you're naïve."

"I'm sure you do. Dinner's ready. Why don't I fill your plate and bring it to the table?"

"Actually, I've got lots of work still to do. I think I'll eat my dinner in my study."

Ellen handed him an empty plate without looking up. "Suit yourself."

8

The Monday morning sky was a canvas of glowing pink and purple when Guy Jones set down his briefcase and walked out on the veranda where Ellen sat reading the newspaper.

"I'm leaving," he said. "I'll call you tonight."

Ellen turned the page, her eyes fixed on the newspaper. "Fine."

Thanks for the lousy weekend! Guy turned around and left, raw determination keeping him from reacting to another of her one-word responses.

He picked up his briefcase and his garment bag on the way out the kitchen door. He got in his Mercedes, backed out of the garage, and headed for Tallahassee, relieved to be away from Ellen's pouting.

He drove through Seaport and Port Smyth, his neck and shoulders tight and his heart empty, wondering when he had gone from being happily married to dreading being alone with his wife. When had they stopped understanding each other? Or stopped listening?

Guy took the Tallahassee exit and merged into the river of traffic going north. He slid a Kenny G disc into the CD player and turned up the volume.

Ellen loaded the breakfast dishes into the dishwasher, then picked up the phone and dialed the Hamiltons' number.

"Hello."

"Julie, it's Ellen. I'm going to have to opt out of going with you and Sarah Beth to the zoo tomorrow."

"What's up?"

"I need to cut back on my activities for a while and be more present to Guy."

"Okay. But I thought he was in Tallahassee till Wednesday."

"He is. But he'd like me to be around the house more and to get back to my writing. When I go too many directions it seems to make him stressed."

"Sarah Beth and I will miss you, but I understand. You sound down. Are you all right?"

"I'm fine. Just trying to focus on my priorities."

"Okay, talk to you later. Wait, Sarah Beth's taking the phone..."

"Hi, what's your name?" said a tiny voice.

"This is Miss Ellen. Is this Sarah Beth?"

"Yes, and my mama take me to see big, big, big, *big* el-fants!"

Ellen smiled. "Have a wonderful time, sweetie. I want to hear all about the zoo when you get back."

"Okay, 'bye."

Ellen heard a muffled sound and then Julie chuckling. "Think she's a little excited?"

"I wish I were going. I'm sorry to saddle you with the long drive by yourself."

"I'll be fine. It's probably good that you're spending the week at home. You have been pretty busy. Are you going to cancel your Bible study with Billy and Lisa?"

"No, those kids are working too hard for me to change the plan. But I'm canceling everything else."

"Okay, I'll check in later in the week and let you know how the zoo adventure turns out."

"Thanks, Julie. Give Sarah Beth a hug for me."

Ellen hung up the phone and redialed.

"Hello?"

"Blanche, it's Ellen. Do you think you can get another ride to the eye doctor this afternoon?"

"Yes, I'm sure I can. Is something wrong?"

"I seem to have overextended myself and I'm feeling a little pushed."

"That's all right, dear. I'll find someone else to drive me. But I'll so miss seeing you."

"Thanks for understanding. We'll get together soon."

Ellen hung up the phone and the doorbell rang. She went to the front door and opened it and saw two men in sport coats standing on the porch.

"Yes?"

"FBI. Are you Ellen Jones?" the older of the two said.

Ellen nodded, her eyes fixed on the ID he held out.

"I'm Special Agent Seth Walker and this is Special Agent Jim Green. We'd like to talk to you about Dr. Ali Tehrani. May we come in, ma'am?"

"Yes, of course."

Ellen held open the door, her heart pounding. She led the men into the living room, seated them on the couch, then sat in the loveseat facing them.

"How can I help you?" she said.

Special Agent Walker studied her with intense brown eyes. "What is your relationship with Dr. Tehrani?"

"My relationship is with his wife, Mina. I met her a few months ago when I was out jogging. I don't know them well, but they seem like very nice people. Dr. Tehrani—Ali—has always been gracious when I've stopped by the house, and I've heard nice things about him from several people at my church who are patients of his."

"What do you know about his daughter?"

"May I ask why you're questioning me about the Tehranis?"

"Please answer the question, ma'am."

Ellen didn't like the tone of Walker's voice and suddenly wished Guy was home. "Sanaz is a junior at FSU. I've only met her once. Seems like a lovely girl. Smart. Polite."

"Have you met Bobak Tehrani?" Walker said.

"No, I haven't."

"Do you know who he is?"

Ellen nodded. "He's Ali's nephew."

"And how do you know that if you've never met him?"

"Mina told me that last month she and Ali had a family get-together, and Bobak was there, spouting off anti-American sentiments. Ali escorted Bobak out of the house and came back alone. He told the others Bobak was no longer welcome. That's the last she saw of him."

"Did Mrs. Tehrani tell you this before or *after* our agents took her husband in for questioning?"

Ellen locked gazes with Special Agent Walker. "Mina had no reason to lie to me."

"Please answer the question, Mrs. Jones."

"After. But why would she tell me something like that before the FBI took her husband away? It was only afterwards that she was going out of her mind, trying to think of a reason why you would suspect him of having ties to terrorists."

"So Mrs. Tehrani spoke to you about that?"

"Yes, of course. She's beside herself with worry about Ali. He's done nothing wrong. She's sure that's the only conclusion you can come to."

Walker looked at Green and then at Ellen. "Did Mrs. Tehrani ever talk about her husband's friends?"

"Not to me."

"So she never gave any indication whether there were anti-war or anti-American sentiments being expressed at the mosque?"

"She's never repeated to me anything that was discussed at the mosque."

"Never?"

"Only in vague generalities."

Walker leaned forward on his elbows. "How about getting *specific* about the vague generalities."

"Mina mentioned that the Muslim women who stayed with her after Ali was taken away were afraid of who the FBI might pick up next. We didn't discuss it beyond that."

"Then what *did* you discuss?"

"You—the FBI. Mina has confidence that you'll see Ali is not a violent man and is not involved in anything wrong. But she's scared."

"If he's innocent, what's she scared of?"

Ellen folded her arms and looked into Walker's eyes. "The *power* you have. She feels helpless. I can appreciate you're doing your job and are trying to keep us safe. But surely you can understand how frightening it must be for Muslim Americans right now."

"We can't worry about it, ma'am. We're fighting a war. We don't have time to mollycoddle every Muslim whose feelings get hurt."

Guy opened the door to his apartment, went in the bedroom, and hung his garment bag in the closet. He spotted the striped shirt Kinsey had used as a nightshirt wadded up on the floor. He reached down and picked it up, aware of the scent of perfume. So much for taking it home with his dirty laundry. He decided to drop it by the cleaners on his way to the office.

He opened the top drawer of the dresser and took out a business card he'd forgotten to put in his briefcase and put it in his shirt pocket.

Suddenly, he was hit with an eerie feeling that someone was in the apartment. He looked over his shoulder, his heart racing, and listened intently. Nothing.

"Hello? Is someone there?"

Guy walked softly out to the living room and surveyed it

with his eyes. He went over and stood in the kitchen doorway and didn't see anyone, then poked his head in the bathroom and saw nothing out of order.

He started to turn around when something propelled him forward, his forehead colliding with the wall above the towel rack.

Guy heard footsteps running behind him and then the front door open. He stood up straight, his hand on the knot that had already started to form on his head. He looked at his hand, relieved to see no blood, then ran out the front door, his eyes darting all over the parking lot. The intruder was gone.

Ellen glanced at her watch and realized that Special Agents Walker and Green had been grilling her for over an hour.

"I think we're about finished," Walker said. "We may have more questions later. If you think of anything else we need to know, give us a call." He handed Ellen a business card. "Being asked to answer questions about your friends must seem cold, but we can't afford to assume anything when we're dealing with terrorists. These people have threatened over and over to attack us again. What we found on that boat should send shivers up your spine."

"It does," Ellen said. "But so does the fear that innocent people like the Tehranis might be sacrificed in an effort to find out who's guilty."

Walker put his pen in his lapel pocket. "We know what we're doing, ma'am. We appreciate your cooperation."

Ellen followed the two agents to the front door and watched as they got in their car and drove away.

She went back to the living room and sat on the couch, her mind reeling with questions. Was Mina being naïve about Bobak? Was the mosque being used to harbor terrorists? What would Guy say when he found out the FBI had involved Ellen?

She leaned her head on the back of the couch and closed her eyes, suddenly aware that her head was throbbing.

Guy put his hand on the antique brass doorknob of the offices of McAllister, Norton, Riley, and Jones and pushed open the door. He spotted Kinsey Abbott at her desk and started walking in her direction.

"There you are," Kinsey said. "I thought maybe you got swallowed up on the freeway."

Guy picked up her hand and put it on the knot just above his hairline. "Feel that?"

"Ouch. What happened?"

"I went by my apartment on the way here and surprised a burglar. The guy shoved me into the bathroom wall and took off."

"How awful! Did you call the police?"

"Yeah, I filed a report, but nothing's missing. I must've walked in right after he did because the place wasn't ransacked."

Kinsey's eyes grew wide and she spoke softly. "I'm sure I pulled the door shut when I left."

"You did. He busted the dining room window."

"Did you get a look at him?"

"Not even a glimpse. I ran outside right afterwards, but I didn't see anyone. The police are going to talk to the neighbors so everyone's on the lookout."

"Surely you're not going back there?"

"Why not? The window should be fixed before the day's over, and there's nothing in my apartment worth his risking a repeat visit. So is Brent in this morning?"

Kinsey nodded toward a closed door. "He's meeting with a client. Kyle and Frank are in court."

"Well, I've got a mountain of paperwork to catch up on. I think I'll hole up in my office and see if I can't knock it out."

Kinsey hugged herself, her eyes fixed on her desk.

"You okay?" Guy said.

"Not really. It gives me the creeps that someone was in your apartment. What if I had been there instead of you?"

"Well, you weren't. Don't waste your time thinking about what might have happened. It's over."

Kinsey looked as if she were going to say something and then didn't.

"Let it go," Guy said.

"I don't have a good feeling about you going back there."

"Well, I'm not spending the night at Holiday Inn Express; that's why I have an apartment. Look, the guy'd have to be an idiot to come back again. He's probably moved on to a different neighborhood."

Kinsey reached up and tucked her hair behind her ear, and he noticed black-and-blue marks on her wrist.

"How'd you get the bruises?"

"Oh, those? I was emptying the bookshelf to clean it, and a stack of books toppled over and fell on it. Don't fuss over my little mishap. You're the wounded one."

He half smiled. "I'm too busy to be wounded. Hold my calls till after lunch and let me get a head start."

Guy studied her for a moment, then walked into his office with the strangest feeling that Kinsey knew something she wasn't telling him.

9

Guy Jones pulled his Mercedes into the assigned parking space outside his apartment. He paused for a moment, then got out of the car and went inside. He flipped on the lights and checked the dining room window, glad to see it had been repaired and a new lock put on.

He got a broom and dustpan and cleaned up the glass fragments, then vacuumed the carpet. He thought about calling Ellen but didn't feel like talking to her yet.

He glanced at his watch, then turned on the TV and surfed until he found news.

"...Also, a spokesperson for the FBI told reporters at a news conference in Seaport today that all five Arab men arrested last Thursday have been linked to the al-Qaeda network, and at least one of the men is believed to have been involved in planning the 9/11 attacks.

"The spokesperson also said that the FBI has reason to believe these five men had been operating as part of a terrorist cell but would not give any details about the intensive investigation currently underway.

"However, an unnamed source at the Seaport Cancer Clinic told a reporter from WRGL-News in that city that one of the clinic's oncologists, Dr. Ali Tehrani, has been questioned by the FBI in connection with the incident. Dr. Tehrani is Iranian born and came to the U.S. fifteen years ago. He has worked at the clinic for the past ten years. The FBI would not comment on whether or not Dr. Tehrani is a suspect, citing security interests and not wanting to compromise the current investigation.

"The Muslim communities in Seaport and Port Smyth are surprisingly quiet, but sources tell us that a joint meeting of Muslim leaders in both cities will take place this evening at an undisclosed location to discuss what their response should be to the new wave of fear and animosity spurred by last Thursday's terrorist threat.

"In local news tonight..."

Guy put the TV on mute and walked out to the kitchen. "Boy, Ellen, you really know how to pick them!"

He popped open a Diet Coke, then went back to the living room and started to sit on the couch when he noticed something stuck behind the cushion. He reached down and pulled out a Baggie filled with white powder.

How did that get there?

He sat on the couch and tossed the Baggie on the end table, thinking the cleaning lady must have dropped it. Then again, since when did she bring her own soap?

He grabbed the Baggie and held it under the light and examined the powder closely. His pulse began to race as he was hit with a sinking feeling that what he held in his hand might be cocaine. But how could cocaine have gotten into his apartment?

He opened the bag and took a whiff—odorless. He'd always heard that cocaine on the tongue leaves a cold, numbing sensation. He touched the powder with his pinkie and dabbed it on his tongue. *Oh, boy.*

Guy's mind began to race in reverse. Who had been in his apartment? The cleaning lady. Brent. Two executives from Brinkmont Labs. The apartment complex maintenance man. A pizza delivery boy. And Kinsey.

Guy sealed the Baggie, his eyes fixated on it. The cleaning lady couldn't afford it. Brent wasn't that stupid. The two execs from Brinkmont had worked only at the dining room table. The maintenance man had walked around marking his checklist, but had never sat. The pizza delivery guy never left the doorway.

Kinsey slept on the couch.

Guy got up and paced, his pulse racing faster than his thoughts. Is this what the intruder was looking for? Was it he who had put those bruises on Kinsey's wrist? What other explanation could there be? She didn't strike him as a user. Was she dealing?

He walked aimlessly around the apartment, not wanting it to be true. What excuse could Kinsey possibly have for getting involved in drugs? She was a beautiful young woman with a respectable career, much too smart for this kind of nonsense. He must be wrong. But what if he wasn't?

Guy got out the phone book and looked up her address and copied it down. He decided to figure out where she lived and pay her a visit. And he didn't plan to call first.

Ellen Jones put her dinner dishes in the dishwasher, her mind racing with the events of the day. How would she defend her friendship with Mina when Guy found out the FBI had questioned Ellen about the Tehranis?

The fact that she had finished the first chapter in her new book should help to placate him, but that was only part of the problem. Ellen still had little hope of ever being published, and spending her days writing a novel that may never have an audience wasn't her idea of doing something significant.

How she longed for the satisfaction she had experienced as a newspaper editor! She had never tired of being immersed in the drama and competing with the electronic media for breaking news. But the intensity was more than Guy had been willing to deal with.

He had convinced her to pursue something tamer and less intrusive to their personal lives. Ellen sighed. Nothing about the life they had now seemed tamer or less intrusive. Had they ever been so cut off from each other—or so miserable? For the first time since their move to Seaport, she longed for the good ol' days.

Guy pulled up in front of a classy two-story townhouse at 106 Allendale Court. *That's her "itty bitty gray house?"* He looked again at the piece of paper on which he had jotted down Kinsey's address. This was the right place.

He got out of the car and went to the front door. Lights were on inside and he heard a TV. He rang the doorbell and waited for what seemed like an inordinate amount of time. Maybe he should have called first.

Finally the door opened and Kinsey stood staring at him, her jaw hanging open. "Guy! What are you doing here?"

"Should I turn around and leave?"

"I'm sorry. I just didn't expect it to be you. Uh, you want to come in?"

"Yes, if you don't mind. I'd like to show you something."

Kinsey held open the door, and he stepped onto a shiny floor of black-and-white marble squares.

He followed her into the living room: Plush white carpet. Huge oil paintings. Glass tables. Black leather furniture. *Nice.*

"Would you like something to drink? I've got Pepsi or water, or I can perk some decaf—French Vanilla or Hazelnut."

"No, thanks. I'm fine."

"Okay. Make yourself comfortable. What is it you wanted to show me?"

Guy sat on the couch, and a second later a gray cat jumped in his lap and startled him.

"Grayson!" Kinsey picked up the cat and put it in another room and closed the door. "Sorry. He's just curious. Where were we?"

"I found something I'm puzzled about." He reached into his sport coat pocket and pulled out the Baggie and held it up.

"What's that?" she said.

"I was hoping you could tell me."

"Tell you what?"

"Come on, Kinsey. I found this stuck down behind a couch cushion. It's not mine. It has to be yours."

She shook her head. "What is it?"

"Well, let's see, it goes by lots of names: Snow. Nose candy. Blow. *Cocaine.*"

"Please tell me you didn't drive all the way over here with that in your pocket? What if the cops had stopped you? You'd be on your way to jail with no defense!"

"I didn't even think about it, that's how upset I am! Now answer my question: Is it yours?"

"I don't do cocaine! I've passed every drug test, and you know it."

"Then where did it come from? You're the only other person who's sat on my couch."

"What about your cleaning lady? She was supposed to be there Friday."

"She couldn't begin to afford this, and if she were dealing, she wouldn't be cleaning apartments." Guy let his eyes glide around the room and then locked gazes with Kinsey. "Nice condo. I'm surprised you can afford a place like this on what *we're* paying you."

"How dare you talk to me like I'm on the stand! I got a good divorce settlement, and I resent the implication! I don't do drugs. And I don't sell them." Her eyes filled with tears and her chin quivered. "I'm hurt you would even think that, much less confront me with it. You know me better than that."

"I'm just trying to determine how an illegal substance got into my apartment."

"Did you ever stop to think the intruder might have left it there?"

"Wedged between the back of the couch and the cushion?"

"Maybe the police were following him and he needed a quick hiding place."

"The police never alluded to that."

"Come on, Guy. If the intruder had been under surveillance, they wouldn't have volunteered anything. Maybe he's a dealer." Kinsey got up and started pacing, her hands moving with every word she spoke. "I just can't believe you think I could be involved in anything illegal. How stupid do you think I am?"

"Actually, I think you're a highly intelligent young woman. So surely you can understand why I have to confront you with it when there's no other explanation."

"There has to be, it's not mine. I swear!"

"Then I suppose your fingerprints won't be on this plastic bag?"

"Absolutely not."

Guy breathed in and let it out. "Okay. You know I had to ask. I'm going down to the police station and turn this over before I get caught with it."

Kinsey stopped, her face ashen. She sat in the chair facing him, her eyes pleading. "Don't do that. Just flush it. Why get the police involved? It'll be embarrassing for both of us."

"Why? We haven't done anything wrong."

"Do you think Brent and the partners want this kind of publicity?"

"Am I supposed to just pretend I didn't find an illegal substance in my apartment?"

"If you get rid of it, no one will ever know and there'll be no harm done."

Guy saw fear in Kinsey's eyes. "Why are you so adamant about this?"

"Look, I know respected professionals who snort coke. I don't. And I don't want to answer a gazillion questions for the police—and especially not the DEA. What other people do is their business. I don't want to be forced to point a finger."

"Why do you care? What they're doing is illegal."

"But not turning them in *isn't*. Look, if it gets out that I knew, it'll look bad for the firm, and Brent will find a way to get rid of me. I'm good at what I do. I've done nothing wrong. Please don't put my job in jeopardy." Kinsey seemed focused on her hands for half a minute and then looked up at him. "Besides, you don't want everyone at the firm to know I spent the night at your apartment. If the police question you, it's going to come out."

"We'll just have to tell the truth. They all know I'm devoted to Ellen."

"Oh, but there's a side of Brent that would just love to prove your religion's a farce."

"Brent *already* believes my religion's a farce. But he knows me and knows I'd never cheat on Ellen or get myself mixed up in drugs."

"Really? Are you sure enough to risk the respect you've earned just to turn in a bag of cocaine the police will probably never be able to trace back to the dealer?

IO

Guy Jones went inside his apartment and bolted the door. He pulled the drapes, took off his sport coat, then removed the bag of cocaine from the pocket and stuck it in the kitchen cupboard next to the sugar.

He went in the living room and flopped on the couch and put up his feet. He probably should have gone to the police and turned over the cocaine. But Kinsey had made a good point.

Was getting involved in this worth risking the respect he had earned, especially if it didn't lead to a conviction? Was it worth losing Kinsey as his secretary? Was he willing to let the media spin the story, knowing that anything that was reported would reflect on the firm—and any mention of Kinsey's overnight at his apartment would sound sleazy? If only he'd told Ellen when he'd had the chance. Was he prepared to deal with all that?

It was all Guy could do not to flush the cocaine down the toilet and forget he'd ever seen it. He wanted to get on the phone and tell Ellen everything that had happened and get her input. But how objective could she be after he hadn't been forthcoming? And how forgiving?

Ellen sat out on the veranda, relieved to feel a cool breeze blowing off the gulf and glad that midnight would mark the end of September.

She glanced at her watch: ten after nine. Guy was taking his sweet time calling her—probably his way of getting back at her for ignoring him over the weekend.

But how had he expected her to react? His sharp criticism had cut a swatch out of their relationship that still needed mending. She hoped it would improve his mood that she had finished the first chapter in her new novel, but doubted it would be enough to stave off his anger when she told him about being questioned by the FBI. She just wanted to get it over with.

The phone rang and she hurried inside to answer it.

"Hello."

"Ellen, it's Mina. Is this bad time to talk?"

"No, I was just sitting outside on the veranda. How is Ali?"

"He stares at nothing and doesn't want to talk."

"No wonder. It has to be horrible having his integrity questioned in the media."

"Ali made FBI see he had nothing to hide. This is his reward?"

"Is the media still hassling you?"

"They wait outside like pack of wolves—not for truth, for lies. Ali will not talk to them."

"Do you know if the FBI found Bobak?"

"Yes, Ali led them to Bobak but was not allowed to talk to him. My husband feels great sorrow turning nephew over to FBI."

"He did the right thing," Ellen said. "They'll let Bobak go if he's innocent. But with all that's at stake, they can't very well disregard his speaking out against the U.S."

"He is young fool with big mouth. But he is not terrorist."

"Then he has nothing to fear." Ellen sat at the breakfast bar. "The FBI questioned me today, too."

"No...I'm so sorry."

"Don't be. If they were going to talk to someone, it's good they came to me. I had nothing but positive things to tell them."

"You are kind, Ellen. And good friend."

"I'm just truthful. I'm sure the FBI has questioned the people Ali works with, and I can't imagine that everyone didn't have nice things to say about him." Ellen heard sniffling. "What is it, Mina?"

"My heart breaks for my husband. He is afraid people will not respect him after he is dishonored this way."

"People are scared. But most are reasonable. Anyone who knows Ali knows what a warm and caring person he is...and what a good doctor. They're not going to change their opinion just because the FBI questioned him."

"I wish it were so, my friend. But I am not so sure."

Ellen heard the call-waiting signal. "Mina, can I call you back? I need to take this call. It's probably Guy."

"You go. I'm going to bed. It's been exhausting few days."

"Sleep well," Ellen said. "I'll touch base with you tomorrow." She switched over to the other caller. "Hello."

"You *are* home," Guy said. "I was beginning to wonder."

"Actually, I've been home all day. I cancelled everything else and worked on the book. I finished the first chapter."

There was a long pause.

"Well, that's a surprise," Guy said. "Are you happy with it?"

"I think so. It's intriguing anyway. So how's your day been?"

"Interesting, to say the least. I stopped by the apartment this morning on my way into the office and surprised a burglar."

"Good heavens! Inside or outside?"

"Inside. I had put my hang up bag in the closet and was standing at the dresser, looking for a client's business card, when I had the weirdest feeling that someone was in there. I looked around the apartment and didn't see anyone; and just as I stuck my head in the bathroom, someone shoved me from behind and I went headlong into the wall."

"Are you hurt?"

"No, just a nasty bump on my head. But the guy got away. I never saw him. By the time I got my wits about me, he'd run out the front door."

"How do you know it was a man?"

"Because he shoved me like Attila the Hun."

"Please tell me you reported it to the police."

"Yeah, I did. But I can't find anything missing. The guy broke the dining room window and let himself in. I had a lot of glass to clean up, but the window's already been fixed. With a better lock this time."

"Good." Ellen paused to let her thoughts catch up with her emotions. "What did the police have to say?"

"They figure it was probably a burglar working the area. I'm sure he's moved on. Regardless, I can't imagine he'd be stupid enough to come back here since I don't have anything valuable."

"What do you mean? You have a TV and a computer."

"Dinosaurs—both of them. Practically worthless."

"Thieves today will kill you for a nickel—or for no reason at all! I can't believe you're being so calm about this!"

"Ellen, get a grip. I wouldn't have told you if I thought you were going to go off." There was a long pause. "Then again, judging from your strong reaction, I might be persuaded to conclude you still care about me."

Ellen was surprised by the tenderness in his tone. "Of course, I still care about you, even if you are a bully."

"Sorry. I have been rather forceful lately."

"The word *controlling* comes to mind."

"But do you understand it's because I see things you don't?"

Oh, please! Ellen breathed in and let it out, letting a few moments of dead air say what she wasn't going to.

"Okay, I know better than to get into these kinds of issues over the telephone," Guy said. "Let's agree to discuss this in a civil manner when I get home Wednesday night. Till then, will you accept my apology for hanging up on you and for raising my voice? No matter how angry I was, it was wrong."

"Yes, it was. I accept your apology. I'm sure both of us can do better."

"I agree. Now, hopefully, each of us will have a better week."

Ellen wanted to bring up the FBI's questioning of her, but she wasn't about to spoil the truce. "So how did everyone at the office react to the burglary?"

"I didn't have time to get into it. It wasn't that big of a deal."

"Could've fooled me. I'm surprised you would downplay it."

"Because I didn't overreact, I'm downplaying it?"

Ellen started to retort and then didn't. "You sound tired, Counselor."

"Yeah, I am. I should probably go. I've still got paperwork to do before I call it a night."

"All right. Lock your doors and windows."

He chuckled. "Yes, Mother. Good night."

"I love you."

"I love you, too."

Guy hung up the phone. *Darn!* Why hadn't he had the courage to tell Ellen about finding the cocaine or about Kinsey spending the night at his apartment? Maybe it would be easier when he could eyeball her.

He went in the living room and lay on the couch. He didn't have any paperwork to do tonight. What possessed him to tell Ellen he did? The last thing he needed was to get comfortable with not telling her the truth.

Guy's mind began to replay his confrontation with Kinsey. Something about it didn't sit right. He'd worked closely with her for over a year and had never before felt as though she was hiding something. He found it hard to believe she would just turn a blind eye to these young professionals who were doing coke. Then again, he knew of several instances when he had questioned Brent's ethics but hadn't told anyone because he didn't feel it was his place.

Guy was pretty sure Kinsey wasn't doing drugs. She didn't

show any signs of it, and the few times she had been required to take a random drug test, she had tested negative.

He just wasn't buying the idea that some intruder stashed a bag of cocaine behind the couch cushion.

II

On Tuesday morning, Guy went into the office early and noticed when Kinsey came in that she didn't have much to say. The dark circles under her eyes told him she probably hadn't slept any better than he had.

She gathered some papers, then came into his office and closed the door behind her.

"Have you got a minute before I go to the courthouse to file these?"

Guy put down his pencil. "Sure."

Kinsey pulled a chair closer to his desk and sat. "Did you talk to the police after you left last night?"

"Actually, I didn't."

Her eyes were wide and questioning.

"*No,* I didn't flush it," he said. "I'm not comfortable destroying evidence. But you made a good point about this being bad publicity for the firm. I don't want to be hasty."

"So what *are* you going to do with it?"

"I don't know, but I'd sure like to know how a bag of cocaine got into my apartment." Guy held her gaze and thought she flinched. "Kinsey, if there's something you need to tell me, now's the time to do it. We've gotten close this past year and I'd like to think you could trust me with anything."

"Of course, I could...if I had anything to tell. I don't."

Guy exhaled. "All right."

"So you're definitely not going to the police?"

"Not at the moment."

"I think it's a big mistake to hang on to it."

"I'm an officer of the court, Kinsey. I don't destroy evidence. You of all people should know better."

"I do. But this is completely outside the norm. Neither of us knows anything about where the cocaine came from, so why should it dictate what we have to do? If you turn it in to the police, they'll want to question me and I'll be forced to either lie or admit I know people who do coke. Some choice. When Brent finds out, he'll find a reason to get rid of me. And the press will turn my sleeping on your couch into some sleazy affair. How do you think that will fly with Ellen?"

Guy felt the heat burn his neck. "I'm not going to do something unethical just to keep from being accused of something that never happened. My track record should mean something."

"I'm sure it does, Guy. *I'm* the one who's going to end up paying for it."

Ellen Jones stopped jogging and looked out over the calm gulf waters, the sound of seagulls filling the expanse. She took a whiff of damp, salty air, and was suddenly reminded of her friend Ned who used to spend his days building sandcastles and giving away bits of wisdom. The water was the color of his eyes and the denim cutoffs he always wore. She could almost picture him, skin tanned and wrinkled, and white wisps of hair blown in all directions.

"When I build my sandcastles," Ned had told her, *"my mind is free and I can do a lot of intercessory praying. I can't explain why, but praying for people makes me feel connected to heaven and earth—and it's something I look forward to every day when I wake up and realize I'm still here."*

But on his eighty-eighth birthday, Ned didn't wake up—at least not in this realm. Ellen looked up at the gold-rimmed cloud that hid the sun and wondered if Ned knew what an impact he had made in her prayer life—or that she had forgiven Blanche Davis and befriended her.

Ellen knelt next to the surf and scooped the wet sand into a mound and patted it until it was hard. Ned's words seemed almost audible.

"You're probably wondering why a grown man's out here all alone, building a sandcastle. It's good therapy. Keeps me out of trouble."

Ellen smiled. "Well, Ned, that's exactly what I need."

As she sculpted the sand, she prayed for Julie, Ross, Sarah Beth, Billy and Lisa, Blanche, and Mina and Ali. She prayed that God would help her understand why Guy objected to her friendship with them. *Lord, help me let go of my anger. Help me to act and not react.*

Ellen heard someone call her name. She looked up and saw Mina Tehrani jogging along the surf about thirty yards from where she was sitting. She waved and motioned for her to come.

Mina came over and dropped down in the dry sand. "It feels good to run. I have been moping around too long."

"Nothing like a little exercise to perk up one's spirits. How's Ali doing?"

"He insisted on going to clinic."

"Then that's probably where he needs to be."

"I think so. His patients were unhappy being passed off to other doctors. Hospital gave me early shift starting tomorrow. It will be good to get busy." Mina glanced over at Ellen. "Is your husband still angry?"

Ellen felt her face get hot. "What makes you ask that?"

"I think he doesn't like you to be friends with us. Too much controversy maybe."

"It's not personal, Mina. Guy's wary of all Muslims right now. It has everything to do with terrorists and nothing to do with you and Ali as people. If he'd take time to get to know you, he'd like you as much as I do."

"But we are Muslim *and* Iranian. How you say...two strikes?"

"Well, you're not terrorists. Has the FBI released Bobak?"

Mina's eyebrows scrunched. "No, and I'm worried. I'm sure he knows nothing about weapons on boat or terrorist cell. But smart aleck attitude will not sit well with FBI."

"Regardless, if Bobak's innocent, they'll clear him."

Mina raised her eyebrows. "*If?* Even you have doubts?"

"I don't know your nephew," Ellen said. "But I have hope that your assessment is right."

Mina looked out over the water. "Ali called his brother in Iran last night. They had words."

"About Bobak?"

"Ali's brother called him traitor for helping FBI find Bobak."

"That's unfair," Ellen said. "If Bobak's innocent, he has nothing to fear. And if he isn't, Ali's refusal to cooperate would make him guilty of harboring a terrorist. Doesn't Ali's brother understand that?"

"He understands only what he hears on Aljazeera. He acts like puppet—much safer for him. We could never go back to that, though nothing will be the same for us now."

"Why do you say that?"

Mina's eyes brimmed with tears and she looked down, her sleek, dark hair falling over her cheeks, her finger making circles in the sand. "From now on, Muslims will not trust Ali because he is friend of U.S. government. And government will not trust Ali because he is friend of Islam." Mina wiped a tear off her cheek and looked at Ellen. "Ali's honesty and patriotism bring only scorn. Where is freedom in that?"

Guy felt a gnawing ache in his stomach. He looked at his watch and realized it was already noon. He put a paperweight on the contract he was reviewing and got up from his desk and stretched his lower back. He noticed Kinsey wasn't at her desk.

He picked up a pencil and wrote on a Post-it note. *Kinsey, I need you to research something for me. Let's plan to meet at four and I'll go over it with you—G.*

Guy stuck the note on the back of Kinsey's chair, then stopped at the receptionist's desk on his way out. "Has Kinsey called in?"

"Yes, sir, around eleven. She said she was at the courthouse and might be a while."

"Okay, thanks."

Guy opened the door and walked down the hall toward the entrance to the building, trying to decide if he was in the mood for a sandwich or a pizza buffet.

He opened the door just as Kinsey reached it. "There you are."

"Sorry," she said. "This took longer than I thought."

"Have you had lunch?"

"No, but I really don't need to eat."

"Come on. Let's grab a bite. The last thing I need is you running out of steam."

"Are you kidding? I could live for a month off the calories I consumed at Savvy's the other night. Plus, I don't feel very conversational at the moment."

Guy was thinking two pouting women in his life was too much. "So don't talk. You can't just stop eating."

"Then let's have lunch at my place. I made up a huge batch of spinach salad and that's a lot healthier than eating out."

"Does sound good, but it seems inappropriate for me to have lunch at your place."

She rolled her eyes. "Suit yourself. But that's the only thing that sounds good to me. See you later." She turned around and started walking toward her car.

"Kinsey, wait. I'll drive."

Guy and Kinsey walked over to his car and got in. He fastened his seatbelt and backed out of the parking space, aware of Kinsey sitting with her arms crossed, ridges across her forehead.

"You okay?"

"Not really."

"You mad at me because I didn't get rid of the cocaine?"

"Mad? No. Disappointed? Very. I might as well start looking for another job."

"Will you stop? Even if I turn the cocaine in and the police question you, Brent's not going to fire you just because you turned a blind eye to some of your friends using cocaine. You may get a slap on the wrist, but you've done a terrific job for the firm, and I'm not about to part with you without a fight."

"You'd fight for me?" she said.

"You don't think I want to train someone else, do you?"

Kinsey raised an eyebrow. "Excuse me, Counselor, who trained who?"

"Okay, so you whipped me into shape. I don't want to start over with someone else. We make a dynamic duo."

Ellen changed out of her running clothes and into a sundress and sandals, justifying in her mind that if she had refused Mina's invitation to take her to lunch, it would have been perceived as rejection. How could she hurt Mina by admitting how vehemently Guy objected to her association with the Tehranis?

Besides, after tomorrow, Mina would be working the day shift at the hospital and Ellen would have limited opportunities to spend time with her, other than their chance meetings while out jogging. And since she had to eat lunch anyway, what difference did it make if she spent that hour with Mina? It seemed the loving thing to do. She could work on her book all afternoon.

Ellen checked her cell phone for messages and didn't find any, then dropped the phone in her purse and left it on. She hoped Guy wouldn't call when she was with Mina, but if he did, at least he couldn't accuse her of being inaccessible.

12

Gordy Jameson was talking with four ladies in the back booth and spotted Ellen Jones and Mina Tehrani coming in the front door of the crab shack. He counted out four coupons and laid them on the table. "Ladies, here's a coupon for each of you for free dessert next time you come in. Enjoy your meal."

Gordy went over and stood with Ellen and Mina. "I didn't know you two knew each other."

Ellen smiled. "We met one day while jogging on the beach."

Gordy saw the dark circles under Mina's eyes. He took her hand and held it, his eyes seeming to search hers. "I was thrilled when I saw your R.S.V.P. I'm so glad you and Dr. Tehrani are coming to the wedding."

Mina's cheeks flushed. "We were planning to, yes. But now I hesitate. Why bring controversy to happy occasion?"

"Mrs. Tehrani, listen to me," Gordy said softly. "As far as Pam and I are concerned, there is no controversy. And the only thing that would take the happy out of the occasion is your lettin' what anybody else thinks keep you from comin'. It means a lot to us to have you there."

Mina's eyes watered. "Thank you for saying so. I will tell Ali."

"That's better. Okay, where would you ladies like to sit?"

Mina looked at Ellen. "Is table in corner by window all right for you?"

Ellen nodded. "Yes, that's fine."

Gordy picked up two menus and led the women to their

chosen table. "Someone will be right with you to take your order." He winked at Ellen and put two coupons on the table. "Enjoy one of Pam's special new desserts—on the house."

Gordy went out to the kitchen looking for Pam and nearly ran headlong into Weezie Taylor, his assistant manager. "I'll bet I know why *you're* here already. Okay, go ahead. Toot your horn."

Weezie let out a robust, contagious laugh. "Whooooeeee! We were up twenty percent last night. And I personally *sold*—notice I did not say *gave away*—seventeen pieces of Pam's melt-in-your-mouth fruit pies, two bread puddings, and five pieces of triple-chocolate mousse cake." Weezie pranced around in a circle and then stopped, her hand out. "Give me five."

Gordy slapped her hand with his. "You're somethin' else. Keep it up and I'll be givin' you a raise."

"I'm tellin' you, boss, the staff was pumped. Didn't I tell you we could get more people in here if you'd let me tend to the advertisin'?"

"Yep, you did. I'm proud of you, Weezie."

Pam Townsend appeared and locked arms with Weezie. "Hey there, girlfriend. I've got six fruit pies hot out of the oven, and six more going in."

Weezie's smile was a half moon. "Excellent. Now if we can just get Mr. Congeniality here to stop *givin'* it away."

Gordy went over and stood between Weezie and Pam, an arm around each. "But I love spoilin' my customers."

"I know," Weezie said. "Can't you spoil 'em a little less often?"

A waitress poked her head in the kitchen. "Boss, the guys are out back. They're wondering if you'll be joining them."

"Yeah, tell 'em I'll be right there." He turned to Weezie. "Hang around here much longer and you're gonna end up workin'."

"All right, I'm leavin'. Think I'll go buy me a new dress with that raise I know I'm gonna get."

Gordy laughed. "Go on, scat."

Weezie left the kitchen, and he turned to Pam and pressed his lips to hers. "We've got plenty of help out front. I'm gonna go have lunch with the guys."

"Good, I need you out of my hair. I've got to make some more pineapple bread pudding and a triple-chocolate mousse cake before Weezie's shift starts." Pam giggled. "This is really fun."

Ellen looked out the window of the crab shack and nodded at Gordy who was having lunch on the back deck with his friends.

"Gordy's such a nice man," Ellen said. "I'm glad he and Pam are getting married."

Mina nodded. "I remember Ali wept with him when Jenny lost fight with cancer. My husband did not think Gordy would recover from deep loss. But now to see he has found love again...well, it's great blessing."

"I didn't know Jenny, but it's easy to see how crazy he is about Pam."

Mina looked out at Gordy and smiled. "Are we ready now to go?"

"Yes, thank you for inviting me. This was so nice."

Ellen's cell phone rang. *Not now, Guy.* "Excuse me," she said to Mina, then reached in her purse, picked up the phone, and pushed the Talk button. "Hello."

"Hi, it's me," Guy said. "Kinsey and I are having lunch and I was thinking of you and thought I'd call and see how your morning went."

"Uh, fine. Pretty uneventful."

"Did you get any more written on the book?"

"No, I just couldn't get into it. You know how that goes. I'll work on it this afternoon. How was your morning?"

"Productive. I got a mound of paperwork done, and Kinsey did some footwork at the courthouse. This afternoon I've got a consultation with a new client and a meeting at four. We're through with lunch and need to get back. I just wanted to check in."

"I'm glad you did."

"Okay, honey. I'll call you tonight. Love you."

"Love you, too. 'Bye."

Ellen put the phone back in her purse, aware of Mina's probing eyes. "That was Guy—just checking to see how my morning went."

There were a few moments of uncomfortable silence.

"You avoided telling him you were with me," Mina said.

Ellen's mind raced with excuses and she finally said, "He's been after me to get back to my writing, and I told him last night that I'd cancelled my other commitments so I could work on the book. I hadn't planned on spending the morning with you—I'm glad I did—but I doubt he would agree that it should have preempted my writing."

Mina's forehead formed deep ridges. "You are kind, Ellen. But your eyes tell me lack of writing is not real issue."

Ellen pulled her Thunderbird into the garage, the image of Mina's hurt expression still fresh in her mind, and her inability to defend Guy picking at her conscience.

She pushed the button and lowered the garage door, then got out of the car and started to open the door to the kitchen and felt something blocking it. She pushed with her shoulder and felt something move, then stepped inside and froze, her heart racing, her eyes flitting around the room. The cupboards were open and everything had been pulled out and dumped on the floor and countertops—silverware, pots and pans, spices, canned goods. Dishes lay broken in pieces across the floor.

Ellen turned around and ran back to the car. She backed out of the garage, drove down the block, then pulled over to the curb. She accessed the menu on her cell phone and found the number for the Seaport Police Department. She hit auto dial, her mind racing with questions.

"Seaport Police Department, how many I direct your call?"

"This is Ellen Jones at 206 Live Oak Place. I just got home and found my kitchen ransacked—maybe my entire house, I'm not sure. I left as soon as I saw the mess. The intruder may still be in there."

"Where are you, ma'am?"

"I'm in my car. I drove down the block from my house and called you."

"Okay. Hold the line, please."

Ellen took a slow, deep breath and wondered what she had been thinking when she talked Guy out of getting an alarm system.

"You still there, Mrs. Jones?"

"Yes."

"Don't go back in the house. Officers will be there in a couple minutes."

"All right, thank you."

Ellen disconnected the call and felt at the same time numb and violated. She thought about calling Guy but decided against it. It was probably better to find out what she was dealing with before she alarmed him.

Ellen started the car, made a U-turn, then drove up the block and pulled over in front of a neighbor's house, her eyes fixed on the front of her own home. She didn't see any sign of forced entry or anything that even looked suspicious. Was someone still in there? Had he found what he wanted?

Ellen felt a chill crawl up her back and was hit with the same eerie feeling she'd had when she was editor of the *Daily News* and was stalked by a kidnapper who wanted her to print his threatening poems to torment the father of his captured victim. She had never before or since encountered such evil and hoped she never would.

In her rearview mirror, she saw a squad car approaching. She got out of her car and walked over to the curb and waved till the car pulled over in front of her house. Two officers got out and one looked familiar.

"Mrs. Jones, Investigator Backus. Chief Seevers and I came and talked to you about the Hamilton case."

Ellen shook his hand. "Yes, I remember."

"This is Officer Rutgers. Tell us what you know."

"I left the house around 11:40 and came home about 1:20. When I tried to push open the door from the garage into the house, it seemed stuck, as if something was blocking it on the other side. I pushed a little harder and felt something move and the door give way. I went inside and everything had been pulled from cabinets and drawers and strewn across the floor and the countertops. I left and called you."

"All right, stay here. Rutgers and I will take a look."

Ellen watched as the two officers drew their guns and jogged over to the front door and tried to open it, then quickly made their way around the side of the house and disappeared. She waited for what seemed an eternity and then saw the officers reappear and walk toward her.

"There's no one in the house now," Backus said. "Whoever was in there broke a back window to get in, and then left by the French doors."

Ellen lifted her eyebrows. "Does the rest of the house look anything like the kitchen?"

"Yeah, I'm afraid so, ma'am. We'll need you to come back in with us and see if you can determine if anything valuable's missing."

13

Ellen Jones stood in the living room with Investigator Backus and Officer Rutgers, disheartened by the destruction. The oil painting of Seaport Beach that once hung over the couch now lay slashed on the floor amidst broken lamps, piles of books, and couch cushions and throw pillows that had been cut open and the stuffing pulled out.

She put her hand on the back of her neck and rubbed, vaguely aware of officers bagging evidence and snapping pictures.

Backus rubbed his nose and resumed his annoying tapping the clipboard with his pencil. "Anyone who'd tear your house apart this way either has a grudge or is after something."

"After what? We're not hiding anything. Nothing valuable was taken."

"Is it possible someone could have a grudge against you or your husband?"

"I can't imagine. We get along with—" Ellen's heart sank. "Oh, wait...the intruder."

"Excuse me?"

"My husband surprised an intruder at his Tallahassee apartment yesterday morning. The man ran off before Guy got a look at him."

Backus rolled his eyes. "And you're just now telling me?"

"I'm sorry. My mind's in a fog." Ellen put her hands to her temples. "Nothing was missing and the police there think it was a thief working the neighborhood."

"So your husband filed a report?"

Ellen nodded.

"Okay, I'll get a copy of it. Maybe there's a connection. Anyone else who might have a beef with either of you?"

"I don't think so. Well, maybe. Guy just won a big toxic chemical case for Brinkmont Labs."

"Tell me about it."

"Some aspiring young litigator convinced the residents of Marble River to sue Brinkmont for allegedly polluting the river and making them sick. Guy presented overwhelming evidence that Brinkmont was operating within EPA guidelines. The jury agreed with him."

"I'll bet that ticked off a few folks."

"Yes, I suppose it did. But enough to do *this*?"

Backus's bushy eyebrows joined in the middle. "Well, *somebody* tore into this place with a vengeance."

Guy Jones sat in his office reading a contract for a new client, aware that Kinsey seemed distant and brooding. He noticed she was on the phone and then heard her voice on the intercom.

"Guy, Ellen's on line one."

"Thanks." He picked up the receiver and pushed the blinking light. "Hi, honey. What's up?"

"The house was broken into. It's a mess. Actually, worse than a mess. Everything that could be cut up *was*—cushions, mattresses, pillows. Things pulled out of cupboards, lamps smashed..."

"Are you all right?"

Ellen sniffled. "Hardly. But I'm not hurt. I wasn't home when it happened."

"When *did* it happen? I thought you were in for the day."

"I planned to be, but I ran into Mina when I was out running this morning and she invited me to lunch. She was just trying to thank me for being a friend." Ellen blew her nose. "I was at

Gordy's when you called. I got home at 1:20 and found the mess."

"Did you call the police?"

"Yes, they're still here, gathering evidence and taking pictures."

"You can't stay there tonight."

"I know. I'm going over to Owen and Hailey's. I'll notify the insurance company and find out what we should do about repairs."

"Hold the line a minute." Guy got up and closed the door. "Are you ever going to listen to me? How could you have lunch with Mina when her husband's name is all over the news? That's what this is about, Ellen! Somebody's trying to send you a message!"

"That's ridiculous. Who even knows Mina and I are friends? I don't think I've ever been seen in public with her except to go jogging. I told the FBI the same—"

"You talked to the FBI?"

"Yes, they came by the house yesterday. But before you get mad, the reason I didn't tell you last night on the phone was because it would've spoiled our truce. It was so nice not to argue."

Guy exhaled as loudly as he could. "What'd the feds want?"

"They asked me general questions about the Tehranis. I told them what I knew. That was it. Did I mention Ali helped the FBI find his nephew?"

"I don't care about Ali! What did the police have to say about the break-in?"

"Will you please lower your voice? Since nothing's missing, they think someone may be angry with one of us. Investigator Backus's antenna went up when he found out you won the Brinkmont case and thinks maybe someone has a grudge against you. It's not at all far-fetched. And it could explain yesterday's intruder at your apartment."

Guy paused, his mind racing in reverse. The last thing he needed was the police thinking the two break-ins were connected and asking questions he wasn't prepared to answer.

"There's no connection, Ellen. I told you it was just a thief working the area."

"Then why didn't he take something?"

"Because I scared him off."

"Well, Investigator Backus is getting a copy of the report you filed with the Tallahassee police. He's interested in pursuing the angle that someone on the losing side of the Brinkmont case is letting you know he's angry. You could be in danger! You can't just blow this off."

"Did you even bother to tell Investigator Backus about your friendship with the Tehranis?"

"Frankly, it never entered my mind. It's preposterous to think someone would act out this kind of anger simply because I've been jogging with Mina and have been to their house a few times."

Ellen walked into the guest bedroom at her son and daughter-in-law's house, Owen on her heels.

"Here you go, Mom," he said, setting her suitcase on the bed. "I'm sorry about your house, but you're welcome to stay with us as long as you want."

Ellen put her arms around him. "Thanks. I'll try not to be a pest."

"Dad sounded rattled when he called. Wanna bet he comes home early?"

"I hope so. I know Investigator Backus is anxious to question him about the details of the Brinkmont case. The more I think about it, the more sense it makes." Ellen looked into her son's eyes and saw her own fear staring back. "You saw the house. Anyone with that kind of anger might be capable of anything."

Owen's eyebrows furrowed and he looked just like his father. "It might not have anything to do with the Brinkmont case. Dad thinks—"

"I *know* what your dad thinks, and he's wrong."

"Mom, Dr. Tehrani's name has been in the news. Everyone knows he's been questioned by the FBI about that boat of explosives and those five terrorists. He's evoked a lot of suspicion. Who's to say some local yokel isn't trying to scare you into backing off?"

"Backing off what, Owen—jogging with a neighbor?"

"People can get really weird about anyone from the Middle East. It's hard to know who you can trust these days."

"Not for me, it isn't. Mina and Ali are wonderful people, and I refuse to make excuses for liking them—or be intimidated into snubbing them."

"Do you have any idea how much strain this is causing your marriage?"

Ellen held her son's gaze. "Since I live with your father, I'm sure I do."

"Mom, look, I know it's not really my place to say anything, but in a way it is—I love you and Dad. I'm scared you're going to let your stubborn attachment to your friends come between you two."

Ellen paused and blinked rapidly until her eyes cleared. "There's more to it than that. I have to be true to who I am."

"Dad wants you to be somebody you're not?"

"Actually it seems as though your dad has lost who *he* is."

"What's that supposed to mean?"

Ellen sat on the bed, her fingers rubbing the raised pattern on the quilt. "It means your dad and I have some work to do. You and Hailey can help by staying neutral. And by praying for us. Your father and I are devoted to each other. Don't ever forget that, Owen. We *will* get through this bump in the road. But you have to let us go through the wounding and not feel responsible to fix us."

A door slammed and seconds later Hailey breezed through the doorway. "I got Owen's message and rushed right home. How awful!" She put her arms around Ellen. "I'm so sorry."

"Me too, honey. Thank the Lord it was only material things that were destroyed. It could have been so much worse."

Guy got out of his car and walked toward his apartment, his mind racing with images of the mess that awaited him at the house and the loose ends here he didn't have time to tie up before heading back to Seaport.

He was confident that Kinsey could handle most of it, though she had turned ashen after Ellen's phone call and seemed more shaken than he was.

Guy put the key in the lock and turned it, then pushed open the door and stepped inside. *What the...?*

His skin was suddenly goose flesh and his shoes felt as though they were nailed to the floor. His eyes darted around the room, assessing the wall-to-wall devastation and feeling as though he were seeing a repeat of what Ellen described in her phone call—couch cushions slashed, lamps broken, books strewn across the floor. He listened carefully for half a minute for any sound, but all he heard was the wild thumping of his heart.

Then he spotted it—something on the dining room mirror. Big letters printed in what appeared to be red lipstick. He shut the front door to cut the glare, and willed his feet to move across the living room carpet until he stood in front of his reflection and read the words that seemed almost suspended across his chest:

You're a dead man!

14

Guy Jones stood leaning on the doorway of his apartment, weak-kneed, and waiting for the police. He took his cell phone out of his pocket and dialed.

"McAllister, Norton, Riley, and Jones. How may I direct your call?"

"This is Guy. Is Kinsey still there?"

"Yes, sir. One moment."

Guy breathed in slowly and then let it out, and then did it again. His heart was racing so fast he felt short of breath.

"Kinsey Abbot."

"It's Guy. My apartment's been ransacked, torn to shreds! Someone wrote, 'You're a dead man' on the dining room mirror! The police are on their way over here. I'm going to have to tell them about the cocaine. Kinsey...? Are you still there...?"

"I'm here. I—I'm just overwhelmed."

"The police investigator that Ellen talked to thinks this reeks of someone having a grudge—maybe one of the disgruntled plaintiffs in the Brinkmont case. If that's true, you could be in danger, too. I don't think you should go home by yourself until we find out more and the police have checked out your place."

"What do you think I should do?"

"Tell Brent what's going on, and then get over here and talk to the police with me. If there's a connection to the case, maybe between the two of us, we can figure it out."

"It doesn't seem plausible that all three incidents are connected. The police seemed sure the first break-in was just a burglary. Why bring up the cocaine? It has nothing to do with the Brinkmont case."

"You don't know that. What if someone planted it there and was trying to set me up."

"Do you really want to have to explain why you held on to it?"

Guy looked up and saw the flashing lights of a squad car. "The police are here. Listen, I think we *have* to tell them everything. Not to do so could put either or both of us at risk. I can't take that chance."

"All right. I'll tell Brent what's going on and get over there as soon as I can."

Ellen sat on the screened-in porch at Owen and Hailey's house, the afternoon sun filtering through a stand of pines, and listened to the clear, melodious song of a cardinal perched on the wrought iron gate.

She closed her eyes and breathed in the unmistakable scent of pine, and for a moment was a girl again, curled up in her grandmother's porch swing reading *Anne of Green Gables*.

She heard footsteps and opened her eyes in time to see Owen sit next to her on the wicker couch, his feet flat on the floor, his hands clasped between his knees.

"What's wrong?"

"Dad's apartment was broken into again. This time it looks about like the house."

Ellen sucked in a breath, her hand on her heart. "Is he all right?"

"Yeah, but there's more...someone wrote a threat on the mirror."

"What kind of threat?"

Owen paused and took her hand in his. "'You're a dead man.'"

Ellen felt a chill. She let go of Owen's hand and took the couch cushion and hugged it to her chest. "What in the world's going on? Who's doing this? And why?"

"The police think it might be the same person. The break-in at Dad's happened at 7:53 this morning—at least that's when his kitchen clock hit the floor, and that would've left—"

"Enough time for someone to drive to Seaport and break into the house."

Owen nodded. "Dad also said whoever did it was probably watching the apartment because he'd left for the office at a quarter till eight."

"When did he call?"

"A couple minutes ago. He couldn't talk long. The police were still there. He told me to tell you that it looks like Investigator Backus might be right about the Brinkmont connection."

Ellen sighed. "Of course, he didn't have the backbone to tell me himself after raking me over the coals about the Tehranis."

"He sounded really uptight, Mom. I think he was more worried that he might sound panicked and upset you even more."

"You're probably right. Have you told Hailey?"

"No, I need to go do that now. The police will get to the bottom of this. Try not to worry, okay?"

Ellen lifted her eyebrows. "Right."

Guy and Kinsey sat in straight-back chairs, arms crossed, and faced Investigator Zack Hamlin who stood leaning against the dining room table.

"All right," Hamlin said, "I've got a clear picture of the break-ins. Let's get back to the cocaine. Mr. Jones, why didn't you just turn it in?"

Guy was aware that Kinsey had shifted her weight. "I fully intended to. But there are extenuating circumstances."

Hamlin raised his eyes. "Why don't you tell me about 'em?"

"The day the verdict came down on the Brinkmont case, my partners threw a victory dinner to celebrate. The wine was flowing all evening, and everybody drank too much, except me. I don't drink. After the party broke up, I made sure everyone went home in cabs—except Kinsey, who never would've made it from the cab to the front door. I decided to drive her myself, but I don't know Tallahassee that well and couldn't find anyone who knew how to find the address on her driver's license. So I let her sleep it off on my couch. Just a friend not letting a friend drive drunk—nothing more."

"So what's the extenuating circumstance here?"

Guy felt the heat flood his cheeks. "I haven't told my wife yet. We've had some disagreements lately. I started to tell her, but then clammed up and never could find the right time."

"Miss Abbot, you look upset. Is there something you wanna say?"

"I didn't realize he hadn't told her, that's all."

Hamlin thumped his fingers on the table. "Go on, Mr. Jones."

"I knew if I turned in the cocaine, you'd have to question Kinsey."

"So you *knew* about the cocaine, Miss Abbot?"

"Well, yes. Since I slept on the sofa, Guy had no choice but to confront me with it. But I don't know anything about it. I wasn't even sure what it was when he showed it to me. I don't do drugs. I've passed every random drug test I've ever taken."

"I see." Hamlin stroked his mustache. "So why did you object to being questioned by the police?"

"Well, because, uh—"

"Because she was afraid that if the media got wind of it, an innocent situation would be made to look like a sleazy affair," Guy said. "It would be an embarrassment to her, me, my wife—and the firm."

"Is that true, Miss Abbot?"

"Yes."

"So where do you think the cocaine came from?"

Kinsey shrugged. "It's baffling. The only thing I can think of is that the intruder either put it there or dropped it by mistake."

"Or it was deliberately planted by one of the plaintiffs in the Brinkmont case," Guy said. "They were expecting to win a huge sum and got nothing. Maybe someone wanted to get even."

Hamlin gave a nod. "Interesting thought. I'll have to check, but to my knowledge, no call was ever made to the Tallahassee police department suggesting we check out your apartment for drugs."

Guy put his briefcase in the car and then walked Kinsey to hers. "Quite a night, eh?"

"My head is spinning and my heart's doing flip flops. At least the cocaine issue isn't going to embarrass either of us now." Kinsey's eyes seemed to search his. "Guy, why didn't you tell me you hadn't told Ellen I spent the night?"

"I don't discuss my private life with you."

"Or with her either, apparently."

"Look, I've come up against a brick wall in my marriage, and it's inappropriate for me to talk to you about it. The person I should be communicating with is Ellen. If I'd done a better job of it, I wouldn't have to go home now and face the music."

"Well, if you need me to back up your story, you know where to find me."

"I really wish you'd stay with a friend until we find out what's going on."

"The police officers said everything's fine at my place."

He looked into her eyes and saw fear. "Why don't you stay at the Holiday Inn Express? I'll pay for it."

"No, I'm fine. Really. If someone wanted to get at me, he'd have done it by now. By all indications, *you're* the target."

Guy rolled his eyes. "Don't remind me."

"I'll go home and lock myself in and turn on the security system. If somebody gets through all that, I'll sic Grayson on him."

Guy smiled without meaning to. "You sure you're all right?"

"I'm a big girl. You'd better get on the road or you're going to be falling asleep at the wheel. I'm sure Ellen will be relieved to see you. She must be beside herself."

Guy opened the door, and Kinsey got in. "I'll call Brent and give him the details. Keep your doors locked. I'll talk to you tomorrow."

Ellen went in the guest room and closed the door. She picked up her cell phone and dialed.

"Hello."

"Mina, it's Ellen."

"I'm glad you called! I saw on TV what happened to your house and could not reach you there. Are you all right?"

"Yes, I'm fine. I'm staying at my son and daughter-in-law's." Ellen told Mina everything that had happened from the time she got home and found the house ransacked until Guy called Owen and told him about the break-in at the apartment.

"This is much worse than I thought," Mina said. "Who would do such things?"

"Everything seems to point to a lawsuit Guy just won. The police think maybe someone on the losing side is angry. The frightening part is we don't know anything for sure, or whether the threat is real or just intended to shake us up."

"I am so sorry. There is enough fear in world today without this. Is there anything I can do for you?"

"Thank you, but no. We just need to work with the police here and in Tallahassee and let them get their heads together. How is Ali?"

"Humiliated and angry. Media people follow him everywhere, shouting questions, taking pictures. Patients see his face on TV, read about him in newspaper. He has done nothing wrong. But he is born in Iran so that makes him terrorist?"

Ellen put her right hand on her left shoulder and pressed her fingers on the tight muscles. "You know, Mina. I think I'm about ready to go live on a deserted island."

Guy got in his car and locked the doors. He looked in the rearview mirror and focused on Kinsey's taillights until they blended into an endless stream of glowing red.

He looked up at the yellow crime scene tape that had been strung across the front door of his apartment, hit again with the bone-chilling, heart-stopping, there's-no-place-to-hide fear that had gripped him when he read the words on the mirror.

Whoever wrote them must have been connected to the Brinkmont case. But how long would it take the police to narrow down the possibilities? There were thirty-six plaintiffs in the case, and probably sympathetic family members and friends who believed Brinkmont was responsible for their health problems and should have been made to pay. How much manpower and money could be spared for that kind of investigation?

Guy gripped the steering wheel and realized his hands were shaking. He turned on the motor and backed out of his parking space.

He took the back streets and turned onto Madison, then drove several miles past the capitol building and stopped at the red light at Trellis. Kinsey's condo was just a few miles down Trellis. What could it hurt to swing by there, just to be sure?

Guy tapped the steering wheel with his fingers. Was he being overprotective? Kinsey was a grown woman, certainly capable of pulling into the garage and letting the door close behind her.

The light turned green and Guy went straight ahead.

15

Guy Jones opened his eyes wide and blinked several times to get rid of the sandy sensation. His headlights spotlighted a row of pink crape myrtle trees up ahead. He pressed gently on the brakes, then turned the car into the driveway and pulled up behind Ellen's white Thunderbird.

He sat for a moment, holding a Styrofoam cup of lukewarm coffee and rehearsing in his mind what he wanted to say to her—what he *had* to say.

He got out of the car and jogged up the porch steps, then took the key from under the mat and opened the front door. The faint aroma of popcorn reminded him that he hadn't eaten dinner.

He walked softly through the living room and down the hall past Owen and Hailey's room, relieved to see light under the doorway to the guest room. He peeked in and saw Ellen lying on the bed atop the comforter, her eyes closed, the afghan she had made Hailey for Christmas draped over her.

"Ellen?" he whispered. "Honey, are you awake?"

The sound of her breathing told him she wasn't. Guy went over and sat in the rocker, longing to put his arms around her and almost forgetting they were at odds. Their differences seemed insignificant in comparison to the looming threat—and his bad decision not to tell Ellen about Kinsey staying at the apartment. He wondered if all the years of being faithful would be enough to offset the doubt, disappointment, and anger that Ellen would likely feel. How he dreaded dumping all that on an already fragile relationship. He prayed for the umpteenth time tonight.

Lord, please help me make it right.

Guy closed his eyes and leaned the back of his head against the rocker. What if the police couldn't figure out who was responsible for threatening him? What if he and Ellen had to live with it, never knowing if or when someone might strike again? And what if whoever threatened him decided to go after Ellen? His imagination displayed one horrible scenario after another. Finally he forced himself to picture only a blank screen...

"When did you get here?" said a sleepy voice.

Guy opened his eyes and almost forgot where he was. He glanced over at the digital clock on the nightstand. "Uh, a couple hours ago. I must've dozed off."

Ellen sat up on the side of the bed and rubbed her eyes. "I'm glad you're home."

"Yeah, me too."

"Help me get this comforter off so you can get under the covers," she said. "I'm sure the drive was exhausting."

"Not as exhausting as what I need to talk to you about."

Ellen yawned. "You want some coffee?"

"No, I don't want to wake Owen and Hailey." Guy got up and sat on the side of the bed next to Ellen. "I need to finish telling you what I was in the process of telling you when Mina's phone call interrupted us."

"About what?"

Guy breathed in and slowly let it out. "The dinner at Savvy's."

"I thought we put it behind us."

"This isn't about your missing the dinner, it's about a decision I made later."

"Can't it wait till morning?"

"No. I need to talk to you while we have some privacy."

Ellen turned to him, a puzzled look on her face. "All right."

"You know how our office get-togethers are—everyone was drinking, except me. After the party broke up, I made sure the others went home in cabs. But Kinsey was too smashed to walk to the front door, and I didn't think sending her home in a cab was a good idea, so I decided to drive her home myself. I looked at the address on her driver's license and had no idea how to find her place, and no one at Savvy's knew either. So I made a decision."

"To do what?"

"Let her sleep it off on the couch at my apartment."

Ellen stared at him blankly.

"As God is my witness, nothing inappropriate happened."

"I thought you had better judgment than that! What were you thinking?"

"It was late. I had no idea *what* to do with her. All I wanted to do was get some sleep. Kinsey crashed on the couch and I slept in the bedroom. The next morning, I drove straight home."

"If your conscience is clear, why are you so bent on telling me this in the middle of the night?"

Guy formed a tent with his fingers. "Because Monday after work, I found a bag of cocaine behind the couch cushion. I figured it had to be Kinsey's, so I confronted her with it."

"And?"

"She didn't even know what it was until I told her. I'm convinced she didn't have anything to do with it."

Ellen turned to him, her eyes probing. "It just magically appeared?"

"Let me back up and put this in perspective." Guy explained how angry he had been that Mina had interrupted their conversation and how he had stubbornly opted not to finish telling Ellen the whole story. He also told her everything that had happened from the first break-in at his apartment until the second, and why he had been reluctant to turn the cocaine over to the police. "I should have told you all this before."

"How could you be so irresponsible?"

"I have no excuse. I'm sorry, honey. I hope you'll forgive me. I've told you everything."

"A day late and a dollar short, Counselor." Ellen grabbed a

pillow and hugged it. "You really think someone related to the Brinkmont case planted the cocaine, hoping to frame you?"

"It makes more sense than anything else."

"But why didn't whoever put it there call the police and tell them you had it? What's the point of planting something if it's not reported?"

"I don't know. That's the one missing link. But I'm convinced it's all related."

Guy sat at the kitchen table with Owen while Hailey made French toast. Ellen shuffled in and poured herself a cup of coffee.

"Morning, Mom," Owen said. "How'd you sleep?"

"Not well. The bed was comfortable, but I just had a lot on my mind. How come you're not at work?"

"I took the day off in case there was something I could help you with."

"How sweet of you. I'm not thinking straight and could probably use a nudge in the right direction."

So now I'm chopped liver? Guy wondered if Owen and Hailey had noticed that Ellen hadn't even acknowledged his presence.

"Dad says he's going to talk to Investigator Backus first thing this morning."

"Good."

"Think you ought to go with him?"

Ellen took a sip of coffee, her eyes fixed on the table. "I don't think that's necessary. While he's doing that, I think I'll get the ball rolling with the insurance company. So many things have to be replaced it's hard to know where to begin."

"Honey, don't forget the DVD we put in the safety deposit box," Guy said. "With all our possessions documented on tape, it shouldn't take long to get a check from the insurance company."

"Was that ever smart thinking," Hailey said. "Leave it to a lawyer."

Ellen took another sip of coffee and said nothing.

"Dad, how about if I go with you to the police station?" Owen said. "It'll be a good way for me to hear all the facts laid out. I've got the big picture, but I'd like to have a better sense of how the three incidents fit together."

Ellen glanced at Guy and then set her gaze on Owen. "Yes, I think that's an excellent idea. I'm sure it will be...*enlightening*."

Gordy Jameson sat in his office at the crab shack, reading Wednesday's newspaper. He heard the front door open. "Good morning, Billy."

"Hi, Mister G. I will work now."

Gordy got up and went out to the dining area and unlocked the door to the deck. "You look mighty chipper this morning."

Billy's head bobbed. "To-day is Bible study. El-len will come to my house."

"Have you talked to her lately?"

"No, but it is Wednes-day. She will come."

Gordy held open the door to the deck and let Billy squeeze past him, then went out to the kitchen.

"Pam, I just read somethin' troubling in the paper: Ellen and Guy Jones's house was ransacked yesterday."

"That's awful. Do they know who did it?"

"Not according to the paper."

"Maybe you should call them."

"Yeah, I think I will."

"What've you got there?" Gordy started to stick his finger into a bowl of something chocolate-looking and quickly pulled it away before Pam could swat him.

"That's the batter for my triple chocolate mousse cake."

"Did we sell out already?"

"Yes, and Weezie left me a note to be sure and make some more."

"You're turnin' out to be a real asset, you know that?"

Pam laughed. "Yes, a real 'cash cow,' to quote Weezie."

"I'm serious. Keep this up and I may have to add a bake shop to this place so you can sell your desserts to go."

"Ah, *sell*. Now that's a novel idea. Why didn't I think of that?"

Gordy smiled. "Hey, I'm gettin' better. I've limited myself to only twelve 'free dessert' coupons per day."

"That's two pies on the house."

"And a dozen happy customers who'll come back again."

"I know." She slid into his arms. "I honestly don't care whether we sell them or give them away. It's just fun being a part of this. Just don't tell Weezie."

Gordy pressed his lips to her cheek. "Think I'll try calling the Joneses."

He went back in his office and flipped through his Rolodex until he found the Js, then picked up the receiver and dialed.

"Hello."

"Ellen?"

"No, this is her daughter-in-law. Hold on, I'll get her."

"Hello."

"Ellen, it's Gordy. I wasn't sure I'd catch you at the house after what happened."

"Actually, you didn't. I've forwarded my calls to Owen and Hailey's."

"I hope I'm not botherin' you, but I was wonderin' if there's anything Pam and I can do?"

"Not really, Gordy. The house is a mess, but the insurance company will get over there today and assess the damage. I hope we'll be able to get back in there soon."

"Any idea who did it?"

"It may be tied to a case Guy was working on. The police have asked us not to give specifics while the investigation is going on."

"That makes sense. By the way, Billy's here workin' this morning and thinks you're gonna do a Bible study today with him and Lisa. You need me to tell him anything?"

"No. As eager as those kids are, I don't have the heart to cancel."

"Sounds like you've got a full plate. Why don't you swing by here any time and I'll send some fish and chips home with you so you and your family won't have to deal with fixing something to eat. It's the least I can do."

Guy left the police station and drove eight blocks before he realized Owen hadn't said a word. "Why are you so quiet?"

Owen shrugged.

"Whatever you're thinking you might as well get off your chest."

"All right," Owen said. "Are you nuts? What possessed you to let Kinsey Abbot spend the night at your apartment?"

"You heard what I told Investigator Backus. She was drunk."

"Come on, Dad. It was completely out of line. You could've just as easily put her up in a motel."

"I was afraid she might fall and hurt herself. Or wander off. She was really smashed."

"So Kinsey's got a drinking problem?"

"She's not a drunk, if that's what you mean. She just likes to party once in a while."

"Fine. Let her. But since when is she *your* responsibility? If you'd treat Mom with as much TLC, maybe you wouldn't be having problems."

"That's a little simplistic."

Owen shook his head. "You'd have chewed me up and spit me out if I had done this to Hailey."

"I didn't do this *to* your mother. Look, I made a bad judgment call. All I wanted to do was keep Kinsey off the street till she sobered up."

"What are you, the enabler? The woman needs to be talking to someone in AA."

"Owen, you're blowing this way out of proportion. I'm done talking about Kinsey."

"Okay. Then let's talk about Mom."

"What about her?"

"I saw the way she avoided you at breakfast. Did you tell her everything?"

"Absolutely."

"Does she believe you?"

"She knows I wouldn't lie to her."

"Did you ask her to forgive you?"

Guy breathed in and forced it out. "Why don't you let *me* handle your mother?"

"Because you're doing a lousy job, Dad!" Owen sat back in his seat and stared out the window. "Look, I don't mean to be disrespectful. But I've watched your relationship with Mom go downhill since Hailey and I moved here, and I don't understand what's going on. You taught me everything I know about respecting women and how to love my wife. You were a great role model. So why'd you stop taking your own advice?"

"I didn't. Marriage requires ongoing adjustments. We've just gotten a little out of sync."

"Is that what you call it? You've hardly said a civil word to Mom in weeks. And then you pull this stunt with Kinsey. What do you expect her to think?"

"I expect her to know that I love her and would never be unfaithful."

"Kind of hard to make that one stick when your actions don't match your words!"

Guy made a sharp turn onto a side street, pulled over to the curb, and clamped his fingers around Owen's wrist. "Don't you *ever* question my faithfulness to your mother! I made a bad judgment call. But I've been committed to Ellen since I slid that ring on her finger. I won't tolerate you or anyone else suggesting otherwise." Guy turned loose of Owen's wrist and clutched the steering wheel, his heart racing.

"You shouldn't have told me to get it off my chest if you didn't want to hear it. If you and Mom had been communicating all along, I doubt if trust would even be an issue. But you have to admit, this looks bad."

"I know how it looks, son."

Guy's cell phone rang. He took it out of his pocket and hit the talk button. "Hello."

"It's Brent. Anything new happening?"

"Owen and I just left the police station. I had a long talk with the investigator who's handling the break-in at the house. He's already talked to Investigator Hamlin up there. They're leaning toward all three break-ins being related to the Brinkmont case."

"I was on the phone this morning with the Brinkmont higher ups," Brent said. "They're pretty rattled about this. A couple of them are considering hiring bodyguards. That's not a bad idea for you either."

"Seems a bit extreme."

"I guarantee you, if I'd gotten the threat, I'd be thinking about it. I've got to run. I need to be in a meeting. Keep me posted on what's happening there. Oh...do you know what Kinsey had on her itinerary today?"

"Yeah, she was going to do some research on that new case you gave us. I think she planned to be out until after lunch."

"All right. Talk to you later."

Guy disconnected the call and put the phone in his pocket.

"What's the deal?" Owen said.

"Uh, nothing. Just Brent checking in." Guy made a U-turn and got back on Main Street. *Bodyguards? This thing is getting out of hand.*

16

Late Wednesday afternoon, Guy Jones stood at the window and watched Ellen pull into the driveway behind his Mercedes. She seemed to be fumbling for something on the passenger seat, then slid out of the car and went up on the porch, holding a white sack under her arm and one in each hand.

Guy opened the front door and held it. "What've you got there?"

"Fish and chips, compliments of Gordy."

"Looks like everybody's on the same page."

"What do you mean?"

"Come see for yourself."

Ellen followed him into the kitchen, surprised to see covered dishes laid out on the countertop and stove. "What's all this?"

Hailey went over and pulled the foil back on several of the containers and closed her eyes, letting the aroma waft under her nose. "Well, let's see. Mina brought over a chicken-and-rice casserole that looks yummy. Blanche brought a brisket. Julie brought a big pan of lasagna with garlic bread and a salad— and a promise to bring tomorrow night's dinner."

Ellen smiled. "How thoughtful of them." She laid the three sacks on the counter. "Add Gordy's fish and chips to that. Also clam chowder."

"We'll never eat all that food," Guy said.

Ellen didn't make eye contact. "It'll keep. We'll get several meals out of it."

"You have the nicest friends," Hailey said. "I can't believe they drove all the way over here just to bring us food."

"So how was your Bible study with Billy and Lisa?" Guy said.

"Fine. Hailey, why don't I help you get this food sorted so we can decide what to serve when."

Thanks for the public brush off. Guy felt his cell phone vibrating. He left the kitchen and took it out of his pocket. "Hello."

"Guy, it's Brent. Have you heard from Kinsey since we talked this morning?"

"No, why?"

"She hasn't been in the office. Hasn't called in. Isn't answering her home or cell phone."

"Maybe she got more involved in the research than she intended."

"But surely she would've called in?"

Guy went in the living room and sat on the couch. "I encouraged her to stay with a friend till we figure all this out. Maybe she did."

"Then why didn't she just call and tell me that?"

"I don't know, Brent. People react differently to stress. Maybe she spaced it out."

"Doesn't she keep an extra house key in her desk?"

"Yeah, it's attached to a magnet in her top file drawer. You going over there?"

"I'll feel better if I take a look. I'll call you back and let you know what I find out."

Ellen sat with Owen and Hailey, watching "Regional News at Six," all too aware of Guy brooding out on the porch swing. She wasn't ready to ease his guilt just because she believed he was telling the truth. How could he have exercised such poor judgment and, at the same time, had the nerve to suggest that *her* friends were having a negative effect on his professional image? The news anchor's voice stole her attention.

"This just in...Seaport police have been dispatched to Bougainvillea Park where a volatile situation developed a short time ago between what appears to be a Muslim family and a group of teenagers. WRGL-TV's Jared Downing is at the scene. Jared..."

"Shannon, what started out as a stroll in the park for one local family has turned into an evening of terror. According to eyewitnesses, the family, whose name we don't yet know, brought their three children to the park and had sat down to eat a picnic dinner when they were confronted by a group of teenage boys. The teens began heckling the family and shouting ethnic slurs.

"Eyewitness Emily Jensen said the family appeared to ignore the heckling until one of the teenagers approached them, wielding a knife, and suggested maybe he should, quote, 'Behead *your* kids to even the score for those beheadings in Iraq.' End quote.

"According to Jensen, the father got up and stood between his children and the teenagers, shouting for someone to call the police. By then Jensen had already placed a 911 call.

"Minutes later, police began arriving on the scene. The troublemakers took off running but were quickly apprehended. These bystanders you see behind me said the teens acted as if they'd been drinking and told police they just meant it as a joke. We don't know yet if any arrests have been made, but we'll bring you the facts as we get them. This is Jared Downing on the scene in Bougainvillea Park. Shannon..."

Ellen threw her hands up. "That's all we need—American youth behaving like terrorists! I hope the police do more than slap those boys on the wrist!"

Hailey put the TV on mute. "I can't believe they'd even threaten something like that in jest."

"It's sad," Owen said. "But it's just a symptom of the fear people have about Muslims. It's only going to get worse."

Guy came in the front door and walked in the living room. "Why do you all look so glum?"

"Because the news is such a downer," Owen said.

"Well, I've got some potentially bad news to add to it. I just got off the phone with Brent. Kinsey didn't show up for work today and no one's heard from her."

"Oh, no..." Ellen closed her eyes and laid her head against the back of the couch.

"Brent went over to her condo and looked around. Her car's there, but she's not. It's completely out of character for her not to have called."

"Did he report it to the police?" Ellen said.

"Not yet. When I left last night, I suggested Kinsey stay with a friend till the police figure out what's going on. We're hoping maybe she did, though it's odd she wouldn't have called the office and told someone. Then again, she was pretty rattled."

"Did Brent see anything at Kinsey's that looked suspicious?"

Guy sat on the couch next to Ellen. "No. There was no sign of a struggle. Nothing out of place—at least nothing that stood out."

"I wonder if she took her purse with her?"

"Why is that important?"

"Because if she took her purse, she probably left by choice."

Guy patted Ellen's hand. "Good point. I'll call Brent back and tell him to check."

Ellen went into the guest room and closed the door. She sat on the bed, got her cell phone out of her purse, and hit the autodial.

"Hello."

"Julie, it's Ellen. Thanks for bringing the wonderful lasagna. How thoughtful of you."

"I still can't believe what happened. Have you found out anything since we talked this morning?"

"No, other than Guy's legal secretary didn't show up for work today and hasn't returned any of her messages. Apparently, Guy suggested to her that she stay with a friend until the police got to the bottom of this. She probably did and just neglected to call the office and let them know. But we'll all feel better when we know where she is."

"Well, just know Ross and I are praying for you. I called the church and put you and Guy on the prayer list."

"Thanks. Blanche told me you had. Oh, darn, I forgot to ask her if she found someone to take her to the eye doctor on Monday. Her car was in the shop."

"Actually, I took her. Sarah Beth and I played in the park across the street from the eye clinic till she was done."

"You're a good friend, Julie. I love and appreciate you so much."

"You know I feel the same about you. Oops, someone's at my door. I've gotta run. Ellen, please be careful. I'm so concerned about this threat."

"We are, too. But we know whose hands we're in. Go answer the door. I'll talk to you later."

Ellen disconnected the call and redialed.

"Hello."

"Mina, it's Ellen. Thank you for bringing us the delicious casserole. It must've taken your entire lunch hour for you to drive over here and back. How thoughtful, especially with all you've got going on. I appreciate not having to think about cooking right now."

"It was my pleasure to return kindness. What did police find out about your situation?"

"They definitely think it's someone's angry response to a recent case Guy won. But they haven't begun to narrow down who's responsible. We're a little edgy, but we've got a lot of prayer support. I suppose you heard on the evening news about the incident at Bougainvillea Park?"

Mina exhaled into the receiver. "Yes, and my stomach is sick. If our children start paying back hate with hate, how will hate ever leave us?"

"There's no excuse for those boys terrifying that family like that. I'm sure they'll be punished."

"Punishment is not cure for hate, my friend."

Ellen drew hearts on the comforter with her finger. "I suppose not. How did Ali do today?"

"You did not see him on news?"

"No, Guy interrupted us, and we didn't finish watching the news. Is the media still following him?"

"Yes, but Ali walks away from them and will not answer questions. All they want is big story. Truth does not matter. Why does life have to be so complicated? Why cannot people just get along? All this hate and violence. It is too much for me."

Guy sat on the porch swing waiting for Brent to call him back, his mind racing with the details of the past two days. He couldn't imagine anyone connected to the Brinkmont case being angry enough with Kinsey to hurt her. Which of the plaintiffs would even understand a legal secretary's role in a case?

He tried to remember exactly what he had said to Kinsey as they parted ways the night before, but his memory of it was a blur. He did remember telling her to keep her doors locked.

His words to Investigator Hamlin echoed in his head: *They were expecting to win a huge sum and got nothing. Maybe someone wanted to get even.*

Guy swatted a mosquito on the back of his neck and scratched the bite on his arm and another on his hand. He started to go back in the house when Ellen came out on the porch and sat next to him in the swing. He could almost hear her thoughts churning.

"I believe what you said about Kinsey spending the night," she said. "I'm sure you know that."

"I had hoped."

"I'm not through feeling angry, but I can't let my anger get in the way of supporting you through this. I'm scared for you, and as concerned about Kinsey as you are. I do like her, you know."

"Yeah, I know."

Ellen reached over and slid her hand under his. "A lot of good it did me to quit the newspaper business. We're right back in the danger zone."

Guy managed a weak smile. "It's not really funny, is it?"

"No, I'm terrified. At least I have a better understanding of how you felt when I was threatened."

"I could always retire."

"Right. And do what?"

"I don't know...buy a banana plantation in Puerto Rico or something. And you could write books to support us." He enjoyed the smile that appeared on Ellen's face.

"I'm afraid at my current rate of publishing success, we'd have to live solely on bananas."

"I love bananas," he said.

"So do I."

"Especially frozen on a stick with that crunchy chocolate coating."

"Or sliced on ice cream with hot butterscotch syrup."

Guy turned to her, his eyebrows raised. "Homemade banana cream pie."

"Warm banana nut bread."

"Creamy banana pudding."

"Bananas sliced on oatmeal smothered with brown sugar." Ellen laughed. "Help, we're going bananas!"

Guy brought her hand to his lips and relished the moment. "I've missed this. Laughing, just being together."

"Me, too. It hasn't been much fun being with you lately."

"I know I've seemed critical. It's difficult when we disagree."

"Only because *you're* difficult when we disagree," Ellen said. "This probably isn't a good time to resume this argument. We've got a lot to deal with and should put this on hold for a while."

"What? Before you've had a chance to throw it up to me that your friends rallied to bring us meals?"

The corners of her mouth turned up slightly. "Ah, I guess actions *do* speak louder than words or education or social class or—"

"I get it, Ellen. You don't have to draw me a picture. It was nice of them. There, I said it. But I still don't know what it is you have in common with them."

Guy's cell phone vibrated and he took it out of his pocket. "Yeah, Brent."

"Donna and I are at Kinsey's place. We've looked everywhere and can't find a purse—except for some empty beaded ones on a shelf in her closet."

"Did you look in her car?"

"Yeah, we did. Her briefcase is there. Cell phone's not in it. Not in the house either. We probably should start phoning her family and friends and find out where she is. Any idea where to begin?"

"Not really." Guy glanced over at Ellen and shook his head. "Kinsey's mother's in a nursing home with Alzheimer's, and her father's deceased. As far as I know, she's an only child. And she really hasn't mentioned any of her friends to me by name."

"What about a boyfriend?"

"No one special that I know of. She hung out at the Starlight Lounge when she was dating a saxophone player—some guy named Vincent. But that was a few months ago. I get the feeling Kinsey goes through men like most of us go though paper towels. It's not something we talk about."

"Maybe her neighbors know who she hangs out with," Brent said. "Donna and I will knock on a few doors. But if that doesn't yield anything, we should probably report it to the police."

"Why don't you check and see if there's an address book near her telephone? That might lead to something. You think I should come up there and help you?"

"No, sit tight. Let me pursue this a little more and call you back. I'm not ready to panic, but I'm getting really bad vibes."

17

Ellen Jones sat in the rocker in the guest bedroom at Owen and Hailey's, waiting for Guy to come looking for her. She could hardly believe he had offered to drive back to Tallahassee to help Brent look for Kinsey.

Look for Kinsey? The thought sent a chill up Ellen's spine. What business did Guy or Brent have looking for Kinsey? For all they knew, whoever had threatened Guy was trying to use her to get to him.

Ellen saw the bedroom door slowly open, and then Guy step inside and close it behind him.

"I figured you were in here," he said.

"Guy, don't get involved in looking for Kinsey. Let the police do it."

"Won't have to. Brent called back. Kinsey apparently went by his place when he was at hers and left a note. She apologized for not calling, said that after last night she was freaked out about the threat and wanted to take two week's vacation. Said she was staying with a friend and didn't want to jeopardize the person's safety by saying who it was."

Ellen stopped to let the words sink in. "She decided just like that to lay low for two weeks?"

"Guess so."

"That leaves you in a real bind. How did Brent react?"

"I think Donna convinced him to cut Kinsey some slack, that she was probably so frightened she wasn't thinking clearly. Plus, she only asked for time off that she's got coming."

Ellen glided her finger along the satin tie on her bathrobe. "Maybe Kinsey's got the right idea."

"Why, you think I should disappear?"

"It certainly couldn't hurt for you to stay out of sight until the police figure out who threatened you."

"I haven't got time to cower. I've got work to do."

"Well, your work sure isn't going to get done if you get killed!"

Guy went over and squatted next to the rocker, his arm around Ellen. "Shhhh. I'm not going to take any chances. But it's more than likely that the threat was intended just to shake me up. I can't imagine anyone being mad enough over the case to kill me. All I did was present the facts to the jury. If anything, I'd expect the jury and/or the Brinkmont people to be targets."

"Then why are you the only one who's been threatened?"

"I don't know. That's what the police are working to find out. Honey, what do you think about me hiring a twenty-four hour security service to watch Hailey and Owen's place—just till we know what's going on?"

"Can you do that?"

"Actually, I already did. They'll have someone over here in the morning. It'll make me feel more at ease. I have to drive back to Tallahassee in the morning."

"Why can't you work here till Monday, like you always do?"

"Where—at the house? How am I supposed to be efficient without an office? Besides, it's not practical now that Kinsey's out."

"Guy, *you're* the one who was threatened! It's just dandy that Kinsey gets to run for cover, but you're the one we should be worried about."

"Honey, the worst thing I could do is take time off right now. It'd put everyone in a bind."

"Then at least hire a bodyguard."

"A bodyguard? Seems rather drastic."

"Wouldn't you rather be safe than sorry? Can you honestly tell me you're not worried about being by yourself?"

Guy tilted her face toward him. "For starters, let's concentrate on making you and the kids feel safe. Just knowing someone's watching the house round the clock would give me peace of mind. When I get back to Tallahassee, I'll decide if I need to do something for me."

Guy sat with Owen and watched the eleven o'clock news until the first commercial, then went in the bathroom, sprayed insect repellent all over himself, and went out on the front porch. He sat in the swing, his arms folded, and glided slowly forward and then backward, relieved when the mosquitoes didn't light.

He was much too tired to expend his energy feeling sorry for Dr. Tehrani or the Muslim couple who had gotten harassed at the park. What did they expect the American public to do—trust them? Of course, the situation was getting out of hand. How would this country ever seem safe with those people living here?

Love your neighbor as yourself.

Guy pushed the floor with his feet and made the swing go faster. Yes, but what was he supposed to do when his neighbor was the enemy?

Love your enemies. Pray for those who persecute you.

Guy breathed in and let it out. He started to get up when Owen came out on the porch and sat beside him.

"You okay?" Owen asked. "You seemed upset by the news."

"I'm just tired. Been a tough couple of days."

"You and Mom still fighting about the Tehranis?"

"We're not fighting, Owen. We just don't agree. Your mom sees nothing wrong with befriending a Muslim, and I don't want to walk on the same side of the street with one."

"I think people are cautious of Muslims with good cause. But what's happening to Dr. Tehrani seems unfair. The FBI let him go.

I don't understand why the media won't leave him alone."

"Because they don't trust him, that's why."

Owen made a tent with his fingers. "Pretty awful what happened to that Muslim family at the park, though. They weren't bothering anyone."

"Then maybe they'll buy a plane ticket back to the Middle East. Don't expect me to feel sorry for them."

"That's kind of cold, don't you think?"

"Maybe. But in my mind, warming up to a Muslim is like getting in the cage with a tiger. Given the right circumstances, they'll turn on you."

There was a long stretch of silence.

"Is Mom okay with you going back to Tallahassee tomorrow?" Owen finally said.

"She's nervous. But she understands Kinsey and I can't both be out at the same time."

"Seems pretty low of Kinsey to take time off and leave you to be a sitting duck. No one threatened her."

"She and I work closely on cases. I'm not surprised she took the threat personally."

"I don't see how you can defend her. This stinks and you know it."

Guy put his arm on the back of the porch swing and let his hand rest on Owen's shoulder. "Kinsey must be terrified to have asked for time off right now."

"She didn't *ask*, Dad. She split."

"If Brent had told her to come in or her job was in jeopardy, she would have."

"Yeah, well, what about your life being in jeopardy? You think she gave that any thought?"

"Look, I know you're disgusted with Kinsey on several levels. But the threat to me is out there whether Kinsey takes time off or not. Do you really expect me to put my life on hold till the police figure out who threatened me? I *need* to stay busy. Frankly, I'm glad for an excuse to keep my mind on something else."

Owen turned and locked gazes with him. "Aren't you scared?"

"I suppose I am. But I'll think about it a whole lot less if I'm busy."

Gordy Jameson sat on the couch in Pam Townsend's living room, scraping the last of the peach ice cream from the bottom of the dish, when his cell phone rang. "There's Will." He handed the dish to Pam and took the cell phone off his belt. "Hello."

"It's me," Police Chief Will Seevers said. "Sorry to be so late returning your call. This Muslim thing's been a real headache. What's up?"

"I was just wonderin' what's gonna happen to the boys who threatened that family at the park?"

"I turned them over to juvy. None of them have a record. I doubt if anything will happen to them other than a slap on the wrist."

"Gimme a break, Will. They were talkin' about beheadin' the couple's kids!"

"They got into some beer and were clowning around."

"Some joke! Supposin' those punks had cornered you and Margaret and threatened to cut off Meagan's head? Think you'd blow it off as a bunch of kids clownin' around? They oughta throw the book at them!"

"You're overreacting, Gordy."

"No, I'm not. You're makin' too little of it."

"Why, because I don't support locking these kids up? There's no way they were going to behead anyone. The knife was plastic."

"The parents didn't know that!"

"Gordy, calm down. No one's saying the boys weren't wrong. But what do you think we should do with them—cane them?

They need to apologize to the couple and finger whoever sold them the beer. Maybe do a little community service. But these kids aren't criminals."

Gordy looked at Pam and rolled his eyes. "What they *did* was. Somebody better make 'em understand that."

"Think I don't know how to do my job?"

"I have a lot of respect for what you do, Will. I've never questioned you before on anything. But I'm tellin' you, you're not bein' objective. I'm not even sure you can be where Muslims are concerned."

"Thank you, Doctor Phil. Anything else?"

Gordy took a slow deep breath. "I don't mean to criticize, but—"

"Could've fooled me."

"I'm tryin' to talk to you as a *friend*. Shoot, we've been pals since we were knee high to a grasshopper. If I can't be truthful with you, who can? All I'm sayin' is you might be a little closed-minded when it comes to Muslims—and protectin' their rights."

"You're entitled to your opinion, Gordy. It's a free country. Just do me a favor and keep that one to yourself. I'm beat. I need to get some sleep."

"Yeah, okay. I'll talk—" *Click.*

Gordy looked at Pam, his eyebrows raised. "He hung up on me."

Pam came over and sat on the side of the chair. "You've been friends too long to let a difference of opinion create hard feelings. Why do you keep pushing Will's hot buttons?"

"All I did was ask what was gonna happen to those boys, then he goes off."

"Then stay away from the subject, Gordy. It's not worth it."

"I don't want the kinda friendship where I have to keep my mouth shut. Will and I have never been that way with each other before."

"We've never been involved in a war on terror before.

Sentiments run deep, and people get passionate about their feel-ings...and their fears."

Gordy shook his head from side to side. "I don't understand Will bein' so blasé about it. It's settin' the wrong precedent to let the boys off easy because they had a little too much beer and thought they'd have some fun. If the Muslim father had threat-ened to behead one of those boys, the feds'd be all over him."

Pam stroked the back of Gordy's hair. "I'm not excusing the behavior, but teenagers don't think like adults. I doubt if they fully understood what they put those parents through."

"Then it's time they did. If the *police chief* thinks they deserve only a slap on the wrist, what's that say about this country? Doesn't protectin' the rights of all our citizens matter anymore?"

Pam got up and stood behind the chair, her hands gently massaging Gordy's shoulders. "I wonder if your reaction to this has anything to do with what's going on with Dr. Tehrani?"

"Maybe. It really gripes me that the media can stalk him, and all that's protected under their first amendment rights. What about *his* rights? The FBI questions him, someone leaks it to the press, and this great man whose life's been dedicated to alleviatin' suffering is suddenly suspected of wantin' to inflict it. It's nuts."

"Let's hope the focus will shift to something else soon."

Gordy took her hand and pressed it to his lips. "Well, I know mine will. Do you realize that ten nights from now we'll be sharin' the king suite at the Pembrooke House as Mr. and Mrs. Gordon Kenneth Jameson?"

18

At five-thirty the next morning, Ellen Jones followed the aroma of freshly brewed coffee down the hall and into Hailey and Owen's kitchen. She filled a mug with steaming coffee, added a splash of cream, then shuffled over to the round oak table and sat staring at the fruit design on the wallpaper. The sound of footsteps caused her to look up.

Guy came into the kitchen, dressed in his olive-green silk suit and gold tie. "I see you found the coffee. Here's the newspaper. I'm going to head out pretty quick."

"I wish you weren't going," Ellen said.

Guy pulled up a chair and sat, then tilted her chin up and looked into her eyes. "I can't just stop living, honey. I'm not going to take any chances."

"Getting us a security guard might ease *your* mind, but it doesn't ease mine. You're the one who was threatened. How safe will you be after you leave the office? Someone could be watching you."

"I've made reservations at the Holiday Inn Express. It has a security guard. Will you stop worrying?"

Ellen squeezed his hand. "Julie put us on the prayer list at church."

"Good, we need it."

Ellen wondered how he could sound so nonchalant about it. "Guy, pray with me before you go."

"All right, honey." He took Ellen's hands in his and paused for a few moments. "Father, Ellen and I have to be away from

134

each other, but we know Your eyes will be on both of us every second and that You know who's behind this threat. We ask you to protect us, to bring the perpetrator to justice, and to give us peace as we leave the situation in Your hands. Be with us while we're apart...and Lord, help us understand each other and not allow our disagreements to make us bitter. In Jesus' name, we pray."

Ellen opened her eyes and held his hand even after he started to let go. "Are you feeling bitter toward me?"

"I didn't say that."

"I know you didn't. I'm asking."

Guy exhaled. "I don't see that we've resolved our differences about the Tehranis—or about any of your friends, for that matter."

"You haven't been home long enough for us to work through it."

"I realize that. But truthfully, I don't see any way to resolve it. I'm not going to forbid you to see them. And you're not going to stop any other way."

"Guy, that's unfair. Except for the Bible study with Billy and Lisa, I haven't seen any of my friends the entire week."

"But you want to, that's the point. I can't change who you are, Ellen. But it's a real problem for me. I just think you should be spending time with people who are more like us and have more in common with us."

"I don't want you leaving angry," Ellen said. "It's hard enough having you gone right now."

"I'm not as angry as I am frustrated. It's obvious from the news that the community's concern that there might be a terrorist cell in the area is escalating, and I find your association with the Tehranis not only embarrassing, but downright unpatriotic. You don't see it that way. So where does that leave us?"

Ellen bit her lip. *Lord, guard my words!* She counted to ten and tried not to let her face show the anger she was feeling. "I suppose it leaves us loving each other and having to work a little harder at understanding each other."

"Yeah, I suppose it does. I need to get going." He brushed her cheek with his lips and rose to his feet. "Call me when the security guard gets here. They promised to have someone over here late morning."

Gordy Jameson sat at his desk and popped the last bite of a sausage biscuit into his mouth and washed it down with a gulp of orange juice. He read the headlines about the boys in the park harassing the Muslim family, then folded the newspaper and tossed it on the chair next to his desk just as the front door opened and closed.

"That you, Billy?"

"Yes, good mor-ning, Mister G!"

Gordy left his office, walked through the dining area, and stopped at the utility closet where Billy Lewis was bent over, gathering his cleaning supplies.

"How was the Bible study?"

Billy turned around, his eyes wide and full of life. "It was very fun. El-len said we did an excel-lent job."

"I'm sure you did. You always give everything 100 percent."

"I will work now." Billy stood up tall, his bucket hung on his arm.

Gordy unlocked the door to the deck and let Billy squeeze past him. He heard the front door open and looked up, shocked to see Ali Tehrani.

Gordy walked over to him, his hand extended. "Doc, what a pleasure to see you."

"Could we talk privately for a few minutes?" Ali said. "Do you have time?"

"You bet. Let's go to my office. Can I offer you some coffee?"

"Yes, thank you. Black."

Gordy walked over to the kitchen and stood in the doorway.

"Pam, darlin', would you bring two cups of black coffee to my office, please?"

Pam caught his gaze, her eyes full of questions.

"There's someone I'd like you to meet." Gordy winked. "Bring that pretty smile, too."

Gordy escorted Ali into his office and offered him a seat. "Here, let me get that newspaper out of your way."

Gordy put the newspaper on his desk, then moved the other chair facing Ali's and sat. "If I'd known you were comin', I would've cleared all the junk out of this office. Pam says I'm a packrat."

Ali smiled. "You should see mine."

A few moments of awkward silence passed, and Gordy took note of the dark circles under Ali's eyes—and how worn he looked.

A gentle knock on the door ended the silence, and Pam came through the doorway, carrying a small tray with two mugs of coffee and a refill pot.

"Here you go, gentlemen." She set the tray on Gordy's desk.

Gordy stood and took her hand in his. "Now I get the privilege of introducin' two of my favorite people. Doc, I want you to meet my fiancée, Pam Townsend. Darlin', this is Dr. Ali Tehrani."

"So this is your lady?" Ali said, rising to his feet.

"Oh, my goodness," Pam said, eagerly shaking his hand. "How nice to finally meet you. Gordy has told me so much about you and how kind you were to him and Jenny. I was looking forward to meeting you at the wedding."

"It's my pleasure to meet you, Pam. I see my friend Gordy has chosen well. Congratulations to you both."

"Thank you."

Gordy put his arm around Pam's shoulder and pulled her close. "I can't stay away from her, so I've got her workin' here. She's turnin' out to be the dessert queen."

"Speaking of that," Pam said, "I need to finish making pies before we open. I'll let you two catch up. Nice to meet you, Dr. Tehrani. I look forward to meeting your wife at the wedding."

Pam left the office, and Gordy noticed rows of deep lines had appeared on Ali's forehead.

"I've been worried about you, Doc. How'd you get in here without the media on your tail?"

Ali smiled weakly. "I left my car parked outside the Bagel Barn, then slipped out the back door and walked over here."

"I'm glad to see you, but I have a feelin' this isn't a social call."

"No." Ali took a sip of coffee. "I regret to tell you that Mina and I will not be attending your wedding."

"Aw, I hate to hear that. You're not lettin' the media scare you off, are you?"

"Mina and I would very much like to be there, but our presence would be disruptive. That's not fair to you and Pam."

"What other people think has nothin' to do with Pam and me. You're a special friend and I'd really be honored if you'd be there."

"It is I who would be honored. But I can't accept the invitation. I simply will not bring to your joyous occasion division and sorrow. When things settle down, Mina and I would like to invite you and Pam to our home for a private time of celebration. But your wedding is not the place to invite trouble. I didn't want to tell you this over the phone. That's why I'm here."

Gordy saw Ali's eyes fill with tears and blinked away the stinging in his own.

"I can't tell you how happy I am for you, Gordy. When Jenny died, I had never seen a man more broken than you were. And now, to see you whole again...well, it just shows how healing is the love of a good woman."

Gordy nodded. "That it is. Pam's terrific. She's not replacin' Jenny. Never even tried to. But what we have is really somethin' special. I already can't imagine my life without her."

Ali's watch beeped. "That's my reminder that I have a new patient evaluation at nine-fifteen. I'm afraid I must leave now."

Gordy stood and shook hands with Ali. "This hurts me, Doc—not that you've decided not to come to the wedding, but the reasons why you felt you couldn't. I hate to see what the media's doin' to you."

"It's more than the media, my friend. It's the American mindset since 9/11. People think all Muslims are violent, but it's the terrorists who are evil. They've twisted the Quran to suit their own purposes, and I have no respect for what they're doing. I understand why people are scared. I'm scared, too. I don't want to see America attacked and all of us living in fear. That is not the America I was drawn to, the one I pledged my allegiance to. I am as disheartened by it as any other citizen."

"Doc, did the FBI question you just because you're Iranian?"

"No. I have a nephew who doesn't use good sense and has been involved in rallies against U.S. foreign policy in the Middle East. He had also been in my home recently, and the FBI knew that. What they didn't know is I had thrown him out and told him not to come back till he stopped spewing his political venom. Long story short, I agreed to help the FBI find my nephew. I knew Bobak was all talk and figured he might as well face the FBI and get it over with. Unfortunately, they are still holding him. And my family in Iran will have nothing more to do with me."

"Wow, that's tough," Gordy said.

"But it's getting dangerous to be a Muslim American. People hate what they fear. So what am I to do? I'm too Americanized ever to go back to Iran, listening day after day only to Aljazeera. That world is much too small for me. I'm a Muslim, yes. But in America, I'm informed and free to make the choices I want. At least, I was."

19

Guy Jones sat at his desk, a mound of paperwork seeming to grow taller before his eyes. How well would he survive two weeks without Kinsey to keep him organized—especially without having had time to prepare in advance?

Much to his chagrin, the temp Brent hired, Marsha what's-her-name, had the personality of a paperweight and reminded him of his ninth-grade history teacher—one more stress he didn't need.

Everyone else must be feeling it, too. The tension in the office seemed almost tangible. No one was talking to him about the threat, but a security guard had been posted outside the main door of the law offices. Brent was fielding all calls from the media.

A voice came over his intercom. "Mr. Jones, your sister is on line one, sir."

Sister? "Which sister?"

"I'm sorry. I didn't ask. Would you like me to find out?"

"No. I'll take it, Marsha. Thanks."

He sat for a moment, his thoughts racing, then picked up the receiver. "Hello, Sis. This is your adoring brother, the one who doesn't have a sister. So who are you with—newspaper, TV, or radio?"

"Guy, keep your voice down. I don't want anyone in the office to hear you."

"Kinsey?"

"Yes. Is your door closed?"

"Yeah, what's wrong? I can hardly hear you."

"I need to see you. Some place where we can talk."

"Are you in trouble?"

"I'll explain when I see you. Just promise you'll come alone."

"Not till I'm sure this isn't some kind of setup." Guy lowered his voice. "Is someone forcing you to call and entice me to meet you?"

"No."

"If someone's forcing you and you can't say so, just cough."

"Guy, no one's forcing me to do anything. Look, I have to see you *today*. I can't explain it over the phone..."

He heard sniffling. Was she crying?

"Where do you want to meet?"

"Holbrook Park. Get on the Eva Holbrook Nature Trail, and I'll find you. Guy, please come alone. I don't trust anyone else with this."

"What time?" he heard himself say.

"Two."

Guy paused to consider what he was about to do. Would Kinsey let him walk into a trap without trying to warn him? His pulse raced so fast he felt lightheaded.

"Kinsey...it's not too late to cough."

"I promise you, no one's forcing me to do anything! But if you don't meet me and hear what I have to say...please, just be there." *Click.*

Ellen closed her Bible and set it on the end table, the words she'd read in Romans 12:16 echoing in her mind: "Live in harmony with one another. Do not be proud, but be willing to associate with people of low position. Do not be conceited."

How was she supposed to reconcile this with Guy's desire that she not associate with the Hamiltons, the Tehranis, the Lewises, or Blanche Davis? She didn't see any of her friends as lesser than herself. She had never even thought about the social differences until Guy had made such an issue of it.

Ellen closed her eyes and allowed the profound sadness to permeate her. What if she and Guy were never able to get past this without doing irreparable harm to their marriage? Ellen hated that she was losing respect for him but couldn't bring herself to tell him so. The last thing she wanted was to hurt him.

"Ellen?"

Ellen looked up and saw Hailey standing in the doorway. "Sorry, I was lost in thought."

"I need to leave for my job interview," Hailey said. "Will you be all right here by yourself?"

"I'll be fine, honey. It helps knowing the security guard is outside. Are you nervous about the interview?"

"I must be. I actually lost my breakfast. I'm not even going to try to eat anything else till I get back."

"You really want this job, don't you?"

Hailey nodded. "I'm going crazy at home. I miss the people contact."

"I can certainly relate to that."

Guy pulled his Mercedes into a parking space at Holbrook Park and turned off the motor. He sat for a moment and observed his surroundings. The neighborhood park was a lush paradise of blooming shrubs, leafy shade trees, and towering pines. Multicolored flowers dotted the ground around a rustic sign that marked the starting point of Eva Holbrook Nature Trail. An arrow pointed to a path that had been carved through the thick ground cover and snaked into the woods.

He counted four cars in the parking lot and made a mental note of each: green GMC Suburban, blue Chevy Impala, white Dodge Caravan, burgundy Ford Taurus. In the rearview mirror, he saw a playground. Three young women were pushing toddlers on the swings, and two little blond boys were climbing a giant yellow tube slide.

An elderly couple sat holding hands on a park bench and appeared to be watching the two little boys. He wondered if he and Ellen would make it to old age together.

A silver Camry pulled into a nearby parking space, and the driver nodded at him.

Guy looked at his watch just as it beeped 2:00. *Okay, Kinsey. Let's get on with it.*

He got out of the car and locked it, then began walking down the nature trail, suddenly wishing he'd worn his Rockports instead of wingtips. He wound his way down the path and deeper into the woods, trying to keep his pant legs from snagging on the thistly branches that seemed to grab at him.

Finally the path widened, and he was able to stroll under a green canopy that opened up enough to allow only glimpses of blue sky. The rich, earthy smell of the woods took him back to his Boy Scout days, but the cawing of a crow gave him an eerie feeling, and he questioned whether he should've agreed to do this.

Guy trudged about a hundred yards down the nature trail and stopped. *Come on, Kinsey. I don't have time for this.*

Up ahead, he saw restroom facilities and a man wearing dark glasses and a ball cap leaning against the building. He stopped, his heart seeming to pound out of his chest. The man in the dark glasses unfolded his arms and stepped away from the building, motioning for him to come.

Guy thought about running, but how fast could he move in these shoes? Plus he didn't relish the thought of a bullet in his back. *Lord, what have I done? Please protect me.*

Guy walked over to the restrooms, weak-kneed, and realized he was at least a half-foot taller than the guy who stood outside. He didn't see a weapon.

"Are you waiting for me?" Guy asked him.

"Quick, let's go inside," said a familiar voice.

In the next instant, Guy stood in the men's room and pulled the sunglasses off Kinsey's face. "Was all this really necessary?"

"You have no idea." Kinsey's voice was shaking.

"Tell me what's going on."

"Did anyone follow you? This has nothing to do with Brinkmont, and I don't want to involve the police."

"I didn't tell the police. But I think I need my head examined. You're obviously in some kind of trouble."

Kinsey's eyes brimmed with tears. "I need to borrow money. My credit cards are maxed out and I can't get a loan."

"For cryin' out loud, Kinsey, why didn't you just meet me for lunch instead of running me all over—"

"I need fifteen thousand dollars—fast."

Guy stared at her dumbfounded. "That's a lot of money."

"I borrowed some money from a loan shark and if I don't pay it back...well, I don't dare think about it."

"A loan shark? You know better than that!"

"I have a gambling problem, okay? I got in over my head and thought I could dig out, but I can't. Please, Guy. I don't know where else to turn."

He searched her eyes, suddenly wishing he had Ellen's ability to read people. "Did the break-ins have anything to do with this?"

"No. Why would you think that?"

"It's odd that you decided to disappear and take two-weeks' vacation at the same time someone threatened me."

"The threat just gave me a convenient excuse to hide till I can scrape up the money. Please, Guy. I'll pay it back as soon as I can. I promise to go to Gamblers Anonymous and get myself straightened out. But if you don't lend me the money, someone's going to really hurt me. This isn't going to go away."

Guy shook his head and started pacing, his hands in his pockets. "Good grief, Kinsey. You're too smart for this!"

"Keep your voice down." She went over to the door and

peeked outside, then came back and looked at him with pleading eyes. "Are you going to help me or not?"

Guy hiked back to where the nature trail had started and stopped to catch his breath. He scanned the playground and parking lot, noting that everything appeared exactly as he had left it. If someone had followed Kinsey, there was no evidence of it.

Guy walked over to the man in the silver Camry. "She's dressed like a man, dark glasses, red ball cap. She should be about five minutes behind me."

"Don't worry, I've been a PI as long as you've been a lawyer. I'll call you when she's on the move."

Guy got in his car and headed for the office, his mind racing with every conceivable way this could go wrong.

He pounded the steering wheel with his palms. How could a woman as educated, bright, and talented as Kinsey even consider borrowing money from a loan shark? And how had he missed the signs of her gambling problem? He knew she enjoyed playing the slots, but she had never seemed obsessed with it. He had thought her recent weekend in Biloxi was merely a getaway with some guy she'd met.

Guy had to think of a way to get his hands on that much cash without involving Ellen. It was just a loan, but she'd never agree to this. Besides, why would he want to give her an opportunity to criticize Kinsey the way she had Brent?

His cell phone vibrated and he took it out of his pocket. "Duncan?"

"Yeah, she's driving the burgundy Taurus," Duncan Manning said.

"Be careful she doesn't spot you. As paranoid as she was about being followed, I'm sure she must've noticed your Camry in the parking lot."

"Hey, give me a little credit. I moved the car where she

couldn't see me and followed her when she pulled out of the park. By the way, there's a Hertz sticker on the car window."

"After what she just told me, I wonder how she can afford to rent a car?"

"What'd she say?"

"That she couldn't pay a gambling debt and borrowed money from a loan shark and can't pay it back. She needs to borrow fifteen thousand dollars ASAP or someone's going to hurt her."

"You believe her?"

"She's never lied to me before…I don't think, anyway. And she wasn't faking the terror on her face."

"You gonna lend her the money?"

"Just see if you can find out where she's staying."

"Okay, I'll get back to you as soon as I know something."

Guy drove several blocks, letting the hard reality of Kinsey's circumstances sink in. Was it wise to get involved in this? But if something awful happened to her because he chose not to help her, could he ever forgive himself?

Guy could still picture the fear on Kinsey's face. Her circumstances had made him acutely aware of his own. Was he being foolish not to do everything possible to protect himself from whoever had threatened him?

He thought back on the devastation in his apartment and the words written on the mirror. He blinked away the image, filled again with dread. He took the phone out of his pocket and hit the autodial.

"Hello."

"Hailey, it's Guy. How'd the interview go?"

"Okay, I think. They never tell you anything."

"Well, let's hope it pans out. Let me talk to Ellen, please."

"Hang on. She's out on the porch."

Guy reached over and turned up the fan on the air conditioner and angled the vent to blow air on his face.

"Hi, how's your day going?" Ellen said. "I've been praying for you."

"I'm fine. Other than being stuck with some way-too-serious temp for the next two weeks."

"Is she that bad?"

"Oh, probably not. I'm just spoiled. How are things there?"

"Good. The insurance company already has the cleanup crew at the house. The painters should be there tomorrow. We'll have to shop for new couches, chairs, lamps, and another oil painting, but I can pick out everything else. I went ahead and ordered the exact same mattress and box springs. I don't see us getting back in the house till late next week."

Guy stopped at a red light and glanced at the patrol car next to him. "So tell me how the security guard is working out."

"Fine, as long as I don't have to share the house with him."

"But you feel safer?"

"A little. But you're the one I'm worried about."

"Well, I'm half tempted to take your advice and hire a body-guard."

There was a long pause.

"What changed your mind?" Ellen said.

"I don't know. It can't hurt—just till the police figure out who's behind the threat."

"Do the police have any leads?"

"Not yet. They've talked to several of the plaintiffs, but no one stands out. Truthfully, I don't know how much manpower they're willing to spare for something like this. I imagine it's going to take time."

"Meanwhile, we're left hanging by our thumbs." Ellen sighed. "Did you have time to talk to the landlord?"

"Uh-huh. My new apartment will be ready tomorrow afternoon, and the rental furniture will be delivered at four. I don't have to be there for that. The manager said he'd take care of it."

"Aren't you scared to go back there?"

"No more than anywhere else. If someone's determined to get to me, it won't matter where I am."

"Thanks for reminding me. Guy, why won't you ask Brent if you can work here for a while?"

"It's not practical, honey, even if I had an office. With Kinsey out, I need to be up here, especially since we both already missed a day. I'll probably work through the weekend. Let's play it by ear. I'll call you tonight. I love you."

"Love you, too."

Guy disconnected the call and stopped for another red light. He spotted his bank up ahead, and it suddenly occurred to him that he could withdraw the money he had put into a special account for an anniversary cruise he was planning for Ellen. She didn't know anything about it so withdrawing the money would be easy and discreet. When Kinsey paid him back, he would just deposit the money back into the account.

He had about twelve thousand dollars saved and could make a cash withdrawal on his credit card for the other three thousand. It's not as though he were doing anything wrong. It was just a loan to help a desperate friend out of a tight spot.

Guy felt the muscles in his neck and shoulders tighten like a drawstring. Deceiving Ellen was getting too easy.

The light turned green and he drove past the bank and turned the car onto Madison and headed for the office. Brent was probably wondering where he was.

20

Police Chief Will Seevers pushed open the side door of the police station and headed down the hall toward his office, thinking an hour from now he'd be feasting on Margaret's Thursday night meatloaf. He heard footsteps, and in the next second Investigator Al Backus was walking beside him.

"I've been waiting for you to come back from your meeting with the mayor," Al said. "We have a situation in the Muslim neighborhood."

"Give me the skinny."

"The custodian at the mosque caught a couple of vandals in the act of spray-painting the floor where the worshippers kneel. He hollered at them, and the next thing he knew they attacked him and then ran off."

"Is he hurt?"

"Beaten pretty badly—taken by ambulance to Seaport Community. I was just on my way over there, hoping to get his statement."

"Have you been to the crime scene?"

"Yeah, the imam's pretty upset—not just about the mosque being desecrated, but because of what was written on the floor." Al arched his eyebrows. "'Muslims are demons and deserve to die.'"

"That ought to light someone's fuse."

"Oh, it gets worse," Al said. "The imam also found a neck chain with a Star of David on the floor. Must've fallen off one of the vandals."

"When did this happen?"

"About an hour and a half ago—just in time to mess up the evening call to prayer at the mosque. Those two clowns probably timed it that way."

"Any idea how they got in?"

"Not for sure. But my guess is the custodian was busy working and didn't have the door locked. There were a few other people working in the offices, but no one saw anything."

Will took off his glasses and rubbed his eyes. *So much for Margaret's meatloaf.* "Okay. Let's go over to the hospital and see what the victim can tell us."

Guy Jones sat at his desk, trying to reach a good stopping point. He glanced at his watch and realized it was already five-thirty—and he still hadn't heard from Duncan.

He pulled Duncan's business card out of his pocket and dialed.

"Yeah."

"This is Guy. Where are you? Why haven't you called?"

"I've got a slight problem. I think Kinsey gave me the slip."

"What do you mean, you *think*?"

"She pulled into the Lamplighter Motel and parked in front of the room on the end. I drove around the back of the building, thinking I'd stay out of sight till she went inside. I didn't have her out of my sight more than forty-five seconds. I guess that's all she needed."

Guy tilted his chair back. "I guess I'll just have to play it her way. I don't know why I cared where she was staying anyway. It's not like I was going to rush over there."

"Hey, it wasn't a waste of time," Duncan said. "I'm pretty sure she'd been staying there. I couldn't get anything out of the manager, so I hung around and watched. Some dude in a black Lexus pulls up in front of the room and knocks on the door. Then he starts banging on the door, shouting obscenities and threatening to beat the tar out of her."

"Did he call her by name?"

"Not any name I can repeat. But I got his license number. A cop friend who owes me a favor says it's registered to a thirty-nine-year-old white guy named Rob Blakely. I'm sitting outside his house as we speak. No sign of him yet."

Guy jotted the name on his desk calendar. "Blakely must be the loan shark. I wonder how he found her."

"Can't be that hard. Maybe he's got his own cronies keeping track of her."

"Why do I get the feeling I'm in way over my head? Maybe I should just call the police and let them handle it."

"Handle what? I'm sure they're gonna care about a gambling junkie who borrowed from a loan shark. Call them if it makes you feel better, but I don't think it'll solve anything."

"Well, I don't want Kinsey to get her legs broken."

"Loan sharks are lowlife, but if you pay them what you owe, they typically disappear."

"Are you saying I should loan Kinsey the money?"

"Nah, that's your choice. I'm just telling you what I know."

Will stood with Investigator Al Backus, looking down at the battered face of the mosque's custodian, who had been admitted to Seaport Community Hospital for observation.

"Sir, are you *sure* you can't single out any distinguishing features of either of the vandals?" Al said. "The smallest detail can be helpful."

The custodian shook his head. "Sorry. Only what I've already told you. One was much taller than the other. They wore ski masks—and black shorts and T-shirts, I think. It all happened so fast."

"Did they say anything to you?"

"Not at first. When I caught them spray-painting the floor, I shouted at them. That's when they charged me and knocked me to the ground. They kept punching me and kicking me over and over. I thought they were going to kill me. Finally one of them said, 'Come on, that's enough. Let's get out of here.' But the guy kept punching me till the other one pulled him off. Then I heard them run away."

"Can you describe his voice?"

"Deep. Young. Really nothing out of the ordinary."

"Would you know it if you heard it again?"

"Maybe."

"Did anything they did or said lead you to think they might be Jewish?"

The custodian snickered. "Other than they defiled our mosque and beat up on a Muslim?"

"The imam found a Star of David on a gold chain on the floor of the mosque," Backus said.

"The infidels probably dropped it on purpose—just another way for them to defile what is holy!"

"I know this must be hard. We're going to do our best to find out who vandalized the mosque and did this to you."

"Allah will not be mocked. They will pay."

"Yeah, well, how about giving *us* a crack at them?"

The nurse came into the room and injected something into the custodian's IV. "You promised not to stay longer than ten minutes."

"So we did." Al gave her a phony smile, then looked down at the custodian. "We *will* get to the bottom of this. All we ask is your patience and cooperation. We may need to ask more questions later."

The custodian nodded, his eyes heavy.

The nurse stood staring at Will and Al, her hand on her hip. "That morphine will make him useless to you for a few hours. The doctor said he needs to rest."

"Yeah, okay," Al said. "We're leaving."

Will got up and followed Al into the hallway. "We need to be prepared for retaliation."

"Maybe not. I doubt the Muslim community wants to draw attention to itself right now."

Will put his hand on Al's shoulder and began walking down the long corridor. "Yeah, right. Have you ever known a Muslim to turn the other cheek?"

Guy walked into his room at the Holiday Inn Express and laid his briefcase on the desk. He took off his suit coat, hung it on the back of the chair, and pulled off his tie. He flopped on the bed, his thoughts racing faster than his pulse. Everything in him wanted to call Ellen and tell her what was going on. But he doubted she would go along with lending Kinsey the money. Was he supposed to just let Kinsey fend for herself?

Ellen hadn't been there to see the terror in Kinsey's eyes or to hear Duncan tell of Rob Blakely beating on her door at the Lamplighter Motel. If loaning Kinsey fifteen thousand dollars would make all that go away and save her from heaven knows what, wasn't it the right thing to do? The poor girl was desperate. It had to be humiliating for her to admit to him the mess she'd gotten herself into.

Guy felt clammy all over. Which sin was greater: not telling Ellen or abandoning Kinsey into the clutches of an angry loan shark?

Lord, I'm in so deep I don't know what to do. Please help me make the right decision.

Guy fell back on the bed and stared at the ceiling. How was he supposed to find time to do everything on his plate: make the bank withdrawals, meet Kinsey, hire a bodyguard, counsel clients, meet with the partners, be in court, keep up with paperwork, ride herd on the temp, get settled in a new apartment?

He got up and ordered a pizza, then flipped on the TV to CNN Headline News. He changed into shorts and a T-shirt, only half listening until he heard the name Seaport mentioned. He picked up the remote and turned up the volume.

"...This small town in the Florida Panhandle just can't seem to stay out of the news. Last evening a group of teenage boys threatened to behead the children of a Muslim couple in one of the city's parks; and late this afternoon, vandals spray-painted a racial slur on the floor of a local mosque, then beat the custodian and fled.

"All this following the FBI's arrest last week of five Arab men, accused of disguising and transporting bomb-making materials and a surface-to-air missile on a fishing boat. The FBI also questioned a Seaport oncologist, Dr. Ali Tehrani, and his nephew Bobak Tehrani, in connection with that incident. Sources told CNN that the FBI expects to make more arrests in the case.

"In Washington today, President..."

Guy took his cell phone out of his shirt pocket. *For cryin' out loud, Ellen, the guy's being named on CNN!* He pushed the auto dial and let it ring once, then changed his mind and turned off his phone. Not now. Not tonight. He just didn't have the energy to argue with her.

Ellen Jones sat in the living room at Owen and Hailey's, thumbing through the latest issue of *Newsweek*—not that she remembered a word she'd read. She couldn't get Guy off her mind.

Owen came in the living room and sat in the La-Z-Boy. "Hailey's already gone to bed. I can't believe she was that wiped out just from a job interview. She doesn't seem to have any energy right now."

"She really wants to find an HR position, Owen. She doesn't find it easy to stay busy at home."

"I'd think she'd be happy to let me handle the pressures of a career. Surely she could find *something* to occupy her time."

Ellen smiled. "Don't you think Hailey wants to feel as though she's doing something significant—not just occupying her time?"

"She could do volunteer work."

"I'm sure she could. But she wants to work in her chosen field. Would you be happy abandoning your CPA background for something to fill in your days?"

Owen pulled up the side lever on the La-Z-Boy and pushed himself back, his feet elevated. "I'm not the one who's going to be a stay-at-home mom someday. I *have* to advance my career."

"I understand that. But Hailey shouldn't stop advancing hers because you might have children someday."

"I guess you're right." Owen seemed to be studying her. "You've been quiet tonight. You worried about Dad?"

"I'm trying to leave him in the Lord's hands. But I'm definitely concerned. I hope he decided to hire a bodyguard."

"You still mad at him for letting Kinsey stay at his apartment?"

"I'm disappointed he used poor judgment."

"You seem mad."

Ellen caught his gaze. "Owen, I'm not going to talk about this with you. Your father and I have a number of issues we're working on."

"Like the Tehranis?"

Ellen turned the page on her magazine. "I told you I don't want to talk about it."

"Mom, you can't blame Dad for being upset. Dr. Tehrani's name is all over the news."

"Yes, and we all know how reliable the news is."

"Why are you being so stubborn? You're not all that close to Mina."

"It's a principle, Owen. Why should I be coerced into distancing myself from the Tehranis just because the media decides to create a story? Mina and Ali are warm, caring people and they're not involved in anything wrong."

"Is it worth antagonizing Dad over some neighbor you met when you were out jogging? Why do you care?"

"Because *God* cares. Since when are we as Christians supposed to act like the world? Mina and Ali are not plotting evil against the United States, and, in fact, are making a positive contribution. I refuse to shut them out just to satisfy your father's ego or the unwarranted suspicions of others!"

"All right, all right, sorry. I was just asking."

Ellen turned the page on the magazine, her temples throbbing, and glanced up at Owen. She closed the magazine and put it on the end table. "I didn't mean to raise my voice. I just feel so strongly that we aren't supposed to judge any group of people by the actions of fanatics. I can't speak for the rest of the Muslim world, but Mina and Ali are fine people who don't deserve to be persecuted."

"People are scared, Mom. They don't know who they can trust."

"So we should assume all Muslims are guilty until proven innocent? That's your answer?"

Owen lifted his eyebrows. "It's probably safer."

Guy was aware of an annoying ringing noise and his stomach feeling as though it were on fire. He sat straight up, his eyes heavy, and realized his cell phone was ringing. He groped his pocket and fumbled for the Talk button.

"Hello."

"It's Duncan. Did I wake you up?"

Guy glanced at the digital clock and could barely make out the numbers: 11:10. "Uh, yeah, I guess so. I must've dozed off. What's up?"

"I'm sitting a few houses down from Blakely's. He's had six

visitors just since he got home around 9:00. Pretty scuzzy-look-ing characters—all males, all driving pricey vehicles: luxury sedans, sports cars, cowboy Cadillacs."

"What's a cowboy Cadillac?"

"One of those big good ol' boy trucks with all the extras— costs almost as much as your Mercedes. Thing is, all of these guys went in empty-handed and came out carrying a bag."

"You think they're Blakely's cronies?"

"I don't know. I need to get a little closer to this."

"What do you mean?"

"Don't ask."

Guy got up and grabbed the bottle of Maalox off the desk and popped two tablets in his mouth. "What's the big secret?"

"It's not a secret, just a hunch. Go back to sleep and let me do my thing. I'll call you when I have something."

"How am I supposed to sleep with this big mystery hanging over me?"

"You'll sleep better than you would if I told you every possi-bility running through my mind. I don't like to speculate till I have more facts, and there's no way I can know anything for sure without more time. You want me to stick with this or not?"

"Of course, I do. Still no idea where Kinsey is?"

"No, sorry. But our one link to her is Blakely."

21

Guy Jones finally got out of bed, wondering if he'd ever really fallen asleep. He turned on the coffeepot, then stepped into a hot shower, his mind racing and last night's pizza feeling like a brick in his stomach.

What would Ellen think of what he was about to do—and what he was paying Duncan Manning to do?

"The thing I love about our relationship," Ellen had said, *"is that we share everything. I'm so blessed being married to a man I totally trust."*

Being dishonest with her wasn't the only thing bothering him. How willing was he to swallow his pride and admit to her that another friend he had perceived to be a class act was completely messed up?

Guy stepped out of the shower and dried off, then wrapped the bath towel around his waist and went out to the desk. He poured a cup of coffee and took the first sip just as his room phone rang. He noticed the red light was blinking.

"Hello."

"Why didn't you call last night?" Ellen said.

Oh, boy. "Sorry, honey. I got in late and was afraid I might wake you." The lie nipped at his conscience.

"Guy, is everything all right?"

"Yeah, I'm fine."

"Well, it would sure be nice if you'd let *me* know that. Why didn't you return my calls?"

"What calls?

"I left a message at the Holiday Inn Express and three messages on your cell phone."

"When?"

Ellen's voice went up an octave. "The first at the Holiday Inn at seven and the other three on your cell phone late—after midnight. When you didn't call back, I lay awake imagining all sorts of awful things."

"Hold on." Guy reached over and picked up his cell phone. "My fault, honey. I accidentally turned off my cell, but I never even noticed the red light blinking on the room phone. Sorry. My mind's on overload. I didn't even think to check."

"Oh...then it is possible that one could care about another and still not think to check for messages?"

"Fair enough, Ellen, you made your point. You going to let it go or do I have to hear about it ad nauseum?"

"I'm not going to turn the knife. All I ask is a little consideration. You just took ten years off my life. Please don't do that again."

"I won't. I'm really sorry."

"Did you hire a bodyguard?"

"Not yet. It's all I can do just to get my work done. I'm not sure you realize how heavily I rely on Kinsey's help. The temp's okay, but I have to get her used to the way I do things, and it's really slowing me down."

There was an uncomfortable stretch of dead air.

"Ellen, I promise I'll look into it as soon as I can. It's not as though I can just hire someone over the phone. There's an interview process involved."

"Then make time, Counselor."

"Don't forget there's a security guard at the office—and there'll be one at the apartment. I should be able to move in tonight."

"That's supposed to make me feel better?"

"Everything's fine. Would you please stop worrying?"

"Then make yourself accessible."

"I promise not to leave you hanging like that again. Listen, I need to get going. I've got a full calendar."

"All right. You're in my prayers. I love you. Be safe."

"Love you, too."

Guy hung up the phone and turned on his cell phone. He cleared Ellen's messages and wondered if it was too early to check with Duncan. He decided he didn't have time to worry about it and pushed the auto dial.

"Yeah," said a sleepy voice.

"Duncan, it's Guy. Were you asleep?"

"Apparently. What time is it?"

"Six-forty."

"Then it's time I got up. I've had my four hours."

Guy went over and sat on the side of the bed. "So did you satisfy your curiosity?"

"I told you I'd call when I had something. I need more time."

"How much time? Kinsey's going to call me today and expect me to meet her with fifteen thousand dollars. I need to allow time to get it together."

There was a long pause.

"What's wrong?" Guy said.

"I think you should hold off giving Kinsey the money...just till I check something out."

"Can you check it out this morning?"

"I don't know. I'm gonna try."

"What's the big mystery?"

"I'm not convinced Blakely's a loan shark."

"You think Kinsey lied to me?"

"I don't know. Maybe."

Guy spent the morning going through his inbox and working with Marsha. He was already drained, and Kinsey hadn't called.

Neither had Duncan. He had a short window to get the money, eat lunch, and get back for a meeting with a client. He got up from his desk, emptied out a zippered portfolio, and went out to Kinsey's desk where Marsha was typing.

"I'll be out of the office for about an hour. Take messages. If my sister calls, tell her to call again at noon."

"Yes, sir," Marsha said. "Don't forget your meetings at one and three."

"Thanks. Call me on my cell if anything comes up."

Guy left the building and drove to the bank. He walked in the front door, relieved to see the teller who had waited on him a number of times he'd made deposits.

He approached her window, a smile on his face. "Hi, Terri, it's nice to see your cheery face."

"What can I do for you today, Mr. Jones?"

"I'd like to withdraw the money I've been saving for the cruise I've been planning for my wife."

"Sure. I can help you with that." Terri reached under the counter and seemed to be groping for something. "Remind me where it is you're going."

"Spain, Portugal, France, Monaco, and Italy. It's going to be fabulous."

"I envy you. I took an excursion once from Key West to the Tortugas, but never a cruise. Okay, let me get you to fill out this form. We always do this when the amount of the withdrawal is over ten thousand dollars. How do you want the cash?"

"Hundreds would be fine." Guy took the form from Terri and stood filling it out while she got the money together. He glanced around the bank, glad that no one seemed to be paying any attention. It was his money. Why did he feel as though he were doing something illegal?

Terri counted out a dozen stacks of ten one-hundred dollar bills while he watched, then put it in the portfolio and handed him the receipt. "Anything else I can do for you?"

"Actually, there is. I'd like to add three-thousand dollars to this by making a cash withdrawal on my credit card."

"All right. No problem."

He handed Terri his Visa card, and she worked up the transaction and handed him the papers to sign.

Terri put her hand over her heart. "I hope your wife appreciates you. This is *so* sweet." She counted out thirty one-hundred-dollar bills, put them in a money folder, and slipped it into the portfolio.

Guy zipped the portfolio and gave Terri the warmest smile he could muster. "It's been fun having you get excited about this trip with me. Maybe I'll bring in pictures when we get back."

"I'd love that."

Guy put the portfolio under his arm and walked out of the bank, feeling like a target carrying around that much cash. Why hadn't Kinsey called? It's not as though he could just drop everything and meet her whenever she wanted. He went over to his Mercedes, put the portfolio in the trunk, and slammed it shut.

He glanced at his watch. No time for lunch out—maybe he'd get a sandwich to go.

At twelve forty-five, Guy sat in his office, preparing for his one o'clock meeting. Neither Kinsey nor Duncan had called. What was he going to do if either of them called while he was with a client? How he hated not being in control of the situation!

He got up from his desk and walked out of the law offices and past the security guard. He walked to the end of the hall and around the corner toward the restrooms.

All of a sudden he sensed someone closing in behind him, then a sharp pressure in the middle of his back.

"Just keep walking," a male voice said. "Don't even think about makin' a sound or I'll run you through. Go out the door to the stairwell."

Guy opened the exit door and stepped into the stairwell. In the next instant, he was in a headlock with a knife blade pressed against his carotid artery.

"Think you're pretty clever, don't you?" The man's voice was deep and raspy. "Well, it's going to cost you—*big.*"

"What're...you...talking about?" Guy could hardly breathe.

"You tell your girlfriend the price just doubled. She's got twenty-four hours, then I'm going to cut her into little pieces."

Suddenly Guy was shoved toward the stairs. He grabbed the railing with one hand and felt his body twist around, his back slamming against the wall, his legs sprawled on the staircase. He heard the exit door close.

He started to get up, but his vision was fuzzy and his skin clammy. He sat on the steps, his heart pounding, and put his head between his legs and took slow, deep breaths. When he was sure he wasn't going to pass out, he slowly got to his feet, his hands shaking, and brushed the dirt off his suit.

His cell phone rang and he fumbled to get it out of his shirt pocket. "Hello."

"It's Duncan. I was right. Blakely's not a loan shark."

Guy splashed water on his face, then combed his hands through his hair. He left the men's room and walked down the hall toward the law offices, wondering if he could refocus enough to get through his one o'clock appointment. He thought about calling the police but decided against it. If the police made the wrong move, Kinsey might end up dead in some back alley. Why hadn't she called? He needed to at least tell her what Duncan had said, and let her speak for herself.

Guy nodded at the security guard and opened the door of the law offices. Marsha got up and walked toward him, a panicked look on her face. "The men are here for your one o'clock. They're waiting in your conference room."

"Okay, thanks. I need you to call my three o'clock and cancel. See if you can reschedule next week."

"Shall I give a reason why, sir?"

Guy tried to mask his impatience. "Just tell them I asked you to."

He turned and went in the room adjacent to his office. He forced a pleasant demeanor and shook hands with three men who were already seated at a round table. "Sorry to keep you waiting. I've got your contract right here."

Guy sat in an empty chair and handed each man a copy of a lengthy contract he had drawn up, then went through the major points one-by-one, relieved each time the men nodded that they understood. He glanced at his watch and realized it was ten after two.

"Do you have any questions?" Guy asked.

One of the men asked him to elaborate further on section four. Guy went through it again, line by line, feeling almost as if someone else were speaking. "Is that clear now?" *Please say yes so I can get out of here.*

The man nodded. "Much clearer, thanks."

"Anything else...? All right, then," Guy rose to his feet, "I'll have the final papers drawn up and call you as soon as they're ready to sign."

He shook hands with the men, then accompanied them to the front door, hoping he didn't seem overly eager to dismiss them. When they were gone, he walked back to Marsha's desk.

"Did you cancel my three o'clock?"

"Yes, sir. I rescheduled it for three on Monday."

"Thanks. I'm going to be out the rest of the afternoon. Take messages. Oh...and if my sister calls, tell her I need to hear from her right away. Be sure she has my cell phone number."

22

G uy Jones pulled into a parking space at Holbrook Park. He turned off the motor and watched the children romping on the playground. What he wouldn't give to feel safe and secure! *Lord, give me wisdom.*

How long should he wait before going to the police? It seemed smarter to confront Kinsey first and find out whether or not Duncan was right. Going to the police too soon could get her killed.

The thug's words kept replaying in his head. *Think you're pretty clever, don't you? It's going to cost you. You tell your girlfriend the price just doubled. She's got twenty-four hours, then I'm going to cut her into little pieces.* What would make the man think Kinsey was his girlfriend?

Guy couldn't help but find the irony in all this. If he'd hired a bodyguard, the thug would never have gotten close enough to hold a knife to his throat and tell him that the price had doubled—and Guy would still believe the fifteen thousand dollars sitting in his trunk was going to save Kinsey's neck.

His phone rang and he jumped. He took a slow, deep breath. *Please be Kinsey.* "Hello?"

"It's me," Ellen said. "Did you get moved in to the new apartment?"

Guy glanced at his watch: 4:20. "Uh, the rental company should be delivering furniture about now. The manager said I didn't have to be there for that."

"Where are you? I called the office and the girl from the temp agency said you were gone for the afternoon."

"Yeah, I had some business-related things I needed to take care of. It's not something I wanted to delegate to Marsha."

"Did you hire a bodyguard?"

"Ellen, I haven't had a minute to myself."

"You're not going to do it, are you? You're just humoring me."

"Honey, I'm really not. I'm just having trouble staying on top of the workload with Kinsey gone."

"You've waited so long now you'll have to go through the weekend without any protection. I can't believe you'd even think of doing that."

After my conversation with Duncan, neither can I. "You're right. I'm going over there right now and do it."

"Promise?"

"Yeah. I'll call you later."

Guy disconnected the call, backed out of the parking space, and headed for downtown. The bodyguard-for-hire place he had seen listed in the phone book was across from Winkler's cafeteria.

Guy's phone rang again and his heart raced. "Hello."

"Hi, it's Kinsey."

"Where have you been?"

"Did you get the money?"

"All fifteen thousand. Where do you want me to meet you?"

"That little corner café on Elm Street we've wanted to try. Come alone. I'll find you."

"Now?"

"Yes, now. You didn't tell anyone, did you?"

"No. I'll be there in about twenty minutes. Might take longer—the traffic's getting heavy."

"All right, hurry. I'm so scared someone might have followed me."

Guy went up the steps to the Elm Street Café and pushed open the glass door. The place was bigger than it looked from outside, and quainter—gingham curtains on the windows, hanging plants, hardwood floors. The aroma of something delicious drew him in.

"Dinner for one?" the waitress said.

"I'm meeting a friend. How about a nice quiet spot?"

"Right this way." The waitress led him to the far corner of the room, away from the windows. "How's this?"

"Fine, thanks."

She handed him a menu. "Our special tonight is Yankee pot roast. Best you'll ever sink your teeth into. All the menu items are available tonight. I'll be back to take your order when your friend gets here."

Guy opened the menu and pretended to be reading. He glanced around the café and saw only two other customers—a gray-haired couple sitting near the entrance. It was ten minutes till five. *Come on, Kinsey. Get here before the dinner crowd starts pouring in.*

Guy's cell phone vibrated. He took it out of his shirt pocket. "Hello."

"Come out to your car," Kinsey said. "I don't have a good feeling about sitting inside."

"All right."

Guy got up and walked over to the waitress. "I'm sorry. My plans have changed, and I'm going to have to leave. Sorry for the trouble."

"That's quite all right. Please come again."

"I will."

Guy walked out the door and down the steps, his eyes searching the parking lot. He didn't see anyone except a person in a red cap sitting at the bus stop. It looked like the same cap Kinsey had worn when he'd met her at the park. He got in his car and the person in the red cap got up and walked to the passenger door and opened it. "Let's go," Kinsey said.

Guy pulled out of the parking lot onto Elm and into a line of traffic.

"Did you bring the money?" she said.

"Yeah, I have the money. What I don't have is the truth."

Kinsey turned to him. "What're you talking about?"

"I don't want to talk about it while I'm driving around in traffic. Let's go somewhere where I can eyeball you."

"Please don't tell me you changed your mind about giving me the money?" Her lower lip quivered. "Guy, I'm in so much trouble. You can't do this to me."

"I didn't change my mind. Someone changed it for me."

Guy had driven for blocks without Kinsey or him saying anything. He kept checking his rearview mirror, and it didn't look as though he was being followed.

"Kinsey, you have to level with me. You pick where you want it to happen, but I'm not letting you out of this car until we agree on that."

"I told you everything when we met at the park. What else is there to say?"

Guy kept driving until he came to Miller's Pond Road, then turned right and drove about a mile before the pavement ended. The car bounced along a rutted gravel road, a trail of white dust behind it. Guy pulled over to the side of the road, the motor still running and the air conditioner on high, and turned to Kinsey.

"Just before one this afternoon, I left the office to go to the men's room. Next thing I know, some guy's got me in a chokehold, a knife at my throat. I think you can guess what he said, but let me tell you." Guy repeated the thug's words verbatim. "It's time to shoot straight with me before we both end up at the bottom of the river. You want to tell me who Rob Blakely is?"

Kinsey didn't respond.

"Okay, then I'll tell *you*. Blakely isn't a loan shark and you don't have a gambling problem. You're a drug dealer, Kinsey. And Rob is either your supplier or your mule."

Her eyes widened.

"I don't have it all figured out, but our friend Duncan Manning followed you out of the park yesterday and was at the Lamplighter Motel when Blakely came banging on your door. Had you been there, the guy would've beaten you to a pulp. You want to fill in the blanks for me?"

"I can't believe you had Duncan follow me!"

"I was afraid for you, Kinsey. I had to do something. I believed you—to the point of drawing fifteen thousand dollars out of the bank. Oh, yeah, it's right there in the trunk. Only now Rob wants thirty grand. Even if I had it, I wouldn't give you a penny to pay a drug debt."

"I never meant for you to get involved! You have to believe me!"

"Believe you? I don't even *know* you! Gotta hand it to you, though, you're good. You had me believing you didn't know anything about the cocaine in my apartment."

Kinsey tucked her hair behind her ear. "The stuff in your apartment was a birthday present for a friend. I'd planned to drop it off on my way home from Savvy's. I was surprised you didn't see it when you were looking for my driver's license."

"Are you kidding? Your cat could be hiding in that purse of yours and nobody would find him."

"When I got ready to leave your apartment, I realized the coke was missing. I couldn't find it and thought maybe I'd lost it at Savvy's. It's not like I could check the lost and found." She rolled her eyes. "Don't look at me like I'm some kind of freak. All I wanted was to make a little money supplying my friends with what they were going to buy anyway."

"You're in a whole lot deeper than just supplying snowball to a few friends! How'd you get in this mess?"

"Believe me, you don't want to know."

Guy yanked her chin toward him and held it. "Someone trashed my home. My apartment. Threatened me. Scared my family to death. And then held me at knifepoint and told me to deliver a message to my *girlfriend*? Oh, yeah. I want to know *everything*!"

Mascara-streaked tears streamed down Kinsey's cheeks. "I'm sorry. I'm so sorry."

"Tell me how I got pulled into this, Kinsey. I have the right to know."

Kinsey took a shuddering breath and dabbed at her eyes with a tissue that Guy handed her. "Rob Blakely supplies me, and I, in turn, supply a half dozen dealers. Rob got in some really good stuff and I wanted in on it. I was having a cash flow problem, so he gave it to me on credit. That part was fine. Is it hot in here?" Kinsey reached up and adjusted the vent so it would blow on her face.

"So what went wrong?"

"Not what, *who*—some guy I met at a club, Jerry something." Kinsey wrung her hands. "We hit it off, had a few drinks, and he spent the night at my place. Only when I woke up, he was gone—and so was my cocaine. I panicked! When I told Rob what happened, he said it was a tough break but not his problem, that he wanted his ten grand. How was I supposed to pay back the money without any coke to sell? My credit cards were nearly maxed out. Plus, my dealers were going elsewhere because I couldn't deliver."

Kinsey seemed reluctant to continue.

"What'd you do?" Guy asked.

"I went back to Rob and begged him to give me more cocaine on consignment, but he just laughed in my face and upped the price to fifteen thousand. Said if I didn't pay it, he'd cut my throat."

"Is he capable?"

"What do you think?"

Guy studied her for a moment, processing everything she'd said. "You still didn't tell me how I ended up in the middle of this."

Kinsey buried her face in her hands. "This is so hard."

Guy gave her a few moments to agonize, then put his hand on her shoulder and squeezed. "Don't lie to me. I want to know what happened."

"Rob must've been following me or had someone else do it because he knows I spent the night at your apartment...and that you came to my place Monday night and again at noon on Tuesday. He—" Kinsey's voice cracked. She paused and wiped the tears off her face. "Rob accused me of making up the story about the guy I met in the club. He thinks...he thinks you and I are having an affair and ripped him off."

"For cryin' out loud, didn't you set him straight?"

"I tried, but he doesn't believe me. I'm sure the man who ransacked your apartment and your house was looking for the missing cocaine."

"You think it was Blakely?"

"I doubt Rob gets that close to the dirty work. He probably pays someone else to *take care* of problems." Kinsey started to sob. "I'm so sorry, Guy. Where am I going to get thirty thousand dollars?"

"Forget the money. You're going to the police and tell them everything. It's over, Kinsey. The only safe way out of this is to turn yourself in."

"I can't do that! I'll have to go prison. My life will be over!"

"Looks to me like it's over either way. But if you want to keep breathing, you need to go to the police."

"No, I can pay this off! I'll figure out something! I'll go see a loan shark for real! There has to be way to fix this!"

Guy grabbed her by the arm and shook her. "There isn't! I'm going to the police and tell them everything. You can either come with me or face the consequences when they catch up to you...or when Blakely does. But I promise you this—Rob Blakely is going down. Duncan already has enough on him to justify a warrant."

"You would actually turn me in?"

"In a heartbeat. What you did was criminal, Kinsey. Don't expect me to be a part of it."

"Please don't go to the police! Just let me work this out! I promise I'll think of something! Rob likes me! He'll listen to reason!"

Guy shook his head. "I'm not turning a blind eye. I can't believe you exposed me and my family to this."

Kinsey turned to him, her eyes vacant, her pretty face suddenly haggard. "Then I'll take my sorry self out of your life. I sure wouldn't want to put a strain on your storybook family!" She pushed open the passenger door, bolted out of the car, and ran through the tall weeds toward the woods.

Guy got out and started to chase her and realized she was too fast. He stopped, his hands cupped around his mouth. "Kinsey, come back! Don't do this! You're going to get yourself killed!"

23

Guy Jones turned his Mercedes into Brent McAllister's driveway and sat for a moment, telling himself he had done the right thing by going to the police.

He got out of the car, his hands on his lower back, and stretched. The soft blue canvas of evening sky looked as though someone had streaked it with a fireball. He wondered if Ellen was admiring it.

He grabbed his weekend bag in one hand and his hang up bag in the other, then went up the walk to the front door of a two-story white-brick mansion. Through the beveled glass, he saw a man and a woman in the entry hall.

Brent opened the door and held it. "You look wiped out."

"It was no picnic having to tell the police about Kinsey. I've hardly had time to assimilate it myself."

"Donna made you some herb tea to settle your stomach."

"Thanks," Guy said. "Sounds good."

"Here, let me put your things in the guest bedroom, and I'll be right out. I'm anxious to hear the whole story."

Guy followed Donna out to the kitchen, wishing Ellen were there.

Donna poured hot tea into a cup, then placed it on a saucer and sat it in front of him. The pleasant aroma compelled him to take a sip.

"Thanks, Donna, this is good."

"You're welcome. I'm sorry about Kinsey. It was a shock to all of us."

"Okay." Brent breezed through the doorway. "Tell me everything."

Guy put his weariness aside and recounted every detail he could remember from the night of the victory dinner when he let Kinsey sleep on his couch until earlier tonight when he watched her run off into the woods. He also told about giving his statement to Investigator Zack Hamlin.

"I feel like a real sap," Guy said. "I should have seen *something*."

Brent shrugged. "Why? No one else did. It's pretty hard to identify a drug dealer who isn't using."

"It breaks my heart to know what may happen to her, and there's nothing I can do to stop it."

"She made her choice, Guy. She's not a kid."

"But she's somebody's kid."

"Well, her mother's got Alzheimer's so she'll never know."

Guy blew on his tea and took a sip. *God knows.*

"I'm disappointed and shocked at Kinsey, and angry that she put you in jeopardy." Brent took off his glasses and rubbed his eyes. "I don't want you talking to the media. Let me do it."

"Be my guest."

"Why don't you drive back to Seaport tomorrow and relax over the weekend. In fact, take all next week off."

"I'd rather stay busy. And it would leave you short-handed."

Brent put his hand on Guy's shoulder. "You need a break from this. Plus you need to be close to Ellen right now."

Guy was thinking that he had never felt more estranged from her.

"Thought any more about a bodyguard?"

"I talked to Investigator Hamlin about it. He seemed to know the going rate, and it sounds cost prohibitive. Plus, there's the problem of having to move back and forth between two locations. He thinks if they get Rob Blakely, that'll be the end of the threat."

"And what if they don't—or they can't find enough to hold him?"

Guy got undressed and put on his pajama bottoms. He picked up his cell phone and lay on the bed in Brent's guestroom, letting the ceiling fan dry his perspiration.

Lord, I don't want to worry Ellen. And I don't want to lie to her. I'm too exhausted to articulate my thoughts. I need Your help.

Guy rested for a moment and let his heart get quiet, then pushed the auto dial.

"Hello, *Guy?*"

"I'm glad you had your cell phone on. I wasn't sure you would."

"I've been worried sick about you. I thought you'd call back after you looked into hiring a bodyguard. So did you get one?"

"Actually, I didn't. The going rate is fifteen hundred dollars a day, ten thousand a week, or twenty-five thousand a month. Seemed a little steep."

"Good heavens, I had no idea!"

"Me either. We really need to talk about it. But don't worry, I'm staying with Brent and Donna tonight and driving home in the morning. I'll see you before lunch."

"I thought you were too busy to come home."

"I have a lot to discuss with you. But I don't want Owen and Hailey in on it. We need to think of someplace private where we can talk."

"Guy, are you okay? You sound funny."

"Actually, I'm not. I found out some disturbing things about Kinsey that I'd like to discuss with you privately—but not over the phone."

"Can't you give me a little hint?"

"She's done something criminal and is in big trouble."

"Oh, no. I hate to hear that. You two worked so well together."

"I'll tell you all about it tomorrow. Right now, I'm so tired I can hardly think." *I wish you were here so I could hold you.* "I love you, Ellen. We haven't been on good terms lately, but I love you so much. I really need us to be okay."

"Guy, you're scaring me. Are you sure you're all right?"

"I'm fine. Just feeling very in touch with what's important to me."

"I love you, too," she said softly. "I'm eager to hear what you have to tell me. Try to get some rest."

"I will. Goodnight, honey."

"Goodnight."

Guy disconnected the call, thinking the conversation had gone much better than he would've ever thought. *Thank you, Lord.*

He was tempted to turn on the news but decided he didn't want to hear anything else upsetting, especially about the unrest in Seaport. He just wanted to go home with a renewed sense of how blessed he was to be grounded in something solid and decent. As fond as he was of Kinsey, her making him privy to the things she'd been involved in made him feel dirty—and profoundly sad that she would now have to face the dire consequences of her choices.

Where was her moral compass? She had repeatedly shut down his attempts to talk about anything spiritual, especially his personal decision to believe in and trust a God he couldn't see or touch—or prove the existence of in a court of law.

But there was one time several months ago when he had taken Kinsey to lunch at The Lobster Pot, and she had given him a small window of opportunity...

"Thanks for an extraordinary job of pulling the research together," Guy had said. "With that off my mind, I can take the weekend to help Ellen get our church's VBS ready to roll."

"What's VBS?" Kinsey said.

"Vacation Bible School."

"Oh. That. I went once when I was a kid. A friend dragged me there."

"You didn't like it?"

"It was all right. What kid doesn't like doing crafts and singing songs? The difficult part was seeing all the perfect mothers picking up their perfect kids and taking them to their perfect homes. My father was a drunk and my mother griped incessantly about how awful her life was. I always wished I belonged to one of those families. It's still a big void. My divorce didn't help any."

Guy held her gaze and searched her eyes. "Kinsey, a lot of us had disappointing families, but we don't have to carry that pain the rest of our lives."

"Sure, I can spend a fortune for therapy and relive it all again. No thanks."

"Or you can enter into a relationship with a Father who *does* love you and will never leave you. Jesus already paid—"

"Guy, don't try to get me saved. I've heard it all before."

"Then why do you run from Him when He's the only One who understands and can heal your wounds?"

"Are you kidding? All I need is another father telling me how I can't do anything right. Thou shalt. Thou shalt not. I'm an adult now. If I mess up, the only one I have to be accountable to is me..."

Guy blinked the stinging from his eyes and turned on his side. He couldn't shake the emptiness he had seen in her eyes then—or today in the car. Her parting words had been replaying in his mind all evening.

Then I'll take my sorry self out of your life. I sure wouldn't want to put a strain on your storybook family!

Guy slid out of the bed and got down on his knees. *Father, Kinsey's so alone. Put someone in her path that will make her understand how much she needs Your Son in her life. Please don't let her die without You.*

24

Before the sun came up on Saturday morning, Ellen Jones was already up and dressed in jogging clothes, feeling as though she would scream if she didn't get out of the house. She went out to the kitchen, tore a sheet off the notepad, and grabbed a pencil.

> Owen and Hailey,
>
> I woke up early and decided to drive down to the beach and watch the sunrise. Don't worry, I'll stay in the car with my doors locked until I'm sure no one has followed me. I'll probably be home before you finish your morning coffee.
>
> Guy called last night and said he'd be here before lunch today. The two of us are going to spend the afternoon tying up some loose ends, so please don't let us get in the way of any plans you have for the weekend.
>
> Love, Mom

Ellen put the note on the kitchen table and set Hailey's mug on top of it, then grabbed her purse and went out the front door.

"Good morning, Mrs. Jones," the security guard said.

"Good morning, Sid. Are you about to die of boredom out here?"

"Oh, no, ma'am. I enjoy time to think."

"Me, too. But I'm used to having my quiet time watching the sunrise. I've missed it so."

"Kind of hard to see the sky with all these trees, eh?"

Ellen smiled. "I love the trees, too. I just need some wide-open space to let my heart run free. It's been a difficult week."

"Yeah, I guess it has. Well, everything's quiet here. I haven't even seen a car go by in hours—just the newspaper van."

"I'll see you later."

"You be careful, ma'am."

"I will."

Ellen got in her car, backed out of the driveway, and headed for the beach. She drove through a maze of residential streets, then turned on Main and drove toward downtown Port Smyth. Hardly anyone was on the road and no one was behind her. She spotted a bakery up ahead and the Open sign lit up.

She pulled up to the drive-through window and ordered a couple of fresh cinnamon rolls and a cup of coffee, thinking she could hardly wait till she was back in her own house and Guy was spoiling her with their long-time Saturday tradition of breakfast in bed.

Ellen paid for the rolls and coffee and then got back on Main Street and drove a few blocks and turned on Beachfront Drive. The road came to a dead end at a public parking lot. She pulled into a parking space, the gulf only about fifty yards in front of her, delighted to see she had the entire place to herself.

Off to the east, a chain of clouds that looked to her like enormous wads of cotton balls covered the horizon. She opened the sack, pulled out a warm cinnamon roll and took a big bite, then licked her fingers and almost giggled at how girlish she felt.

Ellen savored several more bites, then blew on her coffee and took a sip, wondering if Guy had left Tallahassee yet, and what awful thing Kinsey had done. It crossed her mind that Guy might be coming home to confess having an affair with Kinsey, but she quickly dismissed it. In spite of their recent estrangement, Ellen felt sure she would've known intuitively had he been unfaithful. That couldn't be it. Guy told her Kinsey had done something criminal. *Criminal?* No wonder she wanted time off.

Ellen saw the pink color begin to deepen and spread slowly across the expanse. She took several gulps of coffee and put the cup in the holder and closed the sack. She looked in her rearview mirror, then to her right and left and saw no one. She stepped out of the car and slowly filled her lungs with damp, salty air.

Good morning, Lord!

Suddenly invigorated, she trudged across the beach toward the water and began to jog on the wet sand along the surf, her eyes on the horizon, her heart soaring in a different realm. She began to praise God and thank Him for all His blessings.

Ellen ran a considerable distance, then slowed, and finally stopped. The sky had turned the color of hot lava and was streaked with fiery pinks and bluish purples. A billowy cloud shrouded the sun, its rim glowing and seeming to pulsate. The first ray of dawn broke through and then another, and another, until white rays fanned out across the vastness. She breathed in and, for a moment, forgot to exhale.

Ellen stood motionless, even after the magnificence faded and the sun finally rose above the clouds. The presence of God, all encompassing and all protective, paralyzed her with joy.

Gradually, the feeling left her and she turned around to jog back to the car, startled to see a man running toward her. A second later she realized it was Guy and waved. "What are you doing here already?"

He ran to where she was standing and wrapped her in his arms. "I couldn't sleep so I decided to pack up my things and drive back. I saw your note and didn't want to wait any longer to see you. I hope I didn't interrupt your prayer time."

"I'm just glad you're safe." Ellen nestled in his arms for a few moments, then pushed back and looked up at him. "You must be exhausted."

"I just needed to be with you. I have so much to tell you. Some of it will be pretty upsetting."

Ellen looked deep into his eyes and couldn't decide if what she saw was anxiety or guilt. "Maybe I should make you breakfast before we get into this."

"I'd just as soon get it off my chest."

"All right."

Guy took her hand and trudged across the dry sand, then sat in it.

Ellen sat next to him, hugging her knees. "Guy, you're scaring me. Are you in some kind of trouble?"

"Not with the law."

Ellen prayed silently, *Lord, help me hear this with Your ears and react with Your words.*

"Honey, everything I've told you about the break-ins, the cocaine I found, confronting Kinsey with it, and going to the police is true. But some things have happened since then that you need to know about."

Ellen listened as Guy told her about Kinsey calling and asking him to meet her, how reluctant he was to do it, and what she wanted. He told how Duncan Manning had followed Kinsey and soon suspected that the man who had banged on her motel room door was not a loan shark. Guy explained how he had withdrawn fifteen thousand dollars from the bank, and then described his ordeal of being held at knifepoint in the stairwell.

Ellen shuddered. "I'm sure you realize you could've been killed!"

"By the grace of God, I wasn't. And the minute Duncan called back and said he thought Kinsey was dealing drugs, my lending her money was out of the question." Guy seemed pensive and appeared to be staring at nothing. "There's more."

He told Ellen about yesterday's meeting with Kinsey and recounted her explanation of why and how she had gotten involved in cocaine and why her supplier kept upping her debt.

Ellen felt the muscles in her neck tighten. "Kinsey's supplier thinks you're her *boyfriend*, and the two of you ripped him off?"

"She said she tried setting him straight, but he doesn't believe her."

"What would make him think you're her boyfriend?"

"He must've been following her because he knew she had stayed at my place and that I had gone to hers. Remember I told you I went to her condo to confront her about the cocaine?"

"You said you confronted her. You never said *where*."

Guy's eyebrows gathered. "I also went there for lunch one day—for spinach salad. Nothing else."

"How could you be so careless? For a man who's so concerned about his image, not to mention his marriage, you certainly set yourself up to fall!"

"I was looking for answers, honey. Cheating was the furthest thing from my mind."

"And, of course, *you* could never be tempted?" Ellen threw up her hands, then looked out over the water. "If this Blakely is out to get you, why didn't he just kill you when he had the chance?"

"He probably wants what belongs to him. If he kills me, he gets nothing. If he intimidates me, he might get the thirty grand."

"I shudder to think what might happen when he gets tired of trying to collect!" Ellen paused and realized she was shaking. "Who would have ever imagined Kinsey supplying drugs—and dragging you into it?"

"Though she knows it's illegal, I don't think she sees what she's doing as morally wrong. If there's any way she could pay off Blakely and keep dealing, she would."

"That's hard to believe."

"Ellen, she begged me not to turn her in. I told her I had no choice, and that I couldn't believe she had exposed me and my family to this. She just stared at me with eyes so dead they gave me chills. She said she'd get out of my life so she wouldn't put a strain on my storybook family. Then she got out of the car and ran off. I have no idea where she went. I hope and pray Rob Blakely doesn't either."

Guy lay on the porch swing at Owen and Hailey's, his head propped on a cushion and his knees bent, watching a huge, fuzzy spider spinning a web in the corner of the ceiling. He heard a lawn mower in the distance, and the sound of children playing, and Sid's cell phone ringing.

The front door opened and Ellen came outside and stood next to him. "Mind if I sit?"

Guy swung his legs off the side and sat up. "Not at all."

Ellen sat next to him and pulled his arm around her shoulder.

"I'm glad you're still speaking to me," he said. "I hope you know I didn't start out with the intention of withholding information from you."

"And yet you did. The same way I did that time I followed up on a lead and went to Chicago without telling you—then ended up in the middle of a mob vendetta. Deception is easy to justify till we get caught."

"You're right. I knew you'd never agree to my lending Kinsey the money. If it's any consolation, my conscience has tormented me."

"Good." Ellen linked her fingers with his and seemed to be lost in thought. "It's baffling to me that you were willing to go to such extremes to help a drug dealer and yet belittled me for reaching out to people who've done *nothing* wrong...other than not measuring up to your standard of who a prominent attorney should be seen with."

"I know, Ellen. You don't need to remind me."

"I think I do. Julie and Ross, Billy and Lisa, Blanche—and yes, even Mina and Ali—are decent, caring people. But because they don't fit your social mold, you've acted as though they're the dregs of the earth."

Guy just listened.

"You do realize that once they arrest Kinsey, every detail will come out. So much for the perfect image you were worried about."

"Ironic, isn't it?"

"And unfortunate. I'm sure you'll learn to hold your head high, but it's going to be painful for a while. It seems the media is never kind these days—especially if they can turn something into a juicy scandal."

"Brent says he's going to do the damage control. He told me not to talk to the media."

Ellen's hand seemed to go limp. "You told *Brent* before you told me? What's happening to us? We used to be so close I didn't think anything could come between us. Now I'm not so sure. Without communication, what we've got isn't much better than cohabitation."

"It's not *that* bad."

"Yet. At the rate we're going, we might end up old and miserable and stuck with each other. I always envisioned us growing old together—the darling twosome shuffling down the sidewalk hand-in-hand, drawing the attention of couples that hope they'll still be in love when they're our age. Now I picture us eating our meals in front of the television with nothing to say to each other."

"My outlook is more positive than yours."

"Well, Owen's certainly isn't. He won't say it, but I think he's scared we're going to end up divorced."

Guy lifted his eyebrows. "Divorced? How could he even think that?"

"Because he's baffled that we seem to be so much at odds lately."

"Well, divorce is not an option."

Ellen looked at him, her eyes glistening, her nose red. "I know it's not an option. But I don't want us to end up emotionally bankrupt and spend the rest of our days simply tolerating each other because we promised we would."

25

At five o'clock on Saturday evening, Gordy Jameson walked into the crab shack from the back deck and spotted Ellen and Guy Jones coming in the front door. He walked over to them and rested one hand on Ellen's shoulder and shook Guy's hand with the other. "Good to see you two. Are you back in your own house now?"

"No," Ellen said. "It'll be at least Wednesday before the workmen are done."

"Still don't know who tore it up?"

"The police aren't finished investigating," Guy said. "So how're you feeling a week away from tying the knot?"

"Cool as a cucumber, but I'll be happy when it's all over and we get Pam moved in. We just had the place remodeled. It's gonna be great."

"You've got a house on the beach, don't you?" Guy said.

"Yeah, I bought it way back when beachfront property was affordable. The location's great but it needed remodelin'. I turned Pam loose with all that. Looks like a new place."

Ellen linked arms with him. "We're so happy for you, Gordy. We're looking forward to the wedding."

"Yeah, me too. Don't let me hold up your dinner. You wanna sit in your usual spot?"

"That'd be fine," Guy said.

Gordy picked up two menus and led the Joneses to the corner table by the windows. "There you go. How about a couple of limeades—on the house?" He winked at Ellen.

She looked as though she were going to protest and then smiled. "Sure, why not?"

"I'll get those right out to you. Enjoy your meal."

Gordy went over and told the waitress to bring the limeades and noticed Will and Margaret Seevers sitting in a booth. He walked over and slid in beside Margaret and kissed her on the cheek. "How's the matron of honor?"

Margaret laughed. "Starved. I may even order dessert tonight. But we're going to *pay* for it," she quickly added. "We didn't think you'd be here. How come you're working the evening shift?"

"I gave Weezie the weekend off. Told her to rest up since she's gonna work double shifts while Pam and I are on our honeymoon."

"Remind me how long you're going to be gone?"

"Just three days. But I don't trust anyone but Weezie to run the place."

Gordy looked across the booth at Will, who seemed absorbed in the menu and hadn't made eye contact with him. "Hey, Chief, would you mind comin' down to my office for a minute? I need to tap your brain about somethin'."

Will's eyes never left the menu. "And I need to decide what I'm going to order."

"You always end up getting the same thing." Margaret snatched the menu from him. "Go on, I'll order for you."

"You two are so obvious." Will slid out of the booth. "Come on, let's get this over with."

Gordy followed Will down the hall and into his office and shut the door. "How long are you gonna stay sore at me?"

"You as much as told me I'm incapable of doing my job, Gordy. How would you feel if I waltzed in here and told you I didn't think you were treating your customers right—and that you couldn't be objective about it? Frankly, I'm ticked. I don't appreciate your penny ante opinions about stuff you know nothing about."

Gordy sighed. "I apologize for hurtin' your feelings. There's no one I respect more than you. I didn't mean what I said to be a personal attack."

"Sure sounded that way to me."

Gordy didn't say anything for half a minute and then said, "What can I do to make this right? You're about to stand up with me for one of the most important events of my life, which probably wouldn't have happened at all if it hadn't been for you and Margaret. I don't want hard feelings."

Will looked up and caught his gaze. "No matter how I feel about this need you have to defend Muslims, I'm thrilled you and Pam are getting married. I'm honored to be your best man."

Gordy raised his eyebrows. "Sure?"

"Of course I'm sure."

Gordy waited a few seconds, then put one arm around Will's neck and jabbed him playfully in the ribs.

"All right, now that we've settled that," Will said, "I'd like to go eat my dinner before Margaret does. The woman can't be trusted."

Gordy laughed. "What happened to her diet?"

"She's starved herself all week so she can eat whatever she wants on the weekend. And believe me, everything's fair game."

Will ate half of his pineapple bread pudding and laid down his spoon. "All right, Margaret, it's all yours."

"Thanks." She slid the dish over in front of her and took a bite. "Mmm...this is delicious. I think I like it even better than Pam's triple chocolate mousse cake."

"Honey, why don't you just eat sensibly all week instead of starving yourself? You're never going to lose ten pounds binging like this on the weekends."

Will's cell phone vibrated and he took it off his belt clip. "Sorry, I'd better take this. Chief Seevers."

"It's Al Backus. I'm down at the mall with my wife and daughter and just bumped into a security guard friend of mine. He told me a Jewish kid called mall security just after closing last night and reported some thugs had roughed him up in the men's room."

"Why do I need to know this on a Saturday night?"

"Sounds like a hate crime. They allegedly choked the kid till he thought he was a goner, then held his face in the toilet and kicked him repeatedly. They laughed the entire time, and one of them said that Jews were scum and that Hitler had the right idea."

"How many were there? Did he give a description?"

"Never saw their faces. The whole thing was over in a couple of minutes. They left him slumped over the toilet bowl and said if he turned around before they were gone, they'd kill him. All he could tell my friend is that there were at least two, and they sounded about his age, maybe sixteen or seventeen."

"That's it?"

"Yeah, they didn't even rob the kid, and he had fifty bucks on him."

"All right. Jack Rutgers is on duty tonight. I'll send him over to get the boy's statement, jog his memory a little. Maybe he's calmed down and will remember more details. Give me a name and address."

"Unfortunately, the kid wouldn't leave his name. Said he didn't want any trouble but thought they needed to beef up their security at the mall so no one else had to go through what he did."

"Could be a hoax."

"My friend said the kid sounded really shaken."

Will paused to picture the scene Al had described to him. "You thinking what I am—that this could be retaliation for the mosque incident?"

"That Hitler remark is sure a red flag."

"All we need is for this thing to escalate. I don't know what we can do about it, other than make sure we patrol the area around the synagogue."

"Sorry to butt into your night out with Margaret, but I thought you should know."

"Thanks, Al. You did the right thing."

Will put his phone back on his belt.

"What happened?" Margaret said.

"Oh, a Jewish kid got roughed up in the men's room at the mall last night. The thugs told him he was scum and that Hitler had the right idea."

"How awful. Is this because of what happened at the mosque?"

"I'd like to tell you no, but my gut tells me yes." Will lifted his eyebrows. "And just when we thought we got rid of the gangs." He put a five-dollar bill on the table and slid out of the booth. "Put this on the credit card. I'll go get the car and meet you at the end of the pier."

"Please don't let this spoil your mood, Will. I've really been looking forward to this movie and a nice relaxing evening."

"I'm fine, honey. It'll be good to get my mind on something else."

Will picked up a toothpick and went out the front door and walked down the pier. He spotted his Buick and smiled at the thought that he and Margaret were out on a real date. It had been a while since he had parked the squad car for the weekend and given himself permission to enjoy time with just her.

He unlocked the car and started to get in when he felt his cell phone vibrate. He took it off his belt clip and resisted the urge to pitch it across the parking lot. It vibrated again.

"This is Chief Seevers, who happens to be out on a date with his wife, so this better be important."

"It is. It's Rutgers. I'm over at Bougainvillea Park where those boys threatened the Muslim couple's kids. An Iranian student from the junior college was found beaten half to death. He's in an ambulance headed for Seaport Community."

"Good grief. Who called it in?"

"An old couple out for a stroll. They can't really tell us anything."

"Anybody else see anything?"

"If they did, they're not saying."

"Okay, Jack. I'm on my way."

Will pulled the car to the end of the pier, the window rolled down, and saw Margaret approaching, humming a song and looking as content as she had in long time.

She caught his gaze and her countenance fell. "What?"

"Sorry, honey. We may have to catch the late show."

Fifteen minutes later, Will got out of his squad car and hurried over to where he saw his officers sectioning off an area of Bougainvillea Park with yellow crime scene tape. He spotted Jack Rutgers and went over and stood beside him. "Just what we needed."

"Smells like a hate crime, but everyone's suddenly deaf, dumb, and blind."

"How do you know he goes to the junior college?"

"We found his student ID. Name's Dairyoosh something-or-other. I never can pronounce their names. His parents have been notified."

Jack's cell phone rang. "Rutgers... That's too bad. Can't say I'm surprised, though... Yeah, okay. Thanks." He looked at Will. "Our victim's not breathing on his own. I'm sure the organ harvesters are starting to circle."

Will saw the Crime Scene Investigators van pull up. "Keep all these people back and let the CSIs do their work."

Will stood off to the side, his arms folded, his eyes slowly moving across the faces of curiosity seekers standing outside the sectioned off area. One young man in round, thick glasses appeared more anxious than curious. Will casually walked around the perimeter of the crowd and then came and stood next to him.

"It's a terrible thing that happened here," Will said.

The young man didn't take his eyes off the crime scene. "Yeah, I heard."

"Did you know the victim?"

"Victim? Did he die?"

"He's not breathing on his own. Did you know him?"

"He's in my English class."

"What's your name, son?"

"Isaac Kohler."

"I'm Police Chief Will Seevers, Isaac. Can you tell me the victim's name?"

"Yes, sir. Daryoush Fassih. His friends called him Dary."

"Was he your friend?"

"Are you kidding? I'm Jewish. Dary's Muslim."

"Know anything else about him?"

"His family moved here about a year ago from Iran. He's studying to become a citizen and trying to get better at English before he goes to FSU next year."

"How do you know that?"

"We were assigned to critique each other's papers. He wrote an essay about why he wanted to come to America."

"What'd he say?"

Isaac glanced at another youth, then put his hands in his pockets and looked at the ground. "I didn't take it seriously. How can we believe anything Muslims say about stuff like that? Everyone knows they didn't come here looking for the American dream. They hate us and want to convert us all to Islam."

"Is that what you believe Dary wanted?"

Isaac shrugged and pushed a pebble with the side of his foot. "I suppose he wanted a good education."

"Did he ever talk about his religious beliefs?"

"No. He knows I'm Jewish. I was surprised he talked to me at all."

"Did he act resentful toward Jews?"

Isaac lowered his voice. "Dary treated me with respect, all right? I can't speak for anyone else and don't know who did this to him, if that's where you're going."

"You live on campus?"

"No, I live with my parents. My dad's a cardiologist: David Kohler. Maybe you've heard of him."

"How'd you happen to be in the park?"

Isaac pulled a sheet of paper out of his pocket, unfolded it, and handed it to Will. "I needed a quiet place to memorize these for class."

Will glanced at several poems on the paper and recognized "The Road Less Traveled" by Robert Frost. He handed the paper back to Isaac. "Where were you when Dary was attacked?"

"Sitting up there." Isaac pointed to a park bench about a hundred yards away at the top of a gentle slope. "I remember glancing up and seeing people milling around. I didn't pay much attention till I saw flashing lights and realized the police were here."

"Can you tell me anything about the people you saw? Gender? Race? Age? Distinguishing characteristics or clothing?"

Isaac shook his head. "I'm extremely nearsighted. Everything I saw was a blur."

"Okay. I appreciate your cooperation. Here's my card. I want you to call me if you remember anything else that might help us find whoever did this. Where can you be reached if we have more questions?"

The young man's eyebrows scrunched together, the apprehension in his eyes magnified by his thick lenses. "I just told you everything I know."

"Is there a problem with us contacting you?"

The young man shifted from one foot to the other. "Well,

yeah. I mean, if I they see me talking to you about a Muslim, you don't know how miserable they could make my life."

"*They* meaning your Jewish friends?"

Isaac nodded. "My life'll be a nightmare if they think I'm sympathetic to Dary."

"Are you sympathetic?"

Isaac's eyes turned watery and he quickly looked away.

Will laid his hand on the young man's shoulder. "Don't worry. If we need to talk to you, we'll be discreet. I'll need your address and phone number."

Ellen sat out on the porch swing, trying to assimilate the severity of Guy's entanglement with Kinsey and her drug supplier, when Owen came outside and handed her the cordless phone.

"Mrs. Tehrani's on the phone," he whispered. "She sounds upset."

Probably hurt because I haven't called since the incident at the mosque. "Hello." Ellen heard breathing, and then sniffling. "Mina, did something happen? What's wrong?"

"Our friends' son was found brutally beaten at Bougainvillea Park. Police think he was dumped there *after* the beating—just a few yards from where those teens threatened to behead Muslim children." Mina began to sob. "Dary's family is keeping him on life support only long enough to see if organs can be donated."

"Oh, Mina, I'm so sorry. This is the first I've heard about it. Have the police arrested anyone?"

"No one has admitted seeing anything."

Ellen heard voices and wailing in the background. "Where are you?"

"Ali and I are at hospital with Dary's family. I called because I need to hear someone speak of hope. Everyone here is cursing the Jews. Cursing the Christians. Cursing the police, the government, the media. It is too much for me."

"I'm sure they're devastated," Ellen said. "It's probably just anger talking."

"Ali and I are angry, too. We don't understand why anyone would blame all Muslims for actions of extremists. But if our answer for hate is also to hate, then sorrow will never leave us."

Ellen was thinking Guy should be listening to this. "You're right, Mina. I'm going to pray and ask my church family to pray for reconciliation between Muslims, Christians, and Jews in this community. And we'll certainly be praying for Dary's family."

"I thank Allah for you, my friend. You are light in the darkness. I must go now and join the others."

"Please tell the parents how very sorry I am."

"I will tell them."

Ellen hung up, suddenly aware of Guy standing in the doorway.

"What happened now?" he said. "What parents?"

"Friends of Mina and Ali. Their son was brutally beaten and dumped at Bougainvillea Park." Ellen told him everything Mina had told her. "Those poor parents. What a senseless crime!"

Guy came and sat next to her. "I'm surprised something like this hasn't happened before now."

"Well, it can't be tolerated! People in the community need to denounce this kind of violence."

"Some will, but others may find it hard to be sympathetic after all the terrorist attacks and threats. There's an underlying feeling that Muslims have brought it on themselves."

"Why do I bother to talk to you about this?" Ellen jumped up and started walking to the door when she felt Guy take her by the arm.

"Ellen, wait. I'm not putting down Muslims. I thought we were having a discussion. It's important to consider both sides of the issue. Come back and talk to me."

She hesitated, then went back to the swing and sat. "The only valid side to this issue is that every human being was created by God and has value. This is America. What ever happened to equal justice for all?"

"I'm sure justice will be served when they find whoever did this."

"Unless the police don't want to find them."

"Don't underestimate law enforcement. There's no way they can afford to botch this with the whole world watching."

26

On Sunday morning, Guy Jones sat with Ellen in the third row of Crossroads Bible Church, his eyes intent on the pulpit, but his mind only vaguely aware of Pastor Peter Crawford or the words of his sermon.

All he could think about was Kinsey and what might happen to her—or already had. He replayed the events of the past week in his mind and thought back over the year he had worked closely with her. In hindsight, it seemed odd that she almost never referred to any of her friends by name, but nothing in her professional demeanor should have caused him to wonder if something was amiss. *Cocaine trafficking?* How could she throw her life away like that?

Guy could still picture her standing at his bathroom door, swallowed up in his pinstriped shirt, her dark curls softly framing her face, her sleepy blue eyes both innocent and provocative. There had been something strikingly little girlish about her.

All of a sudden, Guy realized the organ was playing and the congregation was standing. He rose to his feet, slid his arm around Ellen's waist, and supported the hymnal with his free hand.

"Are you all right?" she whispered.

Guy nodded without looking up and began to sing.

After the service, Guy stood in the back of the church and dutifully made the rounds with Ellen, greeting people and engaging in small talk. He saw Julie and Ross Hamilton approaching, Sarah Beth riding on Ross's shoulders. He acknowledged the threesome with a fabricated smile and a nod.

"Oh, it's so good to see you." Ellen hugged each of them. "Thanks again for the lasagna. It was so thoughtful." Ellen reached up to Sarah Beth and touched her nose. "Tell Miss Ellen about the zoo."

Guy pretended to listen to the little girl's babble. He glanced at his watch, thinking he was ready to eat lunch, when he saw Billy and Lisa Lewis coming his way.

"How are you do-ing, Guy?" Billy said, extending his hand.

"Fine. Anything going on with you and Lisa?"

Billy's smile was the size of the Grand Canyon. "We are get-ting a new couch!"

"Well, good. That's nice."

"Lisa and I are pray-ing that God will make your house get fixed."

"Thanks." Guy caught Ellen's eye and pointed to his watch.

Ellen nodded and gave him one of her I'll-just-be-another-minute looks.

Guy wondered why Lisa Lewis stared at him, a dopey grin on her face. He didn't ask.

"Well, *there* you are," said a familiar voice. "I've been looking all over for you."

Guy cringed, then turned around and saw Blanche Davis, whose hair seemed even bluer than the last time he saw her. "Hello, Blanche."

"We were all so sorry to hear about your house being ran-sacked—and your apartment. My quilting club is praying for you."

A gossip fest, no doubt. "Thanks." Guy shifted from one foot to the other, wishing Ellen would hurry up.

He felt his phone vibrate and walked outside through the open doors and took it out of his pocket. "Hello."

"Guy, it's Kinsey. I need to see you."

He looked over his shoulder at Ellen and then at the ground, his heart beating wildly. "Where are you?"

"Waiting in the parking lot at Seaport Beach."

"I can't just drop everything. I'm at church with Ellen."

"Can't you make up some excuse? Please? I promise I'm not here to ask for money."

Guy saw Ellen holding Sarah Beth on her hip, the child singing a song that seemed to be entertaining everyone within earshot. "Are you alone?"

"Of course I'm alone. This is not a setup and I'm not here to ask for anything. But I have to leave by two. I need to explain something before—"

Guy heard a loud whooshing sound and then nothing. "Kinsey...? Are you there...? Kinsey...?" *Darn!*

He stood paralyzed for a moment, his heart hammering and his thoughts bouncing off the walls of his mind. What if this was his last chance to make peace with Kinsey and convince her to turn herself in? Was it worth jeopardizing his already fragile relationship with Ellen?

Lord, what should I do? Guy gave himself a few moments to quiet his heart, then dropped the phone in his pocket and walked back inside. He went over to Ellen and put his lips to her ear. "Kinsey just called. You and I need to talk *now*."

Ellen's eyes widened. "Okay, give me a minute."

Guy ambled over to the door and glanced at his watch: 12:15. *Come on, honey. Don't drag this out.*

Ellen kissed Sarah Beth on the cheek and handed her to Ross. She said something to her friends and, seconds later, came over and linked arms with Guy and started walking toward the car. "Tell me everything."

He relayed to her almost verbatim the conversation he'd just had with Kinsey. "My gut tells me I should go talk to her."

"Guy, the woman belongs in jail. Why don't you just let the

police pick her up? She'd be safer behind bars than on the street."

"The police don't have enough to hold her. Everything I told them is just hearsay."

Ellen stopped and looked up at him. "I thought they were about to arrest Rob Blakely?"

"Investigator Hamlin called last night. Blakely's disappeared. They found plenty of evidence in his house to put him away, but nothing that implicates Kinsey. It's really Blakely they want anyway. So if and until he surfaces and produces evidence, the police have nothing to charge her with."

"Why didn't you tell me you talked to Hamlin?"

"You were upset about the Iranian student who was killed. I thought it could wait. Obviously, I didn't know she was going to call. Ellen, the girl has to be scared to death. I'd like another crack at getting her to turn herself in."

"Fine, then I'm going with you."

"I don't think so."

"Well, you're not going alone. What's your objection if you don't believe you're in any danger?"

Guy put his hands on her shoulders. "She might not open up with you there."

"You don't know that. Besides, if what she has to say is all that private, then there must be something else you aren't telling me."

"There isn't, Ellen. I've told you everything."

"Then I'm coming with you."

Guy turned his Mercedes into the public parking area at Seaport Beach and drove slowly down the rows of cars, looking for Kinsey's BMW or the Ford Taurus she had rented. Finally, he pulled into one of the few available parking spaces.

"I don't see her," Ellen said.

"She's here somewhere." Guy moved his eyes slowly across

the beach from left to right. "The two other times Kinsey asked me to meet her, she had on a red ball cap and dark glasses."

"Well, let's get out and start looking. In these clothes, we should stand out a whole lot more than she does."

Guy's cell phone rang. "Hello."

"Who's in the car with you?"

"Ellen."

"I wanted to talk to you privately!"

Guy looked at Ellen and nodded. "Sorry, Kinsey. Whatever you have to say you can to say to both of us. Ellen and I have no secrets."

"Did you call the police?"

"Yes, I told Investigator Hamlin everything."

"No, I mean the Seaport police...before you came here to meet me?"

"Of course not. And I didn't come all the way over here to talk to you on the phone. Where are you?"

"Standing on the beach about thirty yards in front of you." The phone went dead.

Guy looked up and saw a shapely young woman in jeans shorts and a yellow tank top, waving her arms. "There she is. Let's go." He got out of the car, took Ellen's hand, and trudged across the sand.

Kinsey met them half way, then took off her sunglasses exposing the dark circles under her eyes. "Thanks for coming and for not calling the police."

"I certainly considered it," Guy said. "You'd be safe in custody. But the police don't have enough to hold you unless you confess—or until Rob Blakely spills his guts. And he's suddenly gone missing. That should make you nervous enough to turn yourself in."

"I didn't come here to talk about Rob." Kinsey looked over at a group of young people playing volleyball. "Could we go someplace more private and out of the sun?" She glanced at her watch. "My ride leaves at two."

"Why don't we go to the lighthouse?" Ellen nodded toward the red-and-gray structure visible in the distance. "There's a picnic area with several covered shelters. It'll only take a couple minutes to drive down there."

"And you'll get me back here by two?"

Guy nodded. "If that's what you still want."

The three of them walked to Guy's car and Kinsey climbed in the backseat.

No one said anything as they drove down Beach Shore Drive and out to the lighthouse. Guy spotted an empty shelter not far from the road and pulled into the parking area. He got out of the car and took Ellen's arm and walked under the covered shelter to a picnic table.

Ellen gathered the bottom of her skirt and swung her legs over the bench and slid them under the table. Guy sat next to her, Kinsey on the opposite side.

An uncomfortable stretch of silence made him wonder if he should've just insisted Kinsey talk while she was on a roll.

"I know you don't have much time," Ellen finally said, "so I'm going to ask you a question that won't leave me alone. Obviously, you don't have to answer, but what possessed you to get involved in drugs?"

Kinsey sat staring at her hands. "The forty-six thousand a year I made as a legal secretary didn't buy me enough happiness."

"And the extra drug money did?"

Kinsey glanced up at Ellen, her eyes desolate. "Not really. But having it gave me the illusion of happiness. It's surprising how easy you can delude yourself when you're making money hand over fist. But I didn't come here to talk to Guy about that."

"Why did you come?" he said.

"To apologize."

"You already said you were sorry."

"I know. But there's more to the story than I led you to believe." Kinsey looked up at Ellen. "I didn't plan on you listening in on what I'm about to say. But I owe you an apology, too."

Ellen folded her arms on the picnic table and seemed to be listening intently.

"I can't tell you how jealous I was of you, having a man like Guy who loved you and thought of you all the time. I was happy for you, but also angry. It didn't seem fair. No matter how I tried, I could never seem to find a man who treated me the way he treated you. I kept wondering if you even realized how lucky you were. Then when you didn't drive up to join us for Guy's victory dinner, I thought it was the perfect opportunity to..." Kinsey paused, her cheeks flushed with color.

Ellen nodded. "Go on."

Kinsey shifted her gaze to Guy. "That night at Savvy's I pretended to be drunker than I was, hoping we might end up spending the night together." Kinsey's chin quivered. "But you were such a gentleman. You could've easily taken advantage of me—I *wanted* you to take advantage of me—but you didn't. Not even when we were alone in your apartment. I've never had any man respect me like that before."

Ellen's hand found Guy's and gave it a squeeze.

"I'm so ashamed of what I'm about to tell you..." Kinsey wiped a tear off her cheek. "I lied to you. Rob didn't assume we were having an affair, I *told* him we were. I wanted him to believe I was good enough to snag someone like you. So when the cocaine went missing, Rob didn't believe what *really* happened—that some one-night stand whose last name I didn't even know ripped me off. Rob was convinced I made up the story so you and I could sell the stuff without paying him for it. I've begged him to believe me, but he doesn't. I'm so afraid he's going to kill us both. I know you'll never forgive me, but I'm so sorry." Kinsey buried her face in her hands and began to sob.

Guy wanted to shake her. How could she have gambled with his will power, his reputation, and his life?

Several minutes passed without anyone saying anything.

Kinsey wiped her eyes and glanced at her watch. "That's all I came to say. It doesn't change anything, but it's the truth. Would you please take me back now?"

"Who's coming to pick you up?" Guy said. "You mentioned your ride leaves at two."

"Actually, my ride is Greyhound. My bus leaves the station at 2:20, and I need to be there a few minutes early."

"Where are you headed?"

"Atlanta."

"Do you have money?"

"I withdrew three hundred dollars I had left in savings. Don't worry about me. I'll be fine." Kinsey got up and walked toward the car.

Guy followed her, grabbed her arm, and turned her around. He waited until he had eye contact. "Promise me you won't go back to dealing drugs."

"Then how do you propose I get a decent paying job without references—prostitution?"

"Don't even *think* that," Guy said.

"I'm not, but I've got two choices: Go to prison and get three squares a day, or do whatever it takes to stay free."

"You're never going to be free dealing drugs. Brent could make a good case for a judge to be lenient if you turn yourself in and work with the police to get Rob and his supplier."

"Right. Then I can serve my time and wonder every day if the minute I get out someone will be waiting to cut my throat."

"There has to be a way to work this out," Guy said.

"There isn't! I just came to say I'm sorry. I'm so sorry." Kinsey put her fist to her mouth and choked back the emotion.

Ellen walked over and put her hand on Kinsey's shoulder. "*I'd* like to say something. I won't pretend that my emotions have even begun to work through all this, but at least know I forgive you. It took amazing courage to come all the way here to admit the awful truth. I'm grateful you did."

"Thank you..." Kinsey's voice trailed off.

Guy wondered why Ellen was looking at him wide-eyed, her eyebrows raised as if to ask why he wasn't chiming in. He dismissed her with a headshake.

Ellen reached in her purse and pulled out a Gospel tract and handed it to Kinsey. "I want you to have this. There may come a time when it makes sense to you and you'll want to talk about it. My cell number is on the back." Ellen brushed the hair out of Kinsey's eyes. "I'll be praying for you every day, honey. Don't despair. Your Father in heaven won't take His eyes off you—not for a moment."

27

Guy Jones pulled out of the Seaport Bus Terminal parking lot, feeling as though he had just signed Kinsey's death certificate. He drove through downtown and continued on toward Port Smyth, yearning for a sense of normalcy.

"Are you all right?" Ellen said.

"How can I be all right after all that?" Guy glanced over at Ellen. "I was impressed with how calm you were. I don't know how you forgave her so quickly."

"She's just a few years older than Hailey. No matter what the girl's done, it's hard not to care about her."

"I care about her. I'm just too mad right now to forgive her."

Ellen pulled down the visor and put on her sunglasses. "I've found it's easier for me to do it quickly and let the Lord change my heart. But that's me. We're all different."

"I'm glad you gave her the tract. I wasn't feeling very spiritual right then, but I've wondered where Kinsey stands spiritually. I tried broaching the subject with her a few times but could never get past her defenses."

"I don't know that I did either. But I sensed she had a deep need to be forgiven."

"I can't believe she tried to trap me into sleeping with her—with no regard for how it might hurt my marriage."

"At least she's got good taste."

"I'm serious."

"So am I. Though I think she was probably looking for affirmation more than a physical relationship. Behind that perfect size eight is a rejected little girl starving for a father's love. I'm just glad you didn't let your guard down. I might've killed you before I ever had the chance to forgive you."

Guy smiled without meaning to. "Stand in line. I think Rob Blakely has first dibs."

"That's not funny."

"I know. Sorry. But it helps to joke about it."

"I'm uneasy about this Blakely being on the loose," Ellen said. "With Kinsey out of his reach, I'm much more concerned he may come after you. If the man figures out he's not going to get paid, he's bound to take his spite out on someone."

"The thirty thousand Kinsey owed was mostly interest. The guy isn't really out all that much."

"But he thinks you ripped him off," Ellen said. "It's hard to say what he might do, especially if he can't go home without being arrested."

"Well, there's no way I'm shelling out twenty-five thousand a month for a bodyguard. This could go on for a while. We just need to pray the police arrest Rob Blakely...and soon."

Gordy Jameson walked into the kitchen at the crab shack and came up behind Pam Townsend. He put his arms around her and drew her close, his cheek next to hers. "Don't you be wearin' yourself out, now."

Pam rested her back against his chest. "I can't believe the wedding's so close."

"Next week at this time we'll be cozied up under one of those big comforters at the Pembrooke House."

Pam held up her watch. "At two-thirty in the afternoon?"

"Hey, it's allowed."

She turned around in his arms, her eyes seeming to walk into his soul. "I can hardly wait to be married to you, Gordy Jameson."

Gordy cupped her face in his hands and let his lips melt into hers until his heart started to pound, then pulled back and smiled. "I better get outta here before we get in trouble." He kissed the top of her head. "Guess I'll go make sure the Sunday buffet table's been cleared. Keep crankin' out those desserts. They're really catchin' on."

"With *paying* customers?"

Gordy laughed. "You're gonna be more of a pest than Weezie."

He went back out to the dining area and saw Ali Tehrani standing in the waiting area. Gordy walked over to him, his hand extended.

"Hi, Doc. Are you waiting to be seated?"

"No, I was wondering if I could talk to you."

"Sure, let's go down to my office."

Gordy led the way into his office and then shut the door. He pulled a chair up next to Ali's and noticed his eyes looked hollow. "Would you like somethin' to drink?"

"No, I'm fine. Sorry to bring my burdens to you, but there are so few friends I can share with these days. And my Mina is so upset over Dary Fassih's murder that I prescribed tranquilizers for her."

"I can't even imagine how a tragedy like that has affected the Muslim community."

Ali's thick eyebrows furrowed. "You really can't. But it was evident at Dary's burial."

"The boy's already been buried?"

"It is our belief that the dead should be buried as soon as possible." Ali held his gaze. "Muslims are coming from outside the region to comfort the family and denounce this hate crime. I tell you, my friend, the bitterness is fierce. I'm worried about retaliation."

"Against who?"

"The Jews. Imam Bakir found a Star of David on the floor of the mosque where the vandals spray-painted.'"

"I don't remember readin' anything in the newspaper about a Star of David."

"I don't think the police have made it public knowledge. But I know it to be true. And the word has traveled fast among Muslim believers."

"Doc, you gotta talk to them! Gettin' even will just cause more hate!"

"I agree with you, Gordy. But I am just one man. And I've already lost respect because I helped the FBI find my nephew. If I go to the police with this, I'll be considered no better than a traitor. I know you're friends with Chief Seevers. Perhaps you can make him aware of how volatile the situation is. But I ask you, please...do not reveal where you got this information."

"Okay, Doc. But Will knows we're friends. He's liable to make assumptions."

Police Chief Will Seevers sat in his favorite chair, reading the sport's page of the Sunday paper when his wife came in and sat on the couch. He could feel her eyes watching him.

"What is it, Margaret?"

"I'm worried about you."

"Why?"

She got up and took the sport's page out of his hands, folded it, and set it aside, then sat on the arm of the chair. "You've been acting strange since last night after you responded to the beating death of that Muslim student."

"No I haven't. I'm just quiet, that's all."

"I've been waiting for you to talk to me about it."

"Nothing to talk about."

"Since when is a murder *nothing*?"

"The whole thing made me sick. I just need time to sort it out. I'm fine. Really."

Margaret combed his hair with her fingers. "All right. I was just checking."

Will's cell phone vibrated. "I need to take this honey." He picked it up and pushed the talk button. "Chief Seevers."

"It's Jack Rutgers. I hope you're sitting down. We've got another dead male student, this one strangled with some kind of cord or rope."

"Muslim?"

"Nope, Jewish."

Will winced. "That's all we need."

"A couple of coeds saw him lying near the bushes outside the library at the junior college and called 911."

"Is that where you are?"

"Yeah. A crowd's starting to gather, and I heard someone say WRGL News is on the way. Probably couldn't hurt for you to make a statement."

"Okay, I'll be right there."

Will disconnected the call and put the phone on his belt clip.

"What happened now?"

"Another student was murdered—this one Jewish."

"Oh, no."

He told Margaret everything Jack had told him, then kissed her and walked out the front door. His cell phone vibrated again. "Chief Seevers."

"Will, it's Gordy. Have you got a minute?"

"I'm headed over to the junior college. Can I call you later?"

"Uh, this is pretty important. Can you talk to me while you're drivin' over there?"

"Yeah, all right. Hang on till I get situated." Will got in his squad car, fastened his seat belt, and backed out of the driveway. "Okay, what's up?"

"I got a tip that some Muslims might be plannin' to retaliate for yesterday's beating death of the Fassih boy."

"Too late. We just found a dead Jewish student outside the library at SJC. So who gave you the tip?"

"I'm not at liberty to say—just that Muslims outside the region have come here to comfort the Fassih family and may be instigatin' trouble."

"Your source wouldn't happen to be Dr. Tehrani now, would it?"

"You know I never reveal my sources. People come to me and I pass it on."

"Am I that intimidating to talk to?"

"I doubt if it's you he's afraid of."

"Tell your mystery tipper that if he knows something and is withholding it from the police, I can charge him with impeding an investigation."

"He told me what he knows. He's not tryin' to impede anything."

Okay, Gordy, thanks. Get back to me if you hear anything else."

Will disconnected the call and turned right on College Drive, then drove past the giant magnolia trees and made a left on Gleason. He saw flashing lights and a sizable crowd.

He parked his car and jogged over to Jack Rutgers, who was standing a few yards behind the yellow crime scene tape and only a few feet from the body.

Will's mind flashed back to yesterday's hospital room where Dary Fassih lay hooked up to life support, his mother stroking his hair and weeping inconsolably.

"Who's the victim?"

"Name's Isaac Kohler."

Will's heart sank. "Medium build? Thick glasses?"

"Yeah, you know him?"

Will squatted next to the body and pulled back the sheet. "I talked to this boy at yesterday's crime scene. It was obvious he felt bad about what happened to Dary Fassih. Said his Jewish friends would make his life miserable if he showed any sympathy."

"You think *they* did this to him?"

Will pulled the sheet up over Isaac's face and stood. "I don't know. I also got a tip that the Muslim community may retaliate for Dary's death. Maybe they didn't waste any time. What do we know about Isaac?"

"First-year student. Only child. Father's a cardiologist. His parents are attending a medical convention in Miami. We're trying to reach them."

Will lifted his eyebrows. "Can you imagine getting *that* call?"

He stepped back, his hands in his pockets, his eyes surveying the faces of the onlookers. Most of them were young. Probably students. Some were crying. Others were quiet and somber. The vocal ones were pumping the police for information. But each one looked afraid. He thought of his daughter Meagan and cringed at what the world might be like by the time she started college.

"Jack, did anyone see anything?"

"You kidding? They're all deaf, dumb, and blind—just like yesterday."

28

Ellen sat curled up next to Guy on the couch at Owen and Hailey's, watching the six o'clock news.

"Good evening, I'm Shannon Pate..."

"And I'm Stephen Rounds. Welcome to Regional News at Six."

"Seaport Police are investigating the murder of yet *another* college student tonight. Just before three o'clock this afternoon, police responded to a 911 call from a coed at Seaport Junior College who said she and another young woman had spotted what appeared to be a body in the bushes outside the library. Reporter Jared Downing is at the scene. Jared, what can you tell us?"

"Shannon, the mood is solemn here where the strangled body of a male student was discovered earlier today underneath those bushes to my right. He was pronounced dead at the scene, and a preliminary autopsy report puts the time of death between nine and eleven Saturday night. Investigators now believe the victim was killed elsewhere and his body brought here.

"Students and sympathizers have been gathering all evening, consoling each other and asking questions. Police declined to release the name of the victim until they're able to locate his parents, who reportedly are away at a convention. But there's a great deal of speculation that this death may have been a payback from the Muslim community for yesterday's murder of an Iranian student, Daryoush Fassih, who was brutally beaten and left for dead at Bougainvillea Park. Fassih later died at Seaport Community Hospital.

"WRGL News sought Police Chief Will Seevers for comment, and he gave this statement just minutes ago..."

"I can't emphasize strongly enough that speculation is dangerous. People should stay calm and not assume these deaths were ethnically motivated hate crimes. Give my department time to weigh the evidence. I assure you that whoever's responsible will be prosecuted to the fullest extent of the law."

"But, Shannon, the chief's words didn't seem to appease the crowd here. Teachers, students, and parents are angry and scared. They want answers. And right now, no one seems to have any. Back to you..."

"Thanks for that report, Jared. Obviously, we will be following this story closely. Stephen, can you tell us the latest on the Fassih case?"

"Sources tell us that the police have finished combing the area of Bougainvillea Park where the badly beaten body was discovered, and several DNA samples are being analyzed. We haven't been advised of any suspects, but we have learned that police are questioning students and faculty to see if they can find a link to the two murders.

"At one o'clock this afternoon, Fassih's family and friends laid him to rest at a small Muslim burial ground about five miles east of the city. Reporters were respectfully asked not go beyond the gates. WRGL News complied with the family's request, but were able to capture some of it on camera..."

Ellen gripped Guy's hand a little tighter as the footage began to roll.

A dense crowd had gathered some distance beyond the wrought-iron gates, the backs of those closest to the cameras standing almost defiantly against the invasion of privacy. An imam's voice could be heard chanting something foreign and indistinguishable. Then silence. Eerie silence. An unseen woman began to wail, deep and mournful, her anguish needing no words or interpretation.

Ellen blinked to clear her eyes, grateful when the news anchors reappeared on the screen.

"A sad day indeed for the Fassih family and for the entire Muslim community. But today's murder of another student has prompted many people to wonder if this was an eye-for-an-eye response to Fassih's murder. We will stay on top of this developing story and bring you breaking news around the clock."

"At the U.N. today, talks continue..."

Ellen's gaze fell on the picture of Owen on the end table. She could only imagine the anguish of Dary's mother—and of the other student's. Were senseless deaths like these going to become commonplace as the resentment and hatred escalated?

"You okay?" Guy put the sound on mute.

"How could anyone be okay after hearing that?"

"It's a powder keg, honey. That's why I want you to stay out of it."

She turned to him. "I'm not *in* it."

"All right. Sorry. Let's don't go there."

"Can you honestly tell me you don't feel compassion for those boys?"

"No, of course I feel compassion. I can't imagine what it would feel like to lose Owen and Brandon that way. But our boys are smart enough to stay out of the conflict, which is fine by me because I don't want it in our home."

"Well, like it or not, it's already in our home—every day via the news. And now it's on our streets and killing our kids. We can't just ignore it."

"They're not *my* kids, Ellen. And it's not my fight."

"Well, guess what? Kinsey's mess wasn't *my* fight, either, but you didn't see me turn my back on her!" Ellen tried to choke back her tears but couldn't. "Since when do we get to choose who we're supposed to care about? And who gives you the right to choose *for* me? You've bullied me into feeling guilty for wanting to reach out to Mina. Her whole world is upside down, and I haven't seen her in almost two weeks. What kind of message does that convey? She needs Christians to care. And she needs to experience our love, not indifference or rejection."

Guy took her hand. "Calm down, honey. I didn't mean to upset you."

"Well, you did upset me! I wouldn't think of treating Kinsey that way—even after she brought division and violence right to our doorstep!"

"I said I was sorry."

Ellen plucked a Kleenex and blew her nose. "I shouldn't have to sneak around to reach out to Mina or anyone else I think needs a touch from God. You're the last person on earth I ever thought would put me down for it."

"I don't find it easy to care about people I don't understand or have anything in common with. I didn't even handle Kinsey as well as you did."

"I didn't do much."

"Yes, you did. You forgave her. She left knowing you cared about her. And you gave her something spiritual to think about."

"Thanks. But it's not a competition. We have different gifts."

"You obviously understand people better than I do."

"Then trust me to follow my heart and give me the freedom to love the unlovable or least those you find unlovable."

Guy's eyebrows scrunched. "How do I get my ego out of the way? I'd be lying if I said it didn't bother me what other people think."

"I guess you'll have to ask the Lord that question. I honestly think the problem lies in how *you* see them. When I have trouble with someone, I ask God to let me see that person through His eyes. Once that happens, loving them isn't hard."

Guy arched his eyebrows. "Even Blanche, the gossip queen?"

"Deep down she's a sweetheart. You just have to see her with different eyes."

"That would take a miracle after the things she said about you."

"So? Don't forget He changed *my* heart about Blanche." Ellen sat quietly for a few moments, holding Guy's hand. "So are you okay with me reaching out to Mina?"

"Promise you'll stay out of the mosque, out of the news, and off the front page?"

"Above the fold or below?" She smiled. "Just kidding. Yes, I promise I'll do everything in my power not to get noticed by any member of the media, elite or otherwise."

"Thanks. I'm afraid I've earned enough bad press for both of us."

Guy didn't say anything for half a minute, then picked up her hand and pressed it to his lips. "Do you have any idea how much I love you, Ellen—how much I need and value our marriage and the friendship we've built all these years?"

"I thought I did. I admit I've had my doubts lately."

"Well, you can stop doubting." Guy stroked her cheek. "The only thing wrong with this relationship is that my ego needs to be dethroned. And I'm sure the media will gladly do the honors."

Gordy Jameson sat in a chaise lounge under the stars, his hands behind his head, his thoughts on Pam and their upcoming wedding. He closed his eyes and listened to the sound of the waves whooshing up on the sand and imagined himself, Pam in his arms, being lulled to sleep. The doorbell rang and his eyes flew open.

Gordy went inside and through the living room to the front door. He flipped on the light, surprised to see Will Seevers standing on the stoop. He opened the door and ushered him in. "You're out late again."

"I knew you'd be up," Will said. "Mind if I unwind before I go home? It's been a tough day and I don't want to dump on Margaret."

"Nah, come sit. You want somethin' to drink?"

"No, I'm fine."

Gordy led Will to the kitchen, then sat across from him at the table. "Anything in particular got you keyed up?"

"You mean other than pulling back the sheet on today's victim and realizing it was Isaac Kohler, the Jewish kid I talked to yesterday? I couldn't believe it. I just came from his parents' home. He was their only child. Sometimes I hate this job.

"I couldn't sleep last night, trying to get the picture of Dary Fassih out of my mind. I don't know that I've ever seen a beating victim that looked any worse than he did." Will took off his glasses and rubbed his eyes. "I thought I could handle being at the hospital. For some reason, I never expected the Fassihs to be a normal family."

Gordy started to say something and then didn't.

"I mean, most of the Muslims I see on the TV screen are either applauding a suicide bombing, threatening to behead someone, or rioting in the streets like a bunch of lunatics. Truthfully, I've never even talked one-on-one with a Muslim until yesterday afternoon at the hospital." Will made a tent with his fingers. "I sat with Dary's parents while they waited for the doctors to harvest their son's organs..." Will swallowed hard. "It was torture for them, and they were as devastated as I would be if it were Meagan. That's the first time I've ever related to Muslims as people with feelings and as parents who love their kids."

Will seemed lost in thought and Gordy just sat quietly.

"I'll tell you, Gordy, it's really getting to me, thinking about what a volatile world we live in. I just want the killing to stop—and Meagan to grow up without fear."

Gordy lifted his eyebrows. "I suspect that's what the Fassihs and the Kohlers wanted, too."

29

The following Tuesday afternoon, Will Seevers received copies of the final autopsy reports on Daryoush Fassih and Isaac Kohler and wondered if any new information had been included since the preliminary. He picked up the report on Dary Fassih and read through it.

Several dark hairs had been found stuck to the dried blood on Dary's body. These originated from a male and had been typed for DNA, but no match had been found at NCIC.

Several navy blue fibers had also been found stuck to the dried blood. The fibers were cotton and were consistent with those manufactured by Ralph Lauren for Polo shirts.

An odd-shaped indentation had been cut into Dary's left cheek, possibly by something he had been beaten with. The angle of the wound suggested the blow had been delivered by the assailant's left hand.

The image of the boy's disfigured face popped into Will's mind and he blinked it away. But the sound of Dary's mother's wailing lingered in his memory without mercy.

Will put down the report. The information only confirmed what was in the preliminary.

He picked up the report on Isaac Kohler and began reading. The boy had been strangled from behind with a rope. He had fought his attacker, and DNA from blood and skin cells found under his fingernails matched the DNA of the hairs found on Dary Fassih's body.

Will took off his glasses. *The same assailant was involved in both crimes.* He looked up as Investigator Al Backus breezed through the doorway, fell in a chair, and let out an exaggerated sigh.

"We've questioned every student in that English class," Al said, "and every student who even breathed the same air. Nada. Oh, we did finally catch up to the left-handed male student we missed yesterday—some scrawny kid who's been out with mono. There's no way he did it."

"The navy Polo shirt didn't jog anyone's memory?"

"You kidding? In this crowd, that stands out about as much as a cell phone."

"Well, the final autopsy reports gave us an added bonus." Will handed Al the reports. "The same DNA was found on both bodies."

Backus skimmed the pages. "Now we're gettin' somewhere."

"Let's solicit DNA samples from those same left-handed male students. See who's willing to volunteer DNA and who resists."

Guy and Ellen Jones walked from room to room in their home, inspecting the repairs, pleased that the painters had finished a day early.

"Looks great," Guy said. "What do you think?"

Ellen looked up at the walls, and a smile stretched across her cheeks. "I think I'm ready to move back in this second. I don't even care that the living room furniture won't be delivered till Thursday. I'll sit on the floor."

"All right. I'm sure Owen and Hailey are ready to get rid of us. I'll call the security guard service and arrange to have the guards come here."

"Why? Now that we've got an alarm system, we would just be throwing money away. Investigator Backus said he could arrange to have the area patrolled more closely for a few weeks."

"That won't give me enough peace of mind when I'm in Tallahassee."

"Guy, I'd rather you spend the money on a bodyguard."

"Fifteen hundred a day? I don't think so. Let's keep the security guard for now. We've got till Monday to decide."

He slipped his arm around Ellen. "How about making me shrimp pasta for dinner? Maybe light a few candles. Put on some soft music."

"The smell of paint might spoil the ambiance. It's pretty strong."

"I hadn't noticed." He pulled her into his arms and started slow dancing, his cheek next to hers. "I just want the world to go away for a while and let us find our lives again."

The doorbell rang.

Guy went to the front door and looked through the peephole. "It's Blanche. We've been home all of five minutes."

Ellen walked over and stood next to him. "She's missed me and probably needs a little TLC. How about if I take her to the grocery store? We can visit while I shop, and that'll kill two birds with one stone."

"Promise you won't bring her back here?"

"What? And break the spell?" Ellen turned and looked up at him, her arms around his neck. "I can't remember the last time we had a romantic evening at home. I'm not about to invite her in."

Gordy Jameson went in the kitchen at the crab shack and saw his fiancée in front of the open oven door.

"Pam, darlin', would you come out here for a minute? Doc Tehrani and his wife are here and want to talk to us. Here, let me get that for you."

Gordy put on oven mitts and removed four pies from the oven, one by one, and set them on the cooling rack. "Boy, do they ever smell great."

"Where are the Tehranis?"

"They're at the corner table by the windows. Let's go sit with them for a few minutes."

"Any idea what they want?"

"No, but it's the first time I've seen them together in a long time."

Gordy took Pam's hand and walked out to the dining room and over to where the Tehranis were sitting. He introduced Pam and Mina, then seated Pam and sat next to her.

"It's great to see you," Gordy said. "What did you want to talk to us about?"

Ali took a sip of water. "If the invitation to come to your wedding is still open, we would very much like to accept."

Gordy looked at Pam and then at Ali and Mina. "Of course, it's still open. What changed your mind?"

"We just decided that we can no longer remain passive and isolated if we want people to know who we really are. It's time to reach out so there can be no question about our loyalty to this country, this community, to our patients—or our friends. Friends like you."

"Thanks, Doc," Gordy said. "That means a lot."

Mina traced the rim of her water glass with her finger. "We cannot speak for all Muslims, but Ali and I are United States citizens because we value freedom. We must not be silent about this. We must be proactive. And we must build bridges so that people will stop fearing us."

"That also means not dodging the media anymore," Ali said. "I have nothing to hide. I now choose to look at it as an opportunity to build good will."

Gordy reached across the table and took Mina's hand and then Ali's. "That's the spirit. Pam and I join with you in this, don't we darlin'?"

Pam added her hands to the mix. "Absolutely. There is something you should know, though. Dr. David Kohler and his wife are good friends of mine and have been invited to the wedding."

"I know David," Ali said. "And I grieve with him for his murdered son. We realize not everyone will welcome us at your wedding. But we'll reach out as others will let us. We'll try to bring peace and not conflict."

Gordy smiled. "Hey, I'll take you any way I can get you."

Ellen put on a strapless black dress, powdered her nose, and applied a little blush to each cheek. She fluffed her hair and dabbed perfume behind her ears, then stood back and studied her reflection. There was definitely a sparkle in those baby blues.

She went out to the dining room, pleased to see Guy had already lit the candles.

"Wow, do you look nice," he said. "Here, you sit and I'll serve us." He pulled out the chair and waited until Ellen was situated, then pushed her up to the table.

A couple minutes later, he was seated across from her, raving about the shrimp pasta and seeming like his old self.

"It's so nice being home," Ellen said.

"Indeed it is. More Perrier, Madame?"

Ellen nodded. "Thanks. I hope Owen and Hailey's feelings weren't hurt that we decided to stay here tonight."

"Are you kidding? They probably did a dance. They were super about it, but it can't be easy for them having two extra bodies in the house...not to mention a security guard outside."

"Hailey hasn't seemed well lately," Ellen said. "I'm concerned about her."

"She just needs to find a satisfying job. She's wired like her mother-in-law."

Ellen laughed. "Poor dear. Actually, I'm anxious to get back to my writing. I wish I'd hear something from one of the publishers."

"You will."

"Sure, another rejection."

"That's part of it, honey. But one of these days, I'm going to be married to a novelist."

"Think so, huh?"

Guy lifted his glass. "I *know* so. Here's to a bright future." He touched her glass with his.

Ellen heard a ringing noise and couldn't tell where it was coming from. "Oh, for heaven's sake, that's my cell phone."

"Who besides me calls you on your cell?"

"Nobody. Probably a wrong number." She started to take a bite, then dropped her fork and pushed back her chair. "Kinsey! It might be Kinsey!"

Ellen raced down the hall to the bedroom, dug in her purse, and pulled out the phone. It stopped ringing. "Hello...? Is anybody there...? Hello...?" She checked for a message, and there wasn't one.

She took the phone to the kitchen, set it on the countertop, then went into the dining room and resumed her place. "Whoever it was didn't leave a message. What if it was Kinsey, trying to reach me?"

"Then she'll call back. But I seriously doubt you'll hear from her. She'll be lucky if she doesn't end up at the bottom of some river."

"What an awful thing to say."

"We have to be prepared for it, Ellen. There's no way Kinsey can survive on minimum wage—not after the lifestyle she's used to. She's either going to get back into trafficking or something worse."

"Meaning what—prostitution?"

"If she gets desperate enough."

"I'm not going to have this discussion with you. I can't accept that she'd really stoop to that. There has to be another way."

"Honey, why are we talking about Kinsey? This is *our* evening."

Guy got up and pulled Ellen to her feet. He reached around

the corner and turned up the volume on the easy listening CD he'd put in the Bose player, then took her in his arms and began to slowly move his feet, his cheek next to hers.

Ellen closed her eyes and yielded herself to the music and to Guy's lead, hoping she could recapture the mood.

Gordy strolled barefoot along the wet sand, his hand holding tightly to Pam's, his senses alive with the smells and the sounds of the sea.

"What're you thinking about?" Pam said.

"That this time next week we'll be combin' this beach as husband and wife."

Pam squeezed his hand. "I can hardly wait. Being married to you would be wonderful no matter where we lived. But to be home here with the gulf at our backdoor...well, it's more than I ever dreamed."

"You sure it doesn't bother you that Jenny and I lived here?"

"It really doesn't. After all, she lives in your heart, and it's big enough for both of us."

"I just don't ever want you thinkin' that I'm comparin' you to her...or that I expect you to step into her shoes. Because I don't. What I have with you is great, too. It's different."

Pam nodded. "I know. What Todd and I had was special, but it doesn't take away from what we have. I can hardly believe I found it twice in a lifetime."

Gordy stopped and took Pam in his arms. He closed his eyes, his lips seeming one with hers, and let his heart say what words never could. Finally he drew back, one arm around her, and gazed up at the stars—which seemed to him like countless diamonds strewn across black velvet.

"Whaddya suppose God was thinkin' when He created all those galaxies?" he finally said.

"That after all His creative genius, some guy named Edison

was going to invent the light bulb and mess up the view?"

Gordy chuckled and pulled her closer. "I'm glad you feel good about living out here. I think I'd suffocate in a regular neighborhood."

Pam smiled. "I know that."

Gordy took her hand and began walking again. "I can't believe how close we are to the wedding. I'm so glad the Tehranis decided to come."

"Me, too, but I'm preparing myself that their presence might make some people uncomfortable, especially if the Kohlers *do* come. Even your best man's been a pill about the whole Muslim thing."

"Not any more. Bein' with the parents of the two dead kids really did a number on Will."

"That's what you said. Margaret told me the same thing. Let's just hope it lasts through the reception."

30

Guy Jones opened his eyes and for a moment forgot where he was. The first light of dawn filtered through the transom window, and the aroma of freshly brewed coffee seemed to meld with the smell of paint. *Home.*

He lay on his side, Ellen nestled in his arms, remembering the first morning he had awakened with his bride in his arms. He slid his palm under her limp hand, relishing the warm softness, and rubbed his thumb over her wedding ring.

Ellen stirred and stretched, then turned over and faced him, her head on the same pillow. "Hi," she said sleepily.

He kissed her forehead. "Good morning. Isn't it great to be back home in our own bed?"

The corners of her mouth turned up slightly. "Indeed it is, *Romeo.*"

He outlined her features with his finger, then brushed the curls away from her face. "It took me a long time to fall asleep last night. I can't explain it, but this feels like a new beginning. I know I have a long way to go, but I asked the Lord to help me be more sensitive to people. Just be patient while He works on me, okay?"

"Okay."

"You ready for coffee?"

"I hate to move. I've missed the closeness."

"Me, too. I'm sure my being critical was a real turn off."

Ellen's pensive blue eyes agreed with him, but he was glad she didn't say it.

"What's on tap for today?" he said.

"The only thing on my agenda is the Wednesday Bible study with Billy and Lisa. I moved the time up to eleven o'clock so I could spend the afternoon with you."

"Do we need to do any more shopping for the house?"

"We need to find a painting for behind the couch. Though I doubt I'll ever find one I like better than what we had."

"Well, why don't we hit some of the galleries in the old art district and see if we find something? Brent refuses to let me work this week. I haven't got anything else to do."

"Oh, we need to pick up Gordy and Pam's wedding gift, too. I'm sure it's ready."

"All right. Good ol' Sid will watch the house. He's on the day shift."

"I'll be glad when the police catch Rob Blakely and we can stop all this security guard nonsense."

Will Seevers sat at his desk, working through a stack of paperwork when his phone rang. He picked up the receiver and cradled it next to his ear. "Chief Seevers."

"It's Gordy. You got a minute?"

"I'm trying to knock out a mountain of paperwork. What's up?"

"Doc Tehrani and his wife came to see Pam and me yesterday. They've decided to come to the wedding."

"So why are you telling me?"

"One time when we talked about it, you said you wouldn't shake hands with them. Didn't seem right to spring this on you at the reception. Is it gonna be a problem for you?"

"I don't know, Gordy. I just found out about it."

"If you just give them a chance, you'll see they're really nice people. And they're tryin' to be more vocal about where they stand on all the stuff that's been goin' on."

"That's all we need."

"Hey, before you get huffy, let me tell you what they said." Gordy relayed the conversation he and Pam had had with the Tehranis, including Mina's comments about citizenship. "They want people to see they're as loyal and patriotic as any other American."

"All right."

"That's it: *All right?*"

"I promise not to embarrass you, Gordy. I'll be on my best behavior."

"Yeah, okay, Will. Thanks."

"You and Pam getting excited?"

"Yeah, we are. She's off the rest of the week, makin' sure the details come together."

"Well, according to the extended forecast, Saturday afternoon should be picture perfect—bluebird sky and the high around eighty."

Gordy laughed. "I'm so ready to tie the knot, it could snow and it wouldn't wreck it for me. So how're the investigations comin'? Any leads?"

"We're making some headway. The autopsy reports were helpful."

"I sure hope you nail whoever killed those boys."

"We will. I've got to get back to work, bud."

"Okay, talk to you later."

Will hung up the phone and took a bite of his ham-and-cheese on rye. He washed it down with a gulp of milk, then dialed Backus's cell phone.

"This is Backus."

"How're you coming, Al? Any volunteers?"

"Yeah, we got swabs on all left-handed male students except the ones in the evening classes."

"Anybody resist?"

"A couple of jocks dug in their heels and started bumping

their gums about us violating their rights. We told them we could get a court order and they could save themselves a lot of grief if they'd just let us stick a Q-tip in their mouths. They gave in."

"So how many lefties in the night classes?"

"Three, and we're trying to locate them now. With any luck, we'll get it all done before the end of the day."

"How many total?"

"Twenty-one. Thirteen so far with dark hair."

"We're narrowing down the field."

"Yeah, maybe. But these kids don't seem intimidated. If they're nervous, they're sure covering it up well."

Gordy sat out on the back deck of the crab shack, having lunch with his buddies: Captain Jack, Adam Spalding, and Eddie Drummond.

"The big day's almost here," Adam said. "You nervous?"

Gordy shook his head. "Nah, never been calmer."

"It's nice having something upbeat to think about," Captain said. "Anyone else sick and tired of bad news?"

Adam nodded. "I think it's going to get worse before it gets better."

"Yeah, as long as Muslims are here." Eddie put a spoonful of sugar in his iced tea and stirred it. "I wish they'd all go back where they came from and leave the rest of us in peace."

"Peace?" Gordy said. "You think that'd solve our problems?"

"Well, we sure as heck don't need theirs."

Gordy took a sip of his limeade. "It's not that easy to separate ours and theirs, you know. A lot of them are Americans, too."

"Yeah, *that's* the problem." Eddie's eyes narrowed. "We're in a war on terror, yet we're supposed to be tolerant of Muslims living here? Give me a break. All they know is violence. I don't know why we put up with all that religious gobbledygook anyway."

Adam smiled wryly. "The First Amendment?"

"Look, guys," Gordy said. "No law is gonna change people's hearts. You can't legislate brotherhood. But maybe if each of us would decide to treat everyone else with respect, the problem would eventually take care of itself. We can't change the whole world, but we can change our slice of it."

There was a long pause. Gordy's eyes moved from Adam to Captain to Eddie. "What?"

"When'd you decide to get into politics?" Eddie said.

Gordy shoved Eddie's arm. "I'm serious. We're not gonna change anything if we sit around and whine about how bad things are and do nothin' to change it."

"Like what?" Eddie said.

"Well, for starters, how about reachin' out to the families of those two murdered kids?"

Eddie guffawed. "Yeah, right. Why would I wanna do that?"

Gordy raised his eyebrows. "Because you care? Assumin', of course, you do. How hard could it be to write a note? Or send 'em a card?"

"I don't know those people."

"Yeah, well, *those people* are your neighbors. You may need their help someday. All I'm sayin' is we should try treatin' people the way we want to be treated. What goes around, comes around."

Guy strolled hand-in-hand with Ellen through the last art gallery on their list. Suddenly Ellen stopped, her eyes wide, her jaw dropped. He looked up at the painting she was viewing and immediately knew why.

The huge oil painting was lifelike—a close up of an old man building a sandcastle, a pelican so close the man could have touched it.

"It's got to be Ned!" Ellen said. "Look at the detail—the expression on his face and in his eyes. The wispy strands of white hair. The denim cut offs. And the pelican—that's Porky!"

She leaned closer to the canvas and read the artist's name, then turned to a woman arranging a small framed print on an easel. "Excuse me, is Grant Harrington a local artist?"

"As a matter of fact he is. Isn't that a charming painting? Grant brought that one in just last week."

"Did he give you any background on it—whether he used a photograph, or painted it from memory, or actually painted it on the beach?"

"Grant said he used a telephoto lens and photographed this man and the pelican on Seaport Beach. He painted it from the photograph. Looks lifelike, doesn't it?"

"Yes, it's amazing. I knew this man." Ellen stood in front of the painting, seeming mesmerized, then looked at Guy, her eyes pleading. "It's incredible. I love everything about it."

"Don't be too hasty, honey. This is a big decision."

Ellen stretched out her arms. "Look, it's just the right size—from my left fingertips to my right."

"Do you like the frame?"

"It's gorgeous. And the colors would be perfect with the new couch."

Guy smiled and looked over at the woman. "That means we'll take it."

"Excellent choice. Let me go get the paperwork and we'll set up a time to have it delivered and hung for you."

Ellen linked her arm in Guy's and turned her eyes again on the painting. "It seems so real, I feel as though I could walk right into it. What a find this is!"

"You still miss the old guy, don't you?"

Ellen nodded. "I wish I could tell him how much he changed my life."

Guy couldn't deny how dramatically Ellen's attitude changed after she took Ned's advice and began praying for Ross Hamilton and Blanche Davis.

He looked up at the painting and studied the face of the man he'd never met and wondered if Ned were still alive if he would give Guy the same advice.

Guy sat across the table from Ellen at Gordy's Crab Shack, perusing the menu. "Great afternoon, huh?"

"I'm so excited about the painting I can hardly stand it."

"It was a great find, all right. What're you having?"

"Grilled shrimp."

"I'll have blackened mahi-mahi." He set down his menu, then picked up her hand and pressed it to his lips. "I enjoyed spending time with you today. I've really missed it."

Suddenly Ellen seemed to be staring at something beyond him, her eyes wide.

"What's wrong, honey?"

"Guy, don't react, but Mina and Ali Tehrani are walking over to the table. They're almost here..." Ellen's smile looked as though she'd glued it on. "Hi, you two."

A man and woman he guessed to be in their early fifties came and stood at the head of the table. Each had dark hair and dark eyes. The man had a thick mustache, streaked with white.

"This is my husband, Guy. Dear, this is Dr. Ali Tehrani and his wife, Mina."

Guy rose to his feet and shook hands with each of them. "Nice to finally meet you." He felt the lie scald his cheeks.

"The pleasure is ours," Ali said. "We were wondering if you might like to join us. Of course, if this isn't a good time, we will understand."

Guy glanced at Ellen, her eyes filled with raw panic.

"Maybe we could have a rain check," Guy said. "This is a bit of a celebratory dinner for us. We're finally back in our house."

Ali smiled warmly. "Perhaps another time, then."

Mina bent over, her arms around Ellen's neck. "I'm glad you

are home, my friend. I've missed you so."

The Tehranis left the table, and a second later, Guy heard Gordy Jameson's voice. "Hey, Doc...Mina. Good to see you."

If Gordy said anything else, it was drowned out by the screaming silence coming from Ellen.

"Honey, I'm sorry. I got caught off guard. I hope I didn't sound rude."

"You were polite, but they knew they were being brushed off. They know how you feel."

"How could they—unless you told them?"

Ellen lifted her eyebrows. "I didn't have to. Mina picked it up weeks ago in your tone and probably in my evasiveness. I told her it wasn't personal, that you're wary of Muslims in general because of the terrorist threats. I'm sure she wasn't shocked."

"I don't like being talked about."

"And I don't like having to make excuses for your prejudice."

"Prejudice? That's a little harsh."

"Is it? What would you call it?"

"Ellen, honey, look at me. I'm sorry that I hurt you. Please don't let this set us back. I'm trying."

"I know you are. But it's obvious your opinion of the Tehranis hasn't really changed."

"I can't force myself to feel something I don't."

"Then stop trying to do it in your own strength!" Ellen paused for a moment, then looked into his eyes. "Guy, I know it's not my place to instruct you, but I know from experience that the only way you're going to get past this is to admit to the Lord how you feel and let Him change your heart."

31

Guy Jones tossed and turned, vaguely aware of an obnoxious ringing noise that grew louder and louder until he finally realized it was the telephone. He groped the nightstand and picked up the receiver. "Hello."

"Guy, it's Brent. Did I wake you?"

"Yeah, what time is it?"

"Six-thirty. I thought you'd be up."

"I'm supposed to be taking it easy, remember? What day is it anyway?"

"Thursday. Listen, it's over. Some undercover cops busted Rob Blakely a few hours ago. They've got enough to put him and his cohorts away for a long time. Kinsey, too. They've got photographs of her buying snow from Blakely on several occasions."

"Has she been arrested?"

"No, they haven't found her yet."

Guy sat up on the side of the bed. "Well, they're not going to find her in Tallahassee. She's in Atlanta."

"How do you know that?"

"She was here Sunday. She came to tell me the real truth of how I got dragged into it and apologized." Guy told Brent everything Kinsey had told Ellen and him. "We tried to talk her into turning herself in, but she's determined not to do time."

"So you just let her go?"

"What'd you want me to do? The police didn't have enough to arrest her."

"Well, they do now. You need to call Investigator Hamlin and tell him what you just told me."

"All right."

"Brace yourself. I'll do what I can to make sure the facts are disseminated correctly to the media, but your name's going to get batted around and there's nothing I can do to stop it."

"I know, Brent. I'm just sorry it happened."

"I've got the ball rolling to get you another legal secretary I may have some prospects for you to interview Monday."

"All right. See you then."

Guy hung up the phone and sat quietly for a moment.

"What happened?" Ellen said.

He fell back on the bed and told her what Brent had said. "It's not as though I didn't know this was coming, but it's humbling to realize how little I knew about Kinsey. Doesn't say much for my ability to read people."

"Don't be too hard on yourself, Counselor. It just proves the old adage: The true measure of a person's character is who he is when no one's looking."

Will Seevers hung up the phone and for a moment wished he were a kid again, when the biggest problem he had was deciding which baseball card to trade.

Al Backus appeared in the doorway. "You wanted to see me?"

"Yeah, have a seat."

"What's up?"

"The Coast Guard just confiscated another boat full of explosives."

"Where?"

"In Seaport Harbor."

"Coming in or going out?"

Will picked up a bent paper clip and pitched it in the trashcan. "The boat was moored. It appears it was being used as a weapons storage facility. It's registered under a phony name and address. Intelligence is hearing a lot of chatter that terrorists are planning an attack somewhere along the coast. It's going to hit the news any minute."

"So what are we supposed to do?"

"Keep a watchful eye. The threat level has been elevated again to Orange."

"Whatever that means. I hate this."

"We all do. Let's just stay focused on what's in front of us and let the feds deal with it."

Backus folded his arms and tilted his chair back. "Focus on what? We've got nothing."

"Because none of the students' DNA matched what was found on the bodies? Come on, Al. Somebody knows something. Anyone capable of this probably bragged about what he was going to do and maybe even after he did it."

"Yeah, well, mum's the word."

"I saw the look on Isaac's face. He was scared of something. How closely did you scrutinize the Jewish students?"

"Same as everybody else. No one stood out and none of them were left-handed. They all seemed pretty tight. Killing one of their own seems really extreme."

Will arched his eyebrows. "Unless they wanted to shut him up."

"You think Kohler knew who beat up the Muslim kid?"

"Doesn't matter what I think. I need you to find out."

Gordy Jameson went out on the back deck of the crab shack and sat at the lunch table with Captain Jack, Eddie Drummond, and Adam Spalding.

"I'm ready to get off my feet," Gordy said. "Tell me what you know about the latest terrorist threat. I've heard bits and pieces."

"The Coast Guard found another boat of explosives—this

time in the harbor," Captain said. "Intelligence sources are pickin' up all kinda chatter about an imminent attack along the coast."

"People are freakin' out." Eddie tilted his glass and crunched a mouthful of ice.

"Anybody arrested?"

Captain shook his head. "No, but you know they're sniffin' out the Muslim community."

"Still think we should reach out to them, Gordo? Maybe send a card?" Eddie snickered.

"Can it, wise guy." Gordy pitched an ice cube at him. "So what are the authorities sayin'?"

Captain shrugged. "Same thing they always say: be alert. Report anything that looks suspicious."

"You didn't need this with the wedding so close," Adam said.

"Yeah, well, I don't think any of us need this any time. I wonder if Pam's heard."

"Isn't she here?" Adam said.

"Nah, she's off till after our honeymoon."

Eddie nodded toward the back door. "Well, look what the cat drug in."

Assistant Manager Weezie Taylor strutted over to the table and stood, her hand on her hip. "You boys up to no good—same as always?"

"Heck, yes, we are," Eddie said. "You miss us?"

"Unh-unh. And I sure don't miss waitin' tables." Weezie's smile was a bright half moon. "Well...maybe just a little." She sat next to Gordy. "Can you believe the rehearsal dinner's *tomorrow* night?"

"Yeah, and it's about time."

"Look at you, Mr. Cool, Calm, and Collected. My innards would be jitterin' all over the place!" Weezie's hearty laugh turned a few heads toward the table.

"What are you doin' here?" Gordy said. "You're not at the helm till three."

"Oh, I think you should get out of here, concentrate on more important things."

Gordy smiled. "Afraid I'm gonna give away too many desserts, eh? Well, I'll have you know, I'm buyin' us lots of good will."

"Ha! You're gonna *good will* us right into the red. Why don't you step aside and let Weezie, the wise and wonderful, work her charm? Ain't nothin' wrong with makin' a profit."

Adam put his hand over his smile. "The woman's got a point. I haven't paid for dessert since I started coming here."

"You always get the special. Dessert's included."

Weezie turned to Gordy, her elbow on the table, her fist supporting her chin. "Any idea how many desserts you gave away yesterday?"

"I don't keep track. I told you, it's good will."

"Then let me enlighten you." Weezie put her lips to his ear. "You gave away fourteen slices of that good will. At three-fifty each, that's forty-nine dollars—times thirty days is over fourteen hundred a month—times twelve months is over seventeen *thousand* bucks a year in good will."

Gordy chuckled. "I'm more generous than I thought. Haven't you got somethin' better to do than harass me on my lunch hour?"

"Not unless you let me take over your shift so you can go help your fiancée get the last-minute details taken care of."

"You sure? It's gonna be tough on you workin' double shifts when we're on our honeymoon."

"What else have I got to do? Besides, we're closin' early on Saturday."

Gordy pushed himself up from the table, pulled Weezie to her feet, and kissed her on the cheek. "All right. You don't have to ask me twice to spend time with my honey."

Ellen refilled the iced tea glasses, then sat again at the kitchen table. "I'm sorry the intruder smashed the old dishes, but actually, I like these better."

"Well, the tuna salad tasted great," Guy said. "Really hit the spot."

"Want me to make you another sandwich?"

"My taste buds would love it, but my waistline doesn't need it. You want to go to a movie this afternoon?"

Ellen smiled. "That might be fun. How long has it been?"

"I don't even remember. It'd be nice to get my mind on something else."

"All right. Why don't I get the dishes cleaned up while you check the newspaper and see what's on?"

Guy got up and pressed his lips to hers. "I wonder if this is what it'll be like when we retire?"

"Not if we have a banana plantation to run."

He left the kitchen chuckling.

Ellen had just finished stacking the dishes in the dishwasher when the phone rang. She reached for the receiver. "Hello."

"Mrs. Jones, this is Investigator Hamlin with the Tallahassee police. May I speak to your husband, please?"

"Certainly. Hold the line." She put her hand over the receiver and stuck her head in the hallway. "Guy, it's for you."

Guy walked out of the living room and across the hall, and she mouthed the words *Investigator Hamlin* and handed him the phone.

"Hello... No, I haven't talked to Brent since just before I talked to you this morning... When...?" Guy closed his eyes and shook his head. "Any suspects...?"

Ellen sat on a stool at the breakfast bar, watching Guy's expressions, the sound of the investigator's voice audible but his words indistinguishable.

After several minutes, Guy hung up the phone and sat next to her.

"What is it?"

He turned to her, his face ashen. "Kinsey's dead."

Will Seevers sat in Bougainvillea Park on the same wrought-iron bench where Isaac Kohler had sat memorizing his poems. He started to take a bite of his sandwich, then put it back in the sack, thinking it seemed profane to indulge his appetite here and now.

He looked down at the bottom of the grassy slope where Dary Fassih's body had been discovered. The crime scene tape had been removed, and just a few yards away a man was throwing a red Frisbee to his Irish setter. It seemed to Will almost sacrilegious that anyone's feet should be allowed to tramp on the blood-soaked ground where someone's child had lain dying.

He wondered if Isaac had been as nearsighted as he claimed, or if he'd simply chosen not to notice what was happening a hundred yards from where he sat.

"Was Dary your friend?"

"Are you kidding? I'm Jewish. He's Muslim."

Isaac's eyes had belied his feeble denial, and Will felt sure that the young student had made some sort of connection with Dary Fassih—one that may have cost him his life.

Will gathered his uneaten lunch, then got up and trudged down the slope. Why was he so consumed by what had happened here? Why couldn't he just let it go and let Backus fill in the blanks?

The haunting cries of one mother's lamentation seemed to grow louder with each step he took, and he wondered if even solving the case could silence it.

Guy was aware that Ellen was staring at him and wondered if he'd spoken the words or merely thought them.

"Kinsey's *dead?*" Ellen's arms went limp. "How? What happened?"

Guy could barely find his voice. "The Atlanta police found her in—" He swallowed. "A Dumpster." Guy wiped the moisture off his upper lip. "Stabbed in the chest." He reached for Ellen's hand.

"Do they know who did it?"

"Probably a mugger. They found her empty purse in with the garbage. No money or ID—just a business card. They called the office and talked to Brent, then e-mailed her picture to him. Brent confirmed it was Kinsey and called Investigator Hamlin."

"They don't think it was drug related?"

Guy shook his head. "They seem convinced it was a mugging. Brent asked the Atlanta police if Kinsey was wearing any jewelry. They said she wasn't."

"She could have hocked it," Ellen said.

"Yes, but if this was drug related, the assailant would've made sure she was dead. Whoever did this got what he wanted and couldn't have cared less if she lived or died. She probably bled to death."

Ellen closed her eyes, her lip quivering, and wiped a tear off her cheek.

On the walls of his memory, Guy watched a slide show of images of the Kinsey Abbot he had known and respected: Beautiful. Bright. Sensitive. Capable. Efficient. Articulate. Funny. Anything to keep from picturing her dead and stuffed into a Dumpster.

32

Gordy Jameson sat in his office, reading the headlines of Friday's *North Coast Messenger* and decided he wasn't letting the discovery of another boat of explosives quench his enthusiasm for tonight's rehearsal dinner. He folded the newspaper and started to set it aside when a short article at the bottom of the page caught his eye.

LEGAL SECRETARY FOUND DEAD IN DUMPSTER

Kinsey Abbot (35), a legal secretary for the Tallahassee law firm of McAllister, Norton, Riley, and Jones, was found stabbed to death yesterday in an Atlanta Dumpster, just hours after undercover police in Tallahassee arrested Robert Thomas Blakely (33), believed to be a key player in a finely tuned cocaine ring involving Abbot.

Though the Atlanta police concluded that Abbot was likely the victim of a robbery since her jewelry had been removed and her purse was found empty, Tallahassee police have not ruled out the possibility that Blakely may have ordered Abbot's murder.

Blakely denies any connection to Abbott's death, and has been charged with possession and trafficking of an illegal substance. He is being held without bail in the Leon County jail pending today's arraignment.

A source within the Tallahassee police department

told a reporter from the *Democrat* that Guy Jones, one of the firm's partners and Abbott's boss, had previously discovered a small bag of cocaine in his apartment after Ms. Abbot had spent the night there, but did not immediately report it to the Tallahassee police.

Jones, who is married and living in Seaport, was unavailable for comment, but Brent McAllister, a spokesman for the law firm, stated emphatically that Jones and Abbot's relationship was strictly professional, and that Jones had no knowledge of Abbott's ties to drug trafficking until Friday of last week, at which time he filed a report with the Tallahassee Police Department.

The sound of the front door opening and closing caught Gordy's attention.

"That you, Billy?"

"Yes, I am here, Mister G," Billy Lewis said.

Gordy put down the newspaper and went out to the utility closet where Billy squatted, gathering his cleaning supplies into a bucket.

"You remember you're not working tomorrow, right?"

Billy's cheeks stretched and he was suddenly all teeth. "Oh, yes. You and Miss Pam are get-ting mar-ried." Billy stood up and gave Gordy a playful jab with his elbow. "Now you can ask *me* for ad-vice."

Gordy chuckled. "How about that." He unlocked the door to the deck and held it open. "If I don't see you before you leave, I'll look for you at the lighthouse at five o'clock tomorrow night. Pam said to tell you she's gonna have a ton of hushpuppies at the reception."

"I like hush-pup-pies!"

"Well, come hungry and eat to your heart's content."

Billy went out on the deck, and Gordy shut the back door

just as Pam Townsend came in the front door.

"Hi darlin', what're you doin' here?" He walked over and kissed her on the cheek.

Pam smiled and shook her head. "You're not going to believe what just happened. I called the newspaper to cancel my sub-scription. When they asked me my address, I couldn't remember what it was. I had to read it off my driver's license!"

"Sounds like you've got butterflies."

"No kidding. Tell me again what time you get off."

"Weezie's takin' over at three. But I can help you decorate the banquet room any time you want. It's already set for the rehearsal dinner."

"Okay. I'll be back when I get finished running errands. If the florist brings the flowers, just put them in the banquet room and we can arrange them later."

Gordy put both his arms around her. "One day and count-ing. You didn't forget your *new* address, did you?"

Pam pushed back and looked up at him, her palm over his heart. "Right there—as long as we both shall live."

"You got it."

"All right, love. I need to get some things done. You sure seem calm."

"Yeah, I'm fine," Gordy said. "Did you happen to read the paper this morning?"

"No, I didn't want to get depressed. Why?"

"Oh, nothin'. It'll keep."

Pam held his gaze. "You haven't asked me if I've read the news-paper since I've known you. What don't you want me to see?"

"Actually, it's something we both need to be aware of. Hold on." Gordy went to his office and brought back today's paper and read her the article about Guy's secretary. "What impression did it give *you*?"

"That your friend may have been involved with his secretary in more ways than one."

"I hope not. I'm real fond of the Joneses. Could be Doc Tehrani isn't the only one people are gonna be whisperin' about at the wedding.

Guy sat at the breakfast bar, staring at nothing, vaguely aware that Ellen was standing behind him, her fingers massaging his shoulders.

"Is there anything I can do to help you?" she said.

"I don't think so, honey. I just feel like someone kicked the stuffing out of me."

"We'll get through this together."

"Why are you being so understanding? That article was just the beginning."

"I remember what it feels like to be falsely accused. You stood by me when Blanche went to Pastor Crawford with her tall tale of my adulterous affair."

"But you didn't make dumb choices that set you up for the gossip. Some of this is my own fault." Guy closed his eyes and let the kneading of Ellen's fingers soothe him. "I know I talked about it, but I really didn't think Kinsey would get killed."

"It breaks my heart to think what her last minutes must've been like. She had to be terrified. Did she cry out to God? I guess I'll always wonder if she ever read the tract I gave her."

"Sometimes I wish God had just granted forgiveness across the board without requiring such a hard choice from flawed human beings."

Ellen stopped massaging. "Seems to me Jesus made the *hard* choice. Is it asking so much of flawed human beings merely to accept what He did, confess our sins, and follow Him?"

"No, I just feel so helpless when people I care about don't."

Silence settled over them for several minutes, then finally Guy said, "You still want to go to Gordy's wedding tomorrow?"

"Of course. Since when does a little bad press hold me back?

Besides, people's attention will be focused on Pam and Gordy."

"We hope. It could be humiliating for you."

He felt Ellen's arms wrap around his neck, her warm cheek next to his. "Only if I let it. Those who care about us will believe what we tell them. Everyone else will just have to think what they want."

Will Seevers sat in his office bemoaning the stack of paperwork that seemed to pile up as fast as he could work through it. He heard a female voice on the intercom.

"Chief, Gordy's here. He'd like to see you and promises not to keep you long."

"Okay, send him this way."

A minute later, Gordy came through the doorway and flopped in a chair. "Hope you don't mind me droppin' in like this."

"I can take a short break. So how's the groom-to-be holding up?"

"I'm great. With all that's goin' on, you gonna be able to get away on time for the rehearsal and the dinner?"

"Absolutely. Bin Laden himself couldn't stop me. Margaret and I will be there at five-thirty."

Gordy paused for a moment and seemed to be wrestling with something.

"What's on your mind?" Will said.

"Do you know anything about the situation with Guy Jones and that secretary that was murdered—other than what was in the newspaper?"

"What're you asking me, Gordy?"

"Is Guy in trouble over this thing?"

"Not to my knowledge. Backus talked to the Tallahassee PD early this morning, comparing notes on the break-ins and helping to pull the loose ends together. Nobody said anything about him being a suspect. I got the impression that Guy's provided some major leads in this case."

"You think he was involved with the secretary?"

Will raised his eyebrows. "You're pushing the envelope, Gordy. I'm not going to talk about those kinds of details."

"I know. I just feel so bad about it. I'm real fond of the Joneses."

"Anything else on your mind?"

"I was also wonderin' if you got any leads on the murders of the two boys?"

"We're still sorting them out."

"I read where you talked to all the students."

"Yeah, we did."

"By any chance did you talk to the boys who harassed the Muslim couple at the park?"

Will thumped his head with his palm. "Gee, why didn't we think of that? Of course, we did, Gordy. What's with the Columbo routine? You fishing for something specific...like checking to make sure we're giving both boys' deaths equal attention?"

"I didn't say that."

"Listen, Gordy. I want nothing more than to get whoever did this. For me, it's not a Muslim issue or a Jewish issue. I've got two sets of devastated parents, and I want someone held accountable for stealing their sons from them."

"You still losin' sleep over it?"

"What I'm losing is time, bud. I've gotta get back to work."

"Yeah, sure. I need to head back anyway. It's time for the lunch crowd to start rollin' in. See you at 5:30."

Gordy sat in his office at the crab shack and glanced at his watch. In another five minutes, he would officially be gone until after the honeymoon. He heard a gentle knock on the door and looked up and saw Weezie Taylor in the doorway.

"Can I bother you a minute?" she said.

"Sure. Come sit."

"The banquet room looks great. I'm really glad you decided to have the rehearsal dinner here." Weezie sat in the chair next to his desk and fiddled with the hem on her blouse.

"You just gonna bother me or did you have somethin' to say?"

"I'm fixin' to get sentimental and start blubberin' all over myself. Just give me a second."

Gordy put down his pen and scooted his chair over in front of hers. "Well, for cryin' out loud, Weezie, what is it?"

She looked up at him, her dark, round eyes glistening. "I hope you know how very happy I am for you... There I go, blubberin' already." She held up her palm, her eyes closed, and paused for a moment. "Hang on. I need to say this... I stood by and watched you wither and almost die after Jenny passed away." Weezie took hold of his hand. "And now I see you bloomin' again. It's been a real joy for me, too. Watchin' you and Pam fall in love has given me hope that someday I might actually get over the pain of missin' my Joshua—and the Lord might throw some big hunk of a man my way."

"I'm sure He will," Gordy said, "once He finds someone good enough for you."

Weezie's laughter filled the room. "Oh, is *that* it?"

"Okay, my turn to get schmaltzy." Gordy paused until she looked at him. "I don't know that I could've made it through the past three years without you."

"Oh, sure you could've."

"I don't know. Sometimes you were the only reason I got out of bed in the morning."

She waved her hand. "Get outta town!"

"I'm dead serious. I knew that no matter how much I was hurtin', you'd make me laugh. And you'd keep the place runnin' and let everyone think *I* was. You never once tried to take credit, and I always admired that about you. Heck, there were plenty of times when you were the only bright spot in my entire day."

"I had no idea."

"That's what makes you so special, Weezie. You're always too busy thinkin' about the other guy to realize what an asset you are."

"Mercy! You do go on. If I wasn't black, I'd be red in the face."

Gordy smiled and shook his head. "I'm shootin' straight, Weezie. You're my closest friend. If you were a guy, I'd have asked you to be my best man."

"Go on!"

"I would've."

Weezie looked away, her eyes brimming with tears. "It's a privilege knowin' you, Gordy Jameson. You're the most color-blind man I've ever known..." her voice cracked, "and you've always treated me like family. Nobody wishes you more happiness than I do. Tomorrow night when you're sayin' your vows, I'll be cheerin' in my heart, askin' the Lord to give you back the joy you've missed—a hundredfold."

Gordy jumped to his feet. "Enough schmaltz, woman! You're gonna have *me* blubberin'. Come on, you can walk me to the front door."

33

At 4:50 on Saturday afternoon, the sky over Seaport was polished blue marble, its generous swirls of white promising a gorgeous sunset yet to come.

Gordy Jameson stood on the grassy hill that had seemed like a mountain when he was a kid. He inhaled deeply and savored the invigorating smell of salt air. With the red-and-gray lighthouse at his back, he looked out over miles and miles of blue-gray ripples, a balmy October breeze tussling with his shirt. If there was a more perfect spot to avow his commitment to Pam, he didn't know where it was. He closed his eyes and let the sanctity of the moment speak to his heart.

"You about ready, Gordy?" Will Seevers said.

"In a minute. You got the ring?"

Will patted his pocket. "All set."

Gordy spotted a fishing boat in the distance, and behind it a flock of gulls hovering and plunge-diving into the water. He thought of his parents and Jenny and the fun outings the four of them had enjoyed over the years on the old Boston Whaler. His only regret on this glorious day was that they would never know Pamela Jameson.

"It's 4:58, bud. We need to be on other side of the lighthouse."

Gordy breathed in slowly and let it out, then turned and patted Will on the shoulder. "I'm ready."

Ellen Jones stood in the shadow of the lighthouse, her arm linked with Guy's, a gentle sea breeze tickling her hair, and listened to a guitarist sing Paul Stookey's "Wedding Song," surprised that after all these years she still remembered every word.

When the song was over, the bride and groom stood facing each other—Gordy dressed in white trousers and a red-and-white Hawaiian shirt that was not tucked in but didn't quite hide his generous middle, and Pam in a flowing white tea-length dress that set off the radiant glow on her face.

Ellen listened as the minister led Gordy and Pam through their vows and silently renewed her own.

Guy put his lips to her ear. "Leave it to Gordy to do something *different*."

"I think it's sweet."

Ellen smiled when Guy put his arm around her waist and pulled her closer as if to say he agreed.

She thought about love and how it evolves with time and experience. There was something special about two people who had weathered five decades of living with all its joys and sorrows, including the loss of a spouse, entering into the oneness of marriage already knowing so many of its secrets.

A great egret flew overhead, glowing white in the afternoon sun, its graceful wings spread as if it were somehow symbolizing the Creator's blessing on this union.

"You may kiss your bride."

Gordy cupped Pam's face in his hands and tenderly pressed his lips to hers, then broke into a wide grin, a runaway tear dripping down his cheek.

The minister stretched out his arms. "Ladies and gentlemen, I present to you Mr. and Mrs. Gordon Jameson."

By six o'clock the beach was swarming with well-wishers, and Pam and Gordy stood behind a draped table under a huge white canopy, cutting the wedding cake.

Guy Jones put his lips to Ellen's ear. "What kind of cake is that?"

"I think it's supposed to be a crab. Looks like chocolate." The corners of her mouth twitched. "Rather creative, I'd say."

Guy glanced at his watch. "How long do you want to stay?"

"We just got here. I'm sure they're going to have a reception line, and we have to sample the buffet." She looked at him knowingly. "Just hold your head high, Counselor. Most of these people don't know who you are. Oh, look, there's Julie and Ross." Ellen went over and put her arms around them.

Guy stood with hands in his pockets and tried not to make eye contact with any one. He felt someone tap him on the shoulder.

"Hel-lo, Guy." Billy Lewis stood with his wife clutching his arm. He wondered if she grinned even when she slept. "Did you like Mr. G's wed-ding?"

"Yeah, it was very nice."

Billy smiled, his crooked teeth dominating his face. "We are hav-ing hush-pup-pies."

"That's nice." Guy inched away from Billy and Lisa and closer to Ellen. "There must be five hundred people here."

"I wouldn't doubt it. Gordy and Pam have a lot of friends."

Guy saw Will Seevers and his wife mingling with some people he didn't know. He wondered how much the chief knew about his situation.

He let his eyes wander over the crowd. He recognized the mayor. The manager of the Jiffy Lube. His dentist. The church secretary. The lady from the art gallery. Ali and Mina Tehrani. The DA. Weezie from the crab shack. One of the tellers at the bank.

His barber. His eyes stopped on a stocky man in a yarmulke. He studied the man's face and turned to Ellen.

"Honey, isn't that David Kohler, the doctor whose son was killed?"

"I think so. I recognize him from the newspaper."

"I can't believe he's here after what's he's just been through."

Guy noticed Ali Tehrani staring at him and turned away. He heard someone whistle and realized it was Gordy.

The newlyweds stepped away from the cake table and stood with Will and Margaret Seevers. A line was starting to form.

"Oh, good," Ellen said. "I can hardly wait to hug their necks."

Guy dutifully followed Ellen and stood in line, surprised at the diversity of people that Gordy and Pam had chosen to invite. He wondered how many of these guests they actually cared about and how many were just customers they invited because it was good for business.

The aroma of something delicious had made its way to Guy's senses, and he realized he was hungry. Across the way, he spotted another huge white canopy where a buffet table had been set up and dozens of plastic tables and chairs.

He let his eyes flit across a sea of faces and tried to look pleasant as the line inched forward. Every few seconds, he could hear Gordy's voice above the drone, laughing and talking. He leaned closer to Ellen. "Is there anybody Gordy *doesn't* know?"

She chuckled. "I doubt it. What impresses me is how he remembers their names and treats them all as if they were family."

Guy noticed Dr. Kohler standing off to the side and Ali Tehrani walk over and say something to him, surprised when the two men embraced.

"I wonder how calculated that was?" he said to Ellen.

"What?"

He nodded toward the two doctors and noticed he wasn't the only one watching them.

An hour later, Guy had eaten all he could hold and had given up on getting Ellen out of there any time soon. He walked about fifty yards down the beach, the sound of music and laughter at his back, and looked up at the orangey pink sky. The evening breeze was considerably cooler. Out of the corner of his eye, he saw someone ambling toward him and realized it was Ali Tehrani.

"I see you lost your wife, too," Ali said.

Guy nodded. "Last time I saw her, she was with yours."

"What can I say?" Ali threw up his hands. "Women never seem to run out of things to say."

"Yes, it's definitely a curious gender distinction."

"So how do you know Gordy and Pam?" Ali said.

"From the crab shack. Ellen got to know Gordy after the near fiasco with the Hamilton girl's kidnapping. How about you?"

"I was his first wife's oncologist. Gordy and Jenny stole my heart, and I developed a special bond with him that has lasted all this time. I'm so happy he has found love again."

"I didn't know Jenny, but he sure seems crazy about Pam."

Guy listened to the hissing of the surf as it washed up on the sand and wished Ali would move on.

"I am very sorry about your secretary," Ali finally said.

"Thanks."

"Ellen told us the media is trying to turn this into something it isn't. I understand what that feels like."

Guy decided he wasn't about to touch that one.

"If you ever feel a need to talk about it with someone who understands your frustration, I would be glad to listen."

Guy focused on a hermit crab scurrying across the sand. "How have *you* dealt with it?"

"Poorly, I'm afraid. My refusal to answer their questions has only raised more. Why the media persists in portraying all Muslims as violent and dangerous is beyond me."

Guy bit his lip. *Ask me. I could give you a few hundred reasons.*

"It was not my wish to offend you," Ali said.

"I know."

The silence that followed was more obnoxious than the reception noise Guy had just walked away from.

"Please," Ali said, "I would prefer you say what's on your mind."

Guy pushed his hands deeper into his pockets. "All right. What offends me is that while Muslims around the world call for jihad against the United States, Muslim Americans refuse to denounce those threats or the terrorist attacks. Your saying nothing comes across as approval."

Ali nodded. "I have come to realize that and have determined it must change. Muslims are afraid they will be seen as disloyal if they speak out against a brother."

"But you're antagonizing everyone else."

"Guy, much confusion and disagreement exists even among Muslims over the meaning of jihad. Most American Muslims are exposed to a broader scope of world news and generally have a different perception. I agree we must find the courage to denounce the violence and call our brothers to peace."

"When? People are getting increasingly fed up with Muslim communities turning a deaf ear. Just look what's happened here."

Ali's eyebrows gathered. "Daryoush Fassih's murder was a painful wake-up call for me—but Isaac Kohler's even more so. We cannot continue to bequeath hate to our children and think they will have a better life. This is not my way. My daughter Sanaz has been taught to respect *every* person. But my nephew Bobak...he has had no such training."

"Ellen said the FBI cleared him."

"He was not involved in terrorism, but he speaks hate. I told him he was not welcome in my home. He has gone back to Iran."

Too bad you didn't all go with him!

"On behalf of Muslims in this community, I ask your forgiveness for giving you the impression that we are somehow less patriotic than other Americans. We came here with the same hope as any other immigrant—wanting freedom and opportunity and a better life for our children. We are as horrified as you are about the terrorist activity...and embarrassed that Muslim radicals have given all of Islam a bad name. They simply do not represent our values."

Guy caught Ali's gaze. "Then who does?"

The sound of Ellen's laughter distracted him, and he looked up and saw her and Mina walking toward them.

"*There* you are." Approval emanated from Ellen's smile.

"You ready to go?" Guy said, hoping his eyes communicated his desperation.

"Gordy and Pam are getting ready to leave. Why don't we go see them off first?"

Ali turned to Guy and extended his hand. "Perhaps sometime we could continue our conversation over lunch?"

Guy shook his hand and mumbled something noncommittal, thinking that, with his reputation on the line, all he needed was to be seen breaking bread with Ali Tehrani.

34

Gordy Jameson shook Will Seevers's hand and patted
him on the shoulder. "Thanks for standin' with me,
Will—and for pushin' till I agreed to meet Pam. I'll
never be able to thank you enough."

"Seeing you happy is all the thanks I need," Will said. "Are
you lovebirds gonna get out of here, or not?"

Gordy took Pam's hand and pressed it to his lips. "Ready to
go, Mrs. Jameson?"

She turned and looked out at several hundred friendly faces,
her own still radiant. "I want to remember every detail of this day.
It was absolutely perfect."

"It really was, wasn't it? Okay, darlin', get ready to throw your
bouquet, then let's head up the hill."

BOOOOM! A powerful jolt seemed to move the ground, rat-
tling the glassware and evoking gasps and shrieks from the
guests.

Gordy pulled Pam to his chest, his heart pounding madly,
and saw billows of black smoke rising above the trees.

"What was that?" Pam said.

"I dunno. Must've been a humongous explosion."

"That smoke can't be far from city hall," Will said. He
grabbed a chair and stood on it, then cupped his hands around
his mouth and hollered until he had their attention. "Everybody,
stay calm. I know you want to know what happened, but I need
you not to leave just yet so we don't clog the streets with a couple
hundred cars and make it tough for emergency vehicles to get

through." Will jumped down off the chair and looked at the sky over downtown. "I really don't like the looks of this, Gordy. Would you make sure Margaret and Meagan find a ride home?"

"Yeah, sure."

Will said something to Margaret, then ran up the hill toward his squad car.

Gordy stood with his arm around Pam and watched his nervous guests milling around. "So much for the festive mood, eh? Not exactly a great ending to a perfect day."

Margaret Seevers came over and stood with the Jamesons. "I'm sorry this ruined your exit. I wonder what kind of explosion it was?"

Gordy shrugged. "Must've been a humdinger."

All of a sudden, a siren rang out deep and foreboding, increasing to an ear-splitting, almost paralyzing pitch.

Pam put her hands over her ears. "Why is that on?" she hollered.

"I don't know." Gordy spotted the civil defense pole just across Beach Shore Drive. The decibel level was almost unbearable.

"It's a terrorist attack!" someone shouted. "Run!"

Pandemonium broke out, and wedding guests began screaming and knocking over chairs, clambering to get out—many already racing toward their cars.

Gordy tried to spot Meagan Seevers and was relieved to see her clutching her mother's arm.

"We need to get to safety!" Margaret shouted.

Gordy looked at the black smoke spreading across the crimson sky and wondered if any place they ran for cover would be safe.

Will Seevers stood outside city hall and surveyed the smoldering remains of a charred vehicle and the broken windows and damage to the exterior of the building.

"Tell all these curiosity seekers to go home," he ordered Jack Rutgers. "Clear the area of all vehicles—now! I don't want anything within two blocks of here."

Will got on his cell phone and hit the auto dial.

"Hello."

"Margaret, where are you?"

"At our house with Meagan and Gordy and Pam. Tell me what happened. Why did the civil defense sirens go on?"

"A car bomb exploded next to city hall, and we don't know who's behind it. Nobody's hurt, but it's a real mess."

"Will, the media is already calling this a terrorist attack. Was it?"

"It might be. But considering what these people are capable of, this doesn't seem like a big enough bang to me."

"Please be careful. What if they're planning to do something else?"

"I'm fine. You stay inside until the feds give the all clear. Let me talk to Gordy real quick." Will heard a shuffling noise and then Gordy's voice.

"Don't worry, Chief. Your girls are safe."

"Why aren't you and Pam on the road?"

"We thought we'd stay here with Margaret and Meagan."

"That's nice of you, but you might as well go on. There's nothing you can do."

"It's not like Pam and I can just take off on our honeymoon without even knowing what happened."

"Someone exploded a car bomb. Could've been much worse."

"What's with the civil defense siren? You think terrorists did this?"

"That's everyone's gut reaction. But this explosion seems like a firecracker compared to the firepower available to them. I keep asking myself why terrorists would hit some dinky target like Seaport City Hall when they could blow up something significant in Tallahassee or Miami...Listen, bud, I'm really sorry this happened when it did and messed up your wedding."

"It didn't mess it up. The wedding was great. But I'd sure like to know where my bride and I are gonna spend our first night. Maybe we should just go home."

"Go on to Panama City like you planned. Don't let this spoil your honeymoon. The worst is over."

BOOOOM! The deafening sound reverberated and seemed to pick up the ground and slam it down again, evoking shrieks from onlookers. A billow of black smoke rose above the trees on the far edge of town.

Will picked up his walkie-talkie. "Jack, call and request all units from Port Smyth! Gordy, stay with the girls! I'll call you."

Will ran to his car, tossed his cell phone on the passenger seat, and raced down Main Street in the direction of the smoke, wondering if the unthinkable had finally happened and if people here were prepared for what it might mean.

Guy Jones sat with Ellen watching a live report of the explosions on the regional news station.

"I can't believe this is happening," Ellen said.

"I can. It was just a matter of time. We can't police every nook and cranny in a free society." He turned up the volume.

"We're going live to Seaport High School, which was the target of the second blast. Our reporter Jared Downing is on the scene. Jared, tell us what you see."

"Shannon, it's pure chaos here. Behind me, you can see the huge hole in the cafeteria wall and the massive damage to this side of the building. Authorities say a car bomb went off just feet from the building—the identical scenario that played out at city hall about thirty minutes prior to this explosion.

"Firefighters have put the blaze out, but the damage is extensive, and it doesn't look as though classes will be resuming for some time. Thankfully, no students or teachers were in the school at the time of the blast.

"There's a strong feeling here that these were terrorist attacks and that authorities aren't doing enough to uncover the terrorist cell they believe exists somewhere in the region. And considering the carnage that could have resulted had this been a Monday instead of a Saturday night, people are wondering if this is just a prelude to something worse.

"It looks like Chief Will Seevers is about to make a statement. Let's listen."

Will Seevers, still dressed in the Hawaiian shirt he wore at Gordy's wedding, walked over to reporters, his face determined, his voice controlled. "I assure you my department will work twenty-four/seven with the FBI, ATF, sheriff's department, and Homeland Security until we bring to justice the person or persons responsible for these acts of violence. I encourage all citizens of Seaport to stay calm, and to stay alert. No one has yet claimed responsibility. You are urged to call the police department if you have information that might assist us in determining who is responsible. I also urge everyone to refrain from making assumptions about who's behind these attacks. Let law enforcement do its work. I'll update the media periodically and when it's appropriate. Right now, I need to get back to work."

Guy put the TV on mute. "So much for the beautiful little seaside town I talked you into. You may want to move to Tallahassee after all this."

"Hardly." Ellen held tighter to his hand. "But I won't pretend I'm not scared about what's happening. Poor Gordy and Pam. What a horrible way to end their wedding." Ellen paused and seemed to be thinking. "Speaking of wedding, you never said what you and Ali were talking about."

"Does it matter?"

Ellen turned to him. "It might."

"We started out chitchatting about how we came to know Gordy, but it got intense after that." Guy relayed to Ellen the entire conversation, including Guy's venting his frustration over American Muslims not denouncing the violence. "He asked and I told him. I suppose you're mad?"

"No. Actually, I'm glad you cleared the air."

"I don't know how clear it is. Ali didn't have a chance to answer my question. He said radical Muslims don't represent true Islamic values. I'd like to know what he perceives to be true Islamic values."

"Then have lunch with him and ask."

"This is the wrong time to be Muslim friendly."

Ellen arched her eyebrows. "Maybe it's the perfect time. Is that what you are?"

"I don't know *what* I am, honey. But I'm tired of all the Mickey Mouse game playing. American Muslims are either for us or against us. They can't have it both ways."

Will Seevers walked in the front door and listened. The house was completely quiet except for the sound of Margaret's scuffs on the wood floor.

She walked into the entry hall and put her arms around him. "You must be exhausted. You want something to eat?"

"No, thanks, my stomach's upset. Where're Gordy and Pam?"

"In the family room, sacked out on the couch."

"Some honeymoon. How's Meagan?"

"Scared. We entertained her by playing dominoes till she got sleepy, but she didn't want to be alone and brought her sleeping bag in the family room. I guess we all feel a sense of safety in numbers. Will, *were* these terrorist attacks?"

"I don't know, honey. I don't have another explanation right now."

Will peeked in the family room and saw Pam sleeping in Gordy's arms, and Meagan curled up in her sleeping bag on the floor.

"I'm glad someone can sleep," Will said. "Maybe I should try to eat something light. Got any of your homemade chicken noodle soup left?"

"Sure. Come sit and I'll heat it up." Margaret took a Tupperware container out of the refrigerator and poured soup into a mug and put it in the microwave. "I can't believe Gordy and Pam insisted on staying."

"What happened at the reception after I left?"

"That blood-curdling siren went on, and one of guests yelled out that it was a terrorist attack. Everyone panicked and ran in all directions. Gordy took us under his wing and drove us home." Margaret paused and smiled. "The only fun thing in all of this was that Meagan got to ride in Gordy's car—complete with the 'just married' on the back window and the tin cans tied to the bumper. She thought that was pretty cool for an eleven-year-old."

"I just hope that by the time she gets married, the terrorists haven't succeeded in spoiling our freedoms."

Margaret took the mug out of the microwave and sat it in front of Will with a soupspoon. "Give your mind a rest, Chief. You're not going to solve this tonight."

Gordy appeared in the kitchen doorway and covered his yawn with his hand. "Hey, when'd you get home?"

"Just a few minutes ago. Thanks for staying with the girls. I'm really sorry you got stuck here."

"No problem. Any idea who set off the car bombs?"

"Not yet. But we're going to tear this town apart until we get them. Several branches of law enforcement have already pulled together to help."

Gordy moved out of the doorway to let Pam squeeze past, then stood with his arm around her.

"I keep thinking how much worse it could've been," Pam said.

Will nodded. "It's a miracle there weren't any casualties. Can you imagine if this had happened when school was in session?"

"Or if *you'd* been standing outside city hall!" Margaret shuddered. "I don't even want to think about it. Let's change the subject. Wasn't it a beautiful wedding? I'm so glad you two thought of getting married at the lighthouse. The backdrop looked like a picture postcard."

"Yeah, I've loved that place since I was a kid," Gordy said. "The only thing more breathtakin' than the setting was my new bride."

"Pam did have a certain glow. Still does." Will looked at Gordy and prodded him with his eyes.

Gordy glanced at his watch. "You know what? It's only ten after eleven, and I'm so wired I could drive all the way to Panama City without battin' an eye. Whaddya think, Pam?"

"Are you serious?"

"Absolutely. We're only about three hours behind schedule. A couple double espressos, a little time to reminisce about the wedding, and we'll be pullin' up to the Pembrooke House before you know it."

Pam smiled. "Actually, I'm wide awake now."

"Well, you're not leaving without throwing your bouquet," Margaret said. "Let me go wake Meagan up. She had her heart set on being the one to catch it."

35

On Sunday morning, Will Seevers sat in his office, the ceiling fan rustling the papers on his desk, and watched through the window as investigators from the ATF, FBI, and Homeland Security combed the singed grounds around city hall.

Al Backus came in and flopped in a chair. "You feeling as useless as I am?"

"I don't know whether *useless* is the right word. I'll just have to live with the fact that I'm not in the driver's seat on this one."

"The feds are always so arrogant when they claim jurisdiction."

Will folded his hands on his desk. "Let's just stay focused on our two unsolved murders."

"We've got nothing. How long can we keep poring over the case notes?"

"As long as it takes. It's only been a week. I'm convinced whoever killed Fassih and Kohler has told someone. And that someone's bound to slip up."

Al shook his head. "Chief, we've talked to the victims' parents, siblings, extended families, friends, neighbors, classmates, professors, the imam at the mosque, the rabbi at the synagogue—even the college librarian. Nobody's given us anything."

"Then go back and retrace your steps. Either we're missing someone—or the killer's a better actor than we are cops."

"Maybe we're never gonna know."

"*Never* is unacceptable, Al. Stop whining and find me something. By the way, was that Investigator Hamlin I heard you talking to earlier?"

"Yeah. Looks like we can close our investigation of the break-in at the Jones's house. Rob Blakely confessed to all three break-in's—the house and Jones's apartment twice."

"Did he confess to killing the secretary?"

"No. He admitted writing the threat on Jones's mirror and holding a knife on him, but swears it was just an intimidation tactic to try to collect the thirty grand. Blakely swears he never ordered a hit on Kinsey Abbot. Says he didn't even know she'd left Tallahassee."

"Does Hamlin believe him?"

"Yeah, Jones told him that when he and the missus took Ms. Abbot to the bus station, she was confident that absolutely no one knew about her going to Atlanta. Jones said she used a phony name on her bus ticket."

"So her death really was just a random mugging?"

"Looks that way. According to someone at the law firm, she routinely wore a lot of gold jewelry and none was found on her. The medical examiner found scratches where it had been yanked off. You'd think she'd have pawned it if she owed money."

"She probably couldn't scrape up thirty grand no matter what she did." Will shook his head. "Too bad a prominent attorney like Guy Jones let himself get involved with the likes of her."

Guy followed Ellen into the kitchen from the garage and watched as she disarmed the security alarm.

"You've got that down pat," he said. "Feel a little safer?"

Ellen nodded. "I never want to be without it again."

"At least Rob Blakely's locked up." Guy put down his Bible and picked up the Sunday paper and tucked it under his arm. "I might as well read the paper and see what the press is doing to me. Is there any coffee left?"

"Yes, I'll microwave it and bring you a cup."

Guy went out on the veranda and sat in his wicker rocker, aware of church bells ringing in the distance and thinking what a pleasant contrast it was to last night's civil defense siren.

"Here you go." Ellen handed him a mug of coffee, then sat in the other rocker, her arms folded, and seemed to be observing the bird feeders.

"Honey, I'm sorry I insisted we leave church before it was over," Guy said. "I just couldn't face all those people, knowing they probably think I'm a real sleaze."

"I don't know why you won't just go talk to Pastor Crawford about the whole thing—get it out in the open."

"Maybe after the dust settles. Not today." Guy took in a breath and exhaled. "I'm dreading Kinsey's graveside service."

"What time tomorrow is it?"

"I need to call Brent back and ask him. Would you mind bringing me my cell phone?"

Ellen left the veranda and came back with Guy's cell phone and handed it to him. He hit the auto dial and waited.

"Hello."

"Brent, it's Guy."

"Donna and I were just talking about you!" Brent McAllister said. "Has the world gone mad—two car bombings in sleepy little Seaport?"

"It's weird, all right."

"The latest on CNN is that authorities don't have any leads."

"Maybe those Arabs they arrested before will decide to talk. Listen, Brent, did you find out the time for Kinsey's graveside service?"

"Yeah, one o'clock, but you're not going."

"Why not?"

"Because the press will have you for lunch! Nobody from the

office is going. We need to distance ourselves from the situation."

"Kinsey made a huge mistake, but that doesn't erase the fact that she was a tremendous help to me for over a year. I'd like to pay my respects."

"Guy, praying over her dead body isn't going to do a thing for Kinsey...and it could do irreparable harm to your reputation. If you want this thing to *go away* without getting you dirty, you need to stay away."

Guy paused, trying to process the implication. "I don't know, Brent. I need to think about it."

"What you'd better *think* about is how it looks. The press already knows that Kinsey spent the night at your place and that you found cocaine you didn't turn in right away. You think they're going to leave it alone?"

"I haven't done anything wrong!" Guy was surprised at the anger in his tone.

"I know. That's why I'm trying to look out for you."

"Me, or the firm?"

"Both. This may sound cold, but why bother paying your respects to some secretary dumb enough to get mixed up in cocaine trafficking? Kinsey Abbot wasn't worth the dirt they're about to throw on her casket. This was her problem. Don't make it ours."

"You're right, Brent, it sounds cold. I'll see you in the morning." Guy disconnected the call.

"That sounded adversarial," Ellen said.

"Brent doesn't want me going to Kinsey's graveside service." Guy relayed to her everything Brent had said. "Apparently, no one from the firm is going."

"It doesn't surprise me that he's decided not to go, but how dare he dictate what your response should be."

"It really burns me the way he kept downplaying Kinsey, like she didn't matter because she was just a secretary."

"Brent's a master manipulator. Are you going to let him guilt you into not going?" Ellen got up and stood behind him, massaging his shoulders. "What's *really* bothering you?"

Guy breathed in and exhaled. "I guess part of me would like to have a legitimate excuse not to go. I mean, Kinsey died an unbeliever. The idea of her spending eternity in hell...well, that's a tough one. I wish I'd tried harder to get her to listen."

"So now *you're* the Savior?" Ellen paused for a moment, then resumed kneading his shoulders. "Free will is what it is. You can't force a change of heart."

"Why did she have to be so stubborn? It's one thing to bury someone, knowing you'll see them again. But this?"

"So concentrate on the things about Kinsey worth remembering. If you decide to go to the cemetery, I'd like to go with you."

"Even if it means antagonizing my partners?"

"I think we need to consider a higher Authority, Counselor. Which approach seems right to you?"

Will Seevers walked up the steps of a white stucco two-story with a red-tile roof and rang the doorbell. Half a minute later, Simin Fassih opened the door.

"Thank you for seeing me, Mr. Fassih," Will said. "This will just take a minute."

Will walked down an elegant entry hall of polished Spanish tile, a wrought-iron chandelier overhead, and entered the living room. The entire back wall was glass and offered a panoramic view of the gulf.

"This is spectacular," Will said.

Simin nodded. "I originally built this to be the model home in this development, but my wife fell in love with the view."

Will smiled at Mrs. Fassih. "I can see why."

"Please, make yourself comfortable," Simin said. "I cannot tell you how sorry we are about the car bombings. I assume that's why you're here."

"Actually, no." Will sat in a white cushy chair facing the couch and noticed the couple's eyes had grown dull with grief. "I came to reassure you how hard we're working to find Dary's killer."

"You have leads?"

"Not yet. But rest assured, we're going to get him. I just wanted you to know we're retracing our steps and looking for every conceivable angle. This case isn't going to get put on the back burner because of the car bombings."

Simin held tightly to his wife's hand, his eyes brimming with tears. "Thank you. I'm sure public sentiment is not in our favor at the moment."

"Well, I don't run my department based on public sentiment. I want your son's killer punished."

Simin nodded. "We're grateful."

"That's really all I came to say. I wanted to tell you in person, not over the phone."

Will's eyes found a family portrait on the bookshelf, and he remembered Dary was the oldest of four children. What a handsome kid he was. Looked like his mother. Will was glad to have a likeness of the boy to replace the battered image that kept replaying in his memory.

Simin escorted him to the front door and seemed trapped in silence, then finally said, "I cannot tell you how good it feels to be treated with respect, as if you value a Muslim's life as much as everyone else's. We cannot bring Dary back, but hope that through his death, others will come to see that Muslim Americans have the same feelings, hopes, and dreams as everyone. At least then my son's suffering would not have been in vain."

"If it's any consolation, Mr. Fassih, Dary's death has caused me to realize how easy it is for people to misjudge those they don't understand and have little interaction with. Maybe some of the unfounded suspicions would go away if Muslims were integrated into the community and not isolated."

Simin nodded. "I have thought that myself. But I don't know how we would be received when there is so much fear and hostility. It is a frightening time to be Muslim."

Will walked down the front steps and out to his squad car, Mr. Fassih's parting words echoing in his mind, thinking how ironic it was that Muslims were as scared as everyone else.

36

At six o'clock Monday morning, Police Chief Will Seevers sat at his computer, scrolling through the case notes on the Dary Fassih and Isaac Kohler murders. He took a sip of coffee and pushed his glasses higher on his nose. What were they missing? Why did this killer seem silent and invisible?

Al Backus appeared in the doorway and bit off the top half of a doughnut and chased it with a gulp of coffee. "You're here early."

"Why waste time sleeping when I can be trying to solve these murders?"

"Any revelations?"

Will looked over the top of his glasses. "No, but I can see why you're convinced it wasn't a student."

"Plus we already checked out all the siblings and the professors. You want us to go after the custodian and the gardener? They're both right-handed and in their fifties. But hey, who's to say one of them doesn't throw a mean left punch?"

"I don't feel like joking about it, Al."

"Sorry, Chief. A little humor seems to break up the monotony."

Will got up, his hands in his pockets, and stood at the window. "I went by the Fassihs yesterday. I told them we weren't putting this case on the back burner because of the car bombings. I told the Kohlers the same thing."

"What do you want me to do? I'm out of ideas."

"Go back and talk to the rabbi and the imam. See if they've noticed anything strange since the murders—maybe someone who suddenly seems scarce, or more vocal. After the car bombings, I'm sure you'll encounter some resistance in the mosque." Will lifted his eyebrows. "Tread lightly. I know it's not your strongpoint, but I need you to make these religious leaders your best friend. I think I'll go to the college and talk to the English professor."

"Stephen Hardy?"

"Yeah. What's he like?"

"As I recall, late forties, sandy hair and beard. Soft spoken. Nice guy. Real cooperative. Why do you want to talk to him? He didn't know anything."

"I guess because he paired the two boys up for class projects and had a chance to observe any reaction from the students."

"He told us nobody in class paid much attention to it."

"I know. I just want to meet the guy."

"I've never seen you this consumed by a case before, Chief."

"Is it that obvious? I don't usually get emotionally involved."

"Why did you this time?"

Will shrugged. "Maybe because I talked to Isaac the day before he was killed. And the sound of Dary's mother's weeping keeps me up at night. I can't seem to shut it off. I just want to get the person who's wrecked their lives, you know?"

"Yeah, I do. I'll get back out there after this morning's meeting."

Guy Jones pulled his car into Shady Pines Cemetery, glad when he spotted a fresh gravesite not far from the entrance. He looked in his rearview mirror and waited until he saw Ellen's white Thunderbird turn in, then continued on the winding path and pulled up behind a black van and shut off the motor. He glanced at his watch: 12:50.

He got out of the car and looked over at the light gray casket under a yellow canopy and noticed a modest spray of white flowers and greenery draped over it. He counted only five people: one stooped and elderly man; and four people who reeked of media, poised like wolves ready to pounce. This must be the right place.

Guy offered Ellen his arm.

"Brace yourself," she said. "Decide what you want to say, but if you start answering questions, it'll just lead to more."

Guy and Ellen walked across the spongy grass toward the gravesite, and within seconds the reporters were walking along- side.

"Mr. Jones, when did you know Kinsey Abbott was dealing cocaine?"

Ellen squeezed his arm. Did she want him to comment or not comment? He kept walking.

"Sir, did you withhold evidence from the police in order to protect Ms. Abbott? How could you work with her an entire year and not know she was dealing drugs?"

"Were you and Ms. Abbott lovers?"

Guy stopped and locked gazes with the reporter who had the most obnoxious voice. "This is neither the time nor the place to ask these questions. I would appreciate it if you would stay back and respect what we're trying to do here. Excuse us."

Guy continued across the green lawn to the yellow canopy, surprised and relieved when the reporters didn't follow.

He and Ellen were met by a party of one: the stooped, ancient-looking gentleman, wearing a too-small brown suit, green socks, and beige walking shoes. What was left of his white hair was neatly parted and combed to one side.

"Hello, I'm Henry Dibbs, Kinsey's grandfather." The old man offered Guy his withered hand.

"I'm Guy Jones and this is my wife, Ellen."

"Pleased to make your acquaintance," Henry said.

"I wasn't aware that Kinsey had any family except her mother."

"Her mother, Millicent, is my daughter. How do you know Kinsey?"

"She was my legal secretary," Guy said. "And a darned good one. I'll miss her."

Henry looked sheepishly at the casket. "I wasn't expecting anyone to come, so I didn't plan anything. I just knew Millicent would want Kinsey to have a proper burial, even if she was in trouble with the law. That girl always seemed so dark, even when she was little. I knew she was going to be trouble. Kinsey was my flesh and blood, but that didn't mean we loved each other. I don't think she knew how to love anyone, not even her mother. I could count on one hand the times I've seen her in the past twenty-five years. Listen to me jabbering. I'll scoot on out of here so the two of you can pay your respects."

"Wait! Wouldn't you like us to say a prayer?" Guy said.

"Nah, I've never been a praying man. Never saw that it did much good."

"We didn't intend to run you off," Ellen said.

"That's quite all right. I already did what I came to do. You folks do whatever suits you."

Henry Dibbs hobbled across the cemetery lawn toward a white Ford Galaxie parked in front of the van.

"How sad," Ellen said.

"More like pathetic."

Guy stepped closer to the casket and tried not to think about Kinsey's murdered body being inside. He pictured her beautiful face and imagined the sound of her laughter. "What's sad is that a human being can live and die without having made a difference to anyone."

Ellen blinked rapidly. "You're going to make me cry."

Guy put his arm around Ellen. "Kinsey's measure of right and wrong was very different from mine, but I can honestly say she made a positive difference in my life for the year we worked together. I guess that's something."

"I always liked her. I knew she was a lot of help to you."

"How could she end up like this, Ellen? I know she had choices, just like you and I, but she was so wounded. Her father was a drunk. Her mother was unhappy all the time. There was this big void inside her. She never quite felt as though she belonged anywhere." Guy squeezed Ellen's hand. "Before you say it, I know lots of people have a big void, yet they don't sell cocaine. I'm not excusing her, just trying to understand how she could be so lost." He noticed the spray of flowers on the coffin had no ribbon indicating that Kinsey was someone's daughter, granddaughter, wife, sister, friend—nothing. "I prayed she wouldn't die without the Lord. Yet here she is."

Ellen wiped a tear off her cheek. "We have to let it go. God gave her the same choice He gives everyone, Guy."

There was a long stretch of silence and then Guy heard himself say, "I'm still ticked off at Brent for not coming."

"It was certainly in character for him. At least he was honest."

"*Too* honest. How could he just write her off that easily? She did a great job for the firm, regardless of what she was doing on her own time." Guy put his hands in his pockets. "This is awkward. What do we pray over someone who's lost?"

"Let's get quiet," Ellen said. "I'm sure the Lord will impress us with something."

Guy closed his eyes, aware of the muggy air, reporters talking, cars moving along Setzler Boulevard—and the nagging emptiness that served as a reminder that there was nothing to rejoice about.

Suddenly Ellen's voice stole his attention. "Father, thank You for choosing us to be here to commit Kinsey's spirit back to you. To the depths of our being, we know that You valued her, so much so that you sent your Son to die for her sins so that she could be reconciled to You. It's not ours to know how she responded. But thank you that her death has reminded us on a deeper level how we should respect every human being because each has a spirit that is God-breathed and eternal. Father, in Your time and in Your way we ask that you show us what we need to learn from our experiences with Kinsey. We leave her now in Your hands, knowing that You, who *are* love, will deal with her justly."

Guy stood quietly, wondering what he could possibly add to that. "Lord, I'm a new Christian and still learning so many things. I pray that Ellen and I will find something positive in all this..." Guy's voice trailed off.

He let the silence calm his emotions and then reached out and put his palm on the side of the casket. Ellen covered his hand with hers. *Goodbye, Kinsey,* he thought. *I wish things had ended differently.*

Seconds later he removed his hand and dabbed his eyes with his thumb and forefinger. "Thanks for your sensitive prayer, honey. I'm glad you were here. Ready to go?"

"Whenever you are. I'm not in a hurry."

Guy glanced over at the reporters, all too aware that Kinsey Abbot would be remembered as a cocaine dealer, a loose woman, and whatever else Rob Blakely decided to reveal about her to the media.

He stared at the empty space where Henry Dibbs's Ford Galaxie had been parked and wondered if the old man felt satisfied that he'd done his duty.

Will Seevers went in his office, a manila folder under his arm, and picked up the phone and dialed Al Backus's extension.

"This is Al."

"I need you in my office."

"Be right there, Chief."

Seconds later, Al Backus appeared in the doorway.

"Let's sit over here at the table," Will said.

"What've you got there?"

"The break we've been waiting for!"

Will took some photographs out of the manila folder and laid them on the table. "This crushed Mountain Dew can was recovered in the rubble of the first explosion. The DNA on the saliva inside matches the killer's."

Al turned to Will, his eyes wide. "Fassih and Kohler's?"

"Yep. How's that for a shocker? We've got a thumbprint, too."

Al rubbed his hands together. "Now we're cookin'!"

"There's more." Will took another set of photos out of the manila folder and laid them on the table. "A surveillance camera across the street captured these just three minutes before the first explosion—this old VW bus pulls in the circle drive and stops in front of the entrance. Two men get out of the vehicle. Within seconds, both men disappear."

"They look young. Can't they enhance these so we can see more detail?"

"These are enhanced. But look closely at the man getting out on the driver's side. He appears to be Caucasian, dark hair, large build. Notice his left hand."

"Looks like a ring." Al brought the photo closer to his eyes. "The autopsy mentioned an odd indentation cut into the Fassih boy's cheek. Could've been caused by a ring. Must be a pretty substantial ring to show up in a photograph taken from this distance."

"This should breathe new life into the case. From this point on, you're going to be working concurrently with the feds."

"They're not gettin' credit for this one. We've done too much of the ground work."

"Frankly, Al, I couldn't care less who gets credit. I want the killer. How'd you do at the synagogue and mosque?"

"I was a good boy, if that's what you mean. They didn't give me anything, but I feel sure they'll call if anything seems suspicious."

"Good. What was the mood at the mosque?"

"The imam seemed genuinely sad about the explosions—and baffled. I never know how sincere he is, but he seemed like it. Did you talk to the English professor?"

"No, I got tied up in meetings." Will glanced at his watch. "I may try to catch him after his four o'clock class."

37

Will Seevers opened the heavy wood doors in the administration building at Seaport Junior College and walked down a long, shiny hallway toward the faculty lounge. He glanced at his watch, lamenting being seven minutes late, and hoping Professor Stephen Hardy had waited for him.

Will turned into the lounge and saw only one man sitting at a table, seemingly grading papers. "Professor Hardy?"

The bearded man looked up through his round spectacles. "Yes, you must be Chief Seevers."

Will walked over to the table and shook his hand. "Thanks for agreeing to meet. Do you want to talk here, or would you prefer somewhere more private?"

"This is fine," Stephen said. "What's this about?"

Will sat across from him, his arms folded on the table. "My department is stepping up our efforts to solve the murders of your two students, and we're retracing our steps. I realize you've answered questions for Investigator Backus, but I wanted to talk to you myself. I've taken a personal interest in this case, as I'm sure you must have. I just want to brainstorm a bit, if that's okay?"

"Sure, anything I can do to help."

"Would you describe Isaac Kohler to me and any impressions you may have had about him?"

"Isaac was quiet, but very bright. Intuitive. I sensed that he appreciated and understood poetry and literature on a deeper level than my other students, though he rarely volunteered his thoughts."

"Did the other students like him?"

"I don't think they *disliked* him. But he certainly wasn't considered cool."

"How did you determine that?"

"Isaac always seemed to be on the sidelines, watching everyone else. He was the shortest young man in the class and wore unusually thick glasses. It didn't help that he was an introvert...or that he was Jewish. He carried himself as if he expected to be treated as the odd man out. He was a gentle kid. Didn't have a mean bone in his body."

"Anybody give him a hard time?"

"Not that I could tell. Most students tended to ignore him."

"Anything else about him stand out?"

Stephen twisted the hairs on his beard. "Isaac was immensely private. And contemplative. I often wondered what he was thinking. Even on paper, he revealed little about himself, though I perceived him to be full of poetry waiting for expression. I'm sorry that I won't get the chance to find out."

Will jotted a few notes and looked again at the professor. "What can you tell me about Dary Fassih?"

"Dary wasn't intuitive like Isaac, but he was a bright young man. Eager to learn. Outgoing. Good-looking. He tried to make friends, but his broken English caused him to gravitate toward the other Iranian students. I heard him speaking Farsi on a number of occasions."

"Is that Iranian?" Will said.

"Persian. Farsi is the official language of Iran. Of course, I'm determined that all my students become proficient in the English language and don't allow anything else spoken in my classroom. But with such a blend of Latin, Oriental, Iranian, and Israeli students, it's a real challenge."

"Guess there's not much you can do about it."

Stephen raised his eyebrows. "Sure there is. I try to pair each immigrant student with one who will force him to stretch."

"That's what you did with Isaac and Dary?"

"Yes. Both these boys seemed to be social outcasts, and Dary was struggling with the language. Isaac was American born and his English was fine. I thought perhaps these two would make good partners for class projects."

"Weren't you concerned about the strong religious differences?"

"Yes, but I thought they should get over that, too. These boys were both people pleasers. I knew they'd work it out."

"And did they?"

"Very much so. Of course, neither wore it on his sleeve—heaven forbid that a Jew and a Muslim might actually get along. But the work they turned in together proved they were communicating well. And Dary's English had improved considerably just in the few weeks since school started."

Will looked into the professor's eyes. "Who would want to hurt them?"

Stephen shook his head. "I wish I knew."

"This is the only class they had together, Professor. I keep thinking there must be something here to link their murders."

"I wish I could help you, but I've told you and the other investigator everything I know."

Will reached in the manila envelope and pulled out the photograph of the two men getting out of the van minutes before the explosion. "I know these aren't clear, but do you recognize these men?"

"Are they students?"

"I don't know. But they and their VW bus were photographed outside the entrance to city hall minutes before the explosion."

"What does this have to do with Dary and Isaac?"

Will handed him the photo of the crushed Mountain Dew can. "This was found in the rubble. The DNA from the saliva in the can matched the DNA found on Dary and Isaac's bodies. Professor, this can was in the VW bus. One of these men either killed the boys or knows who did."

The lines on the professor's forehead deepened and he moved his eyes to the photograph of the two men and the van and seemed to be studying it.

"Is there something you want to tell me?" Will said.

"Uh, no. I just wanted a thorough look. I'm sorry I can't help you."

Will Seevers walked in the front door and into the dining room where Margaret and Meagan were already seated at the table. "I'm not as late as I thought I'd be."

"I'm glad you got home before we were done. This isn't as good reheated." Margaret filled his plate and handed it to him.

Will cut a piece of baked chicken and put it in his mouth. "Mmm...this is good. I didn't have time to eat lunch."

"So what's happening with the car bombings? Any suspects? Anyone claim responsibility? What did the FBI have to say?"

"I just got home, Margaret. I'd like to at least swallow my food before I start talking shop." He glanced up and saw the hurt on her face. "Sorry, honey. Today's been a zoo. I've barely had time to assimilate it."

"Everybody at my school is freaking out," Meagan said. "Our teacher showed us how they did bomb drills when she was in school back when everybody was scared of the Russians."

"This is a very different kind of threat," Will said. "No one is dropping bombs. In fact, we're beginning to think the terrorists didn't explode the car bombs."

Margaret stopped chewing. "Has someone claimed responsibility?"

"No, but I had a meeting with the feds this afternoon, and we're all thinking the same way."

"Who else would do something like that?"

"That's the question of the hour."

"Can't you at least *speculate*?"

He smiled. "No."

"Gordy and Pam will be home tomorrow," Margaret said.

"Yeah, I'm anxious to see them."

Meagan reached for the rolls. "Maybe we should have them over for dinner this weekend so I can clean Uncle Gordy's plow at dominoes."

Will chuckled. "Clean his plow, huh? You're starting to sound like him."

"Daddy, my friends want to know if I'm scared of the terrorists. Is it okay to say I am? Or should I pretend I'm not because you're the police chief and don't want them to think you're not doing your job?"

"Meagan!" Margaret said. "Of course, your father's doing his job."

"Will it get Daddy in trouble if I say I'm scared, too?"

Will's cell phone vibrated. He heaved a loud sigh. "Sorry, I need to take this. Chief Seevers."

"It's Backus. Where are you?"

"At home having dinner."

"Lucky you. I was leaving the station when I heard the call come in for all units to go to the courthouse. We've got some vocal college students threatening to go house to house in the Muslim neighborhood, looking for terrorists."

Will looked at Margaret and rolled his eyes. "No one in his right mind would do that. They're blowing smoke."

"Probably so, but they're creating quite a stir, and the media's eatin' it up. The feds are preparing to make a statement. Might be good for you to be visible."

Or take a long vacation. "All right. Let me wash down my dinner. I'm on my way."

Ellen Jones lay on the living room couch listening to an instrumental praise and worship tape, thinking about today's experience at the cemetery and the futility of a person struggling through life without a relationship with God. It hadn't been that long ago that she and Guy had clung to their atheism, firmly convinced that their life together was as good as it gets. Had she continued to put her faith in Guy's ability to make her happy, the past few months would have been unbearable.

How much more difficult must it have been for Kinsey, having no one and grasping at anything to fill the void that only God was meant to fill?

Ellen closed her eyes and let the euphonic sound of the music fill her senses and calm her spirit.

Suddenly she was aware of a ringing noise and realized it was her cell phone. She hurried out to the kitchen, took it out of her purse, and pushed the talk button. "Hello."

"Is this Ellen?"

"Yes. Who's calling?"

"My name's Tim Rayburn. I'm the pastor of Morgan Street Ministries near downtown Atlanta. I recently met a young woman, Kinsey Abbot. Do you know her?"

"Yes, why do you ask?"

"I spotted her in a coffee shop last Tuesday, and she looked despondent. I struck up a conversation with her, told her who I was, and one thing led to another. She told me she was in trouble and didn't have anywhere to turn. She showed me a tract you had given her and asked me to explain how a loving God could send people to hell."

"Oh, dear. What did you say?"

"I told her she was looking at it backwards, that God gave us the only way to *avoid* hell. That got her attention."

Ellen's heart raced. "Please, tell me everything that was said! I have an important reason for wanting to know."

"I reiterated what was in the tract—that we're all sinners and the penalty of sin is death, that Jesus' death on the cross paid that penalty for us because we were helpless to do it. And for everyone who receives Jesus, our Father in heaven looks at us as if we had never sinned. Kinsey teared up. I sensed she was hanging on to every word."

"I'm surprised she didn't cut you off."

"Frankly, so was I. I went on to tell her that Jesus' resurrection validates His divinity, that He's both the Giver *and* the Gift. And because of that, she can have the assurance of heaven and a relationship with God here and now."

"She listened to all that?"

"Yes. She asked me what the catch was. I told her salvation was a free gift—that all she had to do is open her heart to Jesus, confess her sins, and start living by the principles in the Bible."

Ellen closed her eyes. "How did she react?"

"Praise God, she let me pray with her right there to trust Jesus as her Savior! That's why I called you. I still have the tract, and your first name and phone number were on it. I think the Lord would like you to know you made an impact on her eternal life."

Ellen tried to swallow the emotion, tears running down her cheeks.

"Ma'am, are you there?"

"Uh, yes, pastor... Give me a minute."

"Why don't you call me Tim?"

Ellen breathed in deeply and let it out slowly. "You should know Kinsey died last Thursday."

"I'm so sorry."

"No, it's okay." Ellen dabbed her eyes. "My husband and I attended her burial today in Tallahassee. We thought she had died an unbeliever. This is astounding."

"May I ask how she died?"

Ellen told Tim what she knew about Kinsey's life and death, and also about her grandfather's peculiar behavior at the cemetery. "I can hardly wait to tell my husband. I'm sure you realize Kinsey wasn't in that coffee shop by chance, nor did she come here by chance. These were divine appointments."

There were a few moments of dead air.

"You know what thrills me to the core, Ellen? Every soul matters to God. Even if nobody on earth besides you and your husband and I gave a hoot about Kinsey Abbot, the Lord and His angels rejoiced over her last Tuesday afternoon."

Guy Jones lay on the couch in his new apartment, wondering if Kinsey's grandfather had given her a second thought after he walked away from the cemetery. He picked up his cell phone and dialed home.

"Hello."

"Hi, honey. Did you make it home without any problems?"

"Uh-huh," Ellen said. "The time went fast. Gave me time to think."

"You sound like you've been crying. Are you upset about Kinsey?"

"Actually, the most wonderful thing happened a little while ago, and I've been praising God ever since."

Guy listened as Ellen told him the details of her phone conversation with Tim Rayburn.

"I started to call you," Ellen said, "but I just needed to be alone with the joy for a while. I can hardly believe it. Kinsey accepted Christ!"

"It would never have happened if you hadn't given her the tract."

"You don't know that. God could've used Tim regardless. But what a gift it is having the assurance she's with the Lord."

Guy couldn't find words to express what he was feeling. Ellen's last words to Kinsey came rushing back to him.

"I'll be praying for you every day, honey. Don't despair. Your Father in heaven won't take His eyes off you—not for a moment."

"Guy, are you there?"

"Yeah, I was just thinking back on what you said to Kinsey when we were out at the lighthouse." He blinked the stinging from his eyes. "Can you imagine what it must've been like for her to experience a Father's love for the first time?"

38

Late Tuesday afternoon, Will Seevers elbowed his way through a mob of reporters and went in the side door of the police station. He waited until Al Backus was inside, then shut the door, reporters still shouting questions at them.

"Give me a few minutes," Will said. "Then come down to my office and let's put our heads together and evaluate where we are."

Will went down to the lounge and got a cup of coffee, then went into his office and flipped the light switch.

His phone rang and he grabbed the receiver. "Seevers."

"Will, it's Gordy."

"Hey, bud. You home?"

"Yeah, Pam and I got in about an hour ago."

"Is that happiness I hear in your voice?"

"It's great being married again. Pam's already in the kitchen, decidin' what to fix for our first dinner at home. Almost seems like she's always been here."

"That's so good to hear. Can I call you back? I'm about to have a meeting."

"Yeah, I was just wonderin' how you're holdin' up."

"Truthfully, I'm exhausted. At least the feds are working *with* us and not throwing their weight around."

"I heard on the news you had some solid leads."

"Yeah, we do." Will looked up and saw Al Backus walk through the doorway. "Gotta go. I'll talk to you soon."

"Yeah, okay. Give our love to Margaret."

Will hung up the phone and took a sip of coffee. "Tell me your impression of today's press conference."

Al held his gaze. "I don't think it placated anyone, if that's what you mean. The media keeps demanding answers we don't have. All we need is for a couple of those college kids to get stupid enough to actually move against the Muslim community. Hard to say what might erupt."

"Yeah, I know." Will looked out the window at the various law enforcement people still combing the grounds outside city hall. "Why hasn't someone claimed responsibility for the car bombings? And why didn't they target something that would draw national outrage? The feds keep talking about domestic terrorism, but even that seems like a stretch to me. Why would anyone pick Seaport where they don't get much bang for their buck?"

"Unless they live here...or nearby."

Will raised his eyebrows. "What would be the motive? And why would they kill Isaac Kohler and Dary Fassih and then set off a car bomb next to city hall and the high school on a Saturday night when there wasn't likely to be anyone there?"

"I don't know. Maybe they were practicing for something bigger."

Guy Jones sat at his desk, aware of someone standing in the doorway. He looked up and saw Brent McAllister. *Here it comes.*

Brent shut the door and sat in a chair next to Guy's desk, his arms folded, his eyes cold and piercing.

"I never agreed not to go to the cemetery," Guy said.

"I thought I made our position clear."

"No, you made *your* position clear." Guy sat quietly for a moment, then took off his reading glasses. "Brent, let's get something straight. I'm one hundred percent onboard when it comes to how we conduct the firm's business, but this was personal business. I accept that you didn't feel a need to acknowledge Kinsey, but she was my right arm for over a year. You don't have the right to tell me I can't pay my respects."

Brent exhaled loudly. "The media's going to turn your life inside out, trying to prove you were lovers and that you knew she was dealing drugs."

"I'm a big boy."

"You're also a partner. It reflects on us."

"Then how about defending my character instead of game playing with the media? For crying out loud, Brent, I wasn't sleeping with her! *I'm* the one who told the police she was dealing cocaine! I'm the good guy in this. How about treating me like it?"

"Why was going to the cemetery so all-fired important anyway?"

Guy leaned back in his chair, his fingers locked together. "I doubt you'd understand if I told you."

"Try me."

"I'd rather not."

"You owe me an explanation, Guy."

"All right. I just didn't think Kinsey deserved to be treated as if she never mattered to anyone."

"What difference could it possibly make to a dead woman?"

"I think it matters to the One who made her."

An awkward silence came between them, and Guy wondered what Brent was thinking.

"Oh, now I get it," Brent finally said. "You're hung up on whether she's going to spend eternity in heaven or hell." He waved his hand. "You know I don't buy any of that religious bunk. Life's over when it's over."

"That's why I didn't want to get into this discussion."

"You can't let your religion dictate the way you represent this firm."

"You know better than that!" Guy looked at Brent and held

his gaze. "I've never pushed my beliefs on you or anyone else. But I can't separate how I function from who I am and what I believe. Not going to the cemetery seemed just plain wrong."

Brent seemed distracted for a few moments, then his eyes grew wide, a grin devouring his face.

"What's so funny?" Guy said.

"Oh, something just occurred to me. If it turns out you Christians were right, I'll see Kinsey again—in hell." Brent laughed. "Should be lot more fun than where you're going."

Guy tuned out everything else Brent had to say, thinking the man was to be pitied, and that Kinsey's change of heart was much too precious to waste on him.

Will Seevers had just finished answering his e-mail when a voice came over the intercom.

"Chief, Professor Hardy has arrived. Would you like me to bring him to your office?"

"Yeah, thanks."

Will popped a breath mint in his mouth, then stood and tucked his shirt in tightly.

Seconds later he heard footsteps and walked out into the hall and saw the receptionist approaching with Stephen Hardy. He shook hands with the professor and led him into his office.

"Why don't we sit here at the table," Will said. "Would you like something to drink?"

"No, I'm fine." Stephen took a seat, his fingers tapping the tabletop.

"What was it you wanted to discuss?" Will said.

"Can I take another look at the picture of the two men getting out of the VW bus—the one you showed me yesterday?"

"Sure. Think you might recognize them?"

Stephen didn't answer and took the picture from Will. He stared at it for several seconds, the photo shaking in his hands.

"Professor, what is it?"

The color drained from Stephen's face. He dropped the photograph on the table and didn't seem to know what to do with his hands. "It's...it's my son. It's Robert. He's the driver. I think the other boy is a neighbor, Lance Pearson."

Will's heart sank. "Did you know this yesterday?"

"I saw the resemblance in the picture but had no reason to think Robert capable of this. But the can of Mountain Dew was the first red flag. Robert drinks it like water, and I finally had to make him buy his own." Stephen looked up at Will, his eyes hollow. "I can't believe I'm so removed from his life. I'm really not a bad parent. Robert's been a handful since his mother died four years ago, and I can only ride herd on him so far. He seems bent on fighting me at every turn, and—"

"Take it easy, Professor. Just tell me why you think he's involved in this."

"Robert's basically a loner. Then a couple months ago, he and Lance Pearson were suddenly inseparable. Robert was cheerful and less combative, and his grades improved. It occurred to me the boys might be gay. I'm ashamed to say I enjoyed the reprieve from our power struggles and chose not to rock the boat by questioning Robert about how they spent their time."

Will leaned forward, his arms on the table. "You mentioned the first red flag. I assume there's a second?"

Stephen nodded. "What I discovered last night in Robert's room. You have to understand that he and I respect each other's privacy. I can't remember the last time I was in there. But after you showed me the photographs, I felt compelled to search his room. I was horrified to find all this white supremacy stuff. Magazines. Newspaper articles. Fliers. Stuff printed off the Internet and plastered all over his computer closet. I got on his PC and read his e-mails..." Stephen's voice cracked. "I think Robert killed Dary Fassih and Isaac Kohler...and made it look like the Jews and the Muslims were killing each other—maybe even to spite me for giving them more attention than I gave him."

Will raked his hands through his hair. "What about the car bombs?"

Stephen nodded. "Robert's been all over Internet sites that give explicit instructions on how to make a car bomb. I have no idea how he got the materials or where he stored them or who else may have been involved." Stephen let out a sob and then stifled it. "I haven't said anything to him. What do I do?"

"Where is Robert now?"

"Probably at home on his computer."

"Okay, we need to pick him up and get a warrant to search his room and his computer."

"What kind of father turns in his own son?"

"One who knows his boy needs help." Will put his hand on the professor's shoulder. "What you just did took more courage than most people could muster in a lifetime."

Guy Jones lay on the couch in his new apartment, the back of his hand on his forehead, his temples throbbing. He had interviewed four applicants for Kinsey's position—none as enthusiastic or vibrant as she. He wondered how long it would be before he was capable of honestly assessing anyone who sought to replace her.

He had already forgiven Brent for being so insensitive. How could the man be expected to understand how asinine he sounded making light of something as serious as where he would spend eternity?

Guy lay quietly, his headache now only a dull throb. Tim Rayburn's call to Ellen was a gift from heaven. He shuddered to think how different things might have been for Kinsey had Ellen not stepped out in faith and forgiven her—or not offered her the tract.

He closed his eyes and tried to picture Kinsey aglow with joy and standing in the presence of God. This was the first time since he'd become a Christian that he experienced rejoicing over a sinner who gets saved.

Suddenly, he had a real desire to rid himself of the callous indifference he had seen mirrored in Brent McAllister. He wondered if his attitude toward Ellen's friends had been any less offensive.

Will Seevers walked in the front door and smiled when he heard the sound of Margaret's scuffs approaching.

She met him in the entry hall and put her arms around his neck. "I'm so proud of you. I can hardly believe it's really over. But I feel bad for Professor Hardy."

"Yeah, he's devastated. My heart goes out to him—and to the Pearson boy's parents."

"You want me to heat up your dinner?"

"Not really. Come sit with me. The eleven o'clock news will be on in a few minutes. I'd like to see how the media's reporting this."

Will sat on the couch, his arm around Margaret, and studied the framed portrait of Meagan on the end table. "How does a nice man like Professor Hardy end up with a monster like Robert?"

"I guess if we knew the answer to that, we could hang out our shingle."

"I went by the Fassihs and the Kohlers on the way home," Will said. "I told them we got the killer and his accomplice."

"I'll bet they were relieved."

"I'm sure. But neither set of parents reacted the way I would've expected."

"What do you mean?"

"They got teary eyed for Professor Hardy and the Pearsons and seemed genuinely concerned for what these other parents were going through. I guess after losing their own sons, they don't get much satisfaction out of seeing two more families torn apart."

"What's Professor Hardy's son like?"

"Big kid. Tall. Quiet. Eyes deader than stone. I kept looking at his hands and thinking about what he did to Dary and Isaac. Makes me shudder. He outweighed those boys by fifty or sixty pounds."

"Did he say *why* he killed them?"

"Yeah, the kid kept ranting even when his attorney tried to shut him up. Says as far as he's concerned, Muslims and Jews are ruining our society. That what happened to Dary and Isaac was nothing compared to the extermination that's coming if we don't keep their kind from taking over. Robert admitted killing Dary to incite the Muslims against the Jews, and killing Isaac to incite the Jews against the Muslims. The car bombs were intended to get everybody scared enough of the Muslims to turn against them."

"Were they the ones who vandalized the mosque?"

Will nodded. "Robert said he deliberately dropped the Star of David on the floor. Everything these boys did was designed to pit Jews and Muslims against each other, and make everyone else turn against both groups. It's hard to comprehend that kind of hate."

"Where'd he get it? Professor Hardy isn't like that, is he?"

"No, not at all. But their relationship's been adversarial since Robert's mother died a few years ago. I guess the kid found an outlet for his anger. It's easy to see from the Web sites he frequented where he picked up his twisted ideas."

"How will we ever put an end to this kind of hate?"

Will held his gaze on the portrait of his daughter. "I don't think we will...unless enough of us are willing to start looking at all people as fellow human beings."

39

O n the following Sunday morning, Guy Jones stood in the balmy October breeze following the church service, his hands in his pockets, and watched the palm fronds swaying as Ellen chitchatted with her friends. For the first time in a long time, it felt good to be home.

"Hi, Guy," Billy Lewis said. "How are you do-ing?"

"I'm fine. How about you?"

"I am won-der-ful. God is good."

Guy noticed Lisa Lewis clinging to Billy's arm, that same disarming grin on her face. He reached for her hand. "Hi, Lisa. You're looking lovely this morning."

"Thank you." Lisa's cheeks flushed with pink. "Bil-ly picked out my dress. He likes me in pur-ple."

Guy didn't miss the adoring look in Billy's eyes and wondered what he saw in this woman that caused him to love her so. Lisa was anything but attractive. Her pointed glasses were out of style and much too heavy-looking for her face. Her body type was stumpy, her skin sallow. And she hardly ever uttered a word. Then again, when had Guy ever tried communicating with her?

He looked over at Ellen who was standing with friends, holding Sarah Beth Hamilton on her hip, and then turned to Billy. "So what have you and Lisa been up to?"

"We a-dop-ted a lit-tle girl! El-len helped us."

Lisa gave an emphatic nod, a twinkle in her eyes.

Guy moved his eyes from Lisa to Billy. They couldn't be serious.

Billy pulled his wallet out of his pocket and showed Guy a photograph of a tiny black child with beautiful dark eyes. From the way she was dressed, Guy guessed her to be African.

"Is this the little girl?" Guy said.

Billy stammered, seemingly beside himself, and then the words came pouring out. "Oh, yes! Her name is Ly-di-a. She is five-years-old. She lives in U-gan-da."

"We will write to her," Lisa said. "She will learn about Je-sus."

Ellen glanced over and saw Billy holding up the picture. She excused herself and came over and stood next to him. "Did Compassion send you information about your child?"

"Oh, yes!" Billy gave her the photograph. "Ly-di-a!" He went on to tell Ellen everything he could remember about the little girl.

From the expression on Ellen's face, one would have thought it was her grandchild they were making a fuss about. She slipped one arm around Billy and the other around Lisa. "I'm thrilled for you—and so proud. I know what a sacrifice it is for you to find the extra money to support a child. God will bless you for it."

Guy was struck by the couple's generosity and couldn't think of a single time when he had given sacrificially.

The Hamiltons came over and joined the circle. "Hey, what's all the excitement about?"

Billy repeated the details, and the Hamiltons exchanged hugs with the Lewises and offered their congratulations.

"You know what?" Guy said. "This calls for a celebration. How about all of us going to Gordy's for lunch—my treat?"

"That's sounds great." Ross Hamilton glanced over at his wife. "We'd love to come."

Billy and Lisa's heads bobbed in unison.

From out of nowhere, Blanche Davis appeared and squeezed in next to Ellen. "What's all the commotion about?"

"Billy and Lisa sponsored a child through Compassion."

Blanche brought her hands to her cheeks. "How wonderful!"

"We're on our way to Gordy's to celebrate," Guy said. "Why don't you come with us?"

"Oh dear, I wouldn't think of intruding."

Guy smiled. *Sure you would.* "Come on, the more the merrier."

Guy sat with Ellen, enjoying his third cup of coffee and feeling surprisingly let down after the last of the guests they'd invited to lunch had gone. He hadn't realized until now how much he missed the friendships he and Ellen had enjoyed in Baxter, and how little time and effort he had invested in building new ones since their move to Seaport.

Ellen reached across the table and put her hand on his. "Thank you. This meant so much to Billy and Lisa."

"You don't need to thank me. I should be thanking you."

"For what?"

"For being an example of how to look for the best in people. I don't know that I really *saw* the Lewises until today. Their slowness always turned me off, and I didn't think I could relate to them. But the way Billy nearly burst his buttons when he held up the picture of that little girl made me realize he's not really that different."

"He's really not. And he and Lisa are so cute together."

"How did you come up with idea of them sponsoring a Compassion child?"

"I read about it in a magazine and sent off for information. I think we should consider it, too. It's surprisingly inexpensive."

"All right. I'll take a look at the information."

"Guy, why do you keep smiling?"

"Can you imagine how exciting it must be for Billy and Lisa to feel on some level as if they're parents? That has to fill a big void in their lives."

"I'm sure it does. But I also think bridging the gap with 'normal' people is equally important to them. It's not often they feel as if they fit in or have anything valuable to contribute. Thanks for making this day special for them...and for me. I was so proud of you."

Guy paused until he was sure he wasn't going to get emotional. "I'm starting to realize something about myself." He looked into Ellen's eyes and knew it was safe to say it. "I'm not a loving person."

"Yes, you are. We've had our problems lately, but you're a wonderful husband—*and* father."

"You don't have to defend me, honey. That's a pitifully small outreach, considering there are billions of people on the planet. I doubt if your old buddy Ned would give me even an *E* for effort. I've thought about him a lot since we bought that painting. It still amazes me how radically your attitude toward Ross and Blanche changed after you took his advice and started praying for them. Yet I still don't do it."

"Even when I pray about it, I don't always find it *easy* to love every person."

"Then how are you able to be so nice to people I would gladly pass by?"

"You'll laugh if I tell you."

"I doubt that."

The corners of Ellen's mouth turned up. "Yes, you will."

"I promise I won't."

She picked up a spoon and stirred what was left of her coffee. "It's something I learned from Billy. I admit it sounds simplistic, but it's had a profound impact on me."

"Ellen, just say it."

"All right." She put down her spoon. "In my mind, I picture myself taking what Billy calls his 'Jesus mask' and putting it on the faces of people I have a hard time with. Seeing His face reminds me that whatever I do to the least of them, I do to Him..." Ellen's voice failed and she looked away, her nose suddenly red and her chin quivering.

"Honey, what's wrong?"

"It was just so awesome," she managed to say.

"What was?"

She wiped a tear from her cheek and paused for a few moments, then lifted her eyes. "I've never told you this, but seeing Jesus' face was the only way I could have reached out to Kinsey. And I'm so glad I did."

40

O n Monday morning, Gordy and Pam Jameson raced down the pier to the front door of the crab shack, giant raindrops falling from a gray cloud that seemed to have appeared out of nowhere.

Gordy fumbled to get the key in the lock, then finally pushed open the front door, lifted Pam into his arms, and carried her across the threshold, both of them laughing so hard they could hardly breathe.

"How long can you keep doing this?" Pam said.

"Till I get tired of it...or too feeble to lift you." Gordy set her down and wiped a water droplet off her cheek with his thumb.

He spotted a new photo hanging next to the 8 x 10 of his parents handing the keys of the crab shack to him and Jenny. He went over and took a closer look, tickled to see a photo of Pam and him holding pies fresh from the oven.

"That rascal Weezie had this blown up." He laughed. "I love you in that chef's hat."

"I have a feeling it's one of her marketing ploys." Pam glanced outside and then at her watch. "Think we should call Billy and tell him not to come in?"

Gordy went back to the front door and opened it. "Nah, I see blue sky already. Probably just a scattered shower. If nothin' else, Billy can dry off the tables and chairs out on the deck. The kid can't afford to lose a day now that he's supportin' Lydia."

"He just glows when he talks about her."

"Yeah, I haven't seen him this excited since he married Lisa. I've got paperwork to do. You gonna make pies?"

"I'd better. Weezie's selling them almost as fast as I pull them out of the oven. If she had her way, I'd have a bakeshop set up in here and would be selling whole pies right and left."

Gordy studied her face. "Would you wanna work that hard?"

"I'd love doing it. I could easily handle a dozen different kinds of pies. Might be good for business. And the added income couldn't hurt."

"Hmm...why don't you start by addin' a few different kinds and we'll see how they do. It's surprisin' how many folks are comin' in just for pie now." Gordy chuckled. "Weezie told me desserts sales were up seventy percent the three days I was gone."

The front door opened. Dr. Ali Tehrani walked in, and the moment he saw them, a warm smile claimed his face. "Oh, it is good to see you looking so happy." He went over to them and took hold of their hands. "I see that being married suits you."

"How about a cup of coffee," Gordy said. "I was just gettin' ready to put on a pot."

"All right, thank you."

"Let me get it," Pam said. "You fellas can visit."

Ali waited until Pam left then turned to Gordy. "I have some-thing I'd like to run by you. It'll just take a couple minutes."

"Sure. Let's go to my office." Gordy walked toward the hall and stopped at the kitchen doors. "Pam, darlin', will you bring our coffee to my office when it's ready?"

"Be glad to."

Gordy led Ali into his office. "Sit wherever you're comfortable."

Ali sat in the same chair as last time, and Gordy pulled his desk chair next to Ali's.

"Okay, Doc, what's on your mind?"

"I'm deeply distressed by the violence, Gordy. I think the threat by those college students to go door-to-door in the Muslim community, looking for terrorists, alarmed me as much as anything that's happened. Not just because it's my neighborhood, but because that kind of anarchy will destroy the freedoms that drew me to this country."

"Aw, things oughta calm down now that they've arrested the two boys who were behind it all."

Ali shook his head. "Those two teenagers weren't behind it *all*. They're merely two misguided kids among many. Do you really think these ethnic killings and the violence won't spread to other cities? How long do you think it will be before more car bombs go off and more children kill each other, thinking they're doing the world a favor?"

Gordy sighed. "It's a cryin' shame."

"The real shame, my friend, is the silence of good people who have the power to shape public opinion. The time to prevent misunderstanding is *before* it happens—not when we're washing our children's blood off the streets."

"Yeah, but somethin' that big is way out of the hands of ordinary folks like you and me."

Ali lifted his eyebrows, his dark eyes wide and soulful. "Maybe not. I have an idea. If it works, it might start a trend that would spread across this country."

Will Seevers started to walk out of his office when his phone rang. He winced, then made an about face and picked up the receiver. "Chief Seevers."

"Will, it's Gordy. You got a minute?"

"I was just about to pick up a sandwich and head for the park. I think I'm craving solitude as much as food."

"You think you could get sprung tonight for a while?"

"Probably. What's up?"

"There's a group of us who'd like to run something by you."

"What group?"

"It's too hard to explain over the phone, but what we wanna talk about is real important—somethin' that should make a positive difference in the community. I'll spring for dinner. Why don't we all meet here in the banquet room at six-thirty? I promise you'll be glad you came."

"How long do you think it'll take?"

"I don't know. Let's just see how it goes. It's excitin'. Could be the start of somethin' really big."

"All right, Gordy, you've got my curiosity up. I know you wouldn't ask unless you thought I'd get on board."

Guy Jones sat at his desk, looking over a contract. The sound of Marsha's voice on the intercom startled him.

"Mr. Jones, a Gordy Jameson is on line one."

Why would Gordy be calling me? "All right, Marsha. Thanks." Guy picked up the receiver and pushed the blinking button on the phone. "How's the new bridegroom? Ellen and I and a group from church were there for lunch yesterday but missed you."

"Doin' great, thanks. Pam and I really appreciate you and Ellen comin' to the wedding."

"We thoroughly enjoyed it. Hope the abrupt ending didn't ruin it for you."

"Nah, we didn't let it. Listen, sorry to bug you at work, but I was wonderin' if you could meet with Mayor Dickson and a group he's workin' with sometime before the weekend? They'd like to hire your legal services."

"Could you be more specific?"

"I think it'd be better to wait and let them tell you. I offered to coordinate gettin' everyone here. The group's meetin' tonight to lay out a specific plan, and then they'd like to get your legal input as soon as possible. I know you won't be back in town until Wednesday night."

"Would Thursday night work?"

"Yeah, that'd be great. They can't really move forward with the idea till they get some legal help. It's a real positive thing. I'm proud to support it."

"Tell me the time and place, Gordy. I'll be there."

41

On the following Saturday morning, Guy Jones whistled as he glided into the bedroom carrying a breakfast tray arranged with warm cinnamon rolls and coffee, and today's issue of the *North Coast Messenger*.

Ellen was sitting in bed, pillows propped behind her, looking like a little girl on Christmas morning. "Mmm...I love the smell of cinnamon rolls."

He placed the breakfast tray across her lap. "Your Saturday treat, Madame."

Ellen leaned down and put her nose to the red rose in the crystal vase and closed her eyes. "Ah, my favorite."

Guy picked up the newspaper and laid it next to her, then crawled over her to the other side of the bed.

"Why are you grinning like a Cheshire cat?" Ellen said.

"Why don't you read the newspaper?"

She gave him a curious look, then opened the newspaper. In the center of the front page was a large box he knew she couldn't miss. Guy read the words printed inside while he waited for Ellen's reaction:

CITY WIDE CALL TO PEACE

In the spirit of forgiveness and in an effort to promote respect and cooperation between all people, we invite every citizen of Seaport to join us on the front lawn of city

hall for an important peace rally and announcement following the Veteran's Day Parade on Saturday, November
11, beginning at 2:00 P.M.

Mayor Jefferson Dickson
Police Chief Will Seevers
Mr. and Mrs. Simin Fassih
Dr. and Mrs. David Kohler
Dr. and Mrs. Ali Tehrani
Professor Stephen Hardy
Mr. and Mrs. Richard Pearson
Rabbi and Mrs. Jacob Goldman
Pastor and Mrs. Peter Crawford
Imam Abdullah Bakir

Ellen looked over at him, her mouth hanging open. "*This* is
what you've been working on?"

"Uh-huh."

"Who in the world managed to get the Fassihs and the
Kohlers to agree to appear with Professor Hardy and the
Pearsons?"

He smiled. "Wait and see. But Ali is paying to have this ad
run in every issue until Veteran's Day."

Ellen mused. "Have you changed your opinion of him?"

"It'd be hard to be around Ali for long and not see what a
caring man he is."

"Was that a yes?"

"It was if you promise not to say 'I told you so.'"

Ellen leaned her head back and slipped her hand into Guy's.
"It's amazing how wrong any of us can be about another person if
we rely on only our own perceptions and prejudices."

"I never thought of myself as being prejudiced. But I was. I
let the media form my opinion of Muslims instead of looking at
each as an individual. I'm not proud of the way I've acted."

She squeezed his hand. "I'm proud of you for admitting it and for doing something about it."

The doorbell rang.

"Let me get rid of whoever it is."

Guy got out of bed, slipped into his bathrobe, and went to the front door. Through the peephole he saw Hailey and Owen standing on the front porch. He opened the door.

"Hi, you two. What brings you out this early on a Saturday?"

"Could we talk to you and Mom for a minute?" Owen said.

"Uh, sure. You want some coffee and cinnamon rolls? I made plenty."

"No, we just ate, thanks."

Guy held open the door and they stepped inside.

"Come down here," Ellen hollered.

Guy followed the kids down the hall and into the bedroom. Owen sat in the chair, Hailey on his lap, but he didn't say anything.

"What's wrong?" Ellen said. "You look so solemn."

"Hailey and I thought you should see this." Owen took a piece of paper out of his pocket, unfolded it, and handed it to them.

Ellen breathed in without exhaling. "Is this what I think it is?"

The glow on Owen's face could have melted an iceberg. "That's the ultrasound of your first grandchild!"

Guy turned to Ellen and in the next second four pairs of arms were intertwined, making it hard to tell who was hugging whom.

"Oh, my word!" Ellen wiped a tear off her cheek. "When's the baby due?"

"April twelfth," Hailey said.

"I ought to break your neck for scaring us to death!" Guy punched Owen on the arm and then pulled him close. "When did you kids find out?"

"Just last week. Hailey's been all messed up with the stress of relocating. Never even occurred to us she might be pregnant till she started throwing up. We decided not to say anything until we had ultrasound pictures to show you."

"Thank heavens, you're not in Raleigh," Ellen said. "I'd be going out of my mind."

Guy looked again at the picture. "Is it a girl or a boy?"

"Definitely."

"Come on," Ellen coaxed, "you have to tell us."

Owen laughed and put his arm around Hailey. "Actually we don't know. There are so few mysteries left in life, we decided to just ride this one out."

42

Veteran's Day fell on a Saturday, and Guy and Ellen met Hailey and Owen downtown for the annual parade and then arrived at city hall at twenty minutes until two. A sizable crowd had already gathered on the front lawn, where rows of folding chairs had been set facing an elevated stage skirted in red, white, and blue.

"This place is half full already," Ellen said. "That's a good sign."

"The way the mayor and police chief have been touting this thing, I'd be surprised if there wasn't a good turnout." Guy took her by the hand, and they found their seats on the front row with a good view of the stage and listened to the Seaport High School band play patriotic songs.

At 1:59, the group whose names had appeared on the announcement in the newspaper filed up on the stage and took their seats, and the crowd noise died down to a whisper.

Mayor Jefferson Dickson stood at the podium and looked out at the crowd. "My fellow citizens, thank you for coming here today. A number of people have worked hard so this event could take place, but they've asked not to be named at this time so nothing will draw attention away from what is about to happen here.

"This momentous occasion might well impact our community for generations to come, and though I'm proud to be a part of it, the idea was born in the heart of Dr. Ali Tehrani, respected oncologist and fellow patriot. I turn this program over to him and pray that you will listen with your hearts."

The crowd applauded politely as Ali got up and stood at the podium, looking very statesmen-like in his black suit and red tie.

"Mayor Dickson, Chief Seevers, distinguished guests, fellow citizens, I doubt there is anyone in Seaport who has not felt anger and revulsion at the events of the past few weeks. Everything from the Coast Guard's discovery of explosives to the murders of two of our young people to the recent car bombings have produced fear and uncertainty...and deep resentment toward those who have vowed to destroy us.

"As a Muslim American, I am appalled and grieved at the actions of radical Muslims who twist the meaning of jihad and use it as a license to dominate and destroy innocent people. For much too long I have been silent on the issue, afraid that speaking out would be perceived as an attack on Islam rather than a rebuke of my misguided brothers. But the escalating violence of the past few weeks has torn at my conscience. You are my neighbors, and I can no longer remain unresponsive. This is *my* country and *my* community—a kaleidoscope of races, religions, and cultures. I do not want harm to befall any person, least of all those with whom I live and work and play and worship.

"Yet, two of our teenagers were brutally murdered by two who were even younger. And though it was not with *our* hands these acts were committed, as a society we bear some responsibility for having failed to communicate to this generation the value of every human being. Diversity should not divide us. America has long been a melting pot of immigrants from every corner of the globe seeking freedom and opportunity. Have we forgotten that none of us has more right to be here than another?

"My friends, if we do not as individuals, as families, as communities, and as a nation work to find common ground, suspicion and misunderstanding will continue to foster hate and erupt into civil violence—and America will become a battleground of diversity instead of a haven for its expression.

"I came to this country too late in life to serve in the military as did these great heroes we honor today. But I love America, and I am determined to defend her honor by fighting against the prejudice, fear, and violence that have raped her soul. But I am just one man. I need your help.

"Each of us must vow to treat all people the way we ourselves wish to be treated, and then live out that commitment in our homes, our neighborhoods, our workplaces, our schools, churches, synagogues, and mosques.

"What I am asking is that here in *this* city we purposefully link arms and defend for each other the basic human right that, 'all men are created equal; that they are endowed by their Creator with certain inalienable rights—among them life, liberty, and the pursuit of happiness.' That's what our Creator intended. That's what our forefathers designed. And that's what so many brave souls, living and dead, have fought to protect. How dare we not endeavor to preserve what has cost so many so much!"

Guy realized he and Ellen and everyone in the audience were on their feet, the applause resounding for perhaps half a minute. Finally everyone sat, and Ali continued.

"And now I would like the others who invited you here to come stand with me."

Each person sitting on the stage rose to his feet and went and stood on either side of Ali.

"Please hold your applause until I have introduced each person."

Ali first acknowledged Mayor Dickson, and then introduced Mrs. Tehrani, Will Seevers, the Fassihs, the Kohlers, Professor Hardy, the Pearsons, the rabbi, the pastor, and the imam. He then reached for the hand of the person on either side of him, and the others followed his lead.

Guy put his lips to Ellen's ear. "I don't know that I could hold hands with the parents of the kid that killed my son."

Ali's voice suddenly sounded emotional. "We stand before you—Muslims, Jews, and Christians—united in our forgiveness and our resolve to see that the senseless violence that has stolen the lives of four of our children will never happen again. We believe that understanding and respect for one another will happen only when we abandon our isolationism and become integrated into the community, committed to a common goal.

"And toward that end, the Fassihs, the Kohlers, and the Tehranis have started a foundation, the money designated for the purchase of land and the construction of The People's Clinic, which will offer free medical and dental care for low-income families and the underprivileged.

"Every nail driven into the walls of this facility will be by the hands of volunteers. The invitation to help in its construction is open to all who are willing to participate. The People's Clinic will be operated by volunteer medical professionals, and already, over forty physicians and nurses have pledged to donate some of their time.

"On the grounds outside the clinic, a life-size bronze sculpture of Daryoush Fassih and Isaac Kohler will stand as a reminder of why we must work together.

"Furthermore, the front walk of The People's Clinic will bear the footprints of school children—another reminder of how important it is that we impart to future generations the virtues of cooperation and mutual respect.

"For every adult or child who lends a hand in the construction—whether in the actual building process or by providing materials or even bringing refreshments to the workers—special tiles with the individual's name will be prominently displayed in the clinic. We want this project to be of the people, by the people, and for the people of Seaport."

Ali got another standing ovation and the applause went on for some time. He looked over at Guy and winked. Finally, he raised his hands to ask for silence and began speaking again.

"We on this stage have written a pledge and signed it. Now we invite you to ponder the words and to sign it, too. This pledge and all the signatures will be put into a scrapbook and displayed in the clinic.

"Mr. Fassih and Dr. Kohler have asked that they be allowed to read it to you." Ali stepped away from the podium and motioned for the two men to approach.

The fathers of the two murdered boys came and stood at the microphone, then began reading in unison:

"We the people of Seaport, having suffered the loss of human life and a frightening attack on our public safety, and having heard the rumblings of civil anarchy, do pledge, from this day forward, to purposefully foster in ourselves, our families, our neighborhoods, our workplaces, schools, and places of worship understanding and respect for our fellow citizens.

"We further pledge that we will seek to be bridge builders within the community, and not become aligned with individuals or groups whose hatred or unlawful actions would threaten the safety and happiness of anyone else. This is our promise to ourselves, our children, our neighbors, and our Creator."

Ali resumed his place at the microphone and stood quietly for a moment with Mr. Fassih and Dr. Kohler, then began speaking again.

"On this Veteran's Day, America is engaged in still another war on its home front, equally insidious and perhaps even more destructive than terrorism. *Patriotism* lies wounded on the battlefield of political disagreement. And, my friends, the death of allegiance has more power to destroy us than any outside enemy.

"Where there is no vision, the people perish. Please…won't you pledge with us to strengthen the bonds between individuals and groups in our community? Together, we *can* heal the past, we *can* promote peace in the present, and thereby, we *will* preserve this great heritage for our children and grandchildren—and all generations to come."

Ali gave a slight nod to the other two men, then the trio

began singing a cappella, "I'm proud to be an American, where at least I know I'm free..."

Guy was aware of rising to his feet, and a tear running down Ellen's cheek, and the November sun filtering through a massive live oak that had withstood the car bombing. But the only voices he heard were those of the three brave men at the podium. Men he'd grown to respect, whose backgrounds and beliefs were vastly different from his, but whose voices now harmonized in an unprecedented show of unity.

Guy slipped one arm around Ellen and the other around Hailey, his hand resting on Owen's shoulder. He sang out with all his heart, deeply grateful for a renewed sense of freedom, for seeing his neighbors with different eyes, and for joining with them to make Seaport a safer place for the grandchild he fully intended to spoil rotten.

AFTERWORD

"'Love the Lord your God with all your heart
and with all your soul and with all your strength
and with all your mind'; and,
'Love your neighbor as yourself.'"

LUKE 10:27

D ear friends,
I had always understood prejudice to be overt dis-
dain for other races and cultures, but I've come to
realize that prejudice begins by deeming *any* group of people to
be of lesser value than ourselves. When we look down on
someone of a different social class, occupation, educational
background, religion, denomination, or even those who are
uncomely, disabled, disadvantaged, we fall painfully short of
Jesus' command in Luke 10:27. For believers, these attitudes
are often repressed because we're ashamed of having feelings we
seem powerless to change.

I began this story with the idea of exposing Guy Jones's attitude about Ellen's friends but never planned for it to evolve into
the volatile conflict between the Joneses over the Tehranis. But
I'm glad it did. As the story progressed, I was surprised to find
myself relating to Guy's attitude toward Muslims as much as

Ellen's and realized I had been nursing a quiet prejudice against Muslims—an attitude born *entirely* out of what I had seen and heard in the media. How unfair! Though I would never have behaved rudely toward a Muslim person, the fear and misunderstanding that "they're *all* out to destroy us" had definitely begun to color my thinking and anesthetized me to the need to pray for their redemption.

Confessing my attitude to God, I began to pray for these people I find hard to understand and who are so culturally and spiritually different—and my heart began to soften. I no longer lump them all together as evil and violent radicals. Most are victims of gross religious manipulation and need to be freed through a saving knowledge of Jesus Christ. They are lost human beings who desperately need a Savior. And that's something I *can* relate to—something that's sufficient to keep me on my knees on their behalf and enough to make them worth reaching out to.

No matter what religious, racial, or social differences may cause us to feel superior to someone else, the best way to conquer that wrong thinking is to develop a servant's attitude. A servant is never greater than the one he serves, and I'm convinced that when we act differently, we will begin to feel differently.

In this century when the media exposes us to the best and the worst of humankind, we would do well to pray that we're able to see our neighbor with our Father's eyes. For each is made in His image and plays a role in His plan. It's never His desire that any should perish—not even one.

I hope you'll join me for the third Seaport Suspense Novel, *All Things Hidden,* where we will find out whether Hailey and Owen have a boy or a girl, and meet up with some interesting new characters who will take us through a maze of twists and turns. As always, it promises to be a page-turner!

I love hearing from my readers. You can write to me through

my publisher at www.letstalkfiction.com or directly through my website at www.kathyherman.com. I read and respond to every e-mail and greatly value your input.

In His love,

Kathy Herman

P.S. If you would like information on how to sponsor a Compassion child, please go online to www.compassion.com and explore the options. The process is easy and so rewarding. My husband and I currently sponsor three children (Guatemala, Uganda, and Rwanda) and have sponsored two others who are now grown. Compassion publishes its operating costs and is proud that a huge percentage of each dollar goes directly to the children, not to administrative costs. Sponsoring a Compassion child is a proven and affordable way to insure that a child's physical and educational needs will be met, and that he or she will hear the message of God's saving grace and will be nurtured in the Word of God.

DISCUSSION GUIDE

1. Do you believe every person is equally valuable to God? Or do you think God loves the saved more than the lost? The beautiful more than the unlovely? The healthy more than the infirm? The intelligent more than the mentally challenged? One ethnic group more than another? Explain your answer.

2. According to James 2:1–9, how are we to treat one another in the church? Do you see this biblical attitude reflected in your own church? Do you practice this attitude yourself? If not, can you pinpoint the reason? What is the difference between prejudice and conceit? Have you been guilty of either?

3. Do you find it difficult to respect people who hold different religious beliefs than you do? Different political views? Does your response to them line up with Luke 10:27, to "love the Lord your God with all your heart and with all your soul and with all your strength and with all your mind, and love your neighbor as yourself?"

4. Read the story of the Good Samaritan in Luke 10: 29–37. Do you believe the actions of the Samaritan man would be practical in today's world? Have you ever had occasion to help someone you would never choose to be associated with? How did it make you feel? Have you

ever passed by someone in need of help because you felt superior—or because you were afraid to get involved? Did you regret it? Are there times when not getting involved is wise? Times when it is an excuse? Explain your answer.

5. Have you ever known a mentally challenged person like Billy or Lisa Lewis? Someone disabled? Disfigured? Chronically ill? Did you tend to avoid them? If so, why? If not, was your experience with that person positive or negative? What types of physical flaws in other people tend to put you off? Can you identify the reason? What should your response be?

6. Have you ever been guilty of judging an entire group of people based on the actions of a proportionately small number? Has anyone ever misjudged you in that way? How did it make you feel? What would you have liked to say in your own defense? Do you think many people are prejudiced against Christians? If so, why? Do you think Christians come across as being prejudiced against certain groups? If so, which ones? What should be our response when we disapprove of unchristian lifestyles or behaviors?

7. Could you relate to Will Seevers and Guy Jones's feelings about Muslims in this story? Do you think their feelings represent the way many Americans feel? If so, why do you think the feeling is so widespread? Is it fair? Is it Christian?

8. Does the way we perceive others affect the way we act toward them? Should it? Is prejudice always related to a person's ethnicity or can it also result from feelings about

social class, job status, physical appearance, educational background, church affiliation?

9. Are we sometimes guilty of being prejudiced even when we don't want to be? Have you ever intentionally or unintentionally passed on prejudices to your children? If being prejudiced is sinful, what should you do about it?

10. Based on Matthew 5:43–48, what do you believe should be the appropriate Christian response to our enemies? Is praying for your enemies difficult for you? Why do you think Jesus told us to do it? Have you ever prayed for someone you were either afraid of or thoroughly disliked and found your perception changed? How do you understand Proverbs 25: 21–22? What does it mean to heap burning coals on an enemy's head?

11. Is the attitude of our heart as important to God as our actions? What do our actions reveal about our true feelings? If you were a character in this story and the attitudes of your heart were revealed, would the reader be appalled at you—or applaud you?

12. Is there an attitude or prejudice you feel God's Spirit nudging you to change? Will you let Him change you?

THE BAXTER SERIES

by Kathy Herman

Welcome to Baxter: the very best of small-town America. Life here is good. People are bonded by a proud heritage—and a hundred-year history unstained by the violence that has seeped into nearly every other American city. But when a powerful explosion shakes not only the windows, but the very foundation on which they've based their safety and security, the door is left open for evil to slither in. The death of innocence is painful to endure, but with it comes the resurgence of faith and hope.

Suspenseful, unforgettable stories that inspire, challenge, and stay with you long after the covers are closed!

TESTED BY FIRE
Book One
ISBN 1-57673-956-2

DAY OF RECKONING
Book Two
ISBN 1-57673-896-5

VITAL SIGNS
Book Three
ISBN 1-59052-040-8

HIGH STAKES
Book Four
ISBN 1-59052-081-5

A FINE LINE
Book Five
ISBN 1-59052-209-5

LEARN MORE ABOUT THESE NOVELS FROM BESTSELLING AUTHOR KATHY HERMAN

LOG ON TO WWW.KATHYHERMAN.COM TODAY!

An excerpt from Kathy Herman's

All Things Hidden,

the next book in the Seaport Suspense series

(available April 2006)

"Do not be deceived:
God cannot be mocked.
A man reaps what he sows."

GALATIANS 6:7

Ellen Jones stood next to her white Thunderbird in the driveway of her father's house in Ocala, Florida, her eyes fixed on the Sold sign in the front yard, and her mind echoing with the sound of her mother's laughter.

She took one last whiff of orange blossoms, wishing she could bottle the sights and sounds and scents that evoked the good memories of this place. It had been a long time since she enjoyed coming here, but the thought of leaving it forever was bittersweet.

"I hope you're happy. You've ruined my life," Lawrence Madison said.

No, Dad, you've had an eighty-seven year head start. Ellen looked in the car at her father sitting in the passenger seat. "We've been over this a dozen times. Your moving in with Roland is the best possible scenario."

"Sure, best for you. Always did think of yourself first."

Ellen bit her lip. She took comfort in the knowledge that her mother would be proud of her, not only for looking after her father but for standing up under his crushing criticism.

"Everything I own is in this dinky U-Haul trailer," Lawrence said. "Why didn't you just sell the shirt off my back?"

"Dad, I asked you what you wanted to keep. If it got sold in the estate sale, it's because you gave the green light. You could at least be grateful those nice young men on the corner loaded it up for us."

Lawrence seemed to be looking in the side mirror. "What do you suppose *she* wants?"

Ellen turned and saw Sybil Armstrong crossing the street. "Dad, please be nice. I'm sure she just came to see us off."

"I brought you some cookies to take with you." Sybil walked over to Ellen and handed her a Baggie. "Oatmeal raisin." She leaned closer and lowered her voice. "I even added a little flax meal. All that fiber will be good for him."

"Thank you, Sybil. That was thoughtful of her, wasn't it, Dad?" Ellen glanced over at her father, surprised to see his eyes welled up.

"Yeah, thanks. Right nice of you. Can we go now?"

"Lawrence," Sybil leaned down by the driver's side window, "don't you be worrying about your flowers. I'll keep them watered till the new owners move in next month. You have my email address. I want to hear all about your new place."

Ellen looked at her watch. "We really should get on the road. It'll only take a couple of hours to get to Seaport, but Guy and Roland are expecting us before noon." She reached over and squeezed Sybil's hand.

Ellen opened the door and slid in behind the wheel. She glanced up at the blue gingham curtains in the kitchen window, and blinked a few times to make her eyes stop stinging.

"You gonna sit here all day or are you going to get this sardine can on the highway?"

Ellen waited for several seconds more, then turned the key and backed out of the driveway, painfully aware of the ending of an era—and the dawning of a potential nightmare.

Ellen opened her eyes wide and blinked several times, feeling the effects of last night's restlessness. She picked up the Styrofoam cup in the holder and drank the last of the lukewarm coffee.

"Dad, would you like a cookie?" She picked up the Baggie on the console.

Lawrence stared out the side window and didn't answer.

Suit yourself.

Ellen took a bite of cookie, her mind wandering back to her mother's kitchen and an incident that happened when she was a junior in high school...

"I'm so proud of you," her mother had said. "I think running for class president is an excellent idea."

"I'll have to really campaign hard. Mary Pat's a cheerleader. And Kent's like the brainiest kid on the planet."

Mother put a plate of oatmeal cookies and a glass of milk in front of Ellen. "Well, you're very smart—and persuasive. Plus, you can get along with anybody. Don't defeat yourself before you even get started."

Her father walked into the kitchen. "Get started with what?"

"Ellen's decided to run for class president. Isn't that something?"

"Big waste of time, if you ask me," her father said. "Why don't you sink your energy into something more useful—like joining the sewing club or becoming a Candy Striper?"

Ellen glanced over at her mother and then locked gazes with her father. "What's wrong with running for class president?"

"It's pointless, Ellen, that's all."

"But Dad—".

"Honestly, Lawrence," her mother said, "why must you be so negative? The entire process will be a good experience for her whether she wins or not. Learning to compete will help her in college."

Lawrence rolled his eyes. "College is a waste of time and money for women. Their place is in the home, taking care of their children."

"What if I don't ever get married and have kids?" Ellen said.

His face softened. "You will." He stroked her cheek. "Just look at that face."

"So if I were ugly, going to college might be worth it. But since I'm not, I should plan on being a housewife? Come on, Dad. That's not fair."

"Listen to me, young lady. What's not fair is women trying to change their natural bent toward being wives and mothers. It's upsetting everything."

"I never said I don't want to get married and have kids. But can't I be a journalist, too?

"Women flooding the workplace is creating problems you have no idea about."

"But all I've ever wanted to do is write."

Her father's eyes were suddenly like stone, his voice stern. "And I'm telling you to spend your time learning things that will benefit your husband and family and not your own selfish ambitions!"

Ellen dropped out of the race for class president. But her father's refusal to fund her college education had only made her more determined. She secured the loans she needed and struggled through all four years without his financial support or approval. But nothing between them had ever been the same...

Ellen spotted the Seaport exit up ahead and put on her right blinker, aware of her father shifting in his seat.

Lord, he brings out the absolute worst in me! Unless You intervene, we're just going to go on making each other miserable.